ADORING KEATON

USA TODAY & WSJ BESTSELLING AUTHOR

SIOBHAN DAVIS

Copyright © Siobhan Davis 2020. Siobhan Davis asserts the moral right to be identified as the author of this work. All rights reserved under International and Pan-American Copyright Conventions.

SIOBHAN DAVIS® and THE KENNEDY BOYS® are registered in U.S. Patent and Trademark Office.

This is a work of fiction. Names, characters, places, incidents and dialogues are products of the author's imagination or are used fictitiously. Any resemblance to actual people, living or dead, or events is entirely coincidental.

This book is sold subject to the condition that it shall not, by way of trade or otherwise be lent, resold, hired out, or otherwise circulated without the prior written consent of the author. No part of this publication may be reproduced, transmitted, decompiled, or stored in or introduced into any information storage and retrieval system, in any form or by any means, whether electronic or mechanical, including photocopying, without the express written permission of the author.

Original paperback published by CreateSpace September 2020

This paperback edition © October 2023

ISBN-13: 978-1-959285-76-2

Edited by Kelly Hartigan www.editing.xterraweb.com

Cover design and logo by Shannon Passmore

www.shanoffdesigns.com

Cover imagery © depositphotos.com

Interior graphics © Robin Harper www.wickedbydesigncovers.com

Formatted by Ciara Turley using Vellum

Keaton
Moving to California was supposed to be my fresh start. A clean slate. An opportunity to drop the façade, escape the lies, find a focus, and just be myself.

But I should have realized it wouldn't be easy, especially when my last name is Kennedy.

I'm not ready to be a gay icon or some celebrity role model. I still haven't admitted the truth to my family or the girl I professed to love, so there's no way I want the public to know I'm into dudes.

Falling for my hot, *straight*, football-player roomie wasn't part of the game plan.

Neither was backing myself into a corner because I trusted the wrong guy.

Now everything is on the line, and it's time to stop pretending.

Austen
From the time I was a little kid, all I wanted is to play football in college and play in the NFL.

As wide receiver for the Golden Bears, I am on track to achieve my goals, but it comes at a heavy price.

Denying who I am—for the sake of my career—goes against everything I believe.

I should never have listened to my high school coach, because all the lies are suffocating me.

Until Keaton Kennedy enters my life, turning it upside down.

Now, there is even more reason to tell the truth, because I'm falling for the famous one and I want the entire world to know.

Note From The Author

While you do not need to have read the previous books in this series to enjoy *Adoring Keaton*, it is recommended you start at the beginning to have a greater understanding of the *Kennedy Boys* world and to avoid spoilers to the earlier books contained within this book. However, you can read it as a **stand-alone romance** if you prefer as it focuses on a brand-new couple with a HEA.

This is a **male-male romance**, focusing on Keaton, the second of the Kennedy triplets to get his story. I understand some readers might not have read this genre before or it's not a favorite genre to read, but if you are enjoying the series so far, I implore you to give this book a chance as it may pleasantly surprise you! Some of my beta readers hadn't read MM romance before, and they loved it; many said Austen and Keaton are now their favorite Kennedy couple!

This is a heartwarming, emotional romance with a sprinkling of angst and drama, a little humor, and some cameos from other characters you have come to know and love. Happy reading!

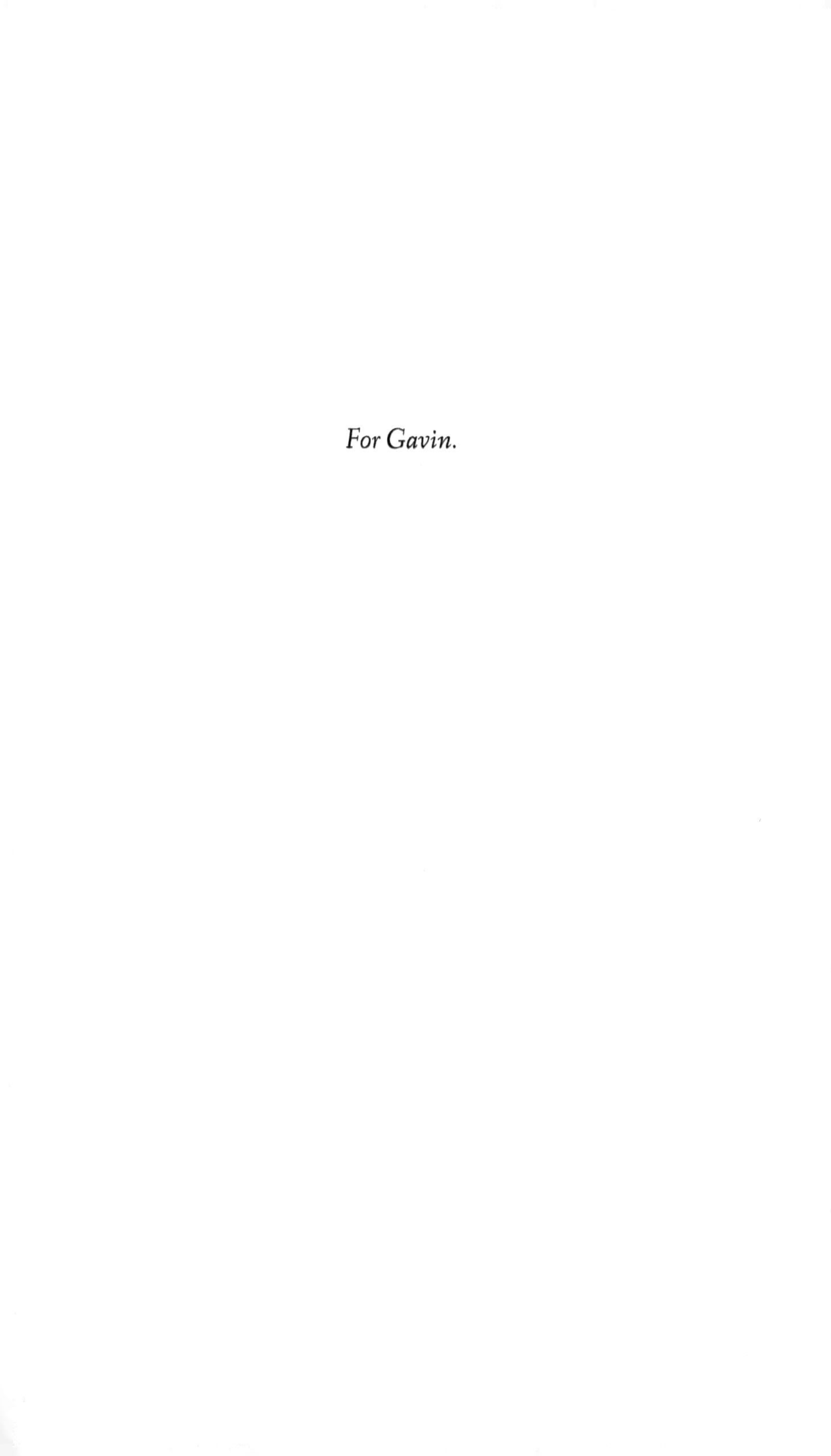

For Gavin.

ADORING KEATON

Prologue
Austen

Spring Semester. Sophomore Year

I tune out Preston and Alan as they flirt up a storm with the fawning sorority girls surrounding them, scanning the packed basement room for my buddy Colton. A concoction of alcohol fumes, weed, and the overpowering scent of perfume and cologne poisons the air, and my nostrils twitch in aggravation. Beats pulse through the large wall-mounted speakers in the four corners of the room, and the party is in full swing with no signs of slowing down.

I like to party as much as the next guy, but these regular Saturday night events are grating on my nerves. I understand the guys want to celebrate or commiserate after the game, but some Saturday nights, I just want to fall into bed and sleep into oblivion, but that's impossible when I live at party central.

At least there's only six weeks until spring semester is over and the torture ends. I'm not rooming with my football buddies next year. My sanity depends upon it.

"What about you, Austen?" a female asks in a sultry voice as a soft hand lands on my bare lower arm.

"What about me?" I inquire, removing the busty redhead's hand.

"We're moving the party upstairs." She waggles her brows suggestively. "You coming?"

"He's taken, ladies," Colton confirms, magically appearing at my side. I flash him a look of gratitude although I had it handled. "Me, on the other hand..." He puffs out his chest, dazzling them with his trademark blinding grin. "I'm as free as a bird and ready to *get it on*."

The girls swoon, practically melting into a puddle at his feet, and my lips tip up at the corners. The only person I know who gets away with that cheesy shit is Colton Barnes. As quarterback of the Cal Bears, there isn't much he can't do. He's as revered as Drake around these parts.

"Catch ya later, man." Colton punches my upper arm, grinning devilishly as he swats the redhead on the ass before trailing her up the stairs.

Grabbing a bottle of beer—my first of the night—I shove my way through the masses, avoiding the grabby hands and shouts directed at me, until I'm pushing through the basement door, out into the rear yard.

The door closes behind me, muting the *thump, thump* of the music, and the quiet darkness is a balm to my sore ears and my tired eyes. A few guys and girls are huddled in lounge chairs, in a semicircle, at the far end of the yard, drinking and talking among themselves. Wanting to avoid them, I walk off in the opposite direction, toward the side of the house.

"Hayes, my man. Come join us," Nolan shouts, jerking his head at me.

"Later, dude. I'm just getting some air." I dismiss him with an effortless smile, and he drops the issue without hesitation.

Ten of us on the team have lived here since freshman year, and they know when to back off and leave me to it.

I'm the only one in the house in a "committed relationship." The only one not banging a different girl every Saturday night.

Drinking another swig of beer, I round the corner of the three-story house, enjoying the fact I can wander around in jeans and a tee. Although the weather is cooler at night, April in California is a vast improvement over April in Colorado. I don't miss the snow or the rain, and I already know I won't be returning to my hometown when I graduate from Berkeley in two years, even if the NFL doesn't come calling.

Tipping my head up, I stare at the starless night sky, wondering how much longer I can keep up pretenses.

My sneakers meet resistance, and I thrust my arm out, slamming my hand against the side of the house, to stop myself from falling over the unexpected obstacle blocking my path. "What the fuck," I mumble, as a strangled groan filters through the air. Regaining my balance, I crouch down over the dark lump at my feet.

The long, lean body is curled into a ball, tucked into the side of the house, and if it wasn't for the low-level moaning escaping his mouth, I might've assumed the dude was dead.

"Hey, man. You okay?"

He shifts, unfurling long jeans-clad legs, while one hand moves to his stomach, rubbing his belly. His shirt lifts a little, revealing toned, tan skin. I say nothing as he sits up, resting his back against the wall.

It's dark on this side of the house, but I can make out his features under the dim glow of the moon.

Holy fuck. *What the hell is the infamous Keaton Kennedy doing passed out on the side of my house?*

"What happened?" he asks, running a hand through his

thick dark hair. His head pivots as he glances around, his brow puckering. "Where am I?"

Alcoholic fumes roll off him in pungent waves, and I'd say it's pretty obvious what happened.

"You're at the football house," I explain. "I'm guessing you passed out as you were leaving." It's the only logical explanation as most guests enter and leave the party via the rear basement door.

"Shit. That's embarrassing." He scrubs his hands down his face.

"Happens to the best of us." I straighten up and offer him my hand. "And no one's around but me."

He takes my hand, and I help him to his feet. He's almost the same height as me, give or take an inch or two, so we're nearly eye level. "Thanks, Austen."

"He knows who I am." I smirk, cocking my head to one side.

He slides his hand from mine, and I miss the warmth of his touch instantly. "That surprises you?" he inquires, looking genuinely curious.

"Nah. That's the point." I'm sure he's familiar with the concept, given how most students on campus know his name too. But he hasn't asked me, and I'm not going to make him more uncomfortable. He just stares at me, and I think I've lost him. "You need help?"

A slow scowl replaces the previously intrigued look on his face. "I'm good." His words are slightly slurred, and he sways on his feet when he attempts to walk away.

"I'm a judgment-free zone. No shame in asking for help if you need it."

"I'm fine," he grits out, forcing a smile on his face. "Thanks for, eh, waking me up."

Shoving my hands in my pockets, I watch him stumble

away, following him at a discreet distance, to ensure he's safe.

My brows pull together when he stops at a blacked-out Land Rover, parked at the curb outside our house, removing keys from his jeans pocket. The keys fall to the ground with a distinct clattering sound, and he curses, bending over, delectable ass up in the air, fingers searching the asphalt.

I stride toward him, purposely not concealing my advance so I don't freak the guy out. He stands, keys in hand again, but he doesn't unlock the car door. Leaning back against it, he tilts his face up, closing his eyes. A low groan rumbles from his chest, as his hand moves to his stomach again. He rubs his hand back and forth across his toned abs, and it's clear he's not doing so hot. Keaton's eyes pop wide at the sound of my approaching footfalls, and he stares at me as if I'm an apparition.

"I'm sober. I can drive," I offer, stopping a couple feet away from him. "You're in no condition to get behind the wheel."

I expect him to argue, but he doesn't. "I know." He sighs, his tone sounding resigned. "Thanks, but I'll just call an Uber."

"Then you'll have to return to pick up your car tomorrow." I flip my palm over for the keys. "Let me drive you home. I'll Uber it back. Problem solved."

His mouth opens and closes rapidly, and I hold still as his gaze roams me from head to toe. I don't need to remind him I'm not exactly a stranger. As wide receiver for the Bears, I'm as well known on campus as he is.

Everyone knows who Keaton Kennedy is, because his arrival at Berkeley turned more than a few heads. His family is as famous as the Kardashians, and everyone knows who the notorious Kennedy boys are.

Unless you've been living under a rock.

Keaton drops the keys in my hand, never breaking eye contact. "Thanks."

"No sweat."

We climb into the car, and I crank up the air-conditioning when I get a good look at his face. He's pale and sweating and on the verge of puking.

"Where to?" I inquire, starting up the engine.

He directs me to an apartment building a couple blocks from campus. I've walked past it several times, so I know where it is.

Keaton leans his head against the window as I glide out onto the empty road, heading in a westerly direction. I cast quick glances at him as I drive one-handed, wondering what his story is.

By all accounts, he keeps his head down and stays out of trouble. We share some classes, and I've noticed how focused he is. How he doesn't like to draw attention. The guy's a bit of an enigma, and I'd be lying if I said he didn't intrigue me. But our paths have rarely crossed, and with my hectic schedule, my friend pool is limited to my football buddies and a couple of acquaintances from my freshman year.

His phone pings in his jeans pocket, and he angles his hips so he can extract his cell. His muscular thighs fit snugly in his dark jeans, and from the way his tight shirt stretches across his firm chest, it's clear he works out. He's definitely broader and more ripped than freshman year. Trust me, I've noticed that too.

"Shit," he murmurs while scrolling through his phone.

"Is everything okay?" I slow down as we reach an inter-section.

"My friends are worried," he admits before hitting the dial button and bringing his cell to his ear. I listen to his one-sided conversation, not even pretending I'm not.

"Seb. It's me." He wets his lips, and I try not to stare at his lush, full mouth. "I'm sorry. I don't know what happened. Guess I passed out by the side of the house." His bloodshot eyes latch on mine. "No. It's cool. I'm, ah, in an Uber." He cringes as the lie leaves his lips, and it's adorably cute. I toss him a smile, letting him know I don't give a rat's ass what he tells his friends. "Okay. I'll text you when I'm home. You too. Tell Kate and Mol I'm sorry for worrying them."

He hangs up, avoiding eye contact, resting his cell on his thigh.

"You know," I say, as I turn the corner toward his apartment building. "Most people would brag about Austen Hayes driving them home."

"I'm not most people," he replies, staring out the window.

"No. You're not," I readily agree.

His head whips around, his startling blue eyes meeting mine. "What does that mean?"

"Relax, man." I drive down the ramp into the basement parking lot. "It wasn't an insult. I like that you don't give a fuck who I am."

"I never said that." He shifts on his seat, looking uncomfortable. "Park over there." He points at a reserved space at the end on the right.

I pull the car into the vacant space and kill the engine. Silence engulfs us as I turn to face him.

"I didn't tell my friend because I thought you might appreciate the privacy." He shrugs, looking a little sheepish.

"I do, and I'm sure you do too."

He exhales heavily. "You know who I am. Great." Sarcasm is thick in his tone.

A smile dances across my lips. "Is there anyone on campus who doesn't?"

"I keep a low profile," he supplies.

"I know that too." I swivel in the driver's seat so I'm looking him straight in the eyes. "I bet you don't realize we're in a lot of the same classes."

Shock splays across his face. "We are?"

I rest my forearm on my knee, smiling. "I'm studying biz admin with a concentration in global management too."

A groan tumbles from the back of his throat. "This just keeps getting better."

"Ouch." I grin, not in the least bit upset.

"Look, man. I'd appreciate it if we kept this between us."

My grin fades. "I would never tell anyone. Your business is your own. I'm the last person to spread gossip."

His broad shoulders relax when he sees I'm sincere. "Thanks, Austen. That means a lot."

"You need me to come up with you?" I ask, because the guy looks a heartbeat away from collapsing or puking.

He shakes his head. "I'll manage."

"You have a roommate?" I ask, as we get out of the car.

"Nope. It's just me." He doesn't look at me as he talks, messing with his phone.

"You sure you're okay?" I ask, reluctant to leave him, for reasons I haven't yet worked out.

The corners of his mouth lift as he pockets his phone and eyeballs me. "I'm drunk, not disabled. I can still make my way into the elevator and up to my apartment without a chaperone, although it's sweet that you care."

I shrug, smirking as I lean back against the side of his car. "Just call me one of the good guys."

His smile expands. "I know you're joking, but I think you *are* one of the good guys, Austen Hayes." He drags a hand through his hair, and my eyes greedily follow the motion, hypnotized by the glorious ink on his arm, the way his muscles flex and roll with the movement, and the elegance of his fingers as he glides them through the silky strands of his dark hair. My libido has noticed this guy on more than one occasion, and simmering attraction lingers in my tissues.

Keaton Kennedy is hot, and his girlfriend is a lucky woman.

But if he knew the thoughts swirling through my brain right now, I doubt he'd be so quick to assert my good guy status. "Maybe. Maybe not." I toss him another smirk, pushing off the door. "And I think that's my cue to leave."

"Your Uber will be here in three minutes," Keaton says to my retreating back. "And I've picked up the tab. Least I could do."

I spin around, talking to him as I walk backward. "I think you're one of the good guys, Kennedy. For real." Truth. The guy oozes goodness and purity from his every pore.

"Good night, Austen." He moves to walk away.

"Drink water and pop a couple pills before you crawl into bed," I shout out.

He narrows his eyes and purses his lips. "Yes, *Dad*."

I chuckle, saluting him one final time. "See you around, dude."

"You can count on it," he replies with a searing-hot grin, before disappearing into the elevator, leaving me open-mouthed and rethinking my theories.

I'm still grinning when the Uber drops me off at the house a short while later.

That was the night I became friends with the hot famous one.

Although, I didn't fully realize the implications of our meeting at the time or how Keaton Kennedy would come to turn my entire world upside down.

Chapter One
Keaton

Fall Semester. Junior Year.

"Sounds like fun," I tell Mom, pressing my cell between my ear and my shoulder as I juggle my overloaded book bag while opening the door to my sixth-floor penthouse apartment.

"Good. Now I only need to work on Kent."

Dropping my bag on the floor in the hall, I shut the door with my foot, putting Mom on speaker. "Don't give him an option. Just tell him you're organizing a party for our twenty-first and he must be there."

I'm one of triplets, and we're the youngest in our family, so our coming of age is a big deal for Mom.

Not that she needs any excuse to throw a party. Kennedy family parties are second nature to Mom now, because she doesn't want to miss a single thing. She spent years building her business, working nonstop, sacrificing so much, missing so much, to give us everything in life. It took its toll on her, and her marriage, and it's only since she sold Kennedy Apparel that she has truly started living. Now, she wastes no opportunity to celebrate, and it wouldn't be a normal year if there aren't at least a few family get-togethers.

Last year, she reunited with Dad after a period of separation, and she's got the biggest smile on her face all the damn time, and I couldn't be happier for them.

Which is why agreeing to this birthday party is a no-brainer.

I love my mom, and I'll do anything to keep that big, bright smile on her face. "I love you, Mom," I blurt, entering the open-plan living area just as Austen emerges from the laundry room.

A knowing smile slips across his mouth, irritating me for a nanosecond, but all I can focus on is how soft and full his lips are, how hot he looks with his freshly cut hair and stylish stubble on his chin and cheeks, and how ripped his inked arms are under his tight tee.

Honestly, I think I must have been missing a few brain cells the night I agreed to let my new *straight* friend move in here with me.

Talk about being a glutton for punishment.

"Sweetheart." Mom's concerned tone yanks me out of my head.

Austen's smile is so wide now it threatens to split his face in two. I flip him the bird, just 'cause I feel like it. He chuckles under his breath, moving into the large kitchen and powering the Keurig on.

"Sorry, Mom. I zoned out for a bit. Blame Austen's new haircut. It's so hideous I checked out in shock."

Austen laughs, knowing full well it's a blatant lie. He's the hottest player on the football team, by a mile, and everyone knows it. His dark hair is long on top and shorn super tight on the sides, with a defined zigzag design etched into the shaved segments.

No one on this campus is cooler than Austen Hayes.

No one.

"Hello, Austen," Mom calls out. "Please excuse my son's rudeness."

"It's all good, Mrs. Kennedy. I know he secretly loves me," Austen shouts back, and I inwardly cringe, because he's no idea how close to the truth he is.

"Honestly, what are they teaching you out there, Keaton?" Mom continues, oblivious. "I told you you should've attended Harvard with your brothers."

"It was a joke, Mom." I twist my head from side to side, attempting to loosen the tense cricks in my neck. I deliberately ignore the Harvard comment, because I'm not going there again.

I shocked everyone when I enrolled at Berkeley instead of Harvard. I hadn't told a soul what I was planning. Not even Kent or Keanu. As triplets, we're the closest of all my brothers, but this was something I needed to do for myself. I knew if I told them my plans they would convince me to drop them, so I purposely plotted behind their backs.

I hurt them, and I know they still don't understand why I did it, but at least they have forgiven me now.

I'd like to say it hasn't damaged our relationship, but that would be delusional, because it has. It's impossible to maintain the same closeness when I'm in California and they're in Boston. We've naturally drifted apart while Keanu and Kent have grown closer.

Keanu married his childhood sweetheart Selena last year, and while they have their own place in Wellesley, they spend the week sharing the condo Keanu and Kent co-own now they are at college.

Despite how everything's turned out, I still don't regret my decision to come here.

"I'm throwing a party for Keaton's twenty-first, and I expect to see you there, Austen," Mom says, ignoring me.

"I wouldn't miss it for the world," Austen smoothly replies while I roll my eyes.

I'm not opposed to bringing Austen home, but I'd rather it wasn't as just my friend.

I glance around, and the world is still spinning. It hasn't crashed down around me because I've finally admitted I'm crushing hard on my new bestie—the one with a steady girl-friend back home in Golden, Colorado.

I'm as much of a lost cause as I've always been.

We say our goodbyes, and I hang up.

"I like your mom," Austen says, handing me a steaming mug of coffee.

Our fingers brush in the exchange, and his touch sends shivers coursing up my arm, like always. "Mom's the best, but I should warn you she'll be all over you like a rash if you come home with me."

He arches a brow, leaning his hip against the marble coun-tertop, waiting for me to elaborate.

"If she still owned her label, she'd be trying to get you to model for her. Especially since your look is supposedly all the rage right now." I wave my hands casually in his direction, not wanting to linger on his tall, tan, ripped body, or the impressive ink covering both arms and most of his chest and back, or meet those gorgeous green eyes that always seem to burn with inten-sity, for fear I'll sprout a boner. God knows, it's happened more times than I can count since fall semester started three weeks ago.

Austen moved in over the summer break when his preseason training commenced, but I only returned from Boston the week before classes resumed, and already I'm hot for him.

Which is stupid.

Because he's straight.

And he has a girlfriend.

However many times I repeat those facts to myself, it doesn't seem to matter. My body will *not* get with the program. And even if he wasn't straight, and he didn't have a girlfriend, it wouldn't matter much when I'm still firmly in the closet, because I'm a chickenshit with no balls and an unhealthy dose of self-loathing.

I had planned on telling my family the truth after the dust had settled on my breakup with Melissa. But my decision to fly to Malibu after Faye and Kyler's going away party put the nail in that coffin.

Now I can't fess up.

Not without telling everyone what happened on that disastrous trip, and how I'm paying the price, and that's just not going to happen.

I made this mess. It's up to me to fix it. Even if I have no clue how to do that.

Austen's smirk rises, and while I curse myself for my honest admission, I'm grateful it's distracted me from my depressive inner monologue.

"He thinks I'm hot." Austen waggles his brows.

"Arrogance is not a good look on you," I retort, feeling heat creep up my neck and onto my face.

"It's only arrogance if I'm the one who believes it, but you were the one pointing it out."

"Forget I said anything. Erase the entire conversation from your brain."

"And miss out on watching you squirm? Where's the fun in that?" He pins me with a shit-eating grin before casually strolling to the refrigerator and opening the door. "What do you want for dinner?"

"You mean there's a choice?" I prop one hand on my hip. It's usually protein and vegetables, though my body is already thanking Austen for it.

Austen is a serious athlete, and he's careful about what he puts into his body. It's why he's usually the one to cook. I don't complain. Having a home-cooked meal handed to me every night is one of the perks of having a roommate. The other is the obvious spank bank material. Though one could argue that's a con.

"You can always cook for yourself," he coolly replies, retrieving two steaks and a broccoli stir fry mix from the refrigerator shelf.

"I'm in a rush," I admit, yanking my shirt up over my head as I head toward the laundry room. "I've got an editorial meeting in an hour. Mol is determined to crack the whip this year."

Molly is one of my small-knit group of friends on campus. She recruited me to *The Daily Californian*, the student-run newspaper on campus, last year when she discovered I was writing on the sly. Having just been promoted to editor, she is intent on making radical changes and stamping her mark all over her predecessor's legacy. I'm hoping she doesn't ruffle too many feathers, but she will have my support, no matter what.

Austen's Adam's apple bobs in his throat as his gaze darts to my bare abs. It's not the first time I've noticed him checking me out, but I've no idea what to make of it. "Someone's been putting extra hours in at the gym," he quips, drilling me with a fiery look.

"My brother Kent created a plan for me when I was home over summer break. He's a hardcore gym rat, and he knows his stuff." I shrug off his veiled compliment, though I'm secretly pleased.

After that shit went down with Brock, I needed something

to distract me until I returned to Berkeley, and the gym was my salvation. It's fair to say I'm in the best shape of my life, even if I'm nowhere near as ripped as Kent or my older brother Keven and I pale into insignificance beside the work of art that is Austen's body.

Austen looks like he's carved from rare stone. He's all sharp lines, curved dips, and cut angles. It speaks to incredible dedication and commitment, and I'm in awe of him. Not just for his stunning otherworldly body but his attitude to life in general.

Austen owns who he is, and he makes no apologies for it. Nothing fazes him, and he seems to take everything in stride. He has a set goal, and he works his butt off in the hopes of achieving it.

Meanwhile, I'm over here in the loser's corner. Directionless. Goalless. Hiding my true self behind a façade I'm beginning to despise. Lying to everyone who means anything to me. Letting scum of the earth manipulate me.

Maybe some of Austen's confidence and strength will rub off on me.

Maybe eventually I'll grow a pair and take back control of my life.

Until then, I'm stuck on this hamster wheel until I find the courage to jump off.

"Okay, everyone. Thanks for your time. Don't forget to download the assignment schedule and take note of your deadline before you leave," Molly says, drawing the meeting to a close. Chairs screech as everyone gets up. I stifle a yawn, glancing at my watch for the umpteenth time, already knowing I'm going to be late.

Fuck him.

He can damn well wait.

I wait until the others have left the room before turning to my friend.

"Well?" she asks, chewing on the corner of her mouth in an obvious tell. "How did I do?"

"You were awesome," I truthfully reply, leaning in to kiss her cheek.

"Honestly?"

"I wouldn't lie to you, Mol." I grab her into a hug. Molly is a teeny-tiny thing, and at five foot nothing, she barely reaches my chest. "Everyone seems excited for your ideas, and I didn't sense any bad vibes." She shucks out of my arms, and I press a kiss to the top of her short blonde head. "You've got this."

"Thanks, Keats." She squeezes my waist. "I don't think I could do this without you."

"Sure, you could, but I'm glad I'm here to support you." I grab my bag, slinging it over my shoulder. "I've got to dash."

"Hot date?" she inquires, lifting a brow.

I snort out a laugh. "Not likely."

Her features soften. "Why not? I thought you and Melissa were done for good this time, or are you having second thoughts?" What she really means to say is fourth, fifth, or sixth thoughts because Melissa and I have been on and off like a yo-yo for the past two years.

I shake my head. "I don't have any doubts. Melissa and I weren't right for one another."

"You were with her a long time though. I'm sure you miss her."

I run a hand through my hair. "Honestly? I do miss talking to her. We'd been together since we were fifteen, but our relationship was more like brother and sister at the end. I made a mess of things since coming here, and I really hurt her. I don't want to keep doing that. A clean break is best for everyone."

I meant what I told Mel the night of my brother's going away party. I care about her, even though I've been stringing her along for years. It wasn't intentional at the start, but I was never going to be the one for her, and she deserved to know that sooner. I feel shitty for how I've treated her, because she's a sweet girl and she didn't deserve to be misled.

My cell pings with a new message, and I don't need to check to know who it's from.

I kiss Mol on the cheek one final time. "We still good for Saturday night?"

"Absolutely. We'll see you at the diner at eight."

Ignoring the incessant pinging of my phone, I make my way to the rendezvous point, my mood souring with every step I take. There can only be one reason why he wants to meet, and it's nothing good. I knew this wasn't the end of it, even if I'd been hoping I was wrong. It seems he's determined to milk this for everything he can get.

I check left and right before ducking into the alleyway, confirming no one is watching me. An arm flies out as I pass an overflowing dumpster, and I'm roughly slammed against a wall.

My bag drops to the ground with a thud as his tatted arm pushes up under my neck. Planting both hands on his shoulders, I shove him back, grateful for the extra muscle I've gained since he last saw me. Working out wasn't just a distraction. It served another purpose too.

"You're fucking late," Brock hisses, drilling dark eyes into me.

"My meeting ran over, and I'm here now."

"You're not calling the shots, Kennedy." He jabs his finger into my chest.

I thrust his finger away. "You don't get to threaten me. We had a deal, and I paid up. I owe you nothing."

His lips curl into a menacing sneer. "We *have* a deal, and you'll stop owing me when I say."

"You made other copies," I surmise, working hard to keep my panic at bay. I'm not surprised. I knew it was too easy. I've been waiting for this to come back at me. It's the fear that haunts me in my sleep every night.

He barks out a derisory laugh, and I wonder how I ever found him attractive.

"Don't play dumb, Kennedy. We both know you're smarter than that. You knew this wasn't over."

"How much?" I ask, just wanting this conversation to be over.

"Fifty thousand." He doesn't even break a sweat.

"Fifty and we're done," I reply, folding my arms and glaring at him.

He laughs. "Cute but stupid." Gripping my chin, he lowers his gaze to my mouth, and bile travels up my throat. "Meet me back here on Sunday. Same time. Bring the cash with you."

Chapter Two
Austen

"You coming to the party Saturday or wimping out on us again?" Nolan asks, as we emerge from the showers after practice with towels wrapped around our hips.

"Hard pass." I open my locker. "I'm all partied out."

"This is what happens when you tie yourself to the same pussy for life." Nolan slaps me on the back, and it's borderline unfriendly. "So much wasted potential. The jersey chasers would go crazy if you dumped that bitch and started living your best life."

I grit my teeth, barely controlling my frustration. "Gia is not a bitch, and I'm sick of repeating myself. Why the fuck do you even care?" I grab my bag and shut my locker, sitting down on the bench as Colton stalks toward me, completely nude, dick flapping about as he towel-dries his wet hair.

"It's called team bonding," Nolan retorts, slamming his locker door shut.

"Let me get this straight," I say, pulling on boxers and

sweatpants. "I'm not being a team player unless I'm banging every jersey chaser and sorority girl in sight?"

"You're the odd man out," Alan adds, supporting the douche. "And it's obvious."

"What's obvious is you two clowns don't know when to shut the fuck up." Colton opens his locker with one hand while drying his balls with the other.

"Your argument lacks merit." I drill Nolan with a pointed look before pulling my shirt on over my head. "But, by all means, bring it to Coach and see what he says."

"It's like you don't like us or something," Alan says.

You think? Schooling my lips into a neutral line, I quirk a brow. "We back in kindergarten now?" My gaze bounces between the two dipshits. "The only thing that matters is how I play on the field and that I have every player's back out there." I shove my wet towel into Nolan's chest. "Judge me on that and only that."

I don't wait to hear their replies, grabbing my bag and exiting the locker room.

"Hey, man. Wait up!" Colton calls out after me, and I slam to a halt, hanging back for him. "You want to grab something to eat?"

"Sure," I say on autopilot, though I'd much rather return to the apartment and eat with Keats.

Which is exactly why I'm going to eat with my best buddy instead.

We settle into our usual booth at our favorite restaurant, ordering steaks and baked potatoes. Stretching my arm out along the back of the booth, I level a look at my bud across the table. "Is Nolan still sore I moved out, or was that shit for some other reason?"

I'm genuinely shocked no one has figured my secret out. I might be living a lie, but I don't hide who I really am. All it would take is someone to properly look at me, to *see* me, and the truth would be staring them in the face.

I suspect Colton knows, and it's not like him to keep shit inside, but he hasn't mentioned a word. I've been tempted to tell him several times, but it's not fair to ask him to keep my secret, so I can only tell him the truth if I'm planning on telling the whole team the truth.

I want to.

Because I'm sick of lying. I never should have agreed with Coach Ramirez. He caught me at a rare vulnerable moment, and I conceded when my gut already knew it was a bad idea.

But I've come this far, so I might as well stick it out.

"Nolan's a dick," Colton says, guzzling his water. "He's pissed you ditched us for Kennedy. Thinks you sold out for his connections."

"He's an idiot." I swirl my bottlecap on the table. "I didn't ditch anyone. I moved out because living in party central was driving me fucking insane. And Keats' connections aren't worth shit to me. His family doesn't move in sporting circles."

Keaton's mom was at the helm of Kennedy Apparel, a billion-dollar global fashion brand, until she sold it a few years back. His entire family are celebrities, initially off the back of their mom's success. But that's changed in recent times.

Keanu and Selena Kennedy are well known in their own right, even though they have now retired from modeling, and Lana Kennedy—she is married to Keaton's brother Kalvin—is a *New York Times* bestselling author. Lana and Kalvin got together under...unusual circumstances that fascinated and disgusted the world at large. His brother Keven's fiancée, Cheryl, is starting to make a name for herself as a shit-hot photographer while Keven is known for keeping a low profile. Keats's brother Kyler was a large presence on the motocross circuit when he was a teen, gaining him a devoted fanbase. His marriage to his cousin Faye was a big scandal even though it's not illegal to marry your cousin in Massachusetts and she's not his blood relative, because Kyler, Kaden, and Keven share a different dad than the other four brothers. Kaden's affair with Eva—the woman who is now his wife—made all the headlines because she was married to a known mobster. And Kent, one of the triplets, is notorious for getting into trouble with the law. He's the so-called black sheep of the family.

The interest in the Kennedys only seems to have multiplied since Alex Kennedy sold her business, helped along by a succession of scandals and dramas that has kept America riveted and fixated on the famous family.

But, as far as I know, their influence doesn't extend to the sports world. So, Nolan is talking out of his ass again.

"You're preaching to the choir," Colton says, gesturing the pretty waitress over. "Two more waters, sweetheart."

"Coming right up, Mr. QB." She shoots him a flirty wink, sashaying her hips as she walks away.

"I know the house wasn't your scene, man," he adds, kicking his sneakers up on the seat beside me. "If I had a girlfriend, I'm sure she'd want me to move out too."

"Gia had nothing to do with it," I truthfully admit. "It was my decision, and I don't regret it. Keats is cool, and he's easy to live with. We have space, and it's quiet, and I can study in peace."

Unlike a lot of the players on the team, my GPA actually matters to me. It's important that I graduate with a degree. I'm realistic enough to know my chances of an NFL career are slim.

Don't get me wrong.

It's my dream.

Always has been, and I'm giving it my all in the hopes I secure a contract, but if I don't, I need to ensure my backup plan becomes a reality.

Getting this degree goes a long way toward achieving that goal.

"Just don't be a stranger, yeah?" Colton smiles as the waitress sets our food down in front of us. "We might not share living space anymore, but you're still the only person I trust completely. On and off the field."

"That doesn't change because I moved out." I cut up my steak. "And I've got your back. Always."

Stifling a yawn, I close my textbook and call it a night. I stand, rotating my shoulders back and forth until the corded knots are less tight. I make a mental note to order a new chair for my desk because this one is a piece of shit that provides little support for my back, despite the manufacturer's claims.

My hand is curled around the door handle when my cell rings. Spotting Gia's glossy auburn waves and striking green eyes staring at me from the screen, I immediately pick up. "Sup, babe?" I lean back against the door, awaiting her response.

"If the rents ask, I'm with you this weekend, 'kay?"

"Sure. Thanks for the heads-up." I cross my feet at the ankles. "Where will you actually be?"

"Hendrix has a gig in Kansas City. I'll be with him and the band."

"He treating you right, Gia?" I ask, like I always do, because I feel a responsibility to check often.

Her heavy sigh filters down the line. "He isn't a bad guy, Austen. I wish everyone would cut him some slack."

To be clear, Hendrix is an ass. I mean, what indie rocker changes their name to Hendrix in a nod to the legendary rock giant? *Could he be any more unoriginal?* Find your own groove. Your own rhythm. And make something of your own name.

Don't hang off someone else's coattails. To me, that just sums the guy up.

While he's never done anything to deliberately hurt Gia—to the best of my knowledge—he's too self-obsessed to truly cherish her the way she deserves. Last time I was home, I heard rumors his drug use is out of control, and that does little to ease my concern.

But he's her choice, and it doesn't look like that's changing anytime soon.

"Be safe. And I'm always here for you. You need me anytime, just call."

"You're my best friend, Woody. You still know that, right?"

I smile. "To infinity and beyond, Jessie." The words glide off my tongue without thought. Gia and I were only six when the first *Toy Story* movie debuted in movie theaters, and we were *obsessed*. We dressed as Woody and Jessie every Halloween for years.

Fun times.

"You're my favorite deputy!" Her light laughter tickles my eardrums, and my gaze drifts to the two framed photos by my bed.

The picture taken last year—at the outdoor market near our homes, the one with our arms wrapped around each other—is purely for show, though the happiness radiating between us was completely genuine, even if the circumstances were fake. The second photo, taken the Halloween we were ten, always brings a smile to my face. We're wearing our *Toy Story* costumes, sporting matching goofy grins as we smile at the camera, carrying bags loaded with candy and goodies.

Most of my childhood memories include Gia, and there isn't anything I won't do for her.

Including fake dating her so she can sneak around with her no-good, talentless rocker boyfriend behind her disapproving parents' backs. She deserves better, and I'm not the only one who knows it.

We hang up, and I saunter out to the kitchen to grab a snack. The TV is on, and Keats is lounging in the leather recliner, staring at the screen in a bit of a daze, looking like he's a million miles away. "You want anything, Kennedy?" I shout out, opening the refrigerator. My question snaps him out of it. Blinking rapidly, he shakes his head, not answering with words. I study the back of his head, wondering what's up. He's been uncharacteristically quiet since he returned from his newspaper meeting last night.

Grabbing a shake and a banana, I head toward the living area, flopping down on the leather sectional. Keats stares straight ahead, not even acknowledging my presence, which is weird, because the guy is politeness personified. My eyes roll to the screen, and my lips curve into a smile. "I didn't know you were into *Ink Master*. I love this show."

He turns his head to me, his eyes roaming the tattoos covering both my arms, the ink fully visible in the sleeveless training top I'm wearing. "That doesn't surprise me in the least."

I grin. "This show started my interest in tattoos. I think I was like eleven or twelve when it first aired. Been hooked ever since."

"I only started watching it when we decided to get inked," he admits.

"We?" I inquire, peeling my banana.

"My brothers and me. We got inked when we turned eighteen. It was Kent's idea. He thought I'd chicken out, but I didn't."

"Why would he think that?" I ask, taking a large bite of the banana.

"Because he thinks I'm a prude." He swallows hard while

watching me finish the banana in three quick bites, squirming on the chair, his eyes dilating a little.

"Why?" I fold the banana peel on the arm of the couch to dispose of later, chugging back my shake as I eyeball my friend with fresh curiosity.

Keaton shrugs. "Kent likes to live on the wild side. Drugs. Booze. Sex. You name it, he's tried it. I've always been too tame, too meek, too good in his eyes."

"Doesn't make you a prude," I say, emptying the contents of the shake down my throat.

"He doesn't understand me. No one does," he quietly adds, and I'm more intrigued than ever.

I sit forward, leaning my elbows on my knees. "Who are you, Keaton?"

His gorgeous blue eyes stab mine, and a whole host of emotions washes over his face. We stare at one another, and a simmering electrical charge ignites the air. It's not the first time, and I doubt I'm the only one who feels it. Just when I believe he's not going to answer, he clears his throat, looking pained when he says, "As soon as I figure it out, you'll be the first to know."

Chapter Three
Keaton

Pushing open the door to the diner, I blow a kiss at Angela, the kind older waitress who always looks after me and my friends when we dine here, as I stride toward our usual booth at the back, with the last-minute dinner guest following in my wake.

"Hey, guys. This is—"

"Austen Hayes," Kate confirms, cutting across my introduction. Tossing her long dark hair over her shoulders, she extends her arm, offering my roommate her hand. "Delighted to meet you. We were beginning to think Keats was making you up."

"I assure you I'm a real boy," Austen quips, and warmth spreads across my chest.

Kate snorts out a laugh, making Austen smile. They shake hands, and then I formally introduce my roommate to Kathryn Whitley aka Kate and Molly Irwin aka Mol. He already knows Sebastien Hewitt, or Seb to his friends, because the three of us share several of the same classes.

The girls have heard all about Austen, including how we met after I finally came clean about the night we attended our first and only party at the notorious football house. They know we became fast friends after that, sitting together in class, texting all the time, and although they joined me at a few of his football games, this is the first time the girls are meeting him in person.

Austen slips into the booth alongside me and Seb, across from the girls. It's a bit of a tight squeeze, and as my thigh brushes against Austen's muscular one, I hope to fuck that won't become a problem, because some days I only have to look at the guy and I'm instantly hard.

"I can't believe you've been hogging this football god all to yourself, Keats," Kate says, pouting up a storm. "Haven't you heard sharing is caring?"

"Austen has a crazy busy schedule and not a lot of free time," I explain, not rising to the bait as I pass a menu to him.

"Congrats on the game today," Mol says. "You were amazing out there."

She's not wrong. He fucking nailed it today. Like always. Austen has oodles of natural talent, and he's got to be a shoo-in for the NFL. Guy sure works hard enough to deserve it, but I know how fiercely competitive it is and that only a small percentage of college football players get signed.

Her cheeks flush a little, and she's working hard not to stare at him. I get it. Austen is drop-dead gorgeous, and it's almost impossible to tear your eyes from him, especially when he gives you his undivided attention.

I probably zone out at least fifty percent of the time during our conversations, because the way he looks at me—with this dark, intense concentration, like every word that comes out of my mouth is the most fascinating word in the English language —turns me into a drooling space monkey.

"Thanks. They were tough competition, and it was touch and go for a while, but we got our shit together." He turns to me, the movement bringing our bodies even closer. "What's good here?" His green eyes are bright and clear, and at this proximity, I can count his long, thick, jet-black lashes and the light smattering of freckles across the bridge of his nose. His lips curve at the corners, as is his habit, and my eyes drop to his lush mouth before I get a grip. Heat floods my cheeks as I look down at my menu, pretending to scan the options I already know by heart. "Depends on what you're in the mood for," I mutter, desperately trying to regain my composure.

Crushing on a taken, straight guy is not cool, Keaton. I remind myself of this at least ten times a day, but it's not helping.

See, this is what happens when you've got the worst case of blue balls this side of the Pacific Ocean.

"What am I in the mood for. Hmm." Austen drums his fingers on the tabletop, and his deep, sultry tone is like a shot of liquid lust straight to my groin.

If I didn't know better, I'd say he was flirting with me.

My cock surges to life, straining against my jeans, and I inwardly cringe as I attempt to focus on unsexy thoughts.

My brain, unhelpfully, returns to that alleyway on Wednesday night, and anger and frustration wipe the board of every other emotion. I've been in the worst mood since Brock made his latest demand, and I was determined to push the asshole from my mind and enjoy tonight, but it's a virtual impossibility, because my life is a clusterfuck of epic proportions right now, and I can see no light at the end of the tunnel.

At least my boner's gone though.

Austen clicks his fingers in my face. "Earth to Keaton. Where'd you go?"

I snap myself out of it, running my hands through my hair as air whooshes out of my mouth. "Sorry. I've a lot on my mind."

"I've noticed." Concern leaks from his eyes, as it has the past couple days. I appreciate that he hasn't pried, but I know he's noticed how introspective I've been.

"Is everything okay?" Seb asks, pressing his back against the side of the booth, pinning me with a strange look.

"I'm fine. It's fine. Just some family stuff." Guilt slams into my gut, and I hate that I'm always lying to my friends.

I'm the shittiest friend.

The shittiest brother.

The shittiest son.

"Saturday night is my cheat night," Austen says, refocusing the conversation. "So, nothing's off-limits."

"Now that sounds like an invitation and a half." Kate waggles her brows suggestively, acting more flirtatious than usual. I don't know if that's to get a rise out of Seb—the guy I'm certain she's secretly crushing on—or if she's genuinely interested in hooking up with Austen.

That thought lands like sour milk in my stomach, and I react without thinking. "He's got a girlfriend," I blurt.

"I know." Kate leans back against the booth, eyeing me curiously. "You've told us about her at least a hundred times," she says, clearly teasing.

"Have the burger," I mumble, unable to look Austen in the eye at this point. "It's their signature dish, and you can't beat it."

Thankfully, the conversation turns lighter after that, and I relax somewhat.

After we've finished eating, we pay the check and head to a local bar we frequent because A. they turn a blind eye to our fake IDs and B. they have five pool tables and run regular pool tournaments where Seb and I have been known to clean up at doubles.

We grab some beers and head to the pool tables, snatching

the last free one. The girls climb onto stools at the high table beside us, talking in hushed voices.

"You play?" Seb asks Austen, while chalking his cue.

"Badly," Austen admits, leaning his arms over the back of a stool. His biceps flex and roll with the motion, and I swear half the damn room notices.

Another reason I like this bar is it's a little off the beaten track, and I don't garner too much interest when I'm here. However, showing up with one of Berkeley's golden boys means there is no flying under the radar.

"Is that the truth, or are you trying to hustle us?" I ask, propping my butt against the edge of the table.

"If I'm hustling, you'd know all about it." Austen shoots me that lopsided, sexy grin, and it gets me hot. "My talents definitely don't extend to pool, but I'm game to play." He shrugs in that cool, casual manner of his, and fuck me, if that isn't one of the sexiest things about him. He knows he's shit, that I'll beat his ass, but he doesn't care. He's in it for fun, not for the win.

Kate and I take on Seb and Austen while Mol sits it out. She's not a big pool fan, and she usually just comes along for the conversation and the craft beer.

Unsurprisingly, Kate and I win because Austen wasn't lying. He sucks. Big-time. But he takes our teasing in good humor. After another couple of games, we call it quits, exiting the bar together.

"The night is still young," Kate announces, looping her arm through Seb's, as we walk along the street. "Let's hit up the football party. We haven't been there since Keats did a disappearing act on us."

I wouldn't mind a few more beers to take the edge off my stress, but I know the main reason Austen moved out of that house was because he was sick of the endless parties.

"We don't have to go," I say, lowering my voice so only

Austen can hear me. "I'm just as happy to go home and drink a few beers there."

Austen's tongue darts out, wetting his lips, and I try not to stare. "I don't mind going as long as we don't stay all night."

"Okay, cool." I call out to the others, and they turn around. "We're in."

"Great." Kate rubs her hands together in glee. "Let's par-tay!"

"Hey." Austen grabs my arm, holding me back as Seb, Kate, and Mol disappear into the basement room ahead of us. Loud rhythmic beats filter out through the door before it swings shut after them. "Just a heads-up. At least one of my teammates believes I ditched the house to move in with you for your connections." Lowering his arm, he shoves his hands deep into his pockets.

I focus on his words and not the fact my skin is tingling from where he touched me. "What connections?" I ask, my brow furrowing. "My family has jack shit to do with the world of sports."

Although, if we wanted to reach out on Austen's behalf, I'm sure Mom could make that happen. I bet she knows someone through someone else who could help. But I already know Austen well enough to know he'd hate that. It'd be the very last reason he moved in with me. "That guy is a total jerk," I add, even though he hasn't identified which one of his teammates is spouting that stupid shit.

Austen grins, staring at me with respect and some indeci-pherable emotion, and I swoon on the inside. My eyes flit to his mouth, very briefly, and I wonder what it would be like to kiss him. To feel those plump lips wrap around my cock and—

Crushing on a taken, straight guy is not cool, Keaton.

I need to get with the program and stop fantasizing about someone I have zero chance of being with.

Forcing myself to concentrate on the here and now, not on the imaginary porno playing out in my head, I blink, focusing on the guy standing in front of me. Except Austen is staring at my mouth, doing nothing to disguise that fact.

Blood travels south, and my cock twitches to life behind my jeans.

Not fucking now.

I will honestly die if I sprout a boner in front of him just because he's looking at my lips. My chest heaves as I watch him watching me, and I wish I was more experienced because I don't know if this means something or nothing at all.

Austen jerks his head up abruptly, taking a step back. Tension is so thick it's almost a tangible substance. My heart pounds behind my rib cage, and blood rushes to my head, making me lightheaded.

"Nolan is a fucking asshole," Austen admits, his voice sounding hoarse. "And he has zero filter. Just ignore him if he says anything."

I clear my throat, rubbing the back of my head. "Duly noted."

I follow Austen inside, and the noise of the crowd elevates to ear-shattering proportions when they notice their wide receiver is in the house. Austen gets swallowed up by the masses and I plunge into the crowd, scanning the room until I find my friends.

"Here." Mol hands me a red cup. "It's warm and cheap as shit, but it's all they've got."

"As long as it has an alcohol count, it'll do." I drain half the cup in one go, and Mol is right, it's nasty, but I'm sure it'll do the trick.

For the first time, I understand why Kent turns to alcohol to handle shit in his life. I don't know what stuff he's dealing with, because he never opens up, but I get the appeal now. I want to drink until I'm in that blank space where my brain stops reminding me of the mess I've made of my life.

"Come dance with me," Mol says, grabbing my elbow. I knock back the rest of my beer, handing the empty cup to Kate. She's pressed in close to Seb, whispering something in his ear, and I wonder if she has plans to finally make a move.

Seb is completely oblivious to her infatuation in a way I hope Austen is with mine.

Mol leads me across the room into the middle of the lively crowd dancing to the hypnotic beats bouncing off the walls. We dance for a few songs before I need to take a piss. She returns to the guys as I make my way to the bathroom.

I'm on my way back when I'm accosted. The guy's shoulders are almost the width of the door he's blocking. It wouldn't be hard to tell he's a football player from his physique, but I made it a point to study all their names when Austen and I first formed a friendship, so I know who he is.

"Hey. It's Keaton? Right?"

I nod. "And you're Nolan."

"You've heard of me." He beams like Keaton Kennedy knowing your name is something to celebrate.

"Austen has mentioned you."

His smile stretches as he steps out of the way, wrapping his large arm around my shoulders. "That's my man. So, I know you're helping him out, but you got any love in your heart for his buddy? I could sure use a leg up, if you know what I mean." He winks, and I puke in my mouth a little.

Is this guy for real? I know he doesn't mean the sexual innuendos because Nolan is as straight as a plank of wood, but he couldn't be any cheesier or any blunter if he tried. No wonder

Austen wanted to leave this place if all his football buddies are as dense as this guy.

I've only met Colton Barnes, and it was a brief meeting, but I know he's a decent guy because Austen wouldn't be tight with him if he wasn't. But the jury is out on everyone else on the team.

I shuck out from under Nolan's arm, turning to face him. "The only way I helped Austen was offering him a room at my place when he needed somewhere quieter to live. That's the extent of it, man. So, whatever you've heard, it's wrong. I don't have those kinds of connections."

His smile is quickly replaced with a scowl. "He warned you off me, didn't he?"

"I don't know what you want me to say. I don't have any sports contacts. Sorry, man." Turning around, I walk off, because I don't want to get into it with a guy who could crush me just by sitting on me.

Austen strides across the room, a look of fierce determination on his face, and it's a lot like watching Moses part the Red Sea. Everyone automatically moves out of his way, leaving a clear path for him to reach me. I watch his long legs eat up the distance between us, and it's impossible not to notice how sexy he is in his tight-fitting black jeans and short-sleeved black Henley.

I am so screwed, because this attraction isn't fading anytime soon.

It's only growing stronger.

Chapter Four
Austen

"Y ou okay?" I ask Keats the second I reach him. The instant I spotted Nolan at his side I was on the move. I don't trust that dipshit around anyone, especially not Keaton.

An amused grin spreads across his delectable mouth. "It's cute you think I need you to ride to the rescue, but I'm a grown-ass man. I can take care of myself."

"Duly noted." I enjoy throwing his words back at him and the slow scowl replacing the amusement on his face. "Come meet my other buddies. If only to prove not everyone is an idiot."

I introduce him to the guys, glad Alan has gravitated to Nolan's side, and they're currently engaged with a couple jersey chasers. With any luck, they'll disappear upstairs. Since I've moved out, I've realized a lot of my issues living here stemmed from those two guys.

My phone vibrates in my pocket, and I'm tempted to ignore it when I see Mom's name flashing across the screen. But she usually only calls me once a week—every Friday night so my family can wish me luck for the game—and the fact she's calling this late on a Saturday means something's up. I gesture to Colton, asking him with my eyes to watch out for Keats, before dashing outside where it's quieter.

There's a gang sitting out on the chairs at the back of the yard, so I walk to the corner of the house, leaning against the brick wall as I return her call. Mom picks up on the second ring.

"Austen. It's Mom. Can you put Gia on the line, please."

Shit. I think fast. "We're at a party, Mom, and she's in the bathroom. I'll get her to call you back."

"Get her to call home. Her mother's been calling her for hours, and she's not picking up."

All the tiny hairs lift on the back of my neck. I hope the only reason Gia isn't answering is because she can't, and not because something or someone is stopping her from picking up. "What's going on?"

"Kendall was in a car accident earlier today. She's been rushed to the hospital, and Anne is frantic with worry. She wants Gia to come home." Mom and Anne, Gia's mom, have been best friends since they were two, and they're as close as sisters.

Fuck. That's rough. Kendall is Gia's fifteen-year old sister, and her only sibling. "Is it serious?" I hate thinking of anything happening to Kendall, because it'd be like something happening to Charlotte. My only sister is thirteen, and I would die if anything happened to her.

"We don't know yet. The last call I had from Anne she said Kendall was in surgery and they were waiting for an update from the doctor."

"Keep me posted, and I'll send Gia home on the next flight." I hope to fuck I can get through to her; otherwise, I may have to fly to Kansas tonight to hunt her ass down.

"Do you want me to book a flight for her?" Mom offers.

"No. I might need to book an Uber too if the next flight is out of San Fran, so it's best if I handle it."

"Okay, honey." There's a short pregnant pause. "When are you coming home? We hardly ever see you anymore. Just once, it might be nice for Gia if she wasn't the one traveling."

Not this shit again. "Mom, you know I have games every Saturday. It's why Gia travels to me. It's why I can't come home until Thanksgiving."

"Everyone asks about you all the time. I know it would be great if you could come back. Maybe attend one of your brother's games. That would mean a lot to him."

Guilt twists my stomach into knots. I hate missing Orwell's games. He attended every one of my football games when I was in high school, but here's the thing—Orwell couldn't give a shit about basketball. He plays it for fun. He has no intention of playing basketball in college after he graduates next year. I know Mom knows this. Orwell doesn't mince his words, but she still loves sticking the knife in any chance she gets, and I'm sick of it.

Even if I wasn't lying to her about Gia, I still wouldn't be able to make it home more regularly. There literally isn't time. Dad understands, and I know he's tried talking to her, but it doesn't seem to register in her brain.

"Mom, you know I'd be there if I could. Orwell gets it. And I'll be home for Thanksgiving. I promise." I rub a tense spot at my brow. "I'd better go find Gia. I'll talk to you later." I don't give her time to reply, hanging up straightaway.

"Is everything okay?" Keaton asks at my back, and I silently curse.

I turn around, facing him. His brows are pinched, his face awash with concern and confusion. "How much did you hear?" I ask.

"Enough."

I nod. "I can explain, but not here, and I need to leave."

"I already called an Uber. Go wait for it at the curb while I let the guys know we're leaving."

I try Gia as I walk around the side of the house, past the spot where I found Keats comatose, striding through the front yard, heading toward the car that has just pulled up at the curb. She doesn't pick up, so I try her again.

Racing footsteps thud behind me as Keats catches up.

We both slide in the back seat, and Keats talks to the driver while I call Gia repeatedly.

The car takes off, and I lean my head back against the headrest, willing Gia to pick the fucking phone up. *Where the fuck is she?*

Keats is quiet, casting troubled glances in my direction every couple of minutes, but he doesn't interfere, and I'm grateful for his calm patience.

After the tenth fucking call, she finally picks up. "Where are you?" I ask, working hard to maintain an even tone.

"At a party," she yells down the phone, and I lift the cell away from my ear before she bursts my damn eardrum. "It's fucking *epic*. You should come, Woody." She titters. "Oh my God. That sounded so wrong." She laughs like a hyena, and acid crawls up my throat.

"Are you high?" I grit out in a clipped voice.

"High on life, dude. S'all good."

"Gia, I need you to get your shit together and call your mom." I hate telling her this when she's high as a fucking kite, but she needs to get her ass on a plane stat. "Kendall's been in a car accident, and you need to get to the hospital."

"Shit, what? Is she okay? Oh my God." She bursts out crying, and I can't make any sense of what she's saying.

"Who is this?" a man with a gruff voice roars down the phone, and my free hand clenches at my side.

"Hendrix, this is Austen. I need you to get Gia on a plane ASAP. She needs to get to the hospital."

"Shit, man. I can't put her on a flight in her current state. I'll make sure she gets on the first flight in the morning."

I grind my teeth to the molars. I hate this asshole. "She needs to get on a plane *now*. Her sister has been in a car accident. I don't know how serious it is. Just go with her. Take care of her until she lands." He knows not to show up at the hospital. Not if he values breathing.

"Aw, fuck, man." The noise of the party rages in the background. "Okay. I've got this." He hangs up, and I've got zero confidence in the dude, but there's nothing more I can do.

"He sounds like a complete fuckwad," Keaton says, breaking the silence in the car, and I throw back my head, laughing heartily.

"You're a good judge of character," I say, as the Uber pulls up in front of our apartment building. Keaton pays on his phone, and we get out. We don't talk as we take the elevator to the top level, but I know he'll have questions, and I'm prepared to give him answers.

We both change into drawstring pants and light sleep shirts, reconvening in the living area a few minutes later. Keaton hands me a bottle of water as he settles into his favorite chair. "Hit me with it," I say, uncapping my water and slowly tipping the cold liquid into my mouth.

"Who is Gia to you?"

I pull my feet up onto the couch, draping my arms over my bent knees. "She's my best friend from back home. Her mom and my mom have been best friends since they were in diapers. They married two guys who were best friends and moved in beside one another. I've grown up with her family like an extension of my own."

"Really?" He quirks a brow.

"Yup." I grin. "Couldn't make this shit up if I tried."

"That's...kinda cool."

I snort out a laugh. "Sometimes, it felt like I had two sets of parents. Definitely *not* cool. Trust me."

Especially after I came out.

"Why does everyone think Gia is your girlfriend?"

That one's a little harder to explain. I want to give him the full truth, but then he'll be a part of the big secret, and I already know Keaton is harboring big enough secrets of his own.

I don't want to add to his burden; I only ever want to lighten his load.

So, I give him the part of the truth I can admit.

"Our parents' greatest wish is to see Gia and me married. We've been super close since we were kids, but it's never been anything more than friendship. For both of us." I take a swig of my water, hating that I have to fudge the truth, because it's not who I am.

I hate how one lie has triggered so many others. How lying has become too commonplace now in my world. For a guy who has always prided himself on being authentic and true to himself, this really kills me.

Keats patiently waits me out, and it's one of the things I really like about the guy.

"She's dating this guy," I continue.

"Hendrix," Keats blurts, letting me know he heard the entire phone conversation. It wouldn't be hard with how loud those two were shouting.

I nod. "Gia is dating Hendrix, and her parents hate him. Like truly hate him with a capital H."

"Why? What's wrong with him besides him having an unfortunate first name."

I chuckle. "There is nothing unfortunate about it. The guy changed his name to that."

Keats' mouth drops open, and I chuckle again. "Getting the picture now?"

"Somewhat."

"He went to our high school, but he was two years older than us. Gia is gorgeous, and she caught his eye. They've been hot and heavy since she was fifteen. Gia's dad caught them fucking in the back of his truck when she was only sixteen, and he blew a gasket. He couldn't do anything about it, except forbid her from seeing him."

"Not that that stopped Gia," Keats surmises.

"That only spurred her on. She's been seeing the guy on and off since she was fifteen. It's caused huge tension in her family, and it came to a head when he was arrested at nineteen for drug possession. He got off on a technicality, but as far as Gia's parents are concerned, the guy is only going to drag her down. They told her they'd withdraw their support for college if she didn't stop seeing him."

"So, you pretended to date her while she continued seeing him in secret," he adds, connecting the dots.

I nod.

"Shit, man. That's rough on you."

"Not really." He doesn't know it served a purpose for me too. "It's not like I have time for dating."

"Both sets of parents will be so mad when they find out."

I shrug. "Let them be mad. If Gia's parents hadn't interfered, I think she might've broken away from him by now. Instead, all they've done is push her closer to him."

And after tonight, I'm realizing how badly I've screwed up too. Gia is a free spirit. A believer that you should be able to live your life however you want to live it. She's never been into peer pressure or following trends just to be cool. Art means the world to her, and getting her art degree is everything. I've never known her to take drugs, although she doesn't judge anyone who does. I've never worried about that possibility even if she was hanging around with that lowlife.

It's clear I've underestimated the power he has over her.

And how much I really know my best friend.

Because the Gia I know and love would never take drugs.

Chapter Five
Keaton

Austen is already planted at the island unit when I wander into the kitchen the following morning. He's up at five a.m. most mornings, but it's unusual to find him awake before me on a Sunday. "You're up early," I remark, opening one of the overhead cupboards to remove a mug.

"Couldn't sleep," he admits, lifting his head from his laptop.

"Is there any news from home?" I inquire, pouring coffee into my mug.

Putting his pen down on his pad, he scrubs his hands down his face. "Kendall is going to be okay. She broke her leg and her arm, but she'll make a full recovery."

"That's good." I eye him carefully. A muscle ticks in his jaw and his shoulders are locked up tight. "So why do you look like someone just kicked your puppy?"

He exhales heavily, rubbing at his eyes. Dark shadows bruise the skin under his eyes, but even tired, Austen is still the most gorgeous guy I've ever seen. "Gia got there a couple hours ago, and Mom ripped me a new one for letting her on a plane in that condition."

I refill his cup before claiming the stool beside him. "That's not on you."

It took me ages to sleep last night after Austen revealed he is in fact single. Not that it makes any difference. Because I'm still the wrong sex, but try telling that to my overactive imagination as it conjured up all kinds of HEAs involving me and my sexy as fuck roomie.

"Thing is, if she'd been with me, I'd have been on that plane with her. Doesn't matter that I'd have to turn around and come straight back. I would never have left her alone if she was smashed."

"The douche didn't go with her, did he?" I sip my coffee, trying not to stare at Austen's fingers as they comb through his hair.

"The asshole didn't even go with her to the airport. I spoke to Gia. She said he needed to network and he couldn't ditch the party."

"Wow. He sounds like a keeper."

"I feel like a piece of shit." He places his elbows on the counter, resting his head in his hands. "I thought I was doing the right thing helping my friend, but I'm only helping her get into trouble. If I was a true friend, I would've said no."

Cautiously, I place my hand on his back, smoothing it up and down his spine. He stills for a second before relaxing into my touch. Swallowing thickly, I clear my throat. "True friends trust their friends to make their own choices. Support them, even if they don't agree. I'm betting you told her your concerns about Hendrix."

"I did," he admits, letting out a little groan as my hand moves more firmly up and down his back. "Fuck, that feels good."

Buoyed by his comment, I stand, keeping one hand on his back as I position myself directly behind him. "You're tense. Let me help." I move my hands to his shoulders and begin kneading the corded muscle through his light top.

Silence engulfs the room, and a crackle of electricity sparks between us. My mouth is dry as I work his knotted shoulders and upper back, savoring the feeling of my hands on his hard, muscular body, even through his clothes.

"I did share my concerns," he says after a few minutes of silence. His voice is deeper and gruffer than usual, and it's doing funny things to my insides. "But she loves him, and she begged me to help her. I couldn't say no."

"Then you have nothing to feel guilty about, and she should have your back now." This girl sounds selfish. Like she's taking advantage of Austen's friendship.

"She does." He shifts on the stool as I press my thumbs into the carved muscle of his back. "Thankfully, our parents think she's only drunk. She told them I was drunk too and that I wanted to go with her, but she refused."

I'm glad to hear it, but she's still selfish in my book. I know Austen said he doesn't have time to date, but he can't even hook up with any girl, because his relationship status is well known on campus and he's too nice of a guy to have anyone think he's cheating on his girlfriend. *Does she even realize how much he has sacrificed for her?*

"Fuck." Austen rests his head down flat on the marble countertop, and my hands stall on his shoulders.

"Am I hurting you?"

"No. It feels good. Don't stop."

I resume kneading his shoulders and upper back, willing the semi I'm sporting to back the fuck down before Austen notices I'm turned on massaging him. But it's a risk I'm willing to take, because the opportunity to put my hands on him is too great to pass up. "Do you have plans today?" I ask, as I continue to work his muscles.

"Nothing except finishing the assignment we have due next week, and I'm almost done."

"Want to catch a movie with me?" Sunday is the only day Austen doesn't have practice or a game or classes and the only chance I have to spend quality time with him. Most Sundays, he uses it to sleep in and catch up on his studies, but we usually do something together, even if it's only grabbing dinner out.

"Sure." His voice sounds strained, and he hisses between his teeth as I move my hands down lower on his back. "What's playing?"

My cheeks heat at having to make this admission, but I soldier on. "*Twilight*," I admit.

Austen picks his head up, twisting around to look at me, his lips curved into a smirk.

"They're playing all the movies for the next few weeks in honor of the new *Twilight* book that just released. The one from Edward's point of view."

Austen stares at me, and I drop my hands to my sides, feeling self-conscious. He sits up, swiveling around on the stool, eyeing me with that penetrating lens of his. His smile broadens, and I wipe my hands down the front of my sweatpants, nervous in case he thinks I'm a freak or a dork because I have a teeny-tiny obsession with the sparkly vampires.

"Team Edward or Team Jacob?" he asks, licking his lips.

"What?" I blurt, blinking rapidly as my gaze dances between his eyes and his mouth.

"Are you Team Edward or Team Jacob?" he repeats, more slowly, his eyes lowering to my mouth for a nanosecond.

"Edward," I reply after a few silent beats.

His lips purse. "We can't be friends anymore." He shakes

his head. "I'm disappointed. Jacob is way hotter and way more interesting than Edward."

Have I wandered into some alternate realm where debating how hot dudes are is normal for straight guys? Has Austen guessed what I've tried so hard to hide? Or have I deliberately misinterpreted all his subtle glances and sly touches? Is he into dudes too?

I rake my gaze over his drool-worthy face and lick-worthy body, and I can't see it.

Fuck.

Has he figured out I'm gay and this is his way of inviting me to open up? My head is a hot mess.

"I've rendered him speechless," Austen says, grinning openly.

I flip up my middle finger, pulling myself together. I'm not ready to fess up, even if I've thought about it before.

No one knows my secret, and I've been tempted to tell Austen so many times, because he's a cool guy and he isn't judgmental, but the fear of losing his friendship always holds my tongue. If I'm wrong, my revelation could ruin what we've built here.

I hated living in the dorms freshman year because I was the center of attention and my roomie was a jerk who tried to use my celebrity status to his benefit. I thought moving into my own place last year would be amazing, but I didn't enjoy living alone, because it was lonely as fuck. I love living with Austen, and we have slotted easily into each other's lives. I don't want anything to mess with that.

Still, this could be an opportunity to test the water, so I roll with it. "Only because anyone who can't appreciate how darkly attractive and inherently intriguing Edward is deserves to be met with a blank face and utter silence." I cross my arms, returning his smirk. "I was giving you a few minutes to come to your senses."

He laughs, and his eyes flare to life, reeling me in to their hidden depths. My cock throbs behind my sweatpants, straining to the point of pain, and if Austen looks down, he will totally notice I'm hard as a rock. "Think you've got that backwards, man."

We stare at one another, and a familiar heady tension pulses between us, growing thicker the longer we remain eye-locked. My hands twitch at my sides with an almost overwhelming craving to touch him. I have never had such a visceral reaction to any guy before. I want to bend him over the counter and fuck him senseless until he's screaming my name.

Austen stands, his chest lifting, as his gaze trails the length of my body. Panic swirls in my chest, but I stand my ground, even knowing he's noticed the monster erection in my pants. My eyes glide down his torso, popping wide when I spot the obvious bulge tenting his pants. I suck in a sharp gasp, as arousal ignites flames in the tiny gap between us. Our eyes meet again, and my heart is pounding in my chest, slamming wildly against my rib cage as my brain grapples to understand the situation.

Austen's eyes bore into me, as if he can see straight through the mask I've spent years perfecting. I hold his gaze, staring back at him with more confidence than I feel.

Kiss me. Fuck me. Love me.

I scream on the inside, pleading with him to hear. Begging whoever is listening up there to let this not be delusion.

Because if this is real—if Austen Hayes is attracted to me in the way I'm attracted to him—then I'm rewriting the playbook.

"I'm surprised it's not busier," Austen admits, a few hours later, when we're seated in the back row of the theater, waiting for the movie to start. He hasn't brought up the kitchen incident, and neither have I. I was worried things would be awkward after he exited the kitchen without commenting on the elephant in the room, but things are normal, and I'm grateful our friendship is intact.

"They've been playing it for weeks," I confirm, grabbing a handful of popcorn as he slides his cell out of his pocket. "They're screening *New Moon* from next week, and tickets are already sold out."

Austen chuckles as he taps out a message on his phone.

"What's so funny?"

"Orwell's giving me crap for watching *Twilight*."

"Heathen. You can tell him I said that." I pop some popcorn in my mouth.

"He thinks I'm a bad influence on you," Austen replies, grinning as he repockets his phone. "If only he knew it was *you* corrupting *me*." He waggles his brows, as I try not to think about the many ways I'd willingly love to corrupt him. His hand dives into the bucket of popcorn the same time mine does, and our fingers tangle in the buttery goodness, sending delicious tingles shooting up my arm.

"I've been wondering," I blurt, ripping my hand from the popcorn before I intertwine my fingers permanently in his. "Which of your parents loves the English classics?"

He arches a brow, slowly dropping popcorn into his delectable mouth, while watching me with mounting amusement.

Heat creeps up my neck, and I hate how flustered I get in his company sometimes. "Austen, Orwell, and Charlotte. It's obvious someone named you after some of the greatest English literary geniuses of our time," I add.

"Top marks, dude," he replies, molding his lips over his straw and pulling deeply from his soda. "Most people don't connect the dots. And it's my mom. She was an English major in college, and she teaches at the local high school now. We have all the classics at home, and she could repeat most of them verbatim."

"Impressive. I'm a fan of that era too. *Wuthering Heights* is one of my favorite books."

He shifts in his chair, and his knee brushes against mine as he pins me with a focused stare. "I've seen some of your journals around the apartment. You write?"

I nod, chewing on the inside of my mouth. "I started journaling a few years ago. It was easier to share my thoughts on the page than out loud. And then I started writing poetry, and I've written a couple of fictional novels." My cheeks are even hotter after admitting that. The only people who know about my writing are my ex and my sisters-in-law, Lana and Faye.

"I'd love to read them some time," Austen says, and I instantly shake my head.

"Nope. Never happening."

He wears a familiar lopsided grin. "If you're going to share them with the world, you should at least test-drive them beforehand."

"I'm not planning on publishing them."

His expression turns more serious. "Why the hell not?"

"For one, the inevitable comparisons with my famous author sister-in-law. And I'm not ready for assholes to pick my words apart. Lots of people love my family, but we have our fair share of haters too. I won't open myself to that."

"That would happen whether you're famous or not. Not everyone will love your words, but you shouldn't let that hold you back."

"It's not just that," I whisper as the lights dim. "I don't

know if I want to be a writer. For now, it's more like personal therapy."

He nods slowly. "I can relate. And it's not like you couldn't change your mind in the future. You could always publish under a pseudonym," he suggests.

I have considered that, and it would offer anonymity. One part of me wishes it was that simple. If it's what I wanted to do with my life, it *would* be that simple. But I have no clue what I'll do when I finish college, and that uncertainty only mirrors the uncertainty in other aspects of my life.

Chapter Six
Austen

Keaton is acting weird. Weirder than he has been lately, and I'm starting to really worry about the guy. From the way he's virtually hugging his backpack, one would think he's hiding the national treasure in there. He kept it close in the theater, and he has it tucked under his arm on the seat in the restaurant, like it's his kid. I sip my water as I watch him glance at his watch for the umpteenth time, noticing how tense his entire body is. If we were at home, I'd return the favor and massage him.

Fuck, his hands on me earlier was hot. He barely touched me, and my cock turned to steel. I know he was hard too, and I thought he'd finally fess up, but he chickened out. I came close to admitting my truth, but I won't ever force someone from the closet. He needs to be the one to open up first, because that indicates he's come to terms with who he is and that he's in the space where he's ready to at least consider the possibility of a relationship.

The waitress places the check on the table, and we both reach for it, but Keats gets there first.

"It's cool," he says, opening his wallet. "I got it."

"No, you don't." I snatch the silver plate away from him, slapping my card down and handing it to the bemused waitress before he can complain. She walks off to process the card, and I lean back in the booth. "You paid for the movie tickets and popcorn. Dinner's on me."

Keaton is generous to a fault. I know he has a trust fund, and his family is fucking loaded, but that doesn't mean he should pay for everything. My family isn't rich, but we're comfortable, and I'm on a full ride, so I can afford to pay my way.

"Next time, dinner is on me," he says, draining the last of his water.

I shrug, because it's no biggie.

"I've got to bail. I'm meeting Mol at the library," he says, sliding out of the booth.

He won't meet my eyes, and that's how I know he's lying. That and his obvious nervous disposition. "Okay."

"I'll meet you back at the apartment." He slides his backpack on over his shoulders, grabbing the straps. "Thanks for today. It was fun."

I rest my ankle on my knee, tilting my head to the side as I look at him. He's so adorable, and he doesn't even know it. "It was. We should watch *New Moon* next. As soon as some tickets open up."

A genuine smile graces his mouth, and my stomach flip-flops. Keaton is a seriously good-looking guy, but when he smiles? Damn. It's like being blinded by the sun. A blanket of heat wraps around me, and fuck it. I want this guy. I want him badly. I just need to be patient and wait for him to get on the same page as me.

But it's hard, in every sense of the word, because I haven't been laid in a long time and I'm dying to fuck him until he passes out.

"I'm all over that," he admits, jerking his head up. "Later, man."

The waitress returns with my card, and I leave a cash tip before hightailing it out of there. I spot Keaton's tall dark head in the distance, and I walk fast to catch up. When I've closed the gap between us, I deliberately hold back, ensuring there are enough people in front of me, in case he turns around.

He turns left, heading away from the campus, and I know my instincts are correct. I trail him from a cautious distance, into a seedier part of town, my trepidation mounting with every step. When he veers right into an alleyway, alongside a dive bar that is known as a hive of illegal activity, my Spidey senses are on full alert.

Pulling up my hood, I risk a peek around the corner. The alley is dark, and I can't see shit from here, so I dip down, keeping my back flat to the wall as I creep after my friend. I slam to a halt when I hear voices and duck behind a dumpster, craning my neck around the edge, instantly not liking what I see.

Keaton is behind another dumpster a little farther ahead. The single red-painted door just behind the dumpster has a subtle overhead light that casts a spotlight on him and his companion.

Keats' stance is defensive as he glares at the tall guy with messy shoulder-length dirty-blond hair and multiple piercings. I recognize him straightaway, because he goes to Berkeley and his rep precedes him.

Brock Jonas is the only son of a media mogul from Malibu. He's another trust fund kid, but unlike Keaton Kennedy, this guy isn't a good guy. He's an arrogant prick with a known drug problem. He plays drums with some seedy indie rock band and drug-and-drink-fueled orgies are their specialty.

What the fuck is Keats doing with him?

Knots twist in my gut as I watch Keaton hand him a thick, large envelope. I'm ready to intervene when the douche shoves Keaton in the chest, but Keats shoves him back, his nostrils flaring as a slew of words leave his mouth. I wish I was closer so I could hear what they're saying, but I can't risk being seen. Keaton would *not* be happy I've followed him. Not when he's gone to such lengths to keep whatever this is from me.

Crouching down, I hide in the dark corner, tucked against the dumpster, as Keaton strides past, frustration and anger rolling off him in waves. I watch that prick Jonas disappear behind the door that leads into the bar before I give chase, but Keaton is nowhere in sight when I emerge on the sidewalk.

I take my time walking back to the apartment, mulling over my options. *Do I fess up and risk Keats' wrath? Or try to find out what's going on before I face him with my suspicions?*

Saying or doing nothing is not an option.

If Keaton is in trouble, and I have a chance to do something about it, then I'm doing something about it.

Keaton isn't home when I return to the apartment, so I finish my assignment, take a shower, and flop down on my bed to call Colton. Colton banned Brock from the football house during freshman year, and he seemed to know something about him, so he's my first port of call.

"That dude is bad news, bro," Colton says, after I've posed my question.

"Tell me something I don't know." Propping my head against a few pillows, I cross my feet at the ankles as we talk. "Can you find out any specifics?"

"I'll ask around."

"Be discreet."

"Obvs." A pregnant pause ensues. "You sure you're not in trouble, man?"

"I promise I'm fine, and I wish I didn't have to be so vague." I didn't tell Colton what I saw tonight or why I want him to dig into Brock because Keaton values his privacy highly, and I'm not about to rat him out when I don't even know what's going on.

"It's cool, man. I'll see what I can find out."

We hang up, and I pull out my sketch pad, picking up the design I've been working on intermittently these past few weeks. Finding time to sketch, or ink, is challenging these past couple years as I have minimal downtime. But it's my passion. My go-to when I need to unwind. However, I can't switch off tonight, and the longer Keaton is gone, the more anxious I feel.

Without stopping to second-guess myself, I hop up and stalk out of my room. Opening the door to Keaton's bedroom, I scan the neat and tidy layout for any evidence of drug para-phernalia, but there is nothing in plain sight. Bile churns in my gut as I step into his room, rifling through the drawers of his desk before moving to his nightstand. My hand falters on the small handle, and air whooshes out of my mouth. I rub at the tightness spreading across my chest.

This is wrong. I can't invade the guy's privacy, even if I'm worried he's got a drug problem. While it seems like the obvious reason behind the exchange in the alleyway, I've seen nothing so far to indicate Keaton has ever taken drugs, and I could be way off base.

Backtracking out of his room, I close the door behind me and return to my room. Throwing myself on my bed, I bury my head in the soft comforter, hating what I just did.

The only way I'll find out if Keaton is in deep shit is if I ask him.

I'll see what I can dig up on Brock Jonas, and then I'll talk to my friend and offer him my help.

Keats has completely closed himself off, and it's like living with a stranger. I can tell he's on edge, and I've asked him what's wrong, but he brushes my concern aside, spending more time out of the apartment than usual, and when he's here, he hides away in his bedroom, avoiding me at all costs.

So, when Colton asks to grab a bite to eat after practice on Thursday, I'm praying he has some intel for me.

"Word on the street is Jonas is estranged from his family and he's cut off from his trust fund," Colton says in between ripping into his steak.

"Is he dealing?"

Colton shakes his head. "Appears not."

I rub my thumb along my bottom lip as I rethink my theories. *If Keaton wasn't paying him for drugs, what was in that padded envelope? Is it possible they are friends? Or their families are connected in some way and he's helping him out?*

Brock doesn't seem like the type of guy Keaton would be friends with, even if their families are close, but Keats wouldn't deny a friend in need, even if he didn't like him. Or maybe it wasn't cash in the envelope and I'm putting square holes into round pegs. "Discover anything else?"

"He's still a Class-A jerk with a chip the size of a planet on his shoulder." Colton pops a fry in his mouth. "And his band is still shit." He wipes his hand on his napkin, eyeballing me. "You sure you're not in trouble, dude? Because you know I've got your back."

"It's not me."

A knowing look appears on his face. "Please don't tell me Kennedy's mixed up with that loser?"

I retain my casual stance even as everything locks up inside me. "Why would you assume this is anything to do with Keats?"

"I can count on one hand the guys you're close to. Apart from me and Kennedy, and maybe Preston, I can't see you sticking your neck out on a limb for anyone else."

"I'm not sure what's going on," I admit, finishing my chicken. "But I intend to find out."

We part ways, and my determination solidifies as I walk back to the apartment. I'm having it out with Keaton tonight. Whatever shit he's gotten himself into, he needs to know he's not in it alone.

Sounds of conversation greet my ears as I enter the apartment, closing the door behind me. My sneakers squelch off the tile floor as I walk the length of the hallway. I slam to a halt the second I round the corner into our open-plan living space, staring in disbelief at the guy sitting on the leather sectional across from Keaton.

Tugging a hand through his long dark hair, he stands, flashing me a megawatt grin. He's wearing his signature ripped jeans, rocker tee, and scuffed boots ensemble, and it takes me back in time.

"Hey, man," Dax says, moving toward me because I'm rooted to the spot. "Long time no see."

"What the hell are you doing here?" I snap. *And what the hell have you been telling my roomie?*

Chapter Seven
Keaton

usten looks shell-shocked, and I'm thinking I made a mistake letting this guy into our place. When he said he was an old friend of Austen's from Golden, I didn't stop to think about whether it was true.

Because I'm still a naïve idiot. Clearly.

"I was in the neighborhood, so I thought I'd stop by," Dax says. His gaze slowly peruses the length of Austen's body, and he's about as subtle as a fucking brick. My brain is going into meltdown mode.

Who the fuck is this guy to Austen?

"Bullshit," Austen says, a muscle pulsing in his jaw. Austen is the epitome of cool, calm, and collected, and I've rarely seen him ruffled. But this guy has him ruffled, and I don't like it one little bit. "And stop fucking looking at me like that."

Dax brings his eyes back to Austen's face, cocking his head to one side. His expression turns more serious. "I just transferred here. I was chosen for the MFA program."

I already know this because he was telling me about the prestigious art program that only supports twelve students a year. He explained he graduated with an arts degree from the University of Denver last spring.

Austen rocks back on his heels, and it's clear the news is a big surprise. "Why here?" he asks in a clipped tone.

"You know why, man." Dax takes a step toward him before glancing briefly over his shoulder at me. Turning his attention back to Austen, he says, "Can we go somewhere private to talk? We have lots to discuss."

I level a stare at the back of his head, shooting invisible daggers into his skull, reversing my original opinion. I thought the guy was cool, but I take it back.

"We have nothing to discuss." Austen's jaw is locked tight, and his eyes burn with anger.

"I'm sorry, man," Dax blurts, grabbing Austen's arm. "I made a mistake, but I want to make it right." He steps even closer until there's barely breathing space between them.

I want to yank him away from Austen, and scream at him to get the fuck out, but it's not my place.

Austen shoves Dax's hand off him, and I silently cheer.

"I know it's bullshit with Gia," Dax continues, oblivious to the hostility rolling off Austen in toxic waves. "I know you miss me as much as I miss you. I know—"

"Not here," Austen snaps, silencing him with a cutting look. "Follow me."

Wait? What? Why the fuck isn't he throwing this douchebag out?

Pain slices across my chest as I watch the guy I have feelings for lead another guy to his bedroom.

Grabbing a beer from the refrigerator, I knock half of it back while I try to figure this out. I need the distraction to stop me from eavesdropping on their conversation.

Dax wasn't subtle.

You don't say that shit in front of another guy unless it's the truth.

You don't blatantly eye fuck another guy unless you're confident in your sexuality.

Dax is gay or into dudes. That's one hundred percent true. I'm sure of it. He clearly has feelings for Austen, and from the anger radiating from my roomie by the bucketload, it's clear there is history between them.

They had some kind of relationship.

Does that mean Austen is gay? Or is he bi?

I don't actually give a fuck about the label if it means what I've begun to suspect—that Austen *is* into guys.

Because that changes everything.

Hope blossoms to life in my chest as I consider the possibilities. Maybe I haven't been imagining the sexual tension between us. Maybe it isn't all one-sided. Maybe Austen *is* attracted to me and there's hope for a romantic relationship after all.

Except he's in a bedroom with his ex-boyfriend or ex-fuck buddy, and my initial burst of euphoria dies an immediate death.

A loud crash echoes from the corridor leading to the bedrooms, and I'm racing there before I've consciously processed the action. Muffled shouts reverberate behind Austen's closed door, and I plant my spine to the wall, heart beating frantically in my chest, as I strain my ears, hoping to hear what they're arguing about. It goes quiet, and blood rushes to my head. As the silence lengthens, I squeeze my eyes shut, attempting to ward off the images forming in my mind.

My chest heaves painfully as a clear groan rings out from behind the door. I hang my head as intense pressure sits on my chest, making breathing difficult. Pain rampages through my body, laying siege to my heart, and I have never felt like this—

like someone's just yanked my beating heart out of my chest—any of the times I ended things with Melissa.

Another groan rips through the air, and a messy ball of emotion clogs the back of my throat. Nausea churns in my gut, and I think I might puke when images of Austen and Dax fucking surface in my mind.

I should move. Because standing outside Austen's bedroom listening to him have sex with another guy is the worst form of torture, but I can't make my limbs move.

Breath stutters in my lungs as a loud thump is followed by fresh shouting. The door swings open unexpectedly, and I'm caught, like a deer in the headlights.

Dax sneers, his gaze raking over me in a quick, derisory fashion. He deliberately shoulder checks me as he storms past, nostrils flaring and fists balled at his side. A minute later, the front door slams, and awkward silence descends.

Austen appears in front of me like an apparition. His hair is messed up, his lips are swollen, and the top button on his jeans is undone.

I swallow over the massive lump in my throat, ignoring the stinging pain behind my eyes, as I attempt to pull off a nonplussed expression.

"Shit." Austen walks toward me, smoothing out the longish strands of hair on top of his head.

I'm rooted in place, unable to move for fear this swirling ball of tempestuous emotion gathering speed inside me will be unleashed.

"I can explain," he says, stopping in the doorway, pinning me with his tortured gaze.

"You don't have to explain anything," I reply, my voice all choked up.

He strides toward me, clasping my face in his large palms. "We both know I do."

I stare at him, feeling my eyes well up, which is ridiculous because Austen has done nothing wrong. We're only friends. He's free to fuck around with whomever he wants. Free to keep the knowledge of his sexuality to himself. It's not like I've been forthcoming about my feelings or my sexuality.

"Fuck, Keaton." His Adam's apple bobs in his throat as he stares into my eyes, and I don't know what he's reading there. Right now, I'm an open book, and I'm probably projecting everything.

He releases my face, grasping my hand and leading me out into the living room. I let him steer me over to the couch and push me down.

He walks off, and I try to get a grip while he grabs my half-finished beer from the kitchen. "You look like you need this," he says, handing it to me. He sits beside me, so close our thighs are brushing, uncapping a bottle of water and chugging the whole thing back. I knock back a mouthful of beer, still dazed.

Austen angles his body so we're facing one another with our knees touching. He holds nothing back as he maintains eye contact with me. "Dax is my ex-boyfriend. I'm gay."

I can only stare at him. I'm unable to form words. This is something I've dreamed about—Austen being gay. Not the ex-boyfriend part, obviously.

He cups one side of my face. "Cat got your tongue?" he teases, and I know it's his way of breaking the stifling tension.

"How long?" I rasp, staring into his eyes, trying to unravel the mysteries there.

"How long have I known I was gay, or how long was he my boyfriend?"

"Both."

Dropping his hand from my face, he settles back on the couch, gently pulling me with him so I've no choice but to relax my tense back muscles. We turn toward one another, our faces so close it wouldn't take much to close the distance and plant one on him. "I came out when I was thirteen," he explains. "Although I knew I was into guys way before that." He maintains eye contact, giving me his full attention. "I dated a couple of guys in high school, much to my parents' dismay, but it wasn't serious until I hooked up with Dax."

My face scrunches into a scowl before I can school my features.

His lips kick up ever so slightly. "You don't like hearing that."

"Not one little bit," I truthfully admit. There's no point holding anything back now.

"He was two years ahead of me, and we dated during his senior year."

It's ironic both he and Gia were dating seniors when they were sophomores, and maybe that's part of the reason why Austen agreed to fake date his bestie when things turned to shit.

"It was intense," Austen admits. "He's an intense kind of guy."

I'll bet he is. Jealousy coats my eyes in a red haze, and I totally regret letting that guy into our home. Not that it really matters. If Dax has come here for Austen, he won't let anything stand in his way. I know I wouldn't if I was lucky enough to ever call Austen mine.

Austen threads his fingers through my hair, and butterflies swoop through my chest. "But it's in the past. We split up just before he left for college." His features soften as he toys with my hair. "This might hurt, but I never want to be anything less than truthful with you. No more lies. No more hiding shit."

I nod, prepared to give him my truths too.

"I was in love with him," he admits, and acid collects at the base of my throat. "But I was only sixteen, and he was my first proper relationship."

"Did you two—" I cut myself off, because it's none of my business, and I'm not so sure I want or need to know the answer when it seems obvious.

"Fuck?" he quietly says, staring into my eyes. "I lost my virginity to him," he adds, and I fucking hate myself for not throwing a punch at that guy when I had a chance.

"I had to ask." My bitter laugh wraps around the heavy tension in the air.

"Keats." Austen clasps my cheeks again. "He doesn't mean that to me anymore. I was brokenhearted when he left. I knew it had to happen, but I struggled to let go. I called and left messages." He flinches before a smile smooths out his features. "Not my finest hour." His jaw hardens and the smile slips off his face. "But I got the message loud and clear when he returned for Christmas with his new boyfriend. Especially when he paraded him around me, ensuring I understood it was well and truly over."

"That was cruel, but I can see that guy doing that," I admit.

"Now I'm older I see the entire relationship in a totally different light. Which is why him turning up here is such a mindfuck. I was someone to fuck around with, for him, while I had convinced myself I was in love. I know now it wasn't that, and I have no desire to reconnect with him."

"Yet you just kissed him." It pains me to say those words, and I drop my eyes, not willing to let him see how much it has hurt me.

"It was a lapse in judgment. He kissed me, and I—" He drops my face, leaning his head back on the headrest, sighing.

I wait for him to gather his thoughts, resting my cheek against the leather.

Austen reclaims my gaze while reaching for my hand. "I'm

sorry if I hurt you. When I took him to my room, it was because I didn't want you to discover the truth like that. Not from him. I told him to get lost, but he kissed me and grabbed my cock, and it's been so fucking long since I had sex my body reacted on autopilot, and I forgot myself for a few minutes. When I woke the fuck up, I pushed him away and told him to get the fuck out."

"It's okay." I squeeze his hand even though it really isn't. But he's not at fault. "You don't owe me any apologies. I'm just glad you didn't fuck him. I'm not sure I wouldn't have barged in there and dragged him off you."

Austen sits up straighter, his eyes flashing with heat. "How long have you been into guys, Keats?"

I draw a brave breath before admitting something I've never told anyone. "All my life, man."

He moves in closer, trailing one hand up my body, before firmly clasping the back of my neck. His eyes drift to my mouth, and I stop breathing. His minty breath fans over my lips as he whispers. "How long have you been into *me*?"

My hand gravitates to the back of his head, and I hold him as firmly as he's holding me. "From the very first second I met you," I admit, praying my thundering heart doesn't find a way to escape my chest, because it would suck to die just as my greatest fantasy is coming to life.

"It was the same for me, and that's all I need to know," Austen says, and I've no time to swoon or celebrate before his wicked mouth is on mine, and we're kissing feverishly, devouring one another like we can't get close enough.

Chapter Eight
Austen

Angling my head, I lick at the seam of Keaton's mouth, and he opens for me without hesitation. Our tongues collide, and a groan slips from the base of my throat. My cock is throbbing painfully behind my jeans, and I pull Keats closer, fisting his tee, until we're chest to chest and his warm, hard body is melting against mine. Our kiss turns savage, and I tug on his lower lip with my teeth, precum leaking from my cock when he moans into my mouth.

Pushing him down on the couch, I nudge his legs apart so I can settle in between them. His hips jerk as our cocks meet behind our clothing, and I rock against him, shoving my tongue in his mouth at the first feel of his long, thick erection pressed against mine. It's everything I'd hoped for, and more, and I want to rip his clothes from his body and drive my cock in his ass until we forget where he starts and I end.

But I can't, because we need to talk more first, and I never want to push him out of his comfort zone.

Keaton grabs hold of my ass through my jeans, and my eyes roll back in my head. His lips move from my mouth to my neck, and his slight hesitation only makes me adore him more. "Fuck. That feels so damn good," I rasp, grinding my pelvis against his.

"I think I could come just like this," he admits, and I prop up on my elbows, grinning down at him.

"Not on my watch." I kiss him again, more softly this time, before easing back. "I want my mouth on your cock." His eyes flare with dark heat, and I know he wants it, but I need to hear him say the words. "Would that be okay?"

He snorts out a laugh. "What do you think?"

I rock my hips against him, grinding down, and the whimper that escapes his mouth has precum leaking from my crown again. Fuck. I think I could probably come just like this too, which is something that didn't happen even as a teenager.

I'm so hot for this guy, and I don't think he knows it.

Palming his face, I trace my fingers through the light layer of stubble on his chin and cheeks. "I need you to say it."

All hints of humor fade from his face as he reaches up, clasping the nape of my neck. "I want whatever you have to offer, Austen." Heat burns like an inferno in his eyes as he lifts himself, bringing his mouth close to mine. "I want it all."

Slamming my lips down on his, I push him back flat on the couch, thrusting my hips against his as desire sweeps through me. Our kissing is wild, and we're thrusting and rubbing against one another, clearly on the same page at last. I sit up, kneeling between his knees, while I yank my gray Henley up over my head. Keats strips out of his tee, revealing his broad shoulders, toned abs, and the impressive ink on one arm. I trail a line of kisses along his jaw, down his neck, and over his collarbone, flicking my tongue against his nipples while rubbing my cock against his.

"Hell." Keaton groans, grabbing my ass cheeks. "You're killing me, man."

I lick a path down the center of his curved abs, grinning as I stare at the dazed look on his face. "All good things come to those who wait," I tease, palming his erection through his sweatpants. My lips move lower while I use my free hand to toy with the happy trail of dark hair leading from his lower belly, snaking beneath his waistband. Keats rocks his hips up as a strangled sound rips from his mouth, and I decide to stop teasing both of us.

We've waited long enough for this moment.

I sit back on my heels, and he lifts his hips so I can tug his pants down. His cock springs free, and I arch a brow at him in surprise. "Commando?"

His cheeks stain red, but he maintains eye contact as he says, "I might've been in the middle of jerking off when I was rudely interrupted by an unwelcome guest."

I flash him a grin. "Rude, indeed," I murmur, letting my gaze roam his hard length. He's big, like me, and his skin is soft to the touch as I wrap my fingers around his shaft. Veins pulse in his cock as I slowly pump him in my hand. My thumb swipes across the precum at his crown, and his hips jerk again.

With one hand, I push my jeans to my knees, releasing my erection.

"And he had the nerve to criticize me," Keaton drawls, noticing I share his apparent love of going boxer-free.

I press down against him, cock to cock, chest to chest, tugging at his lower lip with my teeth. He swallows hard, and his eyes are like two flaming orbs of desire. "You'll never hear me complaining," I whisper against his mouth, as my teeth graze his masculine jawline. "I was a little surprised. Pleasantly so."

"Can we move past the flirty talk and get to the cock sucking part now?" he asks, enthusiasm underscoring his tone, and I burst out laughing.

"Always surprising me," I say, sliding my cock against his.

"Fuck," we chorus at the same time, and I almost come undone at the look on his face. It's a mix of want and fear, of trust and vulnerability, of love and lust. I kiss him as I fist both our cocks in one hand, jerking us off together, while Keats' warm hands knead the cheeks of my ass.

Breaking our lip-lock, I stare deep in his eyes as I check one last time. "You sure you want this?"

"I want it," he groans, as I pump our shafts faster and harder. "I want you."

Sliding down his body, I kiss, nip, and suck a path along his tempting flesh, my tongue pausing when I gently bite his nipples, and then I quit teasing him, nestling between his thighs, as I lower my head and take him into my mouth. I'm not sure what he likes, but I do what I like, because there will be plenty of time to learn each other's kinks. For now, I want to worship his cock and make him feel good.

Gripping the base of his shaft, I work more of him into my mouth, sucking him deep until he hits the back of my throat, while jerking his cock at the same time. I watch him for any sign he's uncomfortable, but all I see is fire and heat and want. Bobbing my head, I trail my lips up and down his cock, while my free hand plays with his balls, maintaining eye contact because the look of raw need on his face is an aphrodisiac.

I take my time, savoring the feel and taste of him, never wanting this to end. I long to bury my fingers in his ass, to massage his prostate until he screams his release from the top of his lungs, but we need to have the ass talk before I go anywhere near his puckered hole, so I rein myself in.

"Austen. Fuck." Keaton's dick pulses in my mouth, straining harder, and his balls tighten against my fingers. "I'm going to come."

With my eyes, I tell him to keep going, and a few seconds later, he explodes, shooting ropes of salty cum into my mouth and down my throat. His back arches off the couch, and the garbled noises leaking from his mouth almost have me coming on the spot. Flushed skin paints his neck and his cheeks a warm pinkish-red color I'm quite partial to, and the way he clamps down on his jaw and bites his bottom lip is sexy as fuck.

He has the hottest cum face *ever*.

I fondle his ball sack while I continue sucking his dick, milking every last delicious drop, until he flops down on the couch and his eyes blink open. I crawl up over him, carefully checking his face for any hint of remorse or regret, relief washing over me when I find none. "You okay?" I ask, running my fingers through my hair.

His answering smile pins me in place. "Holy fuck." His smile expands, and I'm drowning in all things Keaton Kennedy. "That was the best damn blowjob of my life."

I waggle my brows, pleased at his compliment. "My talents extend beyond the field."

He laughs, a carefree kind of laugh that warms every part of me. Tenderly, he cups my face. "They do." Drawing my lips to his, he kisses me passionately, his tongue diving into my mouth. "Is it wrong that I love tasting me on your tongue?" he whispers in my ear.

"There is nothing wrong about that. Or anything we want to do to one another."

"Good." He pushes me off him. "Because I want *you* to taste yourself on *my* tongue."

Fuck. This guy is slaying me. I have a suspicion this is all new to him, but I can't tell for sure, because his earlier nerves have been replaced with quiet confidence that is sexy as fuck.

He drops to the floor, kneeling in front of me. "My turn." Licking his lips, he motions for me to sit up.

Removing my jeans fully, I toss them aside before sitting in front of him with my thighs spread. "You don't have to reciprocate," I tell him even though my balls are fit to burst.

His eyes narrow as his hands move up my legs. "You think I don't want to taste you? That I haven't fantasized about sucking your cock? You think I haven't dreamed about being on my knees before you?" His eyes pop wide. "Shit. I didn't mean to admit that." Renewed vulnerability replaces his previous confidence, and I figure he's getting all up in his head.

Leaning forward, I ruffle his hair. "I've imagined those things as well, Keats. In case I wasn't clear, I'm into you too, and this is so much more than fucking around. I don't do that. I'm more of a relationship kind of guy, and I suspect you are too." I hold his gaze, staring deep into his eyes. "You should never be afraid to tell me what you're thinking."

His hands stall on my knees, and his eyes lock on mine as he admits, "It's just... I've never had a relationship with a guy, and you're clearly more experienced than me."

This isn't a conversation I want to have when his face is inches from my dick and I'm leaking precum like lava, but he needs reassurance, and I'll never deny him that. "There's no manual, Keats," I say, gripping his chin and forcing his gaze to mine. "And your lack of experience only adds to the attraction. We do what feels right. What feels good. For *us*. And trust me when I say there is nothing you could do to me that I wouldn't enjoy." My cock jerks, wanting to get the talking part over and done with. "Especially the feel of your lips wrapped around my cock, but you set the pace, and if you've changed your mind..." I might die of the worst case of blue balls known to mankind. "It's okay," I add, semi-lying.

His brow smooths out, and his shoulders relax as his hands start moving up my legs again. He fixes me with a shy smile as his fingers edge along my thighs. "I'm pretty sure there are plenty of men and women who would kill to be sitting between

Austen Hayes' legs, about to suck his big dick in their mouth. Trust me, I want this."

"He thinks I have a big dick," I quip, gripping his hair as his mouth moves closer to where I ache for him.

His eyes narrow on me again. "Shut up. You know you have a big dick. Don't start acting all humble and shit now."

I chuckle, leaning back and spreading my thighs wider. "Just suck me, man, before I self-combust."

"Fuck," I hiss, throwing my head back when his hand encircles my dick and he starts stroking me. Heat surges through me, and my balls are already tingling. "Shit, Keats." More precum leaks from my cock, and this could be embarrassing. "It's been a while. I'm not going to last long."

I hiss again when his tongue flattens on the tip of my cock, and my hips jerk of their own volition. He stares at me with wanton lust while licking the precum glistening on my crown, and it's hot as fuck.

"Keaton," I warn, thrusting my hips up, needing his mouth on my shaft. And then he's taking me in, a bit at a time, a look of fierce concentration on his face as he slowly slides his mouth up and down my erection. Stars detonate behind my eyes, and I want to hold back, to treasure every second of his warm mouth on me, but I'm too fucking greedy and way too horny, and I need to come.

I thrust into his mouth as he picks up speed, his fingers jerking the base of my cock while his lips slide up and down my shaft, similarly to how I blew him. Every few minutes, he moans and shifts on his heels, and his cock is rock hard again, jutting forward proudly. Knowing he's turned on sucking my dick elevates my arousal, pushing me to the brink of ecstasy.

"Fuck, fuck, fuck," I moan as my balls lift and tighten and tingles zip up my spine. "I'm going to come," I warn, giving him time to pull off me, but he doesn't. He sticks with it like a champ, and I'm even more impressed. His mouth widens, and he takes me deeper, filling his mouth with my cock. The second my crown hits the back of his throat, I shatter, roaring his name as I come and I come and I come, in endless streams of pent-up desire, shooting it all down his throat.

Sweat dots my brow and glistens on my chest as I come down from the most exquisite high. The couch shifts beside me, and I force my eyes open.

"Was that okay?" Keaton asks, his face a mix of self-satisfaction and anxiety.

This guy. Seriously. I must've done something right in my life to be here in this moment with someone so amazing.

Wrapping my arms around his shoulders, I nuzzle his neck. "Dude," I whisper in his ear. "You just rocked my world and then some."

Chapter Nine
Keaton

"This doesn't feel real." I twist my head to stare into Austen's beautiful green eyes. We're still on the couch, both now in sweatpants, arms draped around one another, and I'm afraid to blink in case it all disappears or I wake up and realize it's just a dream.

Austen pinches my nipple. "Feel that?"

"Ouch. Yes. Asshole." I slap his chest, and he chuckles.

He rests his head against my temple. "It's real, babe. We just blew each other."

"And it was epic," I add, because it seems there's no limit to how uncool I am when I finally nail the guy of my dreams. Austen chuckles again, and I fight a blush. "I have zero filter around you," I admit while his fingers rub up and down my arm. "And zero game. It's embarrassing."

"It's cute."

I scowl, slapping his chest again. "I don't want to be cute. I want to be sexy."

Oh. My. Fucking. God. Just shoot me now. I groan, throwing my head back as Austen chuckles. *Again.*

"Stop overthinking. I'm into you just the way you are. I always want you to be yourself." He nips at my earlobe. "You're sexy as fuck, Kennedy. Own that shit."

I peck his lips. "Is this really happening?"

His expression turns serious, and he sits up straighter, keeping his arm around me. "Is that what you want?"

I nod, and a flurry of butterflies invades my chest, taking up residence there, swooping and churning, until it feels like I might throw up. "Do you?" I ask, panic waiting in the wings to go full tilt.

"I do." He is quick to reassure me before I have a coronary.

"How do we do this when we're both in the closet?" I ask.

His face contorts, and I instantly know I've said the wrong thing. "Unless, ugh, you're...not?" I'm confused. He said he came out at thirteen, yet his parents and everyone on campus believes he's straight and dating Gia.

"I am. But I hate it." He sighs, eyeballing me as he talks. I shift on the couch, angling my body so we're more comfortable face to face. His hand lands on my thigh, and mine lands on his knee, and I can't stop the smile breaking out on my face.

Now I know what it's like to touch him, I want to always be doing it.

"I've always known who I am. As soon as I plucked up the courage, I told my parents I was gay, and I didn't hide it from anyone. Not my friends at school. Not my coaches or the other guys on the team. Everyone knew, and most accepted it. There are always a few bigots, but I handled it. Honestly, they never made me regret coming out."

"How come you didn't here?"

A pained look crosses his features. "During senior year, I was getting a lot of attention from scouts, and the head coach of our team pulled me aside to offer some fatherly advice. I really respected Coach Ramirez, but I was pissed when he suggested

I hide my sexuality from the scouts. I stormed off, but a few nights later, he asked to speak to me again, and he explained how difficult it is to be a gay man in football. He'd printed out a bunch of articles, and he shared these poll results with me. It showed that a quarter of those polled believed openly gay athletes hurt sports in general while more than fifty percent believed being openly gay hurt the athlete's career."

He runs his fingers through my hair. "Do you know there is currently only one openly gay male in the four North American professional sports leagues and only nine have come out after they retired? There is one example of an openly gay man who played college football and then went on to play in the NFL. *One.*"

He blows air out his mouth, and it's not hard to see how frustrated he is. "It's such bullshit." He shakes his head, and I squeeze his shoulder. "I took the material home that night and read it all. It was depressing as fuck, but I got the point Coach was making."

He toys with the wispy hairs at the base of my neck, and if he keeps doing that, my dick will be hard as steel again. "I agonized over it for weeks, because it went against everything I stand for to hide who I truly am, but, ultimately, I decided to take my coach's advice."

"I'm sorry." I rest my brow against his. "I know that must've been difficult." I haven't summoned the courage to tell my friends and family yet, but when I do, I know there will be no going back. So, I get how difficult it must've been for someone like Austen who has never struggled with his identity or his sexuality. "I'm in awe of your strength and your courage," I admit.

"I don't feel worthy of that," he quietly replies. "Not when I'm not being true to myself."

Silence filters into the air, and we're both deep in thought.

"It's why you agreed to fake date Gia," I supply, after a few minutes, connecting the dots in my head. "It worked to your advantage too."

Austen nods. "I knew if I came to college as a single, supposedly straight guy, girls would hit on me, and I didn't want the hassle. My parents have always been disapproving of my sexuality, so two birds, one stone." He shrugs, like it's no biggie, when we both know it is.

"They said that?" I blurt, because it's one of my fears. Not my greatest one—that would be the media and the world at large discovering the truth—and, truthfully, I think my parents will be cool with it, but there's still a teeny-tiny sliver of doubt that pricks my nerves any time I think about coming out.

Austen shakes his head. "Never outright. But it was implied. When Gia and I told them we were dating, they looked relieved, and they didn't stop to question it."

"I can't believe they bought it when you'd been openly gay for years and you'd had boyfriends."

"I told them I was bi, and they seemed to accept that easier. They have always hoped Gia and I would get married, so I guess they chose to believe the lie rather than open their eyes and see what's always been staring them in the face. Orwell is the only one who didn't buy it. He correctly guessed what we were doing." He rubs my thigh, and my cock jerks behind my pants. "He was only thirteen, but he begged me not to do it." A veil of sadness shrouds his handsome face, and I want to remove it. "I should've listened to my brother instead of my coach."

"What about the guys on the team? Do any of them know?"

"I think Colton suspects, but he's never said a word."

"You've never been tempted to tell him?"

"So many times, but I don't want to burden him with the secret."

"What if you get signed by the NFL? Will you tell then?"

He lifts his hands from my body, clawing them through his dark hair. "The plan is to wait until after I have a signed contract, if I'm lucky enough to get offered one, and then come out privately to my new team, but I don't know if I can do this anymore. It's killing me lying about who I am. I feel like such a fraud, and the more I lie, the worse it gets."

A messy ball of emotion clogs my throat, and *I* feel like the biggest fraud. I'm a spineless coward. Because I've been lying about who I am my entire life, never having the balls to do what Austen's done. "I know the feeling," I confess, rubbing at the tightness in my chest. "At least you had the courage to admit who you were in the first place. I'm a coward because I've been hiding who I am this entire time, and I couldn't hate myself any more if I tried."

Closing the gap between us, he presses his mouth to mine, and I grab him, holding him close as we kiss. When we pull back, he threads his fingers in mine, fixing me with a look loaded with sympathy. "Everyone's journey is different, and you should never compare yourself to anyone else." He rubs soothing circles on the back of my hand with his thumb. "I am intrigued though. Are you into guys and girls?"

"Just guys." His eyes search mine, and I know what he's asking without him verbalizing. "I'm a piece of shit, Austen, because I've strung Melissa along since I was fifteen, and she doesn't deserve that."

"How did that happen?" He continues to draw circles on my hand with his thumb, and it's hugely comforting.

"I've known I was different from my brothers since I hit puberty, but it only really hit home when I started attending the parties they used to throw, and they were all about the girls while I was only eyeing up the boys. At first, I was confused, and then I was in denial."

I stop, my chest heaving, emotion weighing heavy on my heart and my soul. I wet my dry lips. "I've never admitted this to anyone," I supply. "Except to the pages of my journal."

"We don't have to talk about this now if it makes you uncomfortable," he offers, confirming what I already know. That Austen *is* one of the good guys. A rare gem in a sea of sharks.

"I want to tell you. I want you to know all the hidden parts of me."

An adoring smile graces his gorgeous mouth, and I kiss him. Just 'cause, apparently, now I can, and that shit will never get old.

"I didn't want to be gay. I wanted to be normal." I cringe, because even saying those words pains me. "I wanted to someday get married and have a wife and kids, but I was too naïve or too closed off because I refused to acknowledge to myself that I could still have those things living freely as a gay man." Air whooshes out of my mouth as I remember the anxiety of those years. "I came so close to telling my cousin Faye after she moved in with us, but I always chickened out."

"You couldn't tell your brothers?" he inquires. "Not even the triplets?"

I shake my head. "I was afraid. Not that I think my family will disown me or anything. I know once they find out they'll be shocked, but they'll come around."

"So why haven't you told them?" There's no judgment in his tone or his expression, just curiosity.

"My family can't make a move without the press breathing down our backs, and I know if I officially come out it will mean the entire world knowing, and I...I can't face it, man." Pain annihilates my insides as fear slithers through my veins.

Brock has the power to turn that nightmare into a reality, in the worst possible way, and I have zero control over it. My breathing turns labored as panic races through me at the thought of that recording being in the public domain. There will be no rock big enough to crawl under if that surfaces.

"Breathe, man." Austen rubs my back, his concerned expression examining every inch of my terrified one. "In and out." He breathes with me, until I'm back in control.

"I'm so fucking weak." I squeeze my eyes closed, self-loathing suffocating me.

"Don't be so hard on yourself," Austen says, pulling me into a hug. My arms band around his waist as he holds me to his chest. "That is a lot to take on for anyone, let alone a teen struggling to accept who he is."

"You did it."

He eases back, peering into my eyes. "One of the reasons I chose to heed Coach's advice was this very thing. It's still the one reality stopping me from admitting the truth. I knew if I came here as an openly gay athlete that I'd claim everyone's attention. My teammates. Other students. The media. It's all they would focus on. It would overshadow my stats on the field. I don't want to be defined by my sexual orientation. It should only ever be about my performance on the field. So, I get it, and it doesn't make you weak. It's a very real concern, especially for you because of your family's notoriety."

A layer of stress lifts off my shoulders, and I didn't realize how much I needed to hear that. "I don't want to be a gay icon or a gay role model. I hate the attention my name brings as it is, and I'm not ready for that kind of responsibility. That's been a big driving force behind my decision, but I can't keep denying who I am because it's killing me too, Austen. I have finally accepted who I am in here." I thump on my chest, right in the place where my heart beats. "It's why I properly ended things with Melissa. I'm not into women, and I never will be. Deep down, I've always known that, and I should've been honest with her years ago. She's so sweet, and she deserved better."

I still remember the hurt and the anger on her face the last time we talked, and I hate I put it there. That I turned someone loving and innocent into someone she's not, and I wish there was some way I could make it up to her.

Forcing those thoughts aside, I continue explaining, because Austen needs to know I would never mess with him. I am serious about living my life more authentically, as much as that's possible. "I have accepted it now. I've accepted that the vision I had of the future can still come true with a man, and I'm close to finding the courage to tell my family, but I am *not* ready to let the world know. I am not ready for that level of scrutiny and opinion, and the scary thing is, I don't know if I ever will be."

Chapter Ten
Austen

"We shouldn't have to prepare," I say, feeling his pain as acutely as my own. "No one makes a big deal or is forced into making an announcement if they are hetero, so why the fuck should we have to make any proclamation about our sexuality?" It's a rhetorical question, and we both know it.

"Exactly. Except the worlds we inhabit won't permit us to be true to ourselves without pressure or speculation."

"Or we could just come out and say nothing. Let them draw their own conclusions." It's a spur of the moment comment, not without some merit, but it's not as simple as that for us, and we both know it.

"It would create a media frenzy if we stepped outside hand in hand or were caught kissing." Keaton smooths a hand along his taut jaw. "The vultures would descend on campus, and we'd have to say bye-bye to any form of normal college existence. You'd be hounded after practice and games, and your teammates would be harassed for statements. It'd be a fucking nightmare."

We're both contemplative as the implications of our conversation take root. "We have to keep our relationship a secret," I say, breaking the silence and addressing the elephant in the room.

"Would that be a problem for you?" His big blue eyes search mine.

"No more than for you."

He shakes his head. "You just admitted you are sick of hiding who you are. It's worse for you because you've been out in the open, while I've never known anything different."

"That doesn't mean it'd be easier for you, and it's not a competition."

"So where does that leave us?" he asks, gulping audibly, his nerves returning.

I clasp the back of his head. "Taking things one day at a time," I suggest. "Conducting our relationship behind closed doors."

"Will that be enough?" Fear blazes at the back of his eyes.

"*You're* enough." I peck his lips. "And being with you will make me happy. If we have to hide it, so be it. It's better than not having you in my life as my boyfriend."

Shock splays on his face, and his innocence is showing again. I know Keats is worried about his inexperience, but it's honestly refreshing. I love that he's a blank canvas. That I'm the one who'll get to explore his sexuality with him. It's me who will help him identify what he likes and dislikes.

"Boyfriends," he chokes out, still looking shocked.

"Or no labels, if you prefer." Honestly, I'm not hung up on it. "All I ask is exclusivity. I won't share you."

Red heat creeps up his neck, and I kiss him hard, because he doesn't realize how much I'm into him and how much his inexperience appeals to me. I love we will get to share all this together.

"Boyfriends is good," he says when we finally break for air. "More than good." He smiles, and it's so wide it threatens to split his face in two.

"Cool." I smother a cocky grin. "Boyfriend."

He laughs, pressing his forehead to mine. "My heart is pounding so hard right now, and I can't remember the last time I was this excited or this happy."

Keaton wears his heart on his sleeve, and he's just so inherently good. I hope I'm worthy enough to be in his life. I won't stop trying to prove I am, even if it's only to myself. "Ditto. I haven't had a boyfriend since the summer before senior year, and I love being in a relationship."

He pulls his head back, peering into my eyes. "Can I ask you something?"

"Anything. Don't ever hold back."

"You said it's been a while since you fucked around with anyone. How long is *a while?*"

"I haven't been laid in over a year," I admit, not ashamed by the fact.

His eyes betray his surprise. "Wow. That's...unexpected."

I shrug. "Opportunities to hook up or meet guys are slim. I can't risk it, because of Gia and in case the guy recognizes me. And Grindr dates really aren't me," I add, recalling the few times I used the app with a nasty taste in my mouth.

He looks shocked, but pleased, and I can't help teasing him. "You thought I was a manwhore?"

"No. Definitely not." He is quick to reassure me. "But you're hot as fuck, and you're a football star. You get hit on all the time. I guess I just never really thought it through. It's not like I want to think of you with other people."

"Well, now you know." I deliberately soften my features. "What about you?" His muscles bunch, and I tread carefully. "Does Melissa know you're gay?"

He shakes his head. "No. Although I'll tell her after I've told my parents. She's the only one outside the family I will admit the truth to."

"You haven't been with her consistently though, right?" I ask, easing him into this.

"We've been on and off a lot since college."

"Have you been with any other guys?"

He pales, averting his eyes, and bile collects at the back of my throat. "You can tell me anything. I won't judge."

He tilts his head up. "I've been with two guys. Neither were good experiences."

"I'm sorry." I had a few poor experiences myself when I first came out, and it's almost par for the course, but I would never dismiss his feelings or suggest it's normal or acceptable.

He shrugs, twisting his neck from side to side. "It happens, right?"

I lace my fingers in his as I ask my next question. "Have you ever topped or bottomed? Or you just fucked around with them?"

Withdrawing his hand, he scratches the back of his neck. "I've tried both," he admits, barely maintaining eye contact.

I arch a brow, urging him to continue. If he can't talk about this with me, then he's not ready for a full sexual relationship. Which is okay. We can ease into it. I just need to know what I'm dealing with here, because I never want to make him uncomfortable or push him before he's ready.

"I prefer to top." His eyes examine mine. "What about you?"

"I'm vers. I enjoy both, and I love the thought of your cock driving into me as much as I fantasize about drilling my dick in your ass."

"Hell." He scrubs a hand down his face.

"Does this make you uncomfortable?"

"No. Not really. It's just you're so direct. Melissa and I were sleeping together since we were eighteen, and I've never had this kind of conversation with her."

"I'm not her."

His gaze lowers to my lap. "No, you're most definitely not." He grins, lifting his eyes to mine.

"I'm curious. I've never been with a woman. Can't ever imagine getting aroused by pussy. How did you do it?"

He cringes a little, but before I can retract my question, he answers. "I closed my eyes a lot and imagined she was a guy."

"Any guy?" My lips tip up. "Or you imagined someone in particular?" I want to know everything about Keats. Especially his teenage crushes.

A faraway look appears in his eyes, and he stares off into space for a minute. I wish I had a hotline to his brain so I could read his mind.

Snapping out of it, he locks eyes on mine. "Usually Liam Hemsworth or Shawn Mendes, because they're hot. It was Colton Haynes for a while after he publicly came out because he was my hero for ignoring industry advice and choosing to stay true to himself."

"He's into older men. Noted," I tease.

He laughs before his expression turns serious. "With Melissa, it was very innocent at the start. Mainly kissing. We lost our virginity to each other at eighteen, and it was awkward. We slept together a few more times before I left to come here, but our relationship was never overtly sexual. We were like friends who occasionally slept together."

"And she never wondered about that?" I inquire, popping a brow.

He pulls at his lips. "If she had doubts, she never voiced them to me. It was a first relationship, for both of us. Neither of us had any expectations."

"That's kinda sad."

"I know," he agrees. "And completely selfish of me. I hope she meets someone amazing who can show her how sex and intimacy is supposed to be, because she got shortchanged with me."

"You shortchanged yourself too. I hate you had to pretend, and I can't wait to show you how amazing it is to have sex with the guy you're into."

"Cocky, much?" he asks, tilting his head to one side.

"I've been told I'm good in bed. Not gonna lie about that."

"And you're really okay with it. Me topping?"

"I want to have sex with you, man. There are lots of different ways we can do it. And maybe at some future time, you'll want to try bottoming with me. But if you don't, I'm cool with your dick in my ass."

He splutters, embarrassment mingling with amusement on his face. He straightens his shoulders. "Want my dick in your ass now?"

My cock throbs in response, and there's no need to wait for a verbal reply. The growing bulge in my pants is testament to how badly I want him to fuck me. But there's something else we need to discuss first. A topic which might ruin the mood, but I came home tonight with a purpose, and that hasn't changed.

"So badly, but I need to ask you one more thing." I place my hand on his knee. "You're not going to like it," I warn.

His eyes study mine, and his brow puckers. "What is it?"

"What the hell were you doing in that alley with Brock Jonas?"

Chapter Eleven
Keaton

I tug at my ears to ensure I'm not hearing things. A multitude of competing emotions fry my brain as I try to wrap my head around the horror of Austen's words. "You *followed* me?" I snap, anger winning out.

"Yes, and I'm not sorry I did." His face shows zero remorse, and that only fuels my misguided rage.

"You had no right! It's none of your business." I shove his hand off my knee, rising to my feet. "This is a huge invasion of my privacy. I'm so pissed."

"I'd never have guessed," he drawls, as if this is funny.

I fist handfuls of my hair, glaring at him. "Don't make light of this. How would you feel if I stalked you?"

"Flattered. Aroused. Happy you cared."

"Don't do that." I pace the hardwood floor, panic poisoning my veins as I search for an exit point. "Don't joke."

He stands, planting himself in my path. "Don't deflect. Whether I was right or wrong is inconsequential now. Just tell me what's going on with that asshole?"

"It's none of your business," I hiss. "Just drop it."

"I can't do that. And I won't start a relationship with someone who keeps secrets. This only works if there's complete honesty." He points his finger between us.

"Well, that was the shortest relationship in history," I deadpan, glancing at my watch, hating the pain pressing down on my chest at the thought things are over before they've even begun. "Fifty-three minutes. That's got to be some kind of world record."

His large palms come to rest on my shoulders, and he puts his face all up in mine, forcing me to look at him. "You would end this just so you don't have to tell me?" His nostrils flare. "You would seriously do that over Brock fucking Jonas?"

"It's not what you're thinking." I step back, unable to think clearly with his hands on me.

"I wasn't thinking that, but now I am." His hands ball into fists at his side. "Are you *fucking* him?" he yells.

"No! Do you honestly think I'd do what we did if I was screwing someone else?"

Air expels from his mouth, and his chest heaves as he stares at me, inspecting me like a scientist might study a lab rat. His voice is level again when he speaks. "No, but the Keaton I know is honest to a fault, and this side of you is unexpected and unwelcome."

"Sorry to be such a disappointment already." I push past him, needing to get away because I'm a hot mess and I need to clear my head before I do something pathetic, like cry.

"Keats. Stop." Austen grabs hold of my elbow, stalling my forward trajectory. "Just talk to me." His eyes plead with me. "Please."

Pain slices into me, cutting me into itty bitty pieces until it feels like I'm barely holding all the splintered parts of myself together. "I want to," I whisper, hating the confusion and hurt I see written all over his face. "But I can't."

He lets me go, and tension bleeds into the air. "I can't believe this." He shakes his head, his expression oozing disappointment and sorrow. "And I can't, *won't*, be with someone who keeps things from me." He walks past me, heading in the direction of the bedrooms, and I'm frozen in place, watching his retreating back with pain ripping me apart on all sides.

I can't lose Austen just as we've admitted our feelings, especially because of that blackmailing bastard, but I can't fess up either.

I can't tell him what happened because I'm too ashamed, and I know he'll only think less of me after.

Austen reappears in the kitchen a few minutes later, wearing a hoodie, sweatpants, and unlaced sneakers on his feet. His duffel bag is thrown over his shoulder as he bends down, grabbing his book bag from the floor where he dumped it earlier.

"What're you doing?" I ask, blood slowly draining from my face.

He pins me with a frosty look. "Leaving."

"Don't go!" I plead. Panic jumps up and slaps me in the face.

He spins around, facing me. "Ready to tell me the truth?"

Tension splits the air between us, and I hang my head.

His bitter laugh is like a punch in the gut. "Thought not." His feet squelch on the floor as he approaches, pausing directly in front of me. He tilts my chin up with his finger. "I'll give you some space to think about this, but when I return, I want answers, Keaton." His somber eyes bore holes in my skull. "It's either that or I permanently move out, because I won't share living space with someone who hides shit when I'm only trying to help. It doesn't matter what label we put on our relationship. I cannot handle that."

His shoulders drop, and his voice lowers a few decibels.

"We don't need any more reasons to lie, Keats. Aren't we keeping enough secrets as it is? There should only be honesty between us; otherwise, what's the point?"

I agree. I know he's right, and it's no way to start a relationship, but I'm afraid if I confess he'll want nothing to do with me anyway.

He grabs the strap of his duffel bag. "I'll be at the football house for a couple nights. If you're ready to talk, message me." He doesn't wait for my reply, walking out the door without looking back, and I'm praying it's not prophetic.

I lie in bed, staring at the pristine white ceiling, with my brain tossing my dilemma in a loop through my head, over and over again, until I give myself a pounding headache.

I can't lose Austen.

He's everything I dreamed I'd never have.

Although we'll have to hide our relationship from the outside world, it still means everything to me. Which is why I should tell him, even if I'm terrified he'll judge me. *I know that's not who he is, and he said he's trying to help, so why is this so hard to do?*

Admitting to yourself you're scared isn't easy, but as this spins through my head, I know that's what's really driving my behavior.

This would be so much easier if I could call my computer-genius FBI-agent brother and have him deal with the problem. But I can't expect others to ride to the rescue all the time, and God knows my brother has bailed so many of us out in the past he deserves a break from family drama. Of course, the big issue is the fact I'd have to come clean to my family about my sexuality and the stupid mistake I made last summer, and I hate how disappointed they'll be in me.

I'm not ready to disappoint them again.

I'll find a way of dealing with that snake Brock, and maybe I do need Austen's help.

"Wow, someone got up on the wrong side of bed," Mol says the following day, at lunch, when I slap my tray down on the table in the dining hall and flop into the seat beside her.

"Rough night," I admit, rubbing my tired, red-rimmed eyes.

"Trouble in paradise?" Kate asks, arching a brow. Her words instantly raise my hackles, but I'm probably overreacting. Lack of sleep and a hefty dose of self-pity can do that to a guy.

"I've just got a lot on my mind."

"Anything we can help with?" Seb asks, stealing a fry from my plate.

"No. It's—" I cut off mid-sentence as half the football team enters the noisy room, amid a collective intake of breath.

Austen is at the rear, talking with Colton, laughing at something he's saying, looking like he hasn't a care in the world. Guess he didn't suffer a sleepless night over our first argument, only minutes after we became official.

His head lifts in this direction, as if I called him, and our gazes lock for a few seconds before he looks away. Bile crawls up my throat at his obvious dismissal, but I plaster a fake smile on my face when I refocus on my friends.

"You and Austen have a fight or something?" Kate asks, her warm brown eyes carrying a hint of curiosity.

"Just some roomie teething problems," I lie, because, wow, I'm becoming an expert. "Nothing we can't fix."

"The more important question is what vampire has been

eating you?" Mol asks, smirking as she jabs her finger at the bruised, circular discoloration on Kate's neck. I shoot Mol a grateful look for the purposeful subject change.

"A lady never tells who's biting her or where." Kate winks, and Mol laughs. Seb turns an obvious shade of red, so either he's the one doing the biting or this conversation embarrasses him.

Lucky he wasn't in my apartment last night to hear Austen talk about wanting to drill his cock in my ass.

I sprout an instant semi as that thought lands in my mind, but damn, his straight talking and dirty mouth seriously turn me on.

What am I doing?

I sit back in my chair, pushing my plate toward Seb—he's already devoured half my fries anyway, and I've no appetite—and give myself a stern talking to. The guy I've been dreaming about for months wants to be my boyfriend, and I'm acting like a pathetic teenager with his first crush who's scared of opening himself up for fear of being shamed. I know Austen won't judge me. If anything, he'll probably be mad on my behalf.

So, what the fuck am I doing pushing him away?

My chair scrapes as I stand. "Be back in a sec." I stride toward the two tables where the football team is sitting, heading in Austen's direction.

"Incoming," Colton says to Austen, noticing me first.

"Hey, man." I shove my hands deep in the pockets of my jeans as I stand to the side of Austen's chair.

He looks up, not giving anything away. "Hey, Keats. What's up?"

"Can I talk to you for a minute?"

He nods, standing.

"Hey, Kennedy," someone with a deep voice calls out from behind me.

I turn around, groaning internally when I see who it is. "Hey, Nolan."

"Saw your mom on CNN this morning," he shouts, and my muscles lock up tight, bracing myself for whatever shit he's about to throw at me.

Not like it's my first rodeo.

Kids at school loved spouting crap about my mom, especially when Dad's affair with her psycho assistant became public knowledge. High school was zero fun those days.

"Cool," I lie, knowing it's anything but. I didn't realize Mom was being interviewed this morning, but she's often on TV. She is well known in fashion circles, she does a lot of charity work, and her interior design business is booming, so it's not that unusual to see her on TV screens.

"She's definitely one MILF I'd love to get my hands on." Nolan makes a crude gesture with his hands, and I see red. "How about I come visit next time you're heading home," he adds. "I can show your mom a good time." Rubbing his crotch, he waggles his brows suggestively, as if this is funny.

I'm seconds away from lunging at him, which is something, because I don't lose my temper easily and I'm not the fighter in my family.

But this shit is not cool, and I'm mad as all hell. "How about I slam your head into the wall and see if I can't shake some brain cells loose?" I glare at him, barely controlling my anger.

"Wow. Relax, dude. I'm only yanking your chain." He rolls his eyes, as if I'm the one who's out of line.

"You're an idiot," Austen says. "And you owe Keaton an apology."

Nolan flips Austen the bird. "Fuck you, man. You're not team captain. I don't take orders from you."

"But I am, and you will," Colton interjects, pinning Nolan with a dark glare. "Every time you speak or act, you represent our team. Maybe you should think about that before you open your stupid mouth next time."

Austen jerks his head forward. "C'mon, Keats. Let's get out of here." Wrapping up his lunch, he stuffs it inside his bag before swinging the bag over one shoulder.

I collect my stuff and say goodbye to my friends, following Austen toward the exit. We walk side by side outside, crossing the sidewalk to claim an empty bench.

"You okay?" Austen asks, depositing his bag on the seat beside him as he sits down. He leans forward on his elbows, scrutinizing my face.

"No," I admit, dropping my bag at my feet. "I'm currently trying to think of reasons why I shouldn't walk back in there and knock that jerk flat on his ass for disrespecting my mom."

"He did that on purpose," Austen says. "Don't let him know he got to you."

I rotate my stiff shoulders, pushing all thoughts of the jerk from my mind. I face Austen. "I'm sorry about last night, and you're right. I need to tell you what's going on."

"Thank fuck." Relief washes over his features. He slaps me on the back, giving my shoulder a discreet squeeze.

"Do you have plans after practice?" I inquire.

He shakes his head. "I'll come straight home."

"Don't eat. I'll fix dinner."

I'm not sure what expression he sees on my face, but it's enough for him to reassure me. "Whatever it is, it'll be fine. You don't have to fear the truth."

Well, there's an oxymoron if ever I heard one. My eyes penetrate his. "Let's hope you still think that after I tell you everything."

Chapter Twelve
Austen

The aroma of garlic and tomatoes scents the air as I step foot in the apartment, and my stomach rumbles appreciatively. When I walk into the kitchen, my eyes are glued to Keaton as he stirs something in a pot at the stove. I clear my throat so he's aware of my presence. Looking over his shoulder, he offers me a tentative smile. "Good timing. It's almost ready."

Dumping my duffel bag and my book bag on the floor under the island unit, I glance at the dining table—positioned between the kitchen and living areas of the open-plan room—and my heart does a twisty jump in my chest.

Keaton has set the table, using the white linen tablecloth and napkin set his mom gave him when he moved in. A myriad of small, pale-green tealight holders are scattered across the center of the table, their flames flickering against the glass, and a bottle of red wine is open, warming to room temperature. We rarely use the formal table, choosing to eat at the island unit most times, so the fact he's gone to this much trouble means the world to me.

Without second-guessing myself, I close the distance between us, sliding my arms around his trim waist from behind. "You didn't have to do all this," I murmur, pressing my lips to the side of his neck as I hold him close, his back to my chest.

"I know." Turning off the heat under the large pot, he turns around, and my arms drop from his waist. Our chests are pressed together, our eyes almost level. "But I wanted to," he adds. "Besides, cooking helps to distract me from puking."

I clasp his cheek in my palm, fighting a smile. "I told you you have nothing to fear from telling me the truth. I don't judge. I just want to help." Leaning down slowly, so he knows my intent, I kiss him, pouring reassurance down his throat because I hate seeing him on edge.

Gripping my waist, he pulls me closer, and our kiss deepens, our mouths opening so our tongues can battle for supremacy. Keaton melts under my touch, and I could kiss him nonstop all night long, but that won't resolve the gulf between us. Only conversation can do that. Reluctantly, I pull back, pecking his lips one final time, before my eyes move over his shoulder. "Can I help with anything?" I ask, and he laughs when my stomach emits a loud, gnarly sound.

"Pour the pinot noir," he says, kissing the corner of my mouth, "while I plate up."

"This is delicious," I admit after the first mouthwatering bite of his homemade chicken parmigiana. "I didn't know you were such a good cook." I eat a strict diet, along with most of the guys on the team, so when I moved in here, I offered to cook dinner every night, and Keaton just let me do it. I might have to reassess my strategy and relax my diet a little, if this is any indication of how skilled he is in the kitchen.

"Lana's mom was our housekeeper, growing up, and she cooked all of our meals. She used to let me help her, and I discovered I liked cooking."

"You should've said. I thought I was helping by offering to cook but we can alternate nights, if you want."

"I don't mind eating what you cook," he admits, flattening a hand over his toned stomach. "I'm in the best shape of my life because I'm somewhat following your diet."

"Something tells me it's more to do with good genes," I say, in between mouthfuls of the succulent chicken and noodles. His brows climb to his hairline, and I smirk. "I've seen tons of pics of your family online. Your parents are very good-looking, and it's no wonder their spawn are all so freaking hot."

"He's crushing on my brothers," Keats deadpans. "Awesome."

I stretch my hand across the table, placing it on top of his. "The only Kennedy I'm crushing on is *you*, but I'm not blind, man. Your brothers are hot, but nowhere near as hot as you." That seems to appease him, if the slight stain on his cheeks and soft smile is any measure.

"We can each cook on alternate nights," he says, deliberately not responding. "I will stick to your plan, but we can vary it a little. Steak and broccoli is getting boring."

My lips tug up. "I'm open to try new stuff as long as it's healthy." And it's not like I don't eat carbs, just usually at lunch, before practice.

We chat casually about our day while we eat, and I don't force the conversation, preferring him to relax. If that's even possible, because the dude's wound tighter than a nun in a brothel.

After I've cleared the table and loaded the dishwasher, I join Keaton on the couch, topping up his wine. I've a feeling he'll need it for this talk. I switch to water, because I try to steer clear of alcohol during the week.

I sit beside him, close, but not too close, giving him some breathing space if he needs it. "Whenever you're ready," I say, taking a sip of my water. His tongue darts out, wetting his dry lips and I wish I could remove that terrified look from his face. "Whatever it is, it'll be okay, Keats."

"You say that now, but you're going to realize what a stupid, pathetic idiot I am and you can do better than me."

Setting my water down on the side table, I take his hands in mine. "There is nothing you can tell me, *nothing*, that'll change how I feel about you. Trust me on that." He doesn't look convinced. "Remember, I *see* you? I know who you are. I *like* who you are. You won't scare me away. I'm all in, dude." I stab him with a piercing look. "I'm going nowhere."

Finally, his shoulders relax a smidgeon. His Adam's apple bobs in his throat as he begins explaining. "Last April, I met Brock at one of his band's gigs. Mol dragged me along because she was assigned with writing a review for the paper." He gulps again, and I squeeze his hands in encouragement. "She interviewed the band after the gig, and Brock kept staring at me funny. I didn't think much of it, but after the interview was done, we had a drink with them at the bar, and he was flirting with me."

My brows knit together. "I didn't think he was into guys. He has quite the rep around campus as a ladies' man, and the band's orgies are infamous."

"I don't know whether he is or isn't," Keats says, pulling his hands from mine. "But he certainly led me to believe he was."

Acid floats in my gut, and while I've had an inkling about what Keats had to say, I think it's going to be ten million times worse than I imagined. "What happened?"

"We bumped into each other a few times, and he was always eager to talk to me. He flirted outrageously, and I was massively confused and..." He averts his eyes, knotting his hands as his words die off.

"Flattered and interested," I suggest, because I might hate

that asshole but he's a good-looking asshole. Brock has that whole "bad boy wannabe rock star with a chip on his shoulder" look perfected to an artform. I hate it, but I understand why Brock flirting with Keaton would intrigue and confuse him.

The thing about guys like Brock is they can usually smell vulnerability from a mile away, and Keaton likes to see the good in everyone, so he wouldn't have spent too long questioning Brock's motives.

"Yeah," he admits, clearly embarrassed.

"Don't be embarrassed. Pricks like Brock know how to turn up the charm to get what they want. If he was less than truthful with you, that's on *him*. Not you."

"I'm an idiot, Austen, because I should've known he was messing with me. I mean, I was super cautious at the start, but the more he flirted with me, the more I relaxed around him. When he finally admitted he was into me, I told him I had a girlfriend and I didn't cheat. He told me he respected that and he wouldn't force anything. He let me know he was there if I wanted to act on our attraction."

A tortured scowl whips across his face. "I couldn't get him out of my mind," he sheepishly admits. "And I wasn't in a good place. Melissa was dropping hints about getting engaged, and I was stressed over my exams, and still hating myself for living a lie. Brock became a lifeline I latched on to without giving him proper thought. I was careless." His fingers dig into his thigh. "I should've thought it through. Then maybe I might not have made the biggest mistake of my life."

"What did he do?" At this point, I just need to know.

"I went home for summer break and ended things with Melissa for good. One night, when I was drunk, I stupidly texted Brock that I was single. He replied instantly, inviting me to spend the weekend at his place in Malibu. I was undecided until Melissa showed up at a family party at my house and we got into an argument. I was feeling like a piece of shit, which isn't uncommon around my ex, and I threw caution to the wind. I texted him I would come and booked the next flight."

Air hisses through his gritted teeth, and he's so pale he looks like he might throw up. His tormented eyes meet mine. "You know when you get a bad feeling in the pit of your stomach?" he asks, rubbing a hand over his toned abs.

I nod, because we've all had those instinctual moments.

"I knew I'd made a mistake when I arrived at his beach house. Place was crawling with people. Most either drunk or high or both. He'd led me to believe it would just be us. Said nothing about a party, and I was immediately on guard. My gut was screaming at me to turn around and go home, but I ignored it. I..."

He hangs his head, his shoulders slumping, and I pull him into my arms, hugging him tight. He clings to me, wrapping his muscular arms around my shoulders, and my heart hurts for him. His entire body trembles against me, and I'm already plotting various ways to murder Brock Jonas before I've even heard what he did.

"I was so fucking lonely, man," Keaton admits, easing back. He swipes an angry hand at his damp eyes. "I just needed a connection. I thought that's what was building between Brock and me, but I was such a fool." I brush the tears off his face as they silently roll down his cheeks.

"I won't go into all the details, but I got drunk, and I let him take me to his bedroom after a while. I let him fuck me, and he coaxed me into blowing his buddy Rod while he ..."

I grind my teeth to the molars, and my blood oozes liquid rage. "Did he force you to do it? Did he rape you?" I have to ask, because that lowlife is capable of anything.

"No." Keaton vigorously shakes his head. "I consented to

everything, but I shouldn't have. It was my first time bottoming, and it fucking hurt."

"He didn't prepare you," I surmise, anger crashing through me like a wave.

He shakes his head. "He lubed the condom, but that was it."

More tears leak out of his eyes, and I hug him to my chest again, pressing kisses into his hair. "He's an even bigger asshole than I thought. I'm so sorry, Keats. No one should've treated you like that."

"It gets worse." He swats his tears away as he shucks out of my arms. "The whole thing was a setup. I didn't know he had a hidden camera in his bedroom until he played the video for me the next morning. I vomited everywhere while he and Rod pissed themselves laughing. When I stopped puking, he told me I had to pay up or he'd stream it on the internet."

Chapter Thirteen
Austen

"He's still blackmailing you," I say, working hard to keep my anger in check. Right now, Keaton needs compassion and support, not aggression and murderous rage.

"I paid him off, and he handed over the recording, but he kept copies, and now he wants more money."

"How much did you pay him last week?"

"Fifty thousand."

A string of expletives leaves my mouth. "Jesus Christ."

"It's never going to end, Austen. He's going to keep coming back, asking for more and more. I don't know what to do." Keats buries his head in his hands, and I smooth my hand up and down his back.

"Recording someone without their permission is illegal. Extortion is illegal. You could report him to the cops and get him arrested."

He lifts his head. "I don't trust that he hasn't planned for that. I'm assuming Rod is in on it, though he hasn't shown his face around me since, and I gave the cash to Brock both times.

But I'm guessing Rod has a copy. That he's the backup. I can't risk going to the police because if that tape is made public, my life is over, Austen. I will never live it down. I could never show up on campus again, and I would never be able to look my parents in the eye ever again."

Silence descends, and it's smothering. Anger mixes with frustration and pain in my gut, and I circle my arm around Keats, offering him the only comfort I can.

"We need to get those copies. Then we're going to nail that bastard to the wall."

Keats looks at me curiously. "You're not disgusted with me?"

I'm not surprised he thinks that. Keaton is so hard on himself sometimes. "Of course not. The only mistake you made was trusting the wrong guy." He slants me with a skeptical look, and I stare deep into his eyes. "You're the victim in all this, Keats. What Brock did to you was wrong on so many levels."

When Dax drove a stake through my heart, I quickly realized how fine the line between love and hate is. I remember spending nights wishing him dead. But that pales in comparison to the thoughts racing through my mind now. I want to punch the living daylights out of Brock Jonas until he doesn't exist, but I have a feeling the dude would get off on that. Jonas is a slippery snake, and taking him down requires a carefully laid out strategy.

"I'm so unworthy of you," Keaton says, his eyes glassing over again.

"Hey. Stop stealing my lines." I fuse my mouth to his in a hard kiss. "Thank you for telling me, and we're going to fix this."

"How?" Keats asks.

"I'm not sure yet, but we'll think of something." I kiss him again, and he clasps my shoulders, pulling me flush against his body.

"Thanks, man," Keaton says when we eventually rip our lips from one another. "I've been going out of my freaking mind since all this went down. It feels good to tell someone. To share the burden." It's easy to see he's telling the truth, because his features have softened and his body language is more relaxed. He looks relieved, and I'm glad I could give him that.

"We're in this together. In every single way." I mean every word.

Stepping out of my en suite bathroom, with a towel slung low on my hips, I'm pleasantly surprised to find Keaton waiting on my bed. He is only wearing white Hugo Boss boxers, looking far hotter than any man has a right to. His hair is still damp from the shower, curling around the backs of his ears, and his skin is mostly dry save for a few beads of water stuck to the curves of his abs. My cock surges to life, as blood pools south in my groin.

"Can I sleep in here tonight? I don't want to be alone right now."

I sit on the edge of the bed beside him. "Sure." I plant a tender kiss on his lips. "I assumed we'd be sharing a bed from now on anyway."

Dark heat flashes in his eyes. "I don't want to impose or expect anything."

"Your innocence is such a turn-on."

He pins me with a fierce scowl. "Glad to be such a source of amusement."

"Keaton." I plant my hands on his head. "I was speaking the

truth. It's refreshing to be with someone so good. Someone who has no agenda but to be with me. Don't ever change."

He threads his hands through his hair. "God, I'm such a mess. I don't know how to be. I—"

I silence him with a kiss, plunging my tongue into his mouth and wiping all trace of his self-doubt away with every stroke of my tongue and every brush of my lips.

I rest my forehead against his. "Just be yourself."

"You say that like it's easy," he mumbles.

"With me, it is. That's what makes this special." I push him down flat on his back, holding my body over his, leaving a tiny gap between us. "Within these four walls, we can always be ourselves. No pretense. No lies. Just truth and authenticity."

"I can do that," he says, gripping my hips and pulling me down flush against his body.

We kiss for eternity, crushing our erections against one another, and I get lost in him.

Keaton pulls my towel off, and I remove his boxers, and we reposition ourselves, lying side by side, at opposite ends of the bed, so we can suck each other off at the same time. His warm mouth on my cock feels like heaven, and I moan against his dick as I graze my teeth lightly along his shaft while I play with his balls. When I sense he's ready to come, I release him and pull my dick out of his mouth before kneeling. "Come on my chest." My hand wraps around my straining erection and I pump myself quickly, feeling the tingle spread up my spine.

Keaton mirrors my position, jerking his dick in his hand as we face one another, edging closer to the ledge together. We shoot our loads within seconds of one another, coating our chests with each other's cum, and it's hot as fuck.

Leaning in, I kiss him hard, pressing against him, enjoying the way our chests stick together. "Hmm." I move my lips from his mouth to his jaw to his ear. "I love tasting me on your tongue." Swiping one finger along my cum-slickened chest, I bring it to my mouth, sucking his seed off my flesh in a deliberately slow, seductive fashion. "But I really love tasting *you*." I flatten my hands on my chest, rubbing my fingers in his cum and bringing them to my lips. "So fucking addictive."

"Fucking hell, Austen." Keaton grabs me to him, kissing me passionately. "You're so dirty, but I love it."

"Good," I say, rubbing *my* cum into *his* chest before pulling us both down under the covers. "Because dirty is my middle name and I can't wait to do all sorts of dirty things to you."

We fall asleep facing one another with our arms and legs entwined, sporting matching cheesy grins.

"I need your help again," I tell Colton the next evening when we're walking through campus after practice has ended.

"Shoot," he says before popping a piece of gum in his mouth.

"Can you find out where Brock Jonas and his bandmate Rod live?"

Colton slams to a halt, tugging on my arm to stop me too. He eyes me curiously as he loudly chews his gum. "Do I even want to know?"

"Depends on how involved you want to be."

"Shit, dude. The look on your face right now is scaring me."

I arch a brow, unsure what emotions I'm showcasing. As I held my sleeping boyfriend in my arms last night, my emotions veered between red-hot rage and anguished torment. Any time I think about what Brock did to Keaton, I just want to wrap protective arms around my boyfriend and shield him from any further pain.

Which is why I'm taking action without telling Keaton.

I get that it's hypocritical, because I was supposed to be coming up with a well-thought-out plan, and I shouldn't be going behind Keats' back, but if I tell him what I plan to do, he'll just tell me not to do it and then worry himself sick overanalyzing every single thing that could go wrong.

So, it's better he doesn't know.

I'll fess up afterward, because I agreed there would be no secrets, but I need to do this, because I have to do *something* to keep him safe.

"So, don't ask." I shrug. I can do this alone although I'd rather have Colton as my wingman.

"Scaring me because that wild, reckless expression you're wearing excites me more than it should," he explains, rubbing his hands together. "Whatever you're planning, I'm all in."

I slap him on the back. "Knew I could count on you. How long till you can get the intel?"

"I'll have it for you tomorrow."

"Don't make any post-practice plans and bring a change of clothes with you. Non-branded, and wear dark colors."

"On a scale of one to ten, how illegal is this?"

I'm not sure where breaking and entering fits on the scale, but either way, that won't be Colton's job. "Minus one." I slap him on the back. "I'll be doing the heavy lifting."

"That's *not* disappointing at all," Colton deadpans, looking genuinely upset.

I shake my head, grinning. "I'll make it up to ya," I promise, because if I can't find what I want in Rod's or Brock's place, we'll be paying a little visit to both assholes, and I already know how that'll go down.

"You're sure this is the place?" I ask Colton the next night, looking over at the shabby gray-bricked apartment building across the street with wary eyes. I know the dude is estranged from his family and he's lost his trust fund, but I was still expecting him to live somewhere nicer. This place was built in the nineteen seventies, and you can tell. At least it doesn't have security cameras, which is a major plus, because I intend to get in and out of his apartment undetected, leaving no trace.

Turns out, Rod, whatever his name is, is no longer in the band and no longer at Berkeley. Apparently, he OD'd at the end of the summer, and he's in some expensive rehab in SoCal, so I'm guessing he's no longer involved in this, and we can eliminate him as an immediate threat. He's got his own shit to deal with by the sounds of it.

"Hundo P. My source is reliable." Colton leans back against the wall, and I turn on my side, pressing my shoulder into the red-bricked building.

"Who is your source anyway?" I'm wondering how he knows so much about Brock.

"This girl from my hometown is one of the band's groupies."

"If she's a groupie, why is she helping us?"

She gave Colton a key to Brock's studio apartment, which makes this a lot easier. Colton has also befriended the cute blonde behind the desk in the lobby, so when it's time to make a move, he'll distract her so I can sneak into the elevator. I've got to say, as wingmen go, he's fucking outstanding.

"Because A. She's had a massive crush on me for years." He flashes me a blinding-white smile. "Like it's a giant-sized crush-slash-obsession." I roll my eyes and shake my head. "And B. Brock screwed her one time and then publicly humiliated her. She's wanted revenge ever since."

I probe the empty space above Colton's head with my

gloved hand, and he stares at me like I'm crazy. "What the fuck are you doing, man?" he asks, frowning.

"Performing an ego check." I pat him on the head. "Don't worry, yours is still overinflated and growing exponentially by the minute."

He flips me the bird. "Ego check that."

I chuckle, loving our easygoing friendship. "You didn't tell her anything, right?"

He thumps me in the upper arm. "What kind of wingman do you take me for? Besides, you told me jack shit, so it's not like I had anything to pass on."

I glance across at the building, willing the asshole to hurry up. Colton has it on good authority the band is playing at some dive bar tonight, but Brock has yet to emerge from his place, and it's getting late.

"It's better if you don't know." I slide my hands into the pockets of my black cargo pants.

"This is still about Kennedy," Colton says, and it's not a question.

I nod, because I owe him that much.

He stares at me for a few semi-tense beats, and something shifts in the air. Clearing his throat, he says. "So, are you two officially together now or what?"

I blink profusely, just staring at my best buddy. I've suspected Colton had guessed about me, but I'm still shocked he's gone there. Now that he has, there's no reason to deny it. I choose to trust him. "How did you know about me?"

"Your girlfriend has only visited you once in over two years, and I've overheard enough of your phone conversations to know something wasn't adding up." He scrubs a hand along his prickly jawline. "My best buddy back home is gay. We've been friends since we were little kids. I've watched him struggle with his sexuality. There's something about you that's always reminded me of Jon." His earnest eyes pierce mine. "But I knew for sure last weekend at the party. I saw the way you and Kennedy were checking each other out."

Well shit. We've got to be more careful in public in the future.

"This is new for Keaton, and no one knows," I explain. "You can't tell anyone."

Colton slaps me on the shoulder. "Your secret is safe with me."

"It honestly doesn't bother you?"

His shoulders relax against the brick at his back, and his smile is genuine. "Nope. You love who you love." He shrugs, his smile extending. "I'm just glad you admitted the truth."

"I've wanted to tell you for a long time, but I didn't want to burden you with the secret."

Colton glances over at the building, straightening up. "We should probably talk more about this, but it'll have to wait because our boy's just left the building."

Pulling the hood of my hoodie up over my head, I cast a surreptitious glance at the sidewalk in front of Brock's apartment building, a satisfied grin creeping across my mouth when I spot the asshat hailing a taxi and getting in.

I flash a mad grin at Colton. "Let's get this show on the road."

Chapter Fourteen
Austen

"Fuck it," I say when Colton and I reconvene a half hour later around the corner of the apartment building. "I didn't find anything." Brock's small studio apartment is disgusting. The place is littered with clothes, empty beer cans and bottles, moldy pizza boxes, dirty cigarette butts, and evidence of drug use. It made searching it easy, because no one would ever guess an intruder had broken in and examined every square inch of the place—it's too messy to tell if anything is out of place.

I did discover his drug stash, stowed behind the vent in his poky bathroom. That knowledge might come in handy later— after we've retrieved all the copies he made of that recording. But until we have those in our possession, we can't risk outing him to the cops for any reason. If he suspects Keaton was behind it, it would force his hand, and I won't be responsible for that tape entering the public domain.

"Perhaps I should've stolen his tablet," I say, musing out loud as we head back toward the main part of town. "But that would clue him in, and without his password, it's worthless anyway." It's not like I can just bring it to the local computer shop and ask them to hack it.

Colton frowns, shoving his hands deep in his pockets. "He has something on Kennedy," he says after a couple beats of silence. "That's what you were looking for."

Guy has always been sharp as a tack, so it's no surprise he's figured it out. "Yeah," I admit, striding toward Keaton's SUV. It's still where I parked it, at the curb of a side street. "He's blackmailing him."

Colton cusses. "I always knew Brock was scum of the earth, so I can't say I'm overly surprised."

I unlock the car, and we climb in.

"What now?" Colton asks as I fire up the engine.

I drum my fingers on the steering wheel. "Can you find out which bar they are at?"

He nods, removing his cell from his back pocket. "What're you planning to do?"

I drag my hands through my hair, wondering if this is wise, but I'm at a loss now, and I've got to do *something*. "I'm going to try to talk some sense into him." I pull the car out onto the road.

"You might make things worse," he says, tapping out a message on his cell.

"I can't sit back and do nothing." I take my eyes off the road for a split-second, looking my buddy in the eye. "This has haunted Keaton for months, and it's hovering over him like a bad smell. I have to try."

Slowly, he nods, just as his cell pings with a new message. He gives me the name of the bar, and it's the same one from the night Keaton met him. I swing the SUV around and head in that direction.

"How do cops handle stakeouts? I would literally kill myself out of sheer boredom," Colton says after we've been parked in the alley outside the bar for the past two hours.

"Could be worse," I supply. "At least we're not standing outside, and we have music and shit coffee." I grimace as I swallow another mouthful of the cheap shit they're selling as coffee at the small store around the corner.

"You sure this is smart?" Colton asks again. "If you piss him off, he might take action."

"The prick likes Kennedy's money too much. He knows he's onto a good thing. And it's worth the risk because I might be able to get through to him. He has a lot to lose if this comes out and someone needs to point that out."

"What if he figures out you two are together? That will only give him more ammunition."

"He has no proof." I turn on my side to face him. "And, honestly? If it came out about me, it might be a blessing in disguise."

I've filled him in on my history while we've been stuck out here waiting. We've debated the pros and cons of me coming out to the team at length. Colton is a good sounding board. I know some of the others see him as the joker of the pack, but he's really not. He has a great sense of humor, but he also has a good head on his shoulders, and he's a fantastic listener.

"I know why you'd think that, but that decision should be yours and yours alone. No one should force your hand even if you think it might help in the long run. Controlling the reveal and the timing is crucially important if you decide to do it. No matter what, you have my support."

"And it means the world to me." Knowing our QB and team captain has my back makes the decision easier although it's not something I can decide alone anymore. If I really want to do this—live authentically as an openly gay man—I'll need

Keaton's support too, because this will impact him. My personal life will become a free for all, and some conclusions may be drawn about the nature of our relationship. I won't force Keaton into the open or even into a situation where someone is jokingly questioning his sexuality. I know he's not ready to reveal his true self to the world, and I won't make things harder for him.

So, perhaps Colton is right, and I should forget about confronting Brock Jonas.

But it's too late, because the asshole saunters out of the side door, and I'm out of the car before my conscious mind has even processed the motion. Colton has promised to stay in the car unless something happens that warrants his intervention. If this turns bad, it's better he's not involved. Coach would flip his lid if two of his best players got messed up in an altercation with a known druggie.

I stride toward Brock with purpose, driving my hands into the pockets of my pants to conceal my straining fists. Putting a leash on my anger is challenging, but I do it, because as much as I'd love to flatten the asshole to the ground, that won't achieve anything productive.

"I want a word." I pull no punches as I come to a stop directly in front of him.

Brock is slouched against the wall with his left knee bent, his foot on the brick behind him. A smug grin curves the corners of his mouth as he takes a long drag of his cigarette. His dark-blond hair is stringy, hanging in greasy waves to his shoulders, and a thick layer of stubble covers his chin and jawline. Sweat plasters his Rolling Stones T-shirt to his chest, and he smells like he showered in a bottle of JD.

Just thinking about this smelly fucker putting his hands on my boyfriend ignites a new wave of aggression, and I bite the inside of my cheek to restrain myself before I end up on a murder charge. This prick really has me riled up in a way that is not usual for me.

"That faggot Kennedy has you doing his dirty work for him now, huh?" He blows smoke in my face, smirking like he hasn't a care in the world.

It's not strange that he'd know who I am, but the fact he knows I'm friends with Keaton is alarming. He probably knows we share a place together, which means the fucker is watching my boyfriend.

I don't like it one little bit.

Rage thunders through me, and I take a step closer, glaring at him. "He doesn't know I'm here. And watch what you say about him."

Sloping his head to the side, he continues smoking as he assesses me. "You're very protective of your roomie. I wonder why that is." His beady eyes probe mine, and it's like locking eyes with a cobra.

Brock is even more dangerous than I thought. He doesn't just prey on vulnerability. He's cunning and smart and always looking for an angle in every situation. He's a manipulative nutjob who measures his self-worth through manipulating and controlling others, and I'm guessing he's gotten good at it.

Keaton is not the first person he has tricked and blackmailed.

I'd put money on it, and that makes him a troublesome adversary. Unless we stop Brock, Keaton won't be the last person he does this to either.

I might have made a mistake coming here, but I can't back down now.

"I am loyal to my friends, and I despise lowlife scumbags who take advantage of good people."

"Not my fault Kennedy's a fool. He fell for it so easily." He barks out a derisory laugh. "Dude was so eager to have my cock in his ass it was like taking candy from a baby."

My nostrils flare as images I'd rather not think about surface in my mind. "Don't be an idiot," I hiss, needing to say my piece and get out of here, because I'm seconds away from beating the shit out of this degenerate. "You know who his family is. If you continue this, you will lose everything. They'll go after you because no one fucks with one of theirs and gets away with it. They have the power, the money, and the contacts to bury you. You'll get kicked out of Berkeley. Your fans will turn on the band, and any hopes you have of making it big will be in the toilet."

I lean in closer, almost puking at the noxious fumes that cling to every facet of his being. "You'll go to jail, man. It will ruin your life." I step back, deliberately adopting a cool manner. "You already got a payout. Consider it a win. Hand over the remaining copies, and Keaton will drop it," I lie, because there's no way we're not nailing his ass to the wall. We'll find something to put him behind bars.

Finishing his cigarette, he throws it to the ground, mashing it with the heel of his boot. He pushes off the wall, straightening up, attempting to pull off a look of intimidation, but he's still a few inches shorter than me, and I don't scare that easily.

Folding my arms, I stare him down, frustrated at the obvious amusement now on his face.

"Tell the queer if he makes one move against me, the only one getting ruined will be him." He shoves at my shoulders, and a red mist ghosts over my face.

I shove him back, slamming him into the wall. "Don't fucking touch me."

He smirks as I take a step back. "It's cute you think you can threaten me. Careful, hotshot." He presses his face all up in mine. "It wouldn't take much for me to start some new rumors.

A queer on the football team would be big news. Wonder what your fans would think of that?"

He's clearly bullshitting, but if he realizes how close he is to the truth, I've just royally screwed me and Keats. I let none of that show on my face, maintaining a neutral expression as I stare him down. "As if anyone would listen to a word out of your mouth. You're full of shit, and everyone knows it. But be my guest. Go ahead and make an even bigger fool of yourself. It's no skin off my back."

His eyes drift the length of my body, and I'm losing the battle with my self-control. "I'm not into dudes, but I make an exception from time to time," he says, smirking.

He pushes his chest into mine, and I instantly shove him off, taking a couple steps back. I need to get out of here before I do something I regret. "Drop the blackmail, Jonas, because it won't end well for you. I won't warn you again." I leave him with those words, turning around and heading back toward the car.

"I bet you'd love my cock in your ass," he shouts after me, and I slam to a halt, rage pummeling my insides. "Not like that pussy Kennedy. He tell you my buddy Rod came all over his face while I soaked his ass with my cum?"

My clenched knuckles bleach white as I dig my fingernails into the palms of my hands.

His voice grows louder. "The whole time he was pretending like he didn't enjoy it, but I know he did. He lapped it up like the dirty fucking faggot he is." Grabbing hold of my shirt from behind, Brock yanks me back, wrapping his arm around my neck and squeezing. "Not so fucking high and mighty now, are we hotshot?"

His putrid breath on my ear sours my stomach, but it's his feeble attempt to put me in a chokehold that is his undoing. I let go of my restraint, unleashing every ounce of hatred locked up inside. Shoving my elbow deep into his soft stomach, I slam my head back, whacking his skull with force, and he moans as he stumbles back, relaxing his hold on me.

Pain rattles through the back of my head, but I barely feel it over the liquid aggression charging through my veins. Turning around, I throw myself at him, swinging my fist in his face. He goes down, crashing to the ground like a limp noodle, and I jump on top of him, pummeling him repeatedly, punch after punch, silently rejoicing when blood spurts from his nose and a pained wheezy sound rattles from his chest.

Strong arms pull me away before I can inflict more damage. "Calm the hell down," Colton hisses in my ear as I buck against his hold.

"You really shouldn't have done that, man," Brock groans, spitting blood onto the ground as he struggles to sit up. "I'll have your ass for that."

"No, you fucking won't." Colton kicks him in the ribs, holding out his cell. The screen is open on a photo of Brock with some creepy dude who looks like he'd commit murder just for shits and giggles. "You say one word about what went down here tonight, or you make any move against my buddy, and we'll give the cops the name and address of your dealer. Before he's arrested, we'll tip him off. Let him know you were the one who ratted him out."

I appreciate Colton threatening him, but we all know Brock can go nowhere with this. He swung first, and I was just defending myself. If word got out, no one would believe the druggie over the football player. I'm not saying it to be an ass. Just stating facts. If it comes down to my word against his, I'll win this round, hands down.

Brock climbs to his feet, clutching his torso, and I'm glad he's in pain. He deserves worse for what he's doing to Keats.

"Same goes for Kennedy," Colton adds. "This ends now, asshole."

"Fuck you." He spits more blood on the ground before hobbling toward the door that leads to the bar. "Fuck you both. Motherfucking pricks."

Chapter Fifteen
Keaton

"I can't believe you did that." I grab fistfuls of my hair as I pace the living room floor. Knots tighten in my stomach as anxiety rides me hard.

"I'm sorry. I wanted to help, but I've probably only made things worse." Austen's butt is propped on the edge of the dining table as he watches me prowl the floor with the intensity of a hunter stalking his prey.

I'm still processing. Still utterly shocked at what Austen has done. Because it's out of character for him to act so recklessly.

When he first fessed up, I was freaking out. Instantly checking my cell to see if Austen had forced Brock's hand and he'd released the recording. My breathing only recovered when I didn't see anything trending, and now I've had time to consider it, the overwhelming emotion I'm feeling is gratitude.

No one has ever gone out on a limb like this for me before.

No one has ever put my needs ahead of their own.

And it's everything.

He's everything.

I stop pacing and walk over to him, clasping his face in my hands. "Thank you for trying."

His brows climb to his hairline. "I expected freaking out, not a thank you."

"Oh, I'm most definitely freaking out, but I'm more grateful. Maybe Brock will listen. And if he doesn't, at least he knows I've told someone else. That might make him stop and think. And if what you've told me is true, that his family has washed their hands of him, he needs my money now more than ever."

"You're not giving him another penny," Austen says through gritted teeth, flexing his hands.

Carefully, I take one of his hands in mine, inspecting his reddened knuckles. "Does it hurt?"

"A little, but it's nothing serious. Colton pulled me off him before I could do any real damage."

While I wish I'd been there to see Brock getting his ass beat by my boyfriend, I'm glad Colton stopped Austen before he landed himself in serious trouble. "No one's ever punched someone on my behalf before." I gently knead Austen's hand.

"It's not something to be proud of, and it's not why I went over there."

"I know." I lift my eyes to his. "But you don't understand how much this means to me. No one has ever gone into battle on my behalf before." A messy ball of emotion clogs the back of my throat. "That you accept who I am and go out of your way to protect and support me. It's everything, Austen. It just blows my frigging mind."

"I care about you, and I'll always want to protect you." Emotion shines in his eyes, and I'm glad I'm not the only one turning into a gooey mess.

"That works both ways. I want to protect you too. I can't believe you'd risk your reputation like that. What if he finds out about you? About us? He'll be looking for something to use against you now because that's the kind of nasty, spiteful prick he is." It won't be good enough that he's got me over a barrel. His pride is hurt over the ass-kicking Austen gave him, and he'll want to make him pay. I've no doubt about that.

Austen clasps the nape of my neck, sending delicious tremors cascading along my skin. His touch is electric, and I feel it bone-deep. Soul-deep. Because this guy is working his way into every nook and cranny of my being.

"He won't because we're going to be more careful in public, and Brock doesn't know what we do behind closed doors." He frowns. "Or I hope he doesn't." His eyes lift to mine. "He made it clear he's been watching you. There's no way he could've gotten in here, right?"

It's rare to see Austen rattled, but he's rattled now.

"Security is tight in the building, and I doubt he'd get past our alarm system, but let's make sure." I don't want Austen worrying, and I refuse to look over my shoulder in my own damn apartment. This is our only safe haven. The one place we can be together without worrying about being seen. I'm not about to jeopardize that. Austen's expression is inquisitive as he watches me dial a number on my cell.

My brother picks up on the third ring. "Keats. Everything okay?" Keven asks, instantly assuming I need help. I wonder if he's gotten used to the fact he's the first person we call when we need help or if I should call him more often just to shoot the shit.

"Everything's fine, Kev. Chill. I just need a favor."

"Okay." I hear a door close in the background. "What do you need?"

"Can you send me one of those detector devices? For checking for bugs and hidden cameras."

Deathly silence greets my request. "If you're in some kind of trouble, I—"

"I know I can come to you," I say, cutting across him, because I don't want to outwardly lie. "But I'm fine. Some asshole's been on my case, but I'm handling it. I just want to make sure he hasn't been in my place."

Austen's eyes are glued to mine and he's listening to every word.

"This isn't giving me the warm fuzzies," Kev says. "You sure there isn't something I need to know?"

He's offering me an opening, and I want to take it, but I can't. Not yet. "I'm almost twenty-one, Kev. I can handle things myself. As soon as I can't, I'll let you know. For now, I just need your help with this."

A heavy sigh echoes down the line. "Okay," he finally says. "I'll text you a link to an app you can install on your phone. Just shut your curtains and block out all light and walk around your place with it on. It'll beep and flash red if there is any hidden surveillance equipment in your place. If there is, I expect you to call me back ASAP."

"I will. I promise. Thanks."

"Okay, bro."

"Give my love to Cheryl."

We hang up, and I face my boyfriend as I wait for Kev's message to arrive. "That was my brother Keven."

"I surmised that much," Austen says, tilting his head to one side. "He's the computer genius."

I nod. "He's also an FBI agent, but that's not something that is common knowledge." His bosses understand the importance of keeping his profession a secret, so the couple of occasions a photographer has captured a pic of him at a scene, they have shut it down fast, but it's only a matter of time before the public finds out.

"Wow. That's pretty cool."

I grin. "It is. Especially because he was a computer hacker and he probably should've ended up in jail for some of the stunts he pulled, but instead he was so shit-hot the FBI made him a deal in exchange for immunity."

"I look forward to meeting him. He sounds like he might have some interesting stories to share." Austen grabs my hip, pulling me in closer. "But what I really want to know is why the fuck you haven't asked your brother to help with Brock? I'm guessing he could make it go away like that." He clicks his fingers.

"He probably could, but I—" I hang my head, unable to say it.

"You're embarrassed," Austen says, his voice softening.

I nod, raising my eyes to his. "It would mean telling my family I'm gay, because I couldn't just tell Keven. It wouldn't be fair to ask him to keep it a secret even though I know he'd do it in a heartbeat."

"Your brother sounds awesome."

"He is. He's done so much for our family. I always know he has my back."

Austen holds the nape of my neck. "Then you need to tell your family. Stop torturing yourself unnecessarily. If Keven can help make this go away, it's a no-brainer."

"I'm working up to it," I admit, hating how weak I feel. I know Austen is right. I've thought the same thing a hundred times. "In the meantime, we just have to be careful in public so we don't give Brock any additional ammunition to come after either of us."

Austen drills a hole in my skull, and I know he wants to say more, but he also won't push me out of my comfort zone.

My cell pings, and I open the message from my brother, clicking on the link to download the app.

After a few tense beats, he nods, and I release the breath I'd been holding.

"I'm going to get Gia to pay me a visit," he adds.

My stomach plummets to my toes. "You don't have to do that."

"Actually, I do." He trails his fingers along the downy hairs at the base of my neck, and I bite back a moan. That feels so damn good. "I need to tell her about us. She needs to understand our fake relationship is coming to an end."

Chapter Sixteen
Keaton

"Wait. What?" I splutter. "We agreed we were keeping it secret. I can't—"

He silences me with a kiss, and I wrap my arms around his shoulders, nestling between his legs as he kisses the shit out of me.

"I know you're not ready to face up to things yet," he says when we finally surface for air. "And I will never force you to say or do anything, but it'll happen at some point, and I need to prepare Gia. She has a right to know I'm in a relationship."

When he puts it like that, it makes sense. And I can't deny how happy I am knowing he sees a future for us. Enough to tell his best friend already. "Okay." I trust Austen to do this the right way.

"She can do us this one last favor," he adds, rubbing his thumb along my swollen lower lip. "And, besides, I want her to meet you."

"He wants me to meet his friends," I drawl as warmth suffuses my chest.

Austen pulls me closer, and our crotches collide. His hard dick presses against mine through our clothes, and I love knowing he's aroused from kissing as much as I am.

"I do," he says, his hand flattening over my ass. "And I want to meet yours."

"You already have." I swivel my hips against his. "Seb, Mol, and Kate are my only friends outside of my family."

"You don't have friends from high school?"

I shake my head. "There were a few guys I hung around with, but they were only acquaintances. I find it hard letting people into my life because they always want something from me. I had my brothers, Faye, and Melissa, and I didn't need anyone else," I explain. "At least, not back then. Now, it's different. I want to trust people. To let more in. But it's hard, especially after what happened with Brock because I don't trust my own judgment anymore."

He rubs his nose against mine. "I hate that for you, and I wish it was easier, but I can relate. I had no problem making friends in high school. Sure, I lost some when I came out, but they were never true friends anyway. Since coming to Berkeley, I've found it harder to find genuine people. It's why I haven't really mixed with anyone outside of the football team. Too many want to use me to get to the guys, or they want to jump my bones purely because I'm a football player."

"Just another reason why we're so good together," I say, as the thought occurs to me. "We're both dealing with similar trust issues."

"Good thing we've got each other, right?" Austen grabs my ass in his hands, pulling me onto his hard cock. "See what you do to me?" His eyes dilate, and my cock throbs behind my jeans. "I'm permanently horny around you."

Crashing my lips against his, I push my tongue into his

gorgeous mouth so I can taste him. Our hips rock together, and precum leaks from the tip of my cock. "Want to take this to bed?" I murmur into his ear, grazing my teeth along the column of his neck, inhaling the citrusy scent of his cologne.

"I need a shower first," he says, straightening up and folding his hand around mine. A wicked glint appears in his eye. "Shower with me?"

I don't need to be asked twice, but there's something we must attend to. "I'd like that. But we check for surveillance equipment first."

After we've checked for bugs, and come up empty-handed, thank fuck, we race to Austen's bedroom. I slam into his back when he comes to an abrupt stop in the middle of his bedroom. "What the hell, man?" I ask, my voice muffled against his back.

"You got me a new chair." He twists around to look at me.

"I've heard you complaining, and I've felt your sore shoulder muscles. I spoke to my mom. She's into all that ergonomic shit. She had a couple spare chairs left over after furnishing her new office space. She sent me that one for you."

Austen circles his arms around me, hugging me close. "Thanks, babe."

I shrug, staring into the swirling depths of his green eyes. "It's only a chair."

"It's more than just a chair." He kisses me softly, but it's not long before it heats up, and we're grinding against each other again, arms wrapped tightly around one another.

"I need your cock," Austen says, palming my erection through my jeans. He tugs on my other hand, pulling me toward his en suite bathroom. "Shower. Now."

We strip our clothes off in record time, and I watch Austen's butt cheeks flex as he leans in to turn the shower on.

I want his ass.

Imagining pushing my dick inside of him has more precum leaking from the tip of my cock, and if I don't rein myself in, I'll come like a teenager watching porn for the first time.

Water gushes from the showerhead as Austen looks over his shoulder, his lips twitching when he sees my lust-coated gaze. He steps into the shower stall, ducking his head under the pounding water, and I walk toward him in slow motion, enjoying the view.

Austen tilts his head up, closing his eyes, as water sprays across his face, dripping down over the corded muscle of his shoulders, gliding down his firm chest, trailing over the ink on his upper torso and arms, and trickling through the crevices in his toned six-pack.

My hands are on his body the instant I join him, my palms sliding up and down his chiseled chest, my mouth parted in awe. "Your body is insane, man." Taking the bodywash from the shelf, I dump a load in my hand, lifting my eyes to his. "I want to wash you."

"Work away," he says, his voice oozing like molten chocolate.

Lathering the liquid in my hands, I rub the frothing wash all over his chest and his arms. Water runs down one side of me as I trail my hands over Austen's ripped biceps and the sinewy muscle of his lower arms. Air hisses through his teeth when our dicks brush together, both straining to the point of pain. My eyes lock on his as I grip his hard dick, washing it slowly, my fingers twisting in his dark pubes, tracing a line down the defined V indents on either side of his hips. His eyes roll back in his head before he moves his mouth toward mine.

Fighting a grin, I sink to my knees, enjoying the heated frustration etched across his face at my denial. I wash his powerful thighs with care, savoring every second of this intimate moment.

I have always known I'm a relationship kind of guy. Even though my relationship with Melissa was complicated, and it was never about intimacy or sex with us, I enjoyed sharing the mundane things with her. I enjoyed her company, and there was a certain comfort in having her by my side.

But this.

This is on a whole other playing field.

It's only early days in our relationship, but I'm already addicted to Austen Hayes. I want to spend every second of my free time with him, getting to know him inside and out. Exploring his body is only one part of it. I want to know what makes him tick. To understand who he is on a deeper level. To experience a new side of him as my boyfriend. To finally let go of my inhibitions and the restraints preventing me from truly living.

I finish washing his legs and his feet and I stand, pressing the length of my body flush against his. He rocks his hips into mine, and we move as one, our teeth gnashing when our lips meet in a frenzied kiss I feel in every part of my body.

Austen walks me back until my spine hits the tiled wall. Sliding one hand up my chest, he lightly grips my throat, pressing in gently, and I whimper into his mouth. I squeeze his ass cheeks before sliding my fingers up and down his crack. Our cocks slide against one another and stars burst behind my eyelids.

I have never been so turned on in my life.

Never wanted to fuck anyone as badly as I want to fuck my boyfriend right now.

Austen's tongue plunders my mouth, and I can barely breathe with the brutal way he's kissing me, but I never want it to end.

My fingers prod at his puckered hole, and adrenaline

courses through my veins as anticipation elevates to coronary-inducing proportions.

Austen's hand around my throat tightens as my two fingers breach his asshole, dipping inside. His hips jerk against mine, and I throw an arm out, gripping the edge of the shower as my feet slip a little.

"Damn, Keats." Austen's mouth moves to my jaw, and he nips and sucks his way to my neck.

I suck in greedy lungsful of air, cautioning my dick to calm down before I prematurely shoot my load. My fingers move deeper inside Austen's ass, and he curses. Raising his head, he pins me with eyes so full of dark desire they are almost black. "Fuck me, man. I want your cock inside me."

Nervous excitement bubbles in my chest. I've only done this one other time. With a one-night stand, and I didn't enjoy it as much as I'd hoped because the guy was a stranger, and I was missing a genuine connection with the person writhing underneath me. I know this will be completely different, and while I'm dying to fuck Austen, I'm worried it won't live up to the standards he's come to expect.

"Don't get lost in your head," he says, holding my face in his large palms. "I want this with you. There is no comparison," he adds, proving how well he knows me. "I already know it's going to be amazing, because it's *you*." He kisses me passionately, and my heart swells to bursting point.

I'm falling so hard for this guy, and it's everything I've ever wanted, but I'm terrified because it means I've got so much to lose if I screw this up.

I won't screw it up, I promise myself. He wants me for me, and I never have to hide with him.

"I'm nervous," I admit, tearing my lips from his. "I want to make it good for you."

Austen grabs my hand, circling it around his thick shaft.

"Feel how hard you make me. And that's just from *thoughts* of your dick in my ass. There is no way this won't blow my mind. Trust me, Keats." He rubs his nose against mine. "Trust yourself." He takes my hand, leading me out of the shower. "We've got this."

Chapter Seventeen
Keaton

We crash onto the bed, limbs entangled, beads of water dripping off both our bodies onto the comforter because we are in too much of a hurry to dry off. We lie on our sides, arms and legs entwined, rubbing our dicks together as we thrust forward with mounting need. Austen bites down on my lower lip, and desire coils low in my groin, tightening my dick until it feels like all the blood in my body exists in my cock.

"I need inside you now, man," I rasp.

Austen sits up, opening the drawer of his nightstand, tossing condoms and lube on the bed. I reach for a rubber, but he grabs my wrist, stalling me. "Let me." I kneel in front of him as he slowly rolls the condom on my aching dick, softly biting his shoulder as he gets me ready. He lubes my condom-covered dick before lying flat on his back, easing his slick fingers between the cheeks of his ass.

"I want to do that." I pour the silicone-based liquid on my palms, smothering my fingers with lube before I crouch down between his thighs.

Austen spreads his legs, propping up on his elbows to watch as I insert two fingers into his ass. He's tight, but his muscles relax as I work my fingers in and out of his puckered hole. He hisses when I add a third finger, and my nose nuzzles his ball sack. I lick and suck his balls as my fingers pump harder and faster in his tight hole, and I'm so aroused I don't even realize I'm dry humping the sheets as I prep my lover.

"Keaton." Austen's voice is rigid with restraint, and I know what he needs.

Me.

My cock.

All the way inside his ass.

Adding more lube to my dick, I squeeze the base of my shaft to control myself as I lean over him, kissing him on the mouth. Austen falls back to the bed as I hover over him, my fingers still stroking his ass, while my lips worship his gorgeous mouth. I pull back when it's clear neither of us can wait a second longer. "How do you want this?"

"Like this," he says, grabbing my ass and pulling my dick against his opening. "Put one of my legs on your shoulder," he commands, as I straighten up, withdrawing my fingers and getting into position.

My body is wound tight with nerves, my cock harder than it's ever been as I line my dick up with his ass, placing his right leg on my shoulder. Austen tucks his left leg up and out to the side, opening himself fully to me. His eyes don't leave mine as I slowly inch inside him. His hands are locked behind his head, and every part of him is relaxed and at ease as he watches me enter his body.

"Oh fuck." I hold myself still once I'm all the way inside, wanting to commit this moment to memory.

"Come here." His voice reverberates with raw sex, and I lean down, slanting my mouth against his. He devours my mouth the way one might devour a plate of rich, sinful chocolate cake. Our eyes meet as my cock pulses inside him, and his dick jerks against my stomach.

"You feel so good in me. This feels so good." He grabs the back of my neck, yanking my mouth to his for a hard, fast kiss. "But I need you to fuck me now, Keaton. Fuck me real hard, man. I want you to pound my ass, and stroke my prostate, until I see stars."

I need no further invitation, and I sit back up, rolling my hips as I start to move inside him. The sounds leaving Austen's mouth as I rut into him are purely animalistic, and I press his left leg back as I rise slightly on my feet, ramming my cock into him as deep as it will go. The way his ass hugs my dick is out of this world, and sex has never been this good for me.

Our eyes blaze a trail over one another as I screw him into the bed, driving my dick deeper and harder with each thrust. His cock bobs against his stomach, and I move back to my knees, pumping into him from the same angle, while I grip his erection and stroke his hard length in sync with my thrusts. Sweat coasts down my spine and beads on my chest and my brow as I rock inside him, and every nerve ending in my body is on fire.

Austen yanks me down on top of him, imprisoning my hand between our bodies as he attacks my mouth. A familiar tingle creeps up my spine, and I know I won't last long. His dick pulses against my hand and my stomach as I continue pumping my hips, shoving my cock in and out of his ass, while he ravages my mouth like he'll never get to kiss me again.

"Austen. Fuuuck!" I roar as my orgasm explodes, ripping through me like lightning, waves of pleasure rolling through me, consuming every part of my body. I deposit my seed, in the condom, deep in his ass, and he grits his teeth, hissing, his eyes rolling back in his head as he reaches his own peak. Sticky wetness coats my fingers and my stomach as his cum sprays between our sweat-slickened bodies.

I collapse on top of him, my dick still in his ass, his legs lowering to the bed on either side of my body. Austen snakes his arms around me, holding me close. "Told ya," he whispers in my ear. "Knew you'd fucking rock my world."

After we've cleaned up, we crawl under the covers, lying on our sides, with our legs touching. Austen links his fingers through mine. "You doing okay?"

The cheesiest smile spreads across my mouth. "I am better than okay. That was insanely hot."

"Hotter than you imagined it'd be?" he inquires with a knowing smile.

"Way hotter."

"You look happy," he says as I trace circles on his chest with the tip of my finger.

"I am happy," I honestly admit, and a sudden burst of emotion has tears pricking the back of my eyes.

"It's a good look on you."

"*You're* a good look on me." I hold the back of his neck. "This is serious for me, Austen. I don't fuck around. I'm serious about you."

Pressing his forehead to mine, he says, "I'm serious about you too. This isn't some casual fling for me either."

A shuddering breath escapes my body. "How did I get so lucky? I still can't believe this."

"Believe it, Keaton," he says, pulling me flush against him. He rests his head on my shoulder. "This is the real deal."

We fall into a new routine, and it's as easy as breathing. Our days and evenings are full with our busy schedules, but we both ensure we're home for dinner every night by eight. We take turns cooking, and I'm enjoying coming up with some new menu options. I mention it in passing to Mol, and she suggests a new monthly column in the newspaper with wholesome recipes athletes and other health-conscious students on campus can make. I tell her I'll think about it.

At night, after we've done our homework, we watch TV while we catch up on our day, or we cave to our wild monkey lust, falling into bed and fucking until our limbs ache and we can barely keep our eyes open.

I still haven't bottomed, and Austen hasn't brought the subject up, staying true to his word and letting me set the pace. I know we need to talk about it, and I get seriously turned on every time I think of him sliding into my ass, but my fears always surface, reminding me I need to work up to it.

"That smells good," Austen says, dumping his bag on the floor as he materializes in the kitchen. "Will it stretch to three?"

I glance over my shoulder, spotting Colton Barnes behind my boyfriend.

I know he knows about us, but in the three weeks since Austen confirmed his suspicions, I haven't had any contact with him. A little forewarning would've been nice, but Austen probably knew I'd freak out if I had advance notice. He's eager for me to meet his friends, so I can't be mad at him for springing the Bear's QB on me.

"I can make that work." I smile at Colton. "Make yourself at home, man."

Austen opens the refrigerator, sticking his head inside. "Water, juice, or soda?" he asks his friend. They have an important game tomorrow, against Stanford, their biggest rival, so there's no question either of them will touch a drop of alcohol.

Austen's dedication to football is a huge attraction. The guy gives two hundred percent to everything he commits to, and I'm in awe of him.

"I'll take a water," Colton confirms, dropping his bag on the floor beside Austen's. "Nice place you've got here."

"Thanks." I stir the sauce before putting the lid back on it. I walk to the refrigerator to grab some garlic and unsalted butter to make garlic bread.

"Austen said you lived in the freshman dorms at first," he adds, catching the bottle of water Austen throws at him.

"Yeah." I smile at Austen when he hands me a glass of pinot noir. I take a sip of my wine as I pull lettuce, tomatoes, and peppers to make a salad from the refrigerator. "I wanted the full college experience," I explain, washing the lettuce in the sink. "But it wasn't all it was cracked up to be."

"He was hounded," Austen explains as he sets another place at the table.

"That must suck, man."

I shrug, drying the lettuce with some paper towels. "I'm used to it back home, but I'd stupidly thought coming here would be different. Not so much."

"That's the price of fame." Colton sips his water, looking thoughtful. "I've never stopped to think about it before. And I know what we experience is only a fraction of what it's like for you."

I slice the tomatoes and peppers as we talk. "It's pretty much all I've ever known, but part of the reason why I made the decision to come here was so I could escape the celebrity circus that follows my family. To just be me."

"It must have been upsetting for you then," Colton says, and Austen is right. His friend is easy to talk to.

"I thought about transferring to Harvard with my brothers constantly the first few months," I admit, placing the salad in a bowl. I wipe my hands on the kitchen towel, turning around to face Colton as I sip on my wine. Austen has disappeared to his bedroom. To change, I'm guessing, but also to give me and Colton some time to bond.

"What stopped you?"

"I didn't want to be *that* guy. The one who runs back home with his tail between his legs at the first sign of trouble. I stuck it out, already deciding I would find somewhere else to live the following year. Some place where there wouldn't be people staring at me or knocking on my door at all hours of the day and night. Then I met my friends, settled into my classes, joined the college paper, and gradually found a way to be at peace."

"I'm glad you stuck around." Austen slides up beside me, nuzzling his face into my hair. "We wouldn't have met if you'd left."

Colton chuckles. "Had you pegged as the romantic type, Hayes. I should've put money on it."

Austen flips him the bird. "Bite me."

"I'll leave that up to your lover. Seems like Keaton is fond of digging his teeth into your skin," Colton quips, and my cheeks inflame like an out-of-control bushfire.

Austen told me he's been the butt of some locker room teasing lately thanks to a few bite marks and hickeys I've left on his body. He lied and said his girlfriend surprised him with a visit, but it's another reminder of how careful we need to be. And how much I hate he has to maintain the fake-girlfriend ruse.

Now, I'm the one sporting hickeys and bite marks in non-visible places, which is A-okay with me.

"Shit, sorry, man," Colton says, working hard to hide his amusement, not looking that apologetic. "I didn't mean to embarrass you."

"It's cool." I remove the bread from the bread box. "I'm a novice at all this."

"Austen explained." Colton walks to my side. "And you never have to worry about me. I'd never tell anyone anything about you two."

"Thanks, man. We appreciate that. And thanks for helping with Brock that time."

He nods. "I'm here if you guys need me. Speaking of the douche, has he raised his ugly head lately?"

"He's lying low. Licking his wounds, no doubt," Austen says.

"Hopefully, he got the message," Colton says.

"I think it'll take more than a beatdown to make that snake slither away," I admit. "Although I'd love to take his lack of contact as a good sign, I'm worried he's planning something." I regularly scan the apartment using the app I downloaded to my cell after my phone call with Kev, and at least we are assured the prick hasn't been inside our home.

"If he comes at us again, we'll find a way of making him permanently go away," Austen says, determination underscoring his words. I love how he says "we," and it's a huge weight off my mind to know I'm no longer in this alone.

"I bet he's moved on to someone else. His type usually does."

I pray Colton is right, but for now, I want to push all thoughts of Brock Jonas from my mind and just enjoy the night. "Dinner will be ready in fifteen."

"Can I help?" Colton asks, and I hand him the bread knife.

"Slice that while I prepare the butter. Thanks."

"Austen says you are an amazing cook. I might have to invite myself over more often."

"Yeah, no." Austen pulls himself up onto the counter behind us. "We have little free time to ourselves as it is, and I see enough of your ugly mug."

"You love my pretty-boy face. Admit it." Colton grins.

"You're not my type, Barnes," Austen retorts, and Colton chuckles.

"In more ways than one," he adds, and I fight a grin as they banter back and forth while I finish the dinner prep.

"Man, this is so good I think I'll turn gay and steal your boyfriend," Colton says twenty minutes later when we're seated at the table and diving into our steaks with Tuscan tomato sauce.

"I'd like to see you try," Austen retorts. "Keats is *mine*." He licks his lips as his gaze roams my body in a blatantly obvious manner.

My dick hardens at the dark lust on his face and the jealous possessive tone in his voice. If we didn't have company, I'd drop to my knees under the table and show him just how much his possessiveness turns me on.

Colton chuckles. "Jealous much, Hayes?"

Austen flips him the bird before flashing me a drop-dead-gorgeous smile, and I'm a goner for this guy. Head-over-heels crazy for him.

"Austen is an amazing boyfriend," I admit. "And there isn't a man on the planet who could steal me away from him."

Austen smirks at Colton, wearing the compliment with pride.

"Dude, don't feed the beast," Colton groans. "His ego is already out of control."

"I think you mean *your* ego." Austen shovels another forkful of steak in his mouth.

"Speaking of egos," Colton says, his face almost orgasmic as he finishes off his dinner. "You should open a restaurant or start your own cooking show."

My grin is out of control. "I appreciate the compliment, but cooking is only a hobby. I've seen those restaurant shows on TV, and no thanks. All that stress and pressure is not for me."

Although, the idea of a cooking show *does* hold some appeal, but it's not like I've ever given much thought to cooking as a career.

"What do you plan to do after you graduate"? Colton asks, tearing off a huge chunk of his garlic bread.

"I have no clue. I'll probably start up my own business or something," I mumble, hating that I'm so directionless. Most everyone I've met at Berkeley has a set goal for after they graduate, and I'm still grappling to find a passion I can turn into a career.

"Keaton is a talented writer," Austen says. "And he's acing all his classes. He can do whatever he wants when he graduates. The world is his oyster."

I wish I shared his confidence, but I don't. Not wanting to be a Debbie Downer, I plaster a smile on my face and redirect. "Are you hoping to get signed by an NFL team?" I ask Colton.

"That's the plan," he says. "But if that doesn't work out, I'm going to set up my own personal training business. Maybe start up my own gym franchise. Whatever I end up doing, it will be sports related."

"I've no doubt whatever you do it'll be a huge success."

"While I hate to agree with anything your boyfriend says, Austen is right. The world is our oyster. We can be what we want, do what we want. These are the best years of our lives, and I don't plan on wasting a single second of it."

His words strike a deep chord inside me.

How many more years am I going to waste denying who I am?

It's as if a light bulb goes off in my head, and I see what's been staring me in the face these past few years.

It's no wonder I can't find a passion or a goal when I'm still hiding behind a wall.

Until I fully embrace my identity and my sexuality, I will

never know who I truly am, who I could be, because I'm suppressing that part of myself where the inner passion dwells.

If I want to find a path to my future, it begins with acknowledging who I am in the present.

It's time to tell my family what I should've had the balls to tell them years ago.

I'm ready to tell my family I'm gay.

Chapter Eighteen
Austen

Keaton is waiting with Mol, Kate, and Seb when Colton and I emerge from the locker room after the postgame lecture Coach just laid on us. Knowing my boyfriend was in the crowd, watching us get our asses beat, only adds to my low mood.

"Commiserations, guys," Mol says as we approach the group. "Can I get an official quote for the paper?"

"Mol." Keaton takes her elbow, switching off the recorder on her cell. "We're off duty tonight. Leave the guys alone."

I like Molly. She's sweet and quiet, except when she's looking for a quote or she sniffs a story, and then she transforms from a cute Chihuahua into a ferocious Rottweiler, gnashing teeth at the ready. She's going to make one damn fine reporter someday.

Mol nods tersely, not wanting to let it go, but she values Keaton's friendship too much to persist. I take pity on her. "I'll email you a quote you can use tomorrow. Right now, I just want to drown my sorrow in beer."

Today's game was a big game for us. *The* Big Game.

Against the Cardinals. It's the oldest rivalry in this part of the country, and Stanford has won nine of our last ten meetings. We badly wanted to change that today, and though we came close, we were still the losing team at the end of the second half. I'm fucking sick over handing those smug bastards a victory, especially since they've just cost us our winning streak, and I want to drink my body weight in beer and then crawl into bed with my boyfriend later and get lost in him.

We head to a Thai place for dinner before joining the rest of the team at the sports bar we sometimes frequent. Keaton and I purposely sit on opposite sides of the booth, which I hate, but at least I get to play footsie with him under the table.

Nolan is holding court at the table, and his grating voice drills painful holes in my skull. Keaton chews on his lip as I order another beer, and I know he's concerned I'm drinking too much, but it's not like I'm falling-down drunk every day of the week. And I need to smother all the thoughts screaming in my head.

Losing the game today was a blow, but increasingly, I'm getting frustrated at having to hide my relationship. Like now, I want to wrap my arms around my sexy boyfriend and kiss the shit out of him. I stare at his mouth, remembering his full lips wrapped around my dick last night as he sucked me off while fingering my ass.

Fuck. Sex with Keaton Kennedy is on a whole new orgasmic level, and I literally cannot get enough.

The waitress hands me a beer along with her number written on a napkin. I thank her without looking up at her, never taking my eyes off Keaton, scrunching the napkin, and tossing it on the floor.

Conversation continues around me, but I tune the voices out, drinking my beer as I eye fuck my boyfriend, my dick straining against my jeans, throbbing with need.

Keaton cautions me with his eyes, turning into Seb, whispering in his ear, and a little green-eyed monster makes an appearance, which is ridiculous, because Seb and Kate are clearly into one another, but occasionally, I've wondered if Seb is harboring a secret crush on my man, because I've spotted him staring at him a few times in a way that made me question if he isn't into dudes too.

That shit is catching. Am I right?

I bark out a laugh, draining the rest of my beer as my eyes linger on Keats again. An unexpected burst of pain shoots up my leg as someone levels a swift kick to my shin under the table. Colton glares at me, and I flip him off.

My cell pings with a message from my buddy.

Colton: You're being obvious.

I lift my head from my cell, and Colton jerks his head in the direction of the bathrooms as he sends me another text.

Colton: Go sort your shit out or GO HOME.

Fuck. He's right. I'd hate myself if I did or said anything which outed us. I'll take a piss and then go home before I do any damage.

The room tilts as I stand, and I sway a little on my feet. Ignoring the whoops and hollers at my back, I make my way out of the bar area and into the hallway where the bathrooms are. I have my hand on the door to the men's bathroom when Keaton calls out to me. My eyes whip left and right, but the hallway is empty, so I snag Keaton's arm, pulling him into the accessible bathroom with me and locking the door.

Pushing him up against the door, I drill my hard-on against his crotch as my lips crash against his. Keats grabs the back of my head, kissing me with the same passion, and I get lost in the feel of his hot body flush against mine and the possessive way his lips claim mine.

Reaching between us, I fumble with the buttons of his

jeans, popping the top two open and driving my hand down under the band of his boxers, palming his hard dick.

"Shit, Austen." Keats rips his mouth from mine, holding one hand to my chest. "We can't do this here, man. And not when you're drunk."

"I'm not so drunk that I'm not in control," I truthfully admit. "And I need you, man. I need you, Keats." I grab fistfuls of his hair, peppering kisses along his face and his jawline.

He cusses, and I see the indecision on his face, but right now, my need is too strong. I stroke his cock while I attempt to open my jeans with my left hand.

Keats encircles my wrist, stopping my movement. "We can get an Uber home and be in bed in twenty minutes."

"That's too long," I purr, nipping at his earlobe. "Need you now, babe." I rest my forehead against his. "Please. We can be quick."

Keats moans, tipping his head back, his skull knocking against the wooden door. "You are going to be the death of me."

I love you. I think it, but I don't say it. Thank fuck. Because I don't want to tell him I love him for the first time when I'm drunk in the bathroom of a sports bar. But I need his mouth on my cock and his hands on my body, and that shit can't wait.

He caresses my cheek, and the adoring gaze in his eyes almost has me blurting the truth. "What do you need, boyfriend?" he whispers, trailing a line of feather-soft kisses along my jawline.

"Fuck, Keats." My cock strains painfully against my jeans. "Blow me, dude."

He shoves me back against the sink, making quick work of sliding my jeans and boxers down my legs, and then he's there, exactly where I need him, nudging my thighs apart and lowering his mouth over my throbbing shaft.

I grab the edge of the sink, holding on for dear life, as my boyfriend sucks my dick like a motherfucking pro. When his fingers dive into my ass, I can't hold back any longer, exploding in his mouth as I clamp my lips shut to stop from roaring out his name.

I yank him to his feet, pulling his mouth to mine as I devour him, licking the inside of his mouth, loving the taste of me on his tongue. My hand slides under his boxers again, but he pulls back, tearing his mouth from mine. His lips are swollen, his face flushed, the heady look of lust blazing from his eyes. "Not here. I need to get you home."

I throw my arms around him. "You didn't get off." I never leave my boyfriend unsatisfied, and I'm not about to start now.

His lips purse. "I'm well aware of that fact, Captain Obvious. But we're done with the risk-taking for tonight." He tugs my boxers and my jeans back up, fixing my clothes, and I wrap my arms around his shoulders, holding him tight.

I love you. I fucking love you. I whisper it in my head as I hug my boyfriend, never wanting to let him go.

Keaton chuckles, wriggling out of my arms.

"What's so funny?" I pout as he tucks his cock firmly inside his boxers, buttoning his jeans.

"You. Like this. I've never seen you drunk before."

"Enjoy it," I joke. "Because it doesn't happen often."

"Hold still," he says, and I stare at him as he fixes my hair into place and brushes some lint off my shirt. My heart thumps to a new beat behind my rib cage, and I lace my fingers in his, emotion pinning me in place.

"Do you have any idea how important you are to me?" I say, my voice choked with emotion. "I want to shout it from the rooftops that you are mine. I want everyone to know I have the smartest, most gorgeous, most caring boyfriend in the world."

He grips my face, smiling in amusement. "You're sappy when you're drunk."

I hold him at the waist. "I don't care, and I'm not drunk enough to not know what I'm saying. I hate hiding you from the world. I want everyone to know how much I lo—" I stop myself in time. "How much you mean to me."

"I know, man." His eyes turn glassy. "I know you do." A veil of sadness sweeps over his handsome face, and I hate knowing I put it there.

"Let's go home. I just want to be with you."

Somehow, Keaton manages to get me out of the bathroom and out of the bar without drawing too much attention. Then he's bundling me in the back of a car, talking in a hushed tone with the driver. I drape my arms around him, nuzzling his neck, just needing to be near him. He pushes me off, laughing nervously as he warily eyes the driver. I'm not to be deterred though. I *have* to touch him. Right now, I physically need to be touching some part of him. I can't bear not to be.

Snatching his hand, I hold him tight, lifting it to my mouth to press a kiss there. He wrests his hand from mine, hissing at me to behave, but I can't. I just need to be close to him. Resting my head on his shoulder, I snuggle into his side, shutting my eyes and sighing contentedly.

Keaton exhales heavily, and a few moments pass before he circles his arms around my shoulder, holding me tight. He presses his head into my hair. "It's okay, man. I've got you. Sleep."

Chapter Nineteen
Austen

My stomach lurches, shoving me from sleep, and I stumble from the bed, staggering in the dark as I make my way into the en suite bathroom. Crouching over the toilet bowl, I empty the contents of my stomach as I repeatedly retch. A cool hand brushes damp strands of hair back off my face, and I swat at Keats' hand, not wanting him to see me like this. "Go away, man. I'm gross."

He chuckles. "I've seen worse."

"I doubt that," I mumble, hugging the toilet as my stomach flip-flops and my head pounds like someone is hammering on it from the inside.

"Trust me. I've lost count of the times I watched Kent vomit his guts up."

"Nice visual," I groan, dry heaving as my stomach upends itself.

"Besides, this isn't your first time hugging the porcelain god tonight." He chuckles again, and I slump to the floor, pressing my hot cheek against the cold tile floor.

I don't remember throwing up before. "Kill me now." I am *never* drowning my sorrows in booze again.

He presses a cold cloth to my brow before wiping my face and my neck with it, and patting it gently against my clammy chest. Warmth spreads across my chest as I watch him rinse the cloth under the tap, wring it out, and dab it across my sticky skin.

"Do you think you'll puke again?" he asks, sweeping more hair back off my brow.

"I think I'm done." I move to sit up, but my limbs refuse to cooperate, and I end up half slumped against the shower stall, with my useless legs sprawled across the tile floor.

Keaton smiles as he slides his strong arm underneath me, helping me to stand. "I should've recorded this for posterity," he teases, as I lean on him, trying not to put my full weight on the guy.

"At least it's good experience for when I'm old and decrepit and you've got to take care of me," I blurt.

He steadies his arm around my back, staring straight into my eyes. His gaze is glassy, his face awash with emotion. "You want me around when you're old and gray?"

"Always," I whisper. "I will always want you."

"You slay me, man," he says, his voice cracking at the end. "In all the best ways."

He helps me back to bed before returning with a bottle of water and some toothpaste. I lie helpless against the headrest as he rubs toothpaste over my teeth and then forces me to gargle and spit. Pushing me down under the covers, he tucks them up to my chin, pressing a soft kiss to my brow as he whispers, "Sleep, my love." It's the last thing I remember before I pass out.

"Rise and shine, Sleeping Beauty," Keats says, gently shaking me awake. Forcing my heavy eyelids to open, I curse as he whips the curtains back, and a burst of bright daylight floods my bedroom. Blinking profusely, I ignore the urge to close my eyes again when I spot the time. It's after one, and I've already wasted half the day in bed.

"Fuck. I feel like shit," I admit, hauling myself up in the bed as splintering pain stabs me in the head. My tongue is almost superglued to the roof of my mouth, and the taste in my mouth is like I dined on month-old smelly socks.

Keaton chuckles. "I can imagine. I didn't think you'd drank that much, but man, you were completely trashed."

"That's because you only saw the beer." I rub at my pounding temples. "I did shots at the bar with Preston and a couple of the others when we first arrived." I should've known better. Me and tequila have a checkered past.

Keaton lifts a tray onto the bed, setting it on my lap. He's cooked my favorite vegetable and cheese omelet with whole wheat toast and a glass of orange juice. There's also a bottle of water and a couple of pills. "Eat first, and then take the pills. They should settle your stomach and help with your headache."

He moves to walk out, and I grab hold of his hand. "Thanks for taking care of me."

He bends down, kissing my cheek. "That's what boyfriends do."

"I thought we'd go hiking today. There's still enough time if we leave within the hour," I say.

"You sure you're up to it?"

I nod, because I want to show him one of my favorite places and I want to tell him I love him. I probably also owe him an apology or ten, because God knows what shit I was spouting last night. "I'll be fine. The fresh air will be good for my hangover."

"Okay. Sounds good."

An hour later, we are on the road, and it's a perfect day for a hike. The skies are clear, and there's a soft breeze in the air. It's warm, but not too warm, and the temp is always a few degrees cooler at the peak above El Sobrante, one of my favorite trails in Tilden Park.

"This place is amazing," Keaton says as we hike the trail from Inspiration Point along Nimitz Way.

"I can't believe you've never come here before," I say, because it's popular with Berkeley students.

"I'm not much of a hiker."

"There are tons of walking paths, or you can rent a bike if you prefer." I grip the straps of my backpack, tilting my face up to the sky, relishing the feel of fresh air on my skin. I'm sweating more than normal, and I hope it means I'm sweating the last of the alcohol from my system. Coach will rip me a new one if I'm anything less than focused at practice tomorrow.

"You take all the guys you're dating here?" Keats asks, grinning.

"Cute." If we weren't in public, I'd slap his ass for his sass. "You know you're the only guy I've dated since coming to California. And you should feel privileged because this is my special place, and I wouldn't take just anyone here."

Keaton hands me a bottle of water. "You look like you need that. And thank you. I'm honored."

I flip him the bird, and he laughs.

"I'm being serious, man." His eyes glisten with sincerity. "Thanks for bringing me here."

"You're welcome." I'm happy he's here with me.

"Wow." Keaton stands at the edge of the cliff face, holding one hand over his eyes as he scans the view ahead. Emerald-green hills exist in all directions, and the late afternoon sun glints off the crystal-clear water of the lake. "This is breathtaking."

"I like stopping here because it's more private. If you keep going, you come to a good vantage point where you can see for miles over San Fran Bay." Unzipping my bag, I extract the plaid blanket, setting it on the ground. We sit down, side by side, just taking a moment to inhale the minty, woodsy air and enjoy the gorgeous scenery.

"You might convert me yet," Keats says, pressing his arm against mine. We're far enough off the beaten track not to be noticed here. Shielded by thick, high shrubbery at our backs, it's about as private as we can get outdoors in California.

"During the summer, I want to take you camping back home," I say, unpacking the picnic Keats made before we left. "There's nothing like getting down and dirty with nature." I flash him a flirty grin.

He splutters, almost choking on his water. "I think your mission in life is to corrupt me. Getting me to blow you in the bathroom of the bar last night, and now you want to fuck around out in the open."

"Not out in the open. In a tent," I tease, rubbing his thigh.

He rolls his eyes, but he's fighting a smile. "Like I said, you'll be the death of me."

"Hey." I hold his chin in my fingers, angling his face toward mine. "I'm sorry about last night. If I made you uncomfortable, or I was too pushy, I—"

He silences me with a quick kiss. "There is no need to apologize. You didn't, and you would never force me into anything. I know that." He drags his fingers through the stubble on my cheeks. I was too lazy and too hungover to shave before we left. "I wanted to suck you off, and it was hot."

My cock pulses in agreement. "It was, but it was also dangerous as fuck. Your friends and my teammates were outside. I never want to put you at risk, and I was drunk and sloppy last night. Maybe a little territorial." I grin, because there's no maybe about it. "But it won't happen again. I promise."

"Austen." Keats clasps my cheeks in his hands. "It's okay. Don't beat yourself up over it."

"I never want to treat you with anything less than the respect you deserve." I just go for it. "Because I love you, Keats. I'm in love with you. And that comes with a certain responsibility I never want to forget."

Silence fills the small space between us, and I hope I haven't pushed him too fast too soon, but I can't contain what's in my heart anymore. I've known for some time that Keaton is the guy for me, and I want him to understand he's my future.

"You love me?" Keats croaks, his eyes welling up. "For real?"

I grip his neck. "For real, Keats. I really love you."

He pulls me into his arms, burying his head in my shoulder, his body trembling against mine. "I didn't dare to hope you felt the same because I didn't want to be let down," he whispers against my ear. His hand slides up my chest, his fingers tangling in my hair. He pulls back, keeping his eyes level with mine as he says, "I love you too, man. Have for a while now."

We cling to one another, hugging tightly, his hand on the back of my neck and mine on the back of his head. We rest our foreheads together, letting the magnitude of the moment settle.

"Today's officially the best day of my life," he says when we eventually break apart a little. "You know you're making all my dreams come true," he adds, smiling shyly.

"You give me too much credit, but you better believe I will do everything in my power to make that a reality, because you are everything to me."

"I thought you were just drunk last night when you joked about growing old and gray together."

"I believe I said old and decrepit," I tease, unwrapping the sandwiches. "But we won't nitpick."

He pokes his tongue out, and I laugh, feeling freer than I have in a long time. I hand Keats one-half of the sandwich, taking a large bite out of the other half.

He looks contemplative as he stares straight ahead, his gaze roaming the stunning landscape.

"Penny for your thoughts," I say, demolishing the rest of my sandwich.

"You told me you hated hiding me from the world. That you wanted to shout it from the rooftops," he says, in between slow mouthfuls of the turkey salad sandwich. "And you've said some other stuff when you weren't drunk." He wipes crumbs from the corner of his mouth. "Be honest with me, Austen. How bad are you struggling?"

I uncap a fresh bottle of water, gulping back a few mouthfuls before I answer. I hold his gaze as I admit my truth. "I promised you honesty, so I won't lie. I am struggling big-time, Keats. I was struggling before I met you, and it's worse since you came into my life, because now I have another big reason to be up front about who I am. If I don't enter the draft next year, I'm not going to last till graduation. I can't keep it a secret until then. I can't deny who I am for much longer."

He takes a few moments to reply. "I admire you so much, Austen. You know who you are and what you want, and you just go for it. I get how this is killing you, and I would never ask you to hold back on my account."

"Like I would never ask you to come out on mine."

"I know that, and I've been giving it a lot of thought, especially the past few weeks. I'm ready to tell my family I'm gay and in a relationship with the man I love. I'm going to do it."

A wide smile dances over my mouth. I squeeze his shoulder. "Good for you. I'm proud of you."

"I'm terrified," he admits. "But I know it's the right thing to do." He takes my hand into his lap. "I'm also going to ask Keven for his help. I want my family to know, and for Brock to be out of the picture, and maybe then, at some point, I can find the courage to be publicly open about our relationship, but I don't know how long it'll take me to get there."

"I have no expectations." It's the truth. Obviously, I need to consider Keaton in my decision making, and I would never do anything to hurt him, but my decision to tell my team who I am, is about me at its core. Yes, it will mean not being wholly truthful, but I won't force Keaton until he's ready. I know he will get there. I just hope it's sooner rather than later, but whenever it is, we will get through this together. "It's one step at a time, and I know there will be challenges, but I'm ready to face those with you."

"Me too." He leans in, kissing me sweetly. "With you, I feel like I can scale mountains." I grin at his analogy, and he rolls his eyes. "Just be patient a little longer."

"I can be patient for as long as you need me to be. You set the pace of our relationship. That hasn't changed."

"It's going to work out," he tells me, and I love hearing his confidence, because too often, he's lacking in confidence and so damn hard on himself.

"It is." I squeeze his hand. "Because we love each other too much for it not to."

Chapter Twenty
Keaton

"What are you sketching?" I ask, watching the fierce concentration on Austen's face as he swipes the pencil across the page of his sketch pad. I know he likes to draw. People. Places. Potential designs for tattoos. Because he's told me. But he's never shown me his work, and I've never asked. It's private, and just because we're in a relationship doesn't mean he has to share everything with me.

It's like my journaling and my poetry. He knows I do it, and he's never pried, so I've wanted to offer him the same courtesy. But whatever he's drawing tonight has his sole focus because he's barely lifted his eyes from his pad, not even for *Ink Master*, which is our favorite show, and I'm curious.

"A new tattoo design," he says, lifting his eyes briefly to mine, before returning to his art.

"Must be special." I cross my feet at the ankles. "Because you're in your own little world over there."

He fixes me with a lopsided grin, setting his pencil down.

"He wants my attention." Leaning forward, he grins wider. "What's wrong, baby? Feeling neglected?"

I snort out a laugh, flipping him the bird. "Screw you, man."

"You wish." He waggles his brows, and the air shifts, sexual tension sparking between us.

Austen darts forward, leaning over the arm of my chair to plant a hard kiss on my mouth. "If you must know, I'm designing something for you."

I run my fingers over the top of his head, rubbing the silky strands of his dark hair. "Do I get to see?" I inquire.

"It's not finished." He sits back, picking up his sketch pad. "But I can show you, if you like."

I move over beside him in a flash before he changes his mind. Austen smiles, looking a little...nervous? He holds his pad out to me, and my mouth hangs open at the exquisite drawing. It's a simple concept, but the attention to detail and the fine pencil strokes elevate it to something more complex.

It's a boat wheel with a compass in the center, and a rope weaves around the wheel linking it to an anchor underneath. I immediately understand the symbolism, but the words, written in Austen's distinct penmanship, confirm the sentiment.

Drive your own ship, but let me be the one to anchor you.

Words get stuck behind the messy ball of emotion clogging my throat, and I can't speak. A tear leaks from the corner of one eye as I stare at my boyfriend in complete awe. There are so many things I love and admire about Austen Hayes, but the all-consuming way he cares for me is a thing of beauty.

"Austen," I choke out, carefully putting the pad down and pulling him into my arms. "No one on this planet gets me the way you do, and I want you to be my anchor for all eternity."

His eyes are damp with emotion as we stare at one another. "I want to be that for you, but I would never force the path you travel. I'll be there for the ride. To support and ground you whenever you need it."

"I want you to ink it on me," I say, excitement churning in my gut.

Austen spent a couple summers during high school helping out at a tattoo parlor in Denver, and the owner let him ink some basic designs, having recognized his obvious talent. Austen's Plan B—if the NFL doesn't happen—is to do an apprenticeship at the same parlor, and the owner has already confirmed there is a place for him whenever he wants. Long-term, Austen intends to open his own shop and build it into a franchise business. Hence his business major. Austen is one of the most focused, most determined people I know, and whatever he ends up doing, I already know will be a success. He's too talented and too driven for it not to be.

"It's not finished, and I'm not skilled enough yet, but one day. Sure." He scrubs a hand over his jaw. "You really like it?"

"I love it." I try not to let my sudden disappointment take from the gesture. "Thank you for showing it to me."

I'm en route to the Clark Kerr Campus where Mol and Kate share a dorm when I make a spur of the moment decision. Adrenaline spikes, residing alongside a bucketload of nerves, but my gut tells me to go for it. Pulling my cell from my jeans pocket, I tap out a quick message to Austen.

Me: I'm going to tell my friends. Wish me luck.

My phone rings about thirty seconds later, and a goofy grin spreads across my mouth when I see my boyfriend's gorgeous green eyes flashing at me on the screen. I answer his call straightaway, smiling as I head southeast of the main campus.

"Hey. Why aren't you at practice?" I say in greeting.

"I'm getting changed," he confirms, talking louder over the noise of conversation and laughter in the background. "Are you sure?" he adds.

"Yep. It's a last-minute decision, but it feels right, and it'll be a kind of test run before I tell my family." Initially, I was going to head home this weekend, but Gia is coming up, so I'm heading to Wellesley the following weekend instead.

The noise fades in the background, and the sound of a door slamming reverberates through the line. "What exactly are you planning to say?" he asks, talking quietly into the phone.

"Just about me," I blurt, realizing where his concern is coming from. "I would never tell them about us," I whisper, glancing around me as I walk to ensure no one is listening. "Not without discussing that with you first. I'm just going to tell them I'm gay. That's it."

That's it. As if it's no biggie.

"Do you trust them?"

"With my life." I've zero doubts. I've confided a ton of shit to my friends in the two-plus years we have known one another, and they have never shared anything with anyone, and nothing has made its way into the public domain. "They have given me no reason to ever doubt they are loyal to me."

"Then tell them everything," he says.

Just like that.

"Are you sure?" I splutter.

"I don't want you omitting half the truth because of me. Colton knows. By this weekend, Gia will too. Your friends deserve to know."

"Okay."

"Good." Someone shouts out Austen's name in the background. "I've got to go. I'll see you later. I know you're nervous, but don't be. They're your friends. You've got this."

"Thanks, man. See you at home."

Kate opens the door with a flourish, flinging it back and gesturing me inside. As student accommodations go, this Spanish mission-style complex is the best Berkeley has to offer, in my opinion. The suites are the largest available, and they open out into a decent-sized living area. On either side are the separate bedrooms. There is a large shared bathroom on each floor.

"Come sit with me," Mol says, patting the empty space beside her on the larger of the two couches. "You don't want to be a third wheel."

I arch a brow as I flop down beside Mol, my lips curling into a wide grin when Kate throws herself down on the smaller couch, flinging her arms around Seb and planting a firm kiss on his mouth.

"What'd I miss?" I ask, grabbing a bottle of water from the coffee table.

"We're official," Kate says, and there's no disguising the glee in her voice.

"It's about time," I say, as Seb slides his arm around her shoulders, pulling her into his side. "I'm happy for you guys."

"Our parents are already planning the wedding," Kate says, giggling, totally oblivious to the look of sheer terror lighting up Seb's eyes.

Mol snickers, noticing his expression too. "You might want to cool your jets, sister. Don't want to scare the love of your life away now you've finally gotten him to succumb to your charms."

"Seb knows I'm teasing." She beams up at him, and I love

seeing this different side to her. Seb and Kate are both from New York, and their parents have been close friends for years. It hits me how similar the situation is to Austen and Gia; except with Seb and Kate, the romantic feelings are real.

"Unless you want to give me a coronary, I suggest keeping all talk of weddings to a minimum. Or maybe nonexistent," he says, pressing a kiss to her dark brow.

"Well, I've got news too," I pipe up. Might as well rip the Band-Aid right off. My three friends turn expectant gazes on me. "I'm gay."

A round of applause breaks out in the room, and I stare at my friends like they've just grown extra heads.

Kate jumps out of Seb's embrace, rushing over to hug me first. "Thank fuck you told us. We were afraid we'd be dead and buried before you admitted the truth."

"Wait." My brow scrunches up as I hold her at arm's length. "You knew?" I look at a smiling Mol and a smug-looking Seb. "You *all* knew?"

They nod in sync.

"Well, shit." That doesn't bode well for keeping my secret in the long run. "Is it that obvious?"

"Not really," Mol admits. "In fact, when Seb first told us he thought you were into guys, we laughed in his face. But over time, we've noticed."

"I don't think anyone who didn't know you would guess though," Kate hurriedly adds. "And you get hit on by girls left and right."

"That's just because I'm a Kennedy."

Mol rolls her eyes. "So fucking delusional." She thumps me in the upper arm. "It's because you're hot. Like sex-on-a-stick, drop-your-panties-no-question kind of hot."

"I'm not sure I needed to know that," I murmur.

"Or us," Seb adds.

Mol thumps me again, but she's got the muscle strength of a fly, so I barely feel a twinge. "I'm not hitting on you, because that'd be gross. I'm just pointing out that girls hit on you because you're hot. It's not just because you're famous."

"That's the most backhanded compliment I've ever heard," Kate says. "But what Mol is trying to say is right."

"How did you figure it out?" I ask Seb, leaning back on the couch, relaxing because my friends aren't freaked out by my sexuality, and that is the biggest relief. Warmth blossoms in my chest, spreading all over, and I can't stop smiling.

"I'm bi, and I can usually tell which guys are into guys."

Seb casually drops that bomb and I stare at him with my jaw hanging loose. He smirks, sliding his arm around Kate as she returns to her seat.

"I thought that gaydar nonsense was bullshit," Kate says, crossing her feet at the ankles. "And a way for homophobic jerks to stereotype gay men."

"It's not," Mol interjects. "I did some research on it for an assignment, and these psychologists conducted a study, and they discovered it's real. It's basically an intuitive ability. Some are better at it than others."

"Well, I clearly suck," I say. "Because I had no clue you were bi."

"I don't feel the need to broadcast it," Seb says. "And I wasn't sure if it would help or hinder you in admitting your truth, so I chose to say nothing until you did."

"I'm sorry I didn't tell you sooner. I wanted to, but I've only recently accepted it myself."

"What about your family?" Kate asks, opening a bag of chips and dumping them into a bowl on the coffee table. "Do they know?"

I shake my head. "Not yet, but I'm telling them soon."

"About Austen too?" Seb asks, popping a chip in his mouth.

"You know about me and Austen?" I stare at him in shock. At all of them in shock, because it's obvious they have worked that out too. "Let me guess. Your magical gaydar was at work again?"

"I thought we just determined it's not magic," Mol says, opening a jar of salsa.

A heavy pressure settles on my chest, and I swallow hard. "How did you know we were together?" We thought we were being careful.

"Your eyes naturally gravitate to one another, and the chemistry between you is smokin' hot, man," Seb admits.

"Fuck." I drag a hand through my hair. "We need to keep it a secret."

Mol taps my arm. "It's obvious to us because we're your friends, and we spend time with you both."

"I haven't noticed anyone else noticing," Seb says, trying to reassure me.

"No one knows, and you can't tell anyone." My solemn gaze bounces between them.

"You don't need to worry about us saying anything," Seb says. "We would *never* tell anyone about you or Austen. It's nobody's business but your own."

"We won't tell anyone, and you guys can be yourselves around us," Kate adds. "But I am curious." She shoots me a devilish look, and I prepare myself.

"Oh, boy," Mol titters, dipping a chip in salsa and shoving it in her mouth.

"Do you top or bottom? And who has the biggest cock because—"

Seb plasters his hand over his girlfriend's mouth. "She still has zero filter. In case you were wondering if she'd undergone a personality transplant since lunch."

I chuckle as Kate bites Seb's hand, and he yanks it back, narrowing his eyes on his girlfriend.

"You crack me up, girl, but there's no chance I'll ever answer those questions," I say.

She mock pouts. "You're no fun. Do you have any idea how hot the thought of you guys fucking is?" She fans her face. "Like, hot. Damn. You're both so sexy, and I imagine you wrestling for dominance in the bedroom and pinning each other down, fingering the fuck out of—"

Seb slams his hand over her mouth again. "Sorry, man. She needs another introduction to ethics one-oh-one."

"Or you need to fuck her harder so she's not imagining Austen and Keats screwing their brains out," Mol says.

"Or introduce her to gay porn," I suggest.

Kate jumps up, pulling Seb with her. "That's a wonderful idea. We should start working on it straightaway."

Mol pulls a cushion over her face, mumbling to herself. Kate and Seb laugh.

"What's your deal?" I inquire, ripping the cushion off her face before she smothers.

"They're in the honeymoon phase. Use your imagination," she deadpans.

"Aw, babe. I'm so sorry." Kate leans down, smacking a loud kiss on Mol's cheek. "I'll buy you some earplugs."

"I so need to get laid," Mol grumbles, flipping Kate the bird.

I burst out laughing, unable to keep it in anymore. "You guys crack me up." A well of emotion springs open in my chest, and tears sting the backs of my eyes. I stand, clearing my throat. "You're the best friends I've ever had, and I wish it hadn't taken me so long to remove my head from my ass."

"Hey." Kate pulls me into a hug. "You needed to go at your own pace. We understand that."

"You owe us nothing, Keats, but I'm glad you felt comfortable enough to tell us, and we're here for you." Seb clamps his hand on my shoulder.

"We love you," Mol says, draping herself around me from behind. "And this changes nothing. You're still the same adorable you."

I'm floating on a proverbial cloud as I walk toward home a couple hours later, still on a high after the conversation with my friends. I filled them in on the situation with Brock before I left, and they were all outraged on my behalf, instantly plotting ways we could take the asshole down.

I stop to pick up takeout and a bottle of pinot noir, hoping Austen will be okay to relax his diet tonight, because I'm in the mood to celebrate.

As I round the corner toward our apartment building, a tall, dark form steps out in front of me, blocking my path. My muscles lock up as our gazes meet, and my spine stiffens. "What do you want, Dax?" I ask, in no mood for his bullshit.

He holds his palms up, taking a step closer. "Not a fight, if that's what you're thinking. I'm more of a lover than a fighter. I'm sure Austen has explained that."

The insinuation, combined with his smug smile, rubs me the wrong way. My fist clenches, and an unfamiliar burn races through my veins. "Austen has told me everything. Including how you rejected him and cruelly broke his heart. Think that's all I need to know." I move to walk around him, but he sidesteps me, forcing me back.

"I made a mistake, and I'm here to put things right."

"Unlucky for you, it's too late."

He eyes me from head to toe in a slow perusal. "I'm sure you're a decent guy. Austen wouldn't be with anyone who isn't, but you're not right for him. You should walk away now before you get hurt."

How the fuck does this guy know I'm romantically involved with Austen? And who the fuck does he think he is telling me what to do?

"Go fuck yourself, Dax. Austen wouldn't touch you if you were the last man alive." I shove past him, barely restraining my rage.

He grabs my arm, pulling me back. "That's where you're wrong." He tugs the top of his tee down, exposing the ink on his upper chest. "You never get over your first love, and that's who we are to each other." He points at the crude love heart inked just over his beating heart, "A & D" encased inside. Two words in a foreign language are scrawled in cursive over the heart.

He drops my arm, and I should make my escape, but I'm frozen in place.

"Austen inked that on me himself. It was his idea to add the Latin." He runs the tip of his finger over the text. "Semper iuncti. It means together forever."

My heart feels like a block of stone in my chest, and I'm finding it hard to breathe.

"I'm trying to do you a solid, man. Austen may be resisting now, but he won't resist forever." He thumps a hand over his heart. "Because we're soul mates. He knows it as well as I do. You're just someone to pass the time with. You don't understand him like I do. You couldn't, because what Austen and I shared was intense and deep, and nothing can compare. *No one can compare.*"

He squeezes my shoulder, and I push him aside. Fog swirls through my brain as panic charges through my body, mixing with a tsunami of emotions, threatening to derail me. I'm a hot mess on the inside, but I refuse to let this asshole see that, so I pull myself together. "Believe whatever bullshit you want, but Austen will never be yours. You had your chance, and you blew it. Leave him alone." I stab him with a glare before brushing past him, clutching the takeout bag in a tight grip as I head toward our apartment building with fissures cracking my heart.

Chapter Twenty-One
Austen

The front door slams against the wall as Keats enters the apartment like a raging storm. Tightness spreads across my chest at the thought things haven't gone well. I've been on edge since I arrived home to an empty apartment, hoping it was a good thing my boyfriend wasn't home yet. Praying it meant he was talking it all through with his friends and they were supportive. But if the aggressive way he's opened the door is any indication, things aren't looking good.

Shit. I stand slowly, ready to comfort him as he exits the hallway, stomping into the living area. He puts a takeout bag and bottle of wine down on the coffee table before facing me.

"It didn't go well?" I ask, pain slicing through my heart, like a thousand tiny daggers, at the anguished, tormented look on his face.

"Why won't you ink me?" he barks, catching me completely off guard.

"What?" I'm frowning as I step toward him. He falls back, holding out his arm, keeping me at bay, and damn, if that doesn't hurt. "What's going on, Keats?"

"Answer the question! You designed that tattoo for me, but you won't do it yourself. I want to know why."

I have no clue what's going on here, but he's hurt and he's angry, and if my answers have the ability to soothe his ache, then I'll tell him whatever he wants to know. "Because I'm not skilled enough to ink you."

That was clearly the wrong answer, because the rage misting in his eyes thickens, and the vein at the side of his neck pulses.

"But you were skilled enough to ink Dax," he says, lowering his voice, but not in a way that brings any reassurance.

I work hard to keep my anger at bay, because directing it at Keaton would be wrong. "I should've known he'd reach out to you when his attempt to seduce me failed."

"What?" Keaton's face drops, and he's shielding nothing from me. Fear mixes with hurt, and I wish I could click my fingers and make Dax fucking Madden disappear from the face of the planet.

"He was waiting for me when I left the gym this morning," I admit. "I went for coffee with him because I was afraid he'd make a scene in front of the guys on the team. He declared undying love and begged me to come back to him. I told him I was in a committed relationship and I had no feelings for him anymore. I didn't tell him I was with you, but I guess he must've connected the dots. I was planning on telling you this tonight, but I didn't want it to overshadow your news." I'd actually wanted to call Keats straightaway, but he's prone to overreaction, and I didn't want him freaking out all day or to have that conversation over the phone.

Now, I wish I had called him. At least he would've had a heads-up and been prepared.

I step toward my boyfriend, tentatively holding one side of his face. "What did he say to upset you?"

"He said you were soul mates and no one would compare to him."

I force his eyes to mine. "And you believed that bullshit?" I'm trying not to get mad, because I don't want Dax driving a wedge between me and Keats, but it's difficult. "Hasn't anything I've said registered with you?" I grip his face tighter. "I love you." My nostrils flare. "*You*. Not him! He means less than nothing to me."

"But you tattooed him."

It clicks into place, and I exhale heavily, working hard to quell my anger. Keaton lacking confidence and self-belief isn't anything new. Dax couldn't know how cutting his words would be or how well they would work to foster his agenda. It hurts that Keaton would buy the bullshit he's peddling. That he'd forget everything I've told him and all the ways I've shown him how much I love him. But he's not doing it intentionally, and his self-doubt won't magically evaporate overnight. He deserves my understanding and my compassion, not my frustration and rage.

"Keaton." I hold both sides of his face, eyeballing him as I admit the truth. "I was barely seventeen when I inked that on him. On *him*. Not me." I rip my shirt off to drill my point home, pointing at the empty space above my heart. "It was his idea, and I was working at Pete's shop for the second summer and itching to get more experience. Pete only had me cleaning tools and practicing on leather, so when Dax suggested it, I was excited to ink skin. That's all that was going through my head. I thought nothing else of it. Not even the fact I was a total amateur and I'd be marking my then boyfriend for life." I chuckle, attempting to lighten the tense atmosphere. "If he showed it to you, you've seen how bad it is. I bet a five-year-old would do a better job."

His blue eyes remain latched on mine as he listens. I place

my hand on his chest, right in the place where his heart pounds. "When you told me you loved me, you handed me this." I rub his chest, the steady beat of his heart comforting underneath my palm. "You trusted me with your heart, and that's the greatest honor you could give me. An honor I never forget. I love you, Keaton. Enough to want to ink your skin and leave my mark permanently on you. Trust me. I want that so badly."

I peer deep into his eyes, making sure he's seeing what I'm saying and truly listening to the words. "But, if I tried to ink that design on you, it would look awful, because I have limited experience, and I won't mar your beautiful body." I rest my head against his brow. "You're special to me, Keaton, and when I ink that design on your skin, it will be perfect. Just like you."

When his arms fold around me, I release a shuddering breath. "I didn't care enough about Dax to care how the tat ended up," I continue, talking against his ear. "I didn't feel even a twinge of remorse when it turned out shitty." I pull my head back, needing to look him in the eye when I say this. "Because he wasn't important to me. Not in the way you are. Maybe, if I'd stopped to consider it, I would've realized I wasn't actually ever in love with him."

Keats sucks in a gasp, and I pause to draw a breath. "These past few weeks, I've realized that anything I felt up to now was child's play, because I have never, ever, felt this way about anyone before." I place a tender kiss on his lips. "You're the only man I've truly loved. The only one I ever see myself loving. Please tell me you believe it. That you know Dax means nothing and you won't let a single word that comes out of his mouth impact you in any way."

Keats molds his mouth to mine, kissing me slow and deep, and I hold him close, reaffirming my words with every sweep of our lips. "I'm sorry," he rasps when we break apart. "I got all up in my head and made a big deal out of nothing."

I drag my fingernails through his scalp, in the way I know he likes. "Don't apologize for how you feel. I wish, sometimes, you wouldn't think the things you do, but then you wouldn't be you." I deliberately soften my features, glad to see his shoulders relax and the pained look disappear from his face. "I always want to know what you're thinking. What you're feeling. Even if it frustrates me, and I can't lie—it pisses me off that you believed him so easily. I know you have insecurities, but I've always been honest and never given you any reason to doubt me. I need you to trust me, because without that, we have nothing."

"I do trust you." He grabs the back of my head. "And one of the things I love most about you is how straightforward you are with me, but I still struggle to believe you've chosen me."

I open my mouth to respond to that, but he places his finger against my lips, stalling my words.

"That's all on me. Not you," he says. "You reassure me through your words and your actions, but my insecurities are deep-rooted, and it's going to take more time to work it all out, but I'll get there. And it's not about trust, because I trust you with my life, man."

I could continue laboring the point, but I don't want to argue with him tonight. I still don't know how it went with his friends. "I know you'll get there, and I want that for you, because when your confidence shines through, it's beautiful to behold. Just don't doubt my feelings for you. Don't doubt what I've told you is the truth no matter what any dickhead says."

"I won't. I promise."

"And forget about Dax. He's my problem to handle," I add, as the doorbell chimes.

I frown. "You expecting anyone?"

Keats shakes his head as I put my shirt back on, walking toward the front door with purpose. A muscle pops in my jaw and my fists clench at my side. "If that's my ex, I will not be responsible for my actions." I'm planning on ripping that asshole a new one, and if that's him pounding his fists on our door, I may just throw him off our rooftop terrace.

I yank the door open, ready to let loose on Dax's ass, stumbling back as a tall, beautiful redhead with emerald-green eyes barrels past me, entering the apartment without invitation. "Surprise!" Gia says, darting back to kiss my cheek. She looks out into the hallway, grinning at the tall, lean dark-haired guy who shares my DNA. "And double surprise!"

"What the hell are you doing here?" My question is directed at Orwell but could just as easily be for Gia because she's not supposed to be here until tomorrow night.

"Wow. Good to see you too, dude." Orwell saunters through the door, hands shoved in the pockets of his low-slung jeans, ball cap backward on his head, looking like his shit doesn't stink.

Some things haven't changed.

Shaking my head, I grab both their weekend bags from the corridor, dumping them on the hall floor, before shutting the door. "Do Mom and Dad know you're here?" I ask although I'm pretty sure I already know the answer.

"I'm guessing they've figured out I'm gone by now," he replies, pinning me with a sly grin, and I curse under my breath.

"What'd you do this time?"

"It's not my fault." He's instantly on the defensive. No surprise there either. I cast a glance into the living room where Gia has just thrown herself at my boyfriend. Fuck it. I hadn't even had time to warn Keats about my bestie. This should be fun.

"It never is," I deadpan, steering my brother into the living room. He either got caught smoking dope, fucking someone he shouldn't, or he skipped school.

"They overreacted. Like usual. So what if Romy Saunders is engaged? She's only twenty, and she shouldn't be getting tied down when she's so young and so freaking hot."

I roll my eyes, watching in amusement as Gia grabs Keaton's hand, pulling him down onto the couch beside her, bending his ear.

"Romy Saunders as in Preacher Saunder's daughter?" I ask, pushing my brother down into the recliner chair.

"His pride and joy," Gia says, cutting into our conversation. "The apple of her daddy's eye. The good little virgin who was saving herself for her wedding night until Casanova over there seduced her into taking a walk on the dark side."

Orwell grins, because he truly doesn't see anything wrong with what he did. "What can I say?" He grabs his crotch. "I'm the man. Not my fault she fell on my dick and liked it."

I swat the back of his head. "I'm guessing someone put the idea in her head though, right?"

Orwell shrugs, grinning, and tipping his head at Keaton as he notices him for the first time. "Hey, man. Cool place," he adds, looking around.

"Keaton, meet my brother, Orwell, and my bestie, Gia." I drop down beside Keats, sliding my arm around his shoulders and pulling him into my side. "Keats is my boyfriend," I say, feeling it's best to get straight to the point.

Gia screeches so loud I place my hands over Keaton's ears to protect them. She throws herself on top of us, circling her arms around us in an awkward group hug.

Orwell chuckles. "Welcome to our crazy family."

"Trust me," Keats says when Gia sits back. "I'm well versed in crazy families."

"That's right!" Orwell leans his elbows on his knees, his

eyes lighting up. "Your brother married your cousin, and your other brother's girlfriend cried rape, and twisted fucks tried to hand your brother's girls to shady sex trafficking pervs, and your dad was having an affair with—"

I make a slicing motion with my hand against my throat, and for once, my brother listens.

"I should explain that neither Gia or my brother have any filter and they blurt shit without thinking," I tell Keaton, rubbing my hand up and down his arm. "And they are both the biggest flirts known to mankind. Consider yourself warned."

"I prefer manwhore," Orwell says, not being untruthful in the least. "Or ladies' man, if you want to be more politically correct."

"I'm in a long-term relationship," Gia adds, elbowing me in the ribs. "And being friendly does not equal being flirty."

"She's a big flirt," I pretend to whisper in Keats' ear. "But let's call it friendly. She is our guest after all."

"You're lucky I love you," Gia says, sticking out her tongue. "Otherwise, I'd slap the shit out of you or give you a wedgie like when we were younger."

"You didn't tell me your family was crazy," Keats says, planting his hand on my knee. "We have more in common than I thought."

"My family isn't crazy," I correct. "In fact, our parents are the exact opposite of crazy. Restrained and repressed would be more the words I'd use."

"Truth," Orwell agrees, kicking off his sneakers like he owns the place.

"That's not fair," Gia says. "Pamela and Gary might not be free-spirited like their kids, but they're not repressed." She turns to Keaton. "They are your typical middle-class conserva-tive family. Pamela works at the local high school, so it's important her family is respectable. She likes to be a pillar of the community."

Orwell cracks up laughing, slapping his thigh. "A pillar of the community. Damn, Gia, where'd you come up with this shit?"

"High school," she drawls. "You'd know if you ever showed up there."

I sigh, pulling my cell out of my pocket, dialing Mom's number. Stretching forward, I shove the phone in Orwell's chest. "You need to tell Mom where you are. She's probably freaking out." My parents *are* conservative, and appearances matter, but despite my less than close relationship with them, I can't say they're bad parents, because they're not. They've always wanted what's best for each of us. It's just a shame their version of that is so vastly different from what I want to do with my life.

"Can't you do it?" He throws the phone back at me, and I catch it with a frown.

I stand, pressing it into his palm, as Mom's voice filters through the line. "You made the mess. Now clean it up."

The three of us move into the kitchen to give my brother privacy to talk to Mom.

"Are you hungry?" Keaton asks Gia, carrying the takeout bag over to the counter. "I brought takeout home. It's probably cold, but we can reheat it, and there's more than enough for everyone."

"Sounds good," she says, pulling me into a hug. "I've missed you, Woody."

Behind me, Keaton attempts to disguise his laugh as a cough, and my lips twitch.

"Missed you too, Jess. I'm glad you're here."

"At least now I know why," she says, swinging her long legs

up onto one of the stools. "How long have you two been together?" she asks, as Keaton sorts out dinnerware and silverware.

"A couple months, but we were tiptoeing around one another for a few months before that," I explain.

"I am soooo happy for you." She hugs me again. "Helps me feel less guilty." Sometimes I wonder if Gia knows the meaning of that word, because she hasn't professed any such feelings to me over the course of our two-year-long fake relationship.

"About that," I say, leaning my elbows on the counter. "Our arrangement will be coming to an end at some point, probably sooner rather than later."

"Get out!" Her eyes widen in shock. "You're serious about coming out to the team?"

I nod. "I'm sick of lying all the time."

Her expression turns sad. "I know. It's not a good way to live. It weighs on me too."

I wonder if it truly does, because she seems to cope better with it than me. "It's not imminent, but I know I can't keep the secret until graduation. What will you do?" I inquire, watching Keaton set the table for four.

She shrugs. "I don't know, but I'll figure something out." She holds my face in her hands, and I don't miss the frown on Keaton's face. I'll have to find a private moment to warn Gia to stop being so touchy-feely if she can help it. It's hard because that's always been the nature of our relationship. Most outsiders don't get it. It's one of the reasons her boyfriend Hendrix hates my guts. But I care what Keaton thinks, and if the tables were turned, I wouldn't like his fake girlfriend touching him all the time either. "It's not your problem to solve," she adds, "and you've helped me out so much already. I owe you."

"We've helped one another. Don't forget it suited me too, and I need one final favor from you."

"Anything, you know that."

"Keats and I want to keep our relationship secret for now. It would help if the team saw me with you. Throw them off the scent."

"I can do that." She blows me a kiss. "Just tell me when and where."

"You can come to the game on Saturday and the after-party, and we'll put on a show."

"One last hurrah!" She grins.

Keats walks past me, looking downcast, and I hook my arm around his neck, pulling him into me for a kiss.

"What was that for?" he murmurs when our lips pull apart.

"I need a reason to kiss my boyfriend now?" I tease, not wanting to admit in front of Gia that my boyfriend clearly needs reassuring.

"Never." He pecks my lips twice before moving off, grabbing glasses from the cupboard.

"You two look so good together." Gia smiles. "Good for you, Woody." She moves to hug me again, and I subtly shake my head. She frowns but holds herself back.

"Here." Orwell thrusts the cell at me. "Mom wants to talk to you." His grumpy face tells me all I need to know.

I press the cell to my ear. "Hey, Mom."

"Did you know about this?" Her aggravated tone glides over me like water off a cliff. I learned to tune Mom out years ago for my sanity.

"Nope, but he's here now, so we might as well make the best of it."

"He should be on the next plane back home. Did you hear what he did?"

"Saved the virgin Romy from a lifetime tied to one dick. Seems like we should be patting Orwell on the back." I don't necessarily believe that, but sometimes, I just can't help riling her up.

"Austen! Please."

"Sorry, Mom." I take pity on her. "I'm just trying to lighten the situation. It's not like he murdered anyone. He just had sex."

"With the preacher's daughter! An older woman! And she was engaged to boot!"

"Relax, Ma. You're going to give yourself a coronary. Just let Orwell stay with me this weekend. I'll try to talk some sense into him." I wink at my brother, happy he's here. I don't get to see enough of him, and he's good for my soul. "And it'll give you a break from his crap. You can punish him next week."

Orwell flips his middle finger up at me.

"Okay. But I'm trusting you to look after your brother. You know what he's like. He's even more reckless than you were as a teenager."

I didn't pull half the shit Orwell does. Sure, I went to parties, smoked a little weed, indulged in a few beers every now and then, but I was dedicated to football, and it kept me on the straight and narrow. I never fucked around or missed classes. The only thing I did was date guys and develop a passion for tattoos. Something my mother considers reckless.

Yeah, I'm so done with this conversation.

"I'll make sure he stays out of trouble." I hang up before she can reply.

Orwell whoops, dragging me into a half-assed headlock. "Thanks, big bro. I owe you."

I twist around, locking my arms around his neck, landing a soft punch to his gut. "Do. Not. Make me regret this."

Chapter Twenty-Two
Keaton

"I'm sorry tonight got derailed," Austen says, climbing into my bed alongside me. Setting my book down, I turn to look at him.

"It's okay," I lie, because it's not Austen's fault. Truth is, I could've done without the ambush.

And Gia's wandering hands all over my boyfriend.

Orwell, I like.

Gia, not so much so far, but that could be my jealousy talking.

"It's not." Austen takes my hand. "I didn't even hear how it went with your friends."

A layer of tension flitters off my shoulders as a smile ghosts over my mouth. "It went better than expected. They already knew, man. About me. About you. And they are happy for us."

He pecks my lips, pulling back, smiling. "I knew they wouldn't let you down."

"It's got me thinking," I admit, fisting one hand in the comforter as I speak. "So far, everyone has reacted positively. Maybe, I've been making this out to be worse than it is."

Austen cringes a little, sitting cross-legged in front of me. "I'm glad things have been positive so far, but there are still plenty of assholes in the world, Keats. The people who care about you will be supportive. They might be shocked at first, but they won't stop loving you. However, not everything will be rainbows and unicorns. Social media is full of self-righteous bigoted assholes who will wade in. You're right to be cautious."

I worry my lip between my teeth. "Are we doing the right thing this weekend? With Gia, I mean."

He studies my face for a few seconds. "Are you having second thoughts?"

I shrug, because my emotions are a bit of a clusterfuck when it comes to that girl.

"I'm doing it for us." He threads his fingers in mine. "To deflect suspicion from the team until we're ready to admit the truth."

"That's what I'm worried about. If you parade Gia around this weekend, pushing the girlfriend agenda in their faces, and then you come out as gay, they'll hate you for lying so blatantly." I wish I'd thought of this before Austen arranged for her to come to Cali.

He shrugs. "I'll explain things, but if they're pissed, I'll live with it. I'm not close to most of the guys, and I doubt I'll keep in contact with anyone besides Colton and maybe Preston after we graduate."

"See, that's where I have issues. I don't want them thinking bad of you because you're trying to protect me. Protect us."

"Are you sure that's where the issue lies?" He stares at me in that intense all-knowing, all-seeing way of his.

I exhale heavily, squeezing his hand. "I *am* concerned about that, but I also don't like the way she paws at you."

Austen moves up in the bed, wrapping his arms around me. "That's just the way she is, but I'll talk to her." A pregnant pause ensues, and I attempt to unscramble the mess in my head. He tips my chin up. "I need you to be honest. If you want to call it off, I will. I'll send Gia to her boyfriend for the weekend. I thought this'd help keep our relationship a secret, but if it's going to damage things between us, then I'd rather not do it."

"I don't think I could bear to watch you and her *putting on a show*. I think my reactions would give the game away, which defeats the purpose. So, either you go to the party without me or we call it off."

"It's your call, Keats. You have to make the decision." His gaze challenges me, and I rise to meet it.

"I want to call it off. No one gets to touch you but me."

His lips claim mine, and we clutch one another, kissing and kissing and kissing, only stopping when we need to draw breath. Austen rests his forehead on mine. "Thank fuck."

I ease back, commanding his gaze. "You didn't want to go through with it either?"

He shakes his head. "You think I'd ever want to hurt you like that?" He rubs a hand over his chest. "It was a stupid idea to begin with. I didn't properly think it through."

"You were trying to protect our relationship. I'll never fault you for that."

"I'll tell her first thing, before I head to the gym. Would you be okay to drive her to the airport?"

"Of course. I think I'll skip classes tomorrow anyway and hang out with Orwell."

"You don't have to do that," Austen says, running his fingers through my hair as he smiles adoringly at me.

The effect is like being knocked over by a giant bowling ball. I flatten into a puddle on the bed. "I want to get to know your brother, and this way, I'll ensure he keeps out of trouble."

His shoulders slump in relief. "That is a weight off my mind. Thanks."

"You do so much for me. I want to help where I can."

He kisses me tenderly. "We make a good team."

Those words imprint on my heart, and I melt into the bed. "We do."

Austen moves, sliding down the bed and pulling the comforter off my legs. "What are you doing?" I ask when he tugs on the end of my pajama pants.

"What does it look like?" he teases, eyeing me through hooded lashes, his eyes drenched in lust.

"Your brother is in your room across the hall, and Gia is in the guest bedroom," I say, in case he's forgotten our visitors.

"So?" He yanks my pants down, freeing my semi-hard cock.

"So, we can't do anything sexual. We should just sleep."

Austen's hands crawl up my thighs, and my cock stiffens, making an instant liar of me.

"If every couple thought that, there'd be a lot less babies in the world." He shoves a pillow at my chest. "Scream into that," he adds, grinning as his hand encircles my engorged cock. "Because this is happening, babe." The second his hot mouth wraps around my dick, all protests disappear, and I throw my head back and close my eyes, just enjoying the feel of his skilled lips gliding up and down my shaft.

"I can get an Uber," Gia says the following morning as I grab my car keys and my wallet and leave a note for Austen's brother on the kitchen counter. Orwell is still sleeping, and Gia didn't want to wake him to say goodbye. I take her bag, and she follows me out into the hallway. "Don't be ridiculous." I open the front door for her. "It's the least I can do. Considering."

I don't elaborate because I don't want to get into it with her. She's a virtual stranger, and I don't know her. Austen woke her early to explain, and she was more than happy to let him pay for a plane ticket to Cheyenne, to join her boyfriend and his band for the weekend. I offered to pay, because I didn't want Austen dipping into the savings fund he's been building for his Plan B tattoo dream, and it was ultimately my decision to call a halt to things this weekend, so it only seems fair.

He argued against it, but eventually let me pay for half, and I'm glad he's reasonable when it comes to financial stuff, because arguing over money is unnecessary when I have more than enough to go around. That's not me being arrogant or flippant. I know how fortunate I am. Which is why I think nothing of spending money on my loved ones. As long as we have enough to support ourselves and our dreams, isn't that all that counts?

"It's cool," she says, touching my arm. "I'd rather be with the band, so I'm not at all unhappy with Austen's decision."

Placing her bag in the back of my SUV, I climb behind the wheel and drive us out of the apartment building.

The only flight I could get at the last minute is out of San Fran, so the forty-five-minute journey is bound to be awkward. I switch the radio on, and we're both quiet until I get on I-80 W, and then she lowers the volume and turns to face me. "Austen said he was the one who'd changed his mind, but it was you, right?"

I nod, glancing at her briefly as I drive one-handed along the highway.

"Good." She smiles, bouncing a little in her seat.

"Good?" I inquire, quirking a brow. "Aren't you mad?"

She vigorously shakes her head. "On the contrary. Austen needs someone to put him first. I would've been disappointed if you'd let me publicly pretend he was mine," she adds, popping the cap on an energy drink and knocking it back.

"I couldn't do that. Even watching you put your hands on him last night drove me insane," I truthfully admit.

She smirks. "Knew it." Her eyes dart wildly around the car. "I'm glad he's got you. I know Austen misses being in a relationship."

"You knew his exes," I surmise.

"Yep." She drains the last of her drink, tossing the empty bottle on the floor of the back seat.

Okay, then.

I still can't figure this girl out, except she's not who I imagined Austen's bestie to be. But I won't form a judgment before I even know her. She's important to my boyfriend, so I want to make the effort.

"I've always thought Austen had shit taste in men," she adds, thumping me in the upper arm. "Until you. You're a good catch, Keaton Kennedy, and you make him happy. Happier than I've ever seen him."

"Is that true?" I've no idea if she's blowing smoke up my ass.

"Absolutely." She lifts her legs, planting her dirty sneakers on my clean dash. I try hard not to look offended. "He's different with you. In a good way." She levels a stern look at me, but her unfocused gaze takes away from the intent. Her eyes are flickering all over the place and rolling back in her head.

Shit. *Is she on something? At nine o'clock in the morning?*

I know Austen is concerned about her taking drugs. He talked to her last night before bed, but she assured him there is nothing to worry about. This seems to indicate otherwise.

"You know Dax then," I say, choosing to keep the conversation going. It's not my place to call her out for being high first thing in the morning, but I'll be sharing my suspicions with my boyfriend later. Austen deserves to know, and he can decide if he wants to bring it up with her again.

"I hate that motherfucking prick."

"That makes two of us."

Pulling her legs down, she jumps around in her seat, her eyes out on stalks. "How the fuck do you know about Dax Madden?"

"He's at Berkeley. He got into some prestigious art program just so he could win Austen back, or so he says."

She snorts, and a hiccup erupts from her mouth. "He's a selfish asshole. He never cared about Austen, and I doubt he does now. Probably just wants the notoriety that would come from dating one of the football stars."

That's not a bad theory, and if Dax had his way, Austen would be openly gay, I'm sure.

"If he came here thinking he'd win him back, he's an idiot. Austen would never go back. He won't stay with someone who doesn't treat him right. He might've been blind at the start, but Dax showed his true colors in the end. Woody puts everything into his relationships, and he expects the same in return. It's why none of his previous relationships lasted. The guys were more takers than givers."

I know this, but when she puts it so bluntly, I begin to panic-worry.

Am I taking more than I'm giving?

Those troubling thoughts occupy my mind for the rest of the weekend, eating into my bonding time with Orwell, and though I know Gia meant well, I wish she hadn't opened her mouth at all.

Chapter Twenty-Three
Keaton

"I wish you were here," I admit, from the privacy of my childhood bedroom on Friday night.

"I wish I was there too because I'm already missing the fuck out of you, but we both know this is something you need to do by yourself."

Austen is right.

As usual.

Even if he didn't have a game, I still would've come home alone. "I'm shitting myself." I wipe my clammy hands down the front of my jeans.

"It's only natural," he reassures me. "But this is your family. They love you. It'll be okay. What time is it going down tomorrow?"

"Mom's told everyone to be here for lunch at one."

"Call me the minute the game is over," he says. "I'll be thinking of you."

"I will." I lie spread-eagled on my bed. "Just think, this time tomorrow, my family will know. It'll be a relief, but I'm scared shitless. I doubt I'll be able to sleep tonight."

"I can help with that," he says, his voice dropping to a deep, seductive level that does funny things to my insides. "Did you find the box I put in your bag yet?"

I'm already climbing off the bed as I say, "What box?"

"Go get it and FaceTime me from your tablet." Austen hangs up before I can question him.

Unzipping my duffel, I rummage inside, my fingers landing on the firm box. I pull it out, eyes widening as a gleeful smile tugs my lips up. Excitement and a smattering of nerves creep up my spine. Flipping the lock on my bedroom door, I move back to the bed, exhilaration mounting at the prospect of another first with Austen. Depositing the box on top of the comforter, I power up my tablet and sit up against my headrest to FaceTime my boyfriend.

Although it's past midnight here, it's only a little after nine in California so I'm surprised to find Austen in bed when the screen loads. He's shirtless, slouched in the bed, with his head propped against a mountain of pillows, and the comforter is scrunched at his waist, hiding one of my favorite parts of him. His hair is damp, and beads of water cling to his chest, confirming he's not long out of the shower.

He is the most beautiful man I've ever seen. Inside and out.

How the fuck did I get this lucky?

His sketch pad lies at his side, and I smile as I visualize him naked in bed, working on the design he's going to one day ink on my skin.

"Keats?" Austen's lip curls, and his eyes glint with smug confidence. He knows I zoned out dreaming of him. Shaking my head free, I lift the box onto my thighs. "Where'd you find it?" I inquire, knowing I had it hidden on the top shelf of my closet.

"I borrowed one of your shirts yesterday morning, and I found it by accident. Why'd you hide it from me?"

"It wasn't intentional," I truthfully reply, removing the lid. "I haven't needed my stash of sex toys since we got together. I honestly forgot about it."

"Pity." Austen palms a hand over his washboard abs, and I wish I was there with him. "We could've had some fun." He leans into the camera. "We can now, if you're game."

"Aren't you tired?" I rasp, my dick already hardening in anticipation. It's been a long week, and Austen is usually pretty beat come Friday night.

"I'm never too tired to have video sex with my boyfriend." He pulls one of my dildos out from under the comforter, along with some lube. "Hope you don't mind I stole one."

I grin. "As if." I remove my favorite prostate massager from the box along with lube. "We're really doing this?"

Austen points the dildo at the screen, grinning. "Hell yeah. Strip for me baby. I need to see your hard cock."

Propping the tablet up against the lamp on my bedside table, I slide my sweats and boxers down my legs, kicking them away, watching my boyfriend peel back the comforter to reveal his insanely hot naked body and his beautiful straining cock.

Precum leaks from my crown as I grab hold of my aching shaft, stroking myself while I watch Austen do the same.

"Get comfortable on the bed, babe, and spread those gorgeous thighs," he instructs, his eyes darkening with pure need. I settle myself sideways on the bed, supporting my head on several pillows, ensuring I'm in full view of the screen.

"Lube up," he says, smearing liquid in his palms, expertly coating his fingers. I do the same as I watch him pump his dick and slide two digits into his ass.

"Fuck, that's hot," I admit, mirroring his actions.

Austen's eyes are locked on my hand as I thrust two fingers into my puckered hole, moaning at the tight fit.

"Does that feel good?" he murmurs, jacking his dick while he finger fucks himself.

"So good."

"Imagine it's me," he adds, his breathing heavy. "I'm stroking my fingers inside you, feeling your ass clench around me."

I groan as I visualize it, pretending Austen *is* here and that it is his fingers working inside me. My cock aches with intense longing.

"Open your eyes, babe," Austen commands. "I need to see those baby blues."

"Fuck. I wish you were here." I stare at the look of lust on his face, wishing it were my fingers pumping in and out of his ass.

"Replace your fingers with the massager," he instructs, squeezing lube on the dildo in his hand.

My heart is hammering behind my rib cage as I watch him slowly insert the dildo in his ass, arching his back and moaning.

"Damn. That is hot as fuck," I say, my fingers frozen in place inside me as I'm mesmerized at the sight of my boyfriend pushing a dildo in and out of his ass while he jerks himself off. His abs pull tight as he works his body into a frenzy, staring at me through the screen.

"You're slacking, man," Austen teases, jerking his head at the massager in my hand. "Work it into your ass and pretend it's my cock."

Austen slows his movements, watching me slide the toy into my ass with heated intensity. "That's it, baby. Fuck that ass."

My hand moves faster around my dick, and my eyes roll back in my head as I drive the massager in my ass, moving it up until it presses against my prostate. Black spots burst behind my retinas, and my balls tighten. "Fuck," I grit out. "I'm not going to last much longer."

"We come together," Austen demands, pumping his dick fast as he thrusts the dildo in and out of his ass. "I'm there with you, Keats. I'm driving my dick deep inside you. I'm fucking you hard, and you're clenching around me, your thick cock pulsing against my stomach as I fuck you into the bed so hard you see stars."

My orgasm rips through me out of nowhere, and I briefly bury my head in a pillow to muffle my grunts of pleasure. Warm ropes of cum spray over my abs as I milk every last drop from my dick, hungrily watching my boyfriend cover his body with his own release, wishing I was there to lick it clean.

Our breaths are ragged and our chests are heaving as we grin at one another through our screens. "I love you," I whisper, pressing my forehead to the screen.

"I love you, too." His eyes are swimming in desire. "And I can't wait to fuck you for real."

"I want that too."

"Do you?" he asks, his tone inquisitive, his expression hopeful.

"I do. And I want to work up to it." Austen hasn't pressed me at all in the weeks since we spoke about me bottoming, which I appreciate. It's been on my mind, and instead of thinking about it, I want to start doing something about it, because I want my boyfriend to fuck me. I want to have a normal relationship with him, and I'm done letting that jerk Brock control my life. He doesn't get to take this from me. I'm the one with the power here. I just need to get out of my head and trust my body to my boyfriend, knowing he will always take care of me. That he'll make it good, because he never leaves me unsatisfied.

"Dude." My brother Kalvin instantly grabs me into a hug when I open the door to him and his wife, Lana, the following afternoon. "What's up? We're dying of curiosity here."

"Speak for yourself, Stinky," Lana says. "Not all of us are impatient."

"You'll find out soon enough," I say, wringing my clammy hands, nerves jangling like I'm walking a tightrope. Thanks to my boyfriend, I managed to grab a decent sleep, but I've been barely holding it together since breakfast, and now I just need to get it out before the truth corrodes my insides and I crumple into nothing. "Everyone else is in the living room."

Kal slaps me on the back, letting me go. "It's all good, man."

"Keats." Lana envelops me in a hug, the scent of her delicate floral perfume wafting through the air. "How are you? Doing any writing these days?" she inquires after Kal has headed into the body of the house.

"I'm writing a new column for the college paper," I admit. "It's a weekly cooking column with an emphasis on healthy easy-to-cook meals."

"That's great. Could be a stepping stone to something?" she suggests.

I shrug, closing the front door behind my sister-in-law. "Who knows?" I downplay it because I'm not sure writing a cooking column is my burning desire, and right now, I've got singular focus and no brain capacity to even think about anything else.

I loop my arm through hers. "Who's minding the mini mes?"

As much as I adore my nieces and nephews, I asked my brothers not to bring their kids, because we'd never get to talk otherwise.

"Mom and Dad are staying with us for the weekend. They've taken Hewson and Hayley to the park." Lana squeezes me tight as we make our way across the lobby. "We're not in any rush. We can stay as long as we need to." She stops me, just before we reach the living room. "Is everything okay with you? Faye is worried, and I know she hates that she's not here."

Faye is my brother Kyler's wife. She's also my dad's niece and my cousin. It's complicated. Don't ask. Anyway, I'm closest to Faye out of all the girls, and I wish she and my brother were here today, but after graduating from Harvard, they've taken a year to go traveling, and they are currently in Australia.

They're missing our birthday party next month too, which sucks, but it's too far to ask them to travel. Especially when they've already promised to come home for Christmas. I'm planning on calling them later, as soon as they are awake. It's like three a.m. or something there now.

"I'm fine." Shitting a brick aside. "But it's sweet of you both to care."

"Is it a girl?" Lana asks, her eyes lighting up. "Have you met someone new?"

I smother a laugh. Lana's gaydar is as dysfunctional as my own. "All will be revealed. Come on." I pat her arm, leading her into the noisy living room. I asked Mom if we could talk first and then have lunch because I know my brothers and their significant others. They'd just pester me the whole way through lunch, asking why I'd called this get-together, and I'd rather just get this over and done with.

"Lana, sweetheart." Mom rushes to hug her daughter-in-law. "You look beautiful. As always."

"FYI. She said that to everyone," Kent pipes up, because he always stirs shit. He's sprawled in one of the recliner chairs, already looking bored.

"Because it's true," Mom says, leveling him with a warning look. "My sons, and Brad, are very lucky men."

Brad is Kyler's best friend and a surrogate Kennedy, having lived with us when his family had to flee overseas. Rachel is Faye's best friend from Ireland. She relocated to the US a few years ago, and she's now engaged to Brad. I extended an invite today, because I didn't want to do this without them here, and I'm happy they made it up from New York.

"You tell them, Alex," Rachel says in her lilting Irish accent. "Because *some men* don't understand that women like to be complimented." She shoots a pointed look at her fiancé.

"Don't look at me," Brad protests, placing his hand on his fiancée's knee. They are seated on the large leather sectional, alongside Keanu and Selena and Keven and Cheryl. "I tell you you're beautiful all the damn time."

"If McConaughey is slacking on the boyfriend front, Red," Kent says. "You can always trade up. Women would literally kill to be my girlfriend." He gestures up and down his body. "My offer still stands."

As egotistical as my brother is, it's no lie. Kent is the quintessential bad boy man slut every woman says they don't want, yet they fall at his feet in droves. He always ranks high on social media polls for hottest celebrity bachelor. Kent has never had a girlfriend, and though he likes to flirt outrageously with Rachel—purely to wind Brad up—I doubt even she'd win that honor were she single. Kent shows no sign of giving up his manwhore lifestyle any time soon. Which is fine, if that's what he truly wants. I just happen to think he secretly craves what our brothers have with their women, and I believe finding his person will help him lay his demons to rest.

"As does my threat to knock you flat on your ass," Brad retorts.

These two always play the same parts, but it never gets old. It's entertaining as shit.

"Wow. You'd think I'd be used to it by now," Rachel says, grinning at Kent. "But your monstrous ego still has the power to amaze me. And to think women melt at your feet." She shakes her head. "It's such a mystery."

"There is no denying Kent's charms," Eva says, smiling. Eva is my eldest brother Kaden's wife, and it's no surprise to hear her loyally defending Kent as they have a special bond. Something none of the other women have managed with my troublesome brother. If Kent confides in anyone, it's Eva. Although, even she doesn't know exactly what drives his crazy-ass behavior, because Kent is a steel vault with so many locks and bolts, it'd take heavy-duty explosives to break through. "And someday, one very special, very lucky woman is going to knock him off his feet and take him off the market before he's even noticed it happening."

"Delusional much, Evelina?" Kent smirks, playing his usual game. "There's still plenty of unclaimed pussy awaiting my tongue, my fingers, and my cock."

"Kent!" Mom shrieks, and my eardrums protest. "Please don't. Let's just enjoy today without letting the conversation sink to the gutter."

"You fools all pander to him," Kaden says, slinging his arm around Eva's shoulders, pulling her in closer to him on the couch.

"Agreed, but would we have it any other way?" Dad jokes, carrying a tray laden with drinks into the room. He sets it down on the coffee table, and Mom and I distribute the drinks. The girls get wine, except for Rachel and Selena who stick with water. The guys get beer except for me because Mom was the one who nurtured my love of good wine. She hands me a glass of shiraz, and we clink glasses.

"What's going on, Keaton?" Kev asks, leaning forward and eyeing me carefully. "Does this have anything to do with our last phone call?"

"Not really," I fudge, warning him to say nothing else with my eyes. I fully intend on speaking to him about the Brock situation, but in private. My parents and my other brothers do *not* need to be aware of that recording. I'm hoping to handle it discreetly between Kev and me.

"What phone call?" Mom's eyes crunch at the corners, her mouth turning down. "Are you in trouble?"

Reeling her into my side, I press a kiss to her temple. "Relax, Mom. It's nothing like that." I clear my throat. This is the moment of reckoning. "I have something I need to tell you all. Something I should've told you a long time ago. Something I wanted to say in person." I kiss the top of Mom's head. "You should sit beside Dad for this." Mom's prone to heightened emotion, and I'm not sure how she'll react to my news, so I'd rather she's tucked into Dad's side so he can support her.

Mom pulls me into a hug, whispering in my ear. "Whatever it is, you know we are here for you." She eases back, cupping my face. "Always, my sweet boy."

She cannot know how much those words mean to me in this moment. Or maybe she does, and that's exactly why she said them.

It's a miracle I'm still standing because my legs feel like Jell-O and I can scarcely hold myself upright. My heart is thrashing against my rib cage, and my shirt is stuck to the line of sweat gliding down my spine. My mouth is so dry it's as if mothballs have taken up residence in there.

Pound, pound, pound.

Thump. Thump. Thump.

My heart goes crazy, and nausea swims up my throat, and I genuinely think I could puke.

I set my glass down on the table—I don't trust myself not to spill it—and no one misses the way my hand shakes. Mom sits on the smaller leather couch beside Dad, and they exchange a worried look, holding on to one another as they wait for me to speak.

I scan the room, looking at the faces of all those I love, hoping I have the balls to say this the way I want to say it. Rachel is on her phone, lifting her head up a few seconds later, shooting me a reassuring look.

"Keaton." Keanu claims my attention, and I realize I'm just standing in front of my family like a dummy, shaking and sweating, clearly on the verge of a mini breakdown. "You look like you're going to pass out. Just tell us." My eyes connect with my triplet, and I see the truth there.

He knows. Or he suspects.

My eyes search for my other triplet, but when my gaze locks on Kent, all I see is confusion and a hint of curiosity.

"There's no easy way to say this, so I'm just going to blurt it out first and then explain." I gulp over the football-sized lump in my throat. My heart pounds so fast I hear my pulse ringing in my ears.

Here goes nothing.

"I'm gay."

Chapter Twenty-Four
Keaton

Shocked silence rings out in the room for a few beats until Keanu breaks it. "That's not news to me."

"It isn't?" I ask, disbelief clear in my tone.

Keanu nods. "I mean, I didn't know for sure, but I had my suspicions." He looks me straight in the eye. "I could tell you and Melissa weren't right for one another, and I guess I had a sixth sense about it."

"I did too," Kalvin agrees. "But it was more to do with Keats' love of tight, brightly colored mismatched clothing when he was younger. Now it all makes sense." He flashes me a cheeky grin. "Remember the illuminous pink shirt you wore the night of my eighteenth?"

"My eyeballs still haven't recovered," Kade quips. He turns to his wife. "I'm sure we've got some pictures around here someplace. It has to be seen to be believed."

She elbows him in his side before pinning me with a warm smile. "Don't mind them, Keaton. They've got the maturity of five-year-olds."

I know their ribbing is in good humor and this is just the way we handle things chez Kennedy.

Brad snorts, grinning. "Don't forget the ballet. He was such a pretty little twinkle toes."

I flip him the bird, but I can't keep the grin off my face. "Hey, homophobic assholes. News flash. Wearing pink and doing ballet does not mean you're gay."

"What about ogling the male models in the catalogs Mom used to bring home?" Kev lifts a brow, his lips twitching. "I know I caught you doing that a couple times."

"Try like a hundred times," I admit, gradually feeling the tension seep from my knotted shoulders.

"I caught you checking out Brad's ass one time."

My eyes pop wide at the unexpected familiar voice.

Rachel holds up her phone, and a sleepy-looking Kyler and Faye smile back at me. "I arranged it," Rachel says, answering my unspoken question as she hands me her cell. "I knew they'd want to be a part of this."

"You heard," I stupidly say, talking to my brother and his wife.

"We did," Kyler says. "I'm proud of you, dude."

The lump in my throat swells, and my heart is fit to burst.

"We love you, Keats." Faye blows me a kiss, her gorgeous brown eyes glassy with unshed tears. "I wish I was there so I could hug you and show you how much."

"I wish you were here too, but it means a lot that you stayed up for this."

"Family is everything," Ky says, hugging his wife to his chest. Faye leans back, tilting her head up to look at her husband, and they share one of their lovestruck looks.

All my brothers are crazy in love with their women, but the way Faye and Kyler look at one another is on a whole other level. They are so in love, and I hope that years down the line

Austen and I are as wrapped up in one another as they are. Couple goals, for sure.

"Sweetheart." Mom calls out, drawing my attention. "Come sit beside us." She pats the space in between her and Dad, and emotion sweeps through the room like fog.

"For the record," I say, eyeballing Brad. "I never checked you out. My brother's a dick." I sit down on the couch between my parents, propping Rach's cell up against a vase on the coffee table.

"Aw, you're not his type, McConaughey," Kyler quips. "Try not to slit your wrists."

Faye slaps her husband on the chest. "Jesus, Ky. You can't say stuff like that."

"It's okay, Faye," Brad says, brushing Rachel's long hair off her shoulder. "Ky's just jealous because he knows I have the better ass."

"Boys," Mom says. "I'd like to get serious for a minute."

The room instantly mutes, and my entire body trembles again because this sounds intense. Mom clasps my hand, smiling at me as her eyes well up. Dad puts his hand on my shoulder, squeezing gently in a silent show of support, his eyes conveying I have nothing to panic over.

I can hardly breathe over the swelling of emotion in my throat. Austen's reassurances about my family were on the money, and this has gone better than I hoped for.

"My sweet, darling boy." Mom scrunches my face in her hands, kissing my cheeks. "We love you. So, so much."

"All we've ever wanted for each of you is to be happy," Dad adds, his voice cracking a little. "We've gone through our fair share of trials and tribulations as a family, and we always come out stronger. But more than that, what we've lived through highlights the importance of staying true to yourself." He squeezes my shoulder a little harder, fighting to hold on to his composure.

Watching the emotion on my dad's face almost makes me lose the tenuous control on my own emotions.

"We never want you to be afraid to be yourself, and we will always support you, because we love you." His gaze drifts quickly around the room. "We love all of you. Your mom and I will always support your dreams and your ambitions because we want you all to live your best lives."

Mom smiles at Dad, and they share a moment. My gaze catches Lana's, and she smiles, swiping tears from her face as she snuggles into Kal. Kal nods at me, all trace of humor gone from his face, his expression dripping in emotion.

Mom swipes an errant tear rolling down her face. "How long have you known, honey?"

"I've always known deep down, but it became more real when I was like fourteen, fifteen, and I realized I wasn't the same as Keanu or Kent."

I glance over at Kent for the first time, because he hasn't said a word, and that concerns me. He's looking at the floor with his head in his hands, so I can't see his expression to gauge his reaction.

"They were into girls," I continue, refocusing on Mom, "and I was more interested in boys." Nerves fire at me, but I draw a deep breath, keeping my cool. "I was confused," I admit, and Mom takes both my hands in hers, holding me tight. "And I didn't want to be gay," I add. "I wanted what you all had." I look around the room at my brothers and Brad. "I wanted a girl-friend and to one day be married and have kids."

A sob rips from Mom's throat. "Oh, honey. I hate that you were so lost for all those years. That you didn't feel you could come to us. That we didn't notice."

"Let's get real, Ma," Kalvin says. "Look at all the shit we

were dealing with, and we all know Keats. He always puts everyone else before himself. He was never going to put that on us."

"I came close to telling Faye so many times," I admit, smiling at my sister-in-law-slash-cousin on the screen. "But I was scared of admitting it even to myself."

"Oh, Keaton." Tears stream down Faye's face, and Kyler's arms band around her stomach as he holds her even closer. "I knew you were trying to tell me something. I thought I was right to not push it, but maybe I should have."

I shake my head. "I needed to do this at my own pace. When I was ready, and I've only just reached that point. I still have so much stuff I need to work through."

"Does Melissa know?" Kaden asks.

"No. I wanted all of you to know first, but I will tell her. I plan to visit her tomorrow before I leave for the airport."

"This will devastate her," Cheryl says, speaking up for the first time.

"I know, and my biggest regret is not having the balls to end things with her properly when I first left for Berkeley, because I've only hurt her more these past couple years."

"Or it might free her," Selena suggests, her soft voice matching her tender smile. Keanu presses a kiss into her hair, smiling at her adoringly in a way that gives Kyler a run for his money.

"It might help her gain closure," Lana agrees. "And you shouldn't apologize for who you are, Keaton. We all know you're a good person with a good heart. You didn't hurt her intentionally."

Kent snorts, and it's his first reaction. My muscles lock up, and I brace myself for whatever is about to come. Several heads whip in Kent's direction, but he doesn't look up, and my nerves are jangling again. Acid crawls up my throat when I lock eyes with Keanu, spotting the same anxiousness on his face.

"Just be honest with her," Rachel says, deliberately slicing through the sudden tension in the air. "Tell her what you've told us, and hopefully, she can find it in her heart to forgive you."

Kent barks out a laugh, finally lifting his head. "Not fucking likely." His eyes burn with dark resentment, and I flinch. The look of pure venom on his face has me wishing the ground could open and swallow me.

"Kent. I—" I cut myself off, unable to form words. I don't know what to say in the face of such blatant hostility. From experience, I know it's better to let Kent stew. I'll try to talk to him when he's calmed down. The very last thing I want is to say something that will drive an even greater divide between us or cause a full-scale family argument.

Kent's lips curl into a snarl as he stands, glaring at me. "If I ever needed further proof that I'm not like the rest of you, this is it." He casts a scathing look around the room. "Look at you all tripping over yourselves to act like this is no big deal."

"I can see you're pissed, but at least give Keats a chance to get his story out," Keanu says, pleading with his eyes as he stares at Kent. "It's not like this is really a big surprise to either one of us."

"Isn't it?" Kent snaps. "Don't put words in my mouth."

Kade stands. "Don't make this about you. For once in your Goddamned life, can you think about someone else?"

"And I resent the insinuation that we're faking our reactions," Kalvin adds. "So what if Keaton is into guys? He's our *brother*. Your *triplet*. And this isn't the dark ages. Many people are bi or gay or pan these days. Who the fuck cares?" He jabs his finger in Kent's direction. "Keats being gay doesn't change who he is to us."

"I understand if you feel hurt because you're closest to Keaton and Keanu," Ky says. "Maybe you and Keats should discuss it privately when you've calmed down."

"Go fuck yourself, Ky," Kent seethes. "You don't fucking know what's in my head." He scrubs a hand down his cheek. "You're all a bunch of self-serving assholes," he hisses, and I don't understand where this deep hatred is coming from. "And you have the nerve to call me selfish?" He drills a loaded look at Kade.

"Kent." Dad's voice holds considerable warning. "You're upsetting everyone. If you could just explain what's going on so we can—"

"What?" Kent roars, throwing up his hands. "Pretend like you understand me? Like you honestly give a shit?"

I glare at my brother as Mom quietly sobs into my shoulder. Out of all of us, Kent is the one to always make her cry, and I hate it. I hate seeing my mother cry. It destroys something inherent inside me, and I just want to bundle her up and protect her from anyone who wants to hurt her.

I don't know what's gotten into Kent. He's always been volatile and prone to slinging hurtful words and cruel accusations, but he hasn't been this bad in years.

He's an attention whore, and he'll tell you he isn't loved, that our parents never cared for him, when the truth is he claimed a huge chunk of their attention when we were growing up because he was always getting into trouble and acting out purely to provoke them. Mom and Dad spent more time bailing him out, bringing him to different shrinks and therapy sessions, and trying to understand him than they did with any of my brothers. We don't begrudge him that or at least I don't. I can't speak for my brothers even though it doesn't appear any of them hold any grudges, but it's not like we've ever openly spoken about it.

We tolerate Kent's behavior because we love him. It's part of who he is. I wish I knew what demon my brother worships at the altar of, because I've never understood why he lashes out. Why he always seems so angry with the world. But he is who he is, and we can't force him to be someone he's not. We've all tried getting him to open up, but he never does. So, we do what we can to make allowances for him and just accept him the way he is.

But this shit is way out of line.

"Hate me all you want," I say, sending a daggered look at my brother. "But don't you dare take this out on Mom or anyone else."

Chapter Twenty-Five
Keaton

"I do hate you," Kent spits, stalking to where I'm sitting, leaning over me with a dark look. Pain stabs me in the chest. "You make me sick," he adds, casting a derisory glance up and down my body. "Fucking pervert," he snaps before storming out of the room, leaving bloody wreckage in his wake.

A thousand pinpricks stab me through the heart, and intense pain presses down on my chest to the point I can scarcely breathe. I try to swallow over the anguished lump in my throat, and it almost chokes me. Tears prick my eyes, and I squeeze them shut, folding my arms around myself in a desperate bid to maintain my composure.

How can he say that to me? Is that really what he thinks? Why? Am I that disgusting to him now?

Anger smashes through the hurt, charging through me, and I snap my eyes open, lowering my arms and clenching my fists.

Fuck. Him.

He doesn't get to take his petty narrow-minded prejudices

out on me. I've never understood him, and he doesn't understand me, and maybe that's always the way it will be.

In this moment, I'm more concerned about Mom because she's shaking and sobbing at my side, hurting as much as I am at Kent's cruel words.

"Where did we go wrong with him?" Mom cries, looking to my dad with red-rimmed eyes and flushed cheeks.

Dad nudges me, and I stand, letting him take my place and comfort her. "Shush, darling. Kent is a grown man, and it's time he started taking responsibility for his actions and who he is." Dad offers me a sad smile. "Like Keaton is doing today."

Cheryl stands, hauling me into a hug. "Don't let Kent take away from today. He loves you, and he's hurting. He didn't mean it, and I'm sure he'll come around." She runs a hand up and down my back in a comforting gesture.

I'm honestly not sure he will, and after what he's just said, I don't know if I'll ever be able to forgive him, but I keep those thoughts to myself.

"I'm proud of you," she adds, easing out of our embrace. "And I hope you're happy now because we could all see you were struggling."

"Thanks, Cher Bear." Cheryl was Keven's childhood sweetheart and a permanent fixture in our home when we were growing up. Until Kev messed everything up and lost her for a few years. Thankfully, they found their way back to one another, and now they're getting married next year. I couldn't be happier for my brother, because Cheryl is an angel and she has the purest heart.

"I'm sorry, Keaton," Mom says, and I turn back around. "Kent should not have said what he said. He was way out of line."

"Don't apologize for Kent, Mom. It's not your place. He just needs to process." I don't know why he's so upset, and I doubt he'll tell me, because he's always closed off where his emotions are concerned. "I'm so grateful for your support. That goes for all of you," I add, offering a fragile smile to the rest of my family. "It's taken me months to pluck up the courage to tell you the truth. Along with Austen's encouragement."

"Austen knows?" Mom asks.

I wet my suddenly dry lips. "Eh, yeah. Actually, that's the other part of what I have to tell you." I scratch the back of my head. "Austen's not just my roommate. He's my, ah, boyfriend."

Rachel jumps up, squealing and enveloping me in a bone-crushing hug. "Way to go, Keats."

She high-fives me.

Like we're ten.

"Austen Hayes is a total fucking ride," she supplies, grinning.

"Is he now?" Brad asks, pouting slightly.

She rolls her eyes. "Get over yourself, McConaughey. If you're allowed to drool over Camila Cabello, then I'm allowed to drool over Austen Hayes."

"Eh, yeah, no." I narrow my eyes playfully. "The only one allowed to drool over Austen Hayes is me, but I can appreciate your good taste."

"And don't pretend like you don't drool over Shawn Mendes," Brad adds, because those two just can't help one-upping each other. "I totally know that's why you bought tickets to his last gig."

"Shawn is super sweet," Selena says. "I met him at a charity event one time. He's a really nice guy."

"We should reach out to him for help promoting Moonlight," Keanu says, weaving his fingers through his wife's long blonde hair.

Moonlight is the facility Selena and Keanu are building to provide support services for victims of sex abuse. It's an ambitious plan that will take years to put in place, but they are already making good progress with the build. Everyone in the family is contributing in some way, and we're all invested in making it a success.

"That's a good idea," Selena says, beaming at Keanu. "I'll add his name to our list."

"Oh my God," Lana gasps, eyes locked on her cell. "Your boyfriend is seriously hot."

"Give that here," Kalvin says, snatching the cell from his wife's hand.

Cheryl, Rachel, and Eva crowd around Kalvin, angling for a look at the phone. Oohs and aahs ring out, and I can't wait to tell Austen about this later.

"Meh." Kalvin scoffs. "He's not that hot." His lips twitch.

"He is totally hot," Lana protests, pursing her lips. "Don't tell me your masculinity is offended."

Kalvin shrugs, letting his grin loose. "I'm just winding Keats up." He eyeballs me. "Your man is hot as fuck. That ink? Those biceps and abs?" He winks suggestively, and I roll my eyes. He's such a clown. "Go you."

"Oh my God. I have no words," Faye says, smiling over a yawn.

"Let me see." I hold out my hand and Kal places Lana's cell in my palm. I can't contain my grin as I stare at the photo Lana pulled up on Google. It's a photo from Austen's last game, and the photographer captured him just as he pulled off his helmet. His hair is flat on top of his head, but you barely notice because the massive smile on his handsome face is all you see when you look at the pic.

"He looks happy," Mom says, sneaking a peek.

"They won that game by a landslide, and it was his best game so far this season," I explain.

"I think it's because he's in love," she says, squeezing my arm.

Kal barks out a laugh. "Here we go."

"What's wrong with loving the fact my boys are in love and happy. It warms my heart." Her smile fades a little, and I know she's thinking of Kent, because he's the only one not paired up now. I know how much she worries about him. She's previously confessed she's scared he won't find a girl strong enough to take him on.

"There is nothing wrong with that, Mom." I pull her into my arms. "And I can't wait for you to meet Austen. I already know you'll love him."

She pats my face. "I will, sweetheart. He's your choice, and that's a given." A wicked gleam appears in her eye. "Of course, it helps that he's so pretty to look at."

A chorus of groans rings out.

"That's gross, Mom," Kev says. "You can't hit on Keaton's boyfriend."

She laughs, her face full of joy. "Oh, lighten up. I'm not hitting on him. Why would I when I have my own sexy stud right here?" She swats Dad's ass, winking at him in a way I never want to witness again. A fresh round of complaints bounces off the walls, and my brothers share my nauseated look.

"I swear you want us to puke," Kal says. "Knock that shit off, and act your age."

"Kalvin Edward Kennedy." Mom swats the back of his head. "I'll have you know that you're never too old for sex. Especially second-chance sex. It's the best."

Thank fuck we haven't eaten yet, because I'm pretty sure I'd have just lost my lunch after that comment. I wish I could rewind time and unhear it. No kid wants to know about their parents' sex life. Ugh. So gross.

Dad bursts out laughing, hauling Mom into his arms. "I think you've made your point, love. If you continue, you might just scar them for life."

"The point is," Mom adds, losing the humorous expression as her gaze jumps around the room. "I have eyes, and I've always admired beauty in all its shapes and sizes. If I'm allowed to tell your girls they're beautiful, I'm allowed to tell Keaton's boyfriend he's beautiful too."

"That's a valid point," Keven says. "But you know we were just yanking your chain."

"I wouldn't have it any other way," Mom says, snuggling into Dad and smiling. "You all keep me young."

"I love that photo," I tell Lana, handing her back her cell.

"I can't wait to meet him," she says, her joy for me obvious.

Warmth spreads across my chest, and I deliberately ignore the pain I'm working hard to mask, thanks to Kent's cutting words.

"How long have you and Austen been together?" Eva asks.

"A couple months, so it's still early days, but it's going well. He's great."

"You're positively glowing." Mom's smile expands. "You're definitely in love."

"I am." Heat floods my cheeks, but I'm not ashamed to tell my family I love him. "He's amazing, and he's helped me accept who I am."

"I cannot wait to meet him." Mom pins me with a look I know all too well. "He is still coming to your birthday celebration, right?"

"Yes, Mom. He'll be here." She drops her hands, reaching behind me to grab my forgotten glass of wine.

She hands it to me, smiling. "I want to make a toast." We all reach for our drinks. Everyone gets up, forming a circle around Mom and me. Rach holds her cell out, ensuring Faye and Ky are included. Their love wraps around me, and tears threaten to spill. Right now, it feels like I can handle anything—even Kent's obvious disgust and disappointment—because my family understands and they accept and support me. Support us.

As Mom looks at me, with nothing but love and pride shining in her eyes, I realize how truly wealthy I am. All the money in the world pales in comparison to this. "To Keaton and Austen. To courage and truth."

Chapter Twenty-Six
Austen

"What are you doing here?" Keats asks, a massive smile appearing when he exits through the gate and finds me waiting for him.

"What does it look like?" I push off the pillar I'm leaning on, grinning at the look of complete and utter adoration on my boyfriend's face. Fuck. Seeing that will never get old.

Casting a quick glance around, to ensure no one is paying us attention, I lean into his ear and whisper, "I wanted to pick my boyfriend up from the airport. Shoot me if that's a crime." Keats gave me his SUV this weekend as he knew I wanted to hike. His plan was to take an Uber home from here, but there was no way I wasn't picking him up.

"I missed you like crazy, man," he says, as we walk off in the direction of the parking lot.

"Tell me about it." I grab his carry-on in an attempt to stop myself from reaching for him.

My skin crawls with the need to touch him, to hold him, to kiss him.

I know. I've got it bad.

"I hate the overnights with away games, but two nights' separation was hell," I admit. "We're not doing that again."

The second we climb in the car, we're all over one another, and I thank God for whoever invented black-out windows.

Keaton pulls me into the back seat, kissing me with fierce passion as we tear at each other's clothes.

He lies naked on top of me as we kiss, jacking both of us off in his hand, while my hands roam his body, kneading his ass, my finger flirting cautiously against his puckered hole. He hisses as I gently push the tip of my finger in, his cock jerking against my stomach, but he doesn't flinch or pull back, so I slowly ease my finger all the way in. I've wanted this. So much. And I memorize every second of him clenching around me, so happy he's trusting me to take care of his pleasure.

We climax in record time, seconds after one another, and I can't stop kissing him as we come down from our high.

We sport matching grins as we freshen up, using wipes to remove the cum from our stomachs and to clean our hands. I pull Keats back into my chest, wrapping my arms around him, just needing to hold him. "I'm glad you're home, and I'm happy it went well." Mostly. I'm still pissed at what Kent said to him, but I don't want to make this about me. Keats called me after our win yesterday, filling me in. I rub a hand up and down his arm. "How was your talk with Melissa?"

He angles his head, looking up at me as his fingers toy with the dark hair on my arms. "I didn't get to speak with her. She wasn't at home. I texted the family group, telling them not to say a word to her. Just in case they bump into her someplace. I'm going to arrange to meet her when I'm home in a few weeks for my birthday."

"And what about Kent? Did you speak to him before you left?"

He sighs, and I feel his pain as acutely as if it was mine.

"He went back to Boston last night." He grips my arms, holding me tight. "It was probably for the best. I'm still so hurt. I don't think either one of us is ready to talk yet."

"You think he's hurt because he's your triplet and you didn't tell him?" I ask, pressing kisses into his hair.

"That could be part of it, but I didn't tell Keanu, and he was fine with it."

"Because he suspected the truth, so it wasn't as much of a shock for him." From the way Keaton explained it, it seems like Kent had no clue. "I find it a little weird, if I'm honest. The three of you were close growing up, so how come Keanu read the signs, but Kent didn't?"

"Keanu wasn't around as much because of modeling, but I confided things in him about my relationship with Melissa, so him reading between the lines isn't surprising. Kent was around more but he's...It's hard to describe Kent when you don't know him. He's a lot like an island. Like, he's part of our family, but he's detached at the same time. He drifts out to sea, and he doesn't get involved. He was always wrapped up in his own shit, so maybe he wasn't as observational as Keanu was." He shrugs. "I don't know. I never know what's going on in Kent's head. This is no different."

He sounds like a selfish, immature jerk to me, but I don't articulate that thought. I haven't met the guy, and all I know is he's troubled and prone to wild, reckless behavior. I hate he's the reason my boyfriend is melancholy at a time when he should be ecstatically happy. And I want to punch his lights out for calling his brother a pervert. Can't guarantee I won't when I meet him. If he says one nasty thing to my boyfriend in my presence, I'm not sure I'll be able to hold myself back.

But, Kent is his brother. Keaton loves him, and even though he's upset, I know he wouldn't want me hating on him or throwing punches. I know how important it is for Keats to have both his triplets on his side, so I'll take my cues from him. This is for Keaton to handle, and I can't interfere. I don't like it, but I understand it.

For now, my mission is to distract him. "Have you eaten? Or do you want to grab some dinner?"

"I could eat." Keaton sits up, turning around to bend down and kiss me. "I love you. I couldn't have done this without your encouragement. Thank you."

I grab the back of his head. "I always have your back." I peer into his beautiful blue eyes, basking in the warmth I see there. "I love you too, and I can't wait to meet your family."

A lopsided grin appears on his mouth. "They can't wait to meet you too. Especially my sisters-in-law. They Googled you." His grin stretches as his fingers trace a path along my collarbone. His touch sears bone-deep, heating every corner of me. "And they think you're hot."

"They have good taste. I like them already," I tease, brushing my fingers along the stubble on his chin.

"Just prepare yourself for the crazy and you're good," he adds, pulling our clothes off the floor, and tossing my jeans and tee at me. "Let's go before the parking ticket expires."

"You've got to be kidding me," Keaton hisses under his breath as Dax walks past our table in the restaurant, sending daggers in our direction.

I stretch my hand across the table before I remember we're in public. It physically pains me to pull back when every inch of my being wants to comfort him. "I told you I spoke to him and it's handled. Let him glare at us if he wants. Who cares?" I refuse to give my ex any more space in my head.

"What if he outs you or us?" Keaton asks, viciously stabbing his chicken like he's imagining it's Dax's head.

"He told me he won't." I pop a carrot in my mouth.

"That doesn't instill confidence. If he wants to put a strain on our relationship, all he has to do is talk to the media and he'll bring a shitstorm down upon us."

"Maybe we should ask Keven to dig through his stuff too. If he finds something incriminating, we can use it to guarantee his silence."

Keats gave me a complete run-through of his discussion with his FBI-agent brother. Keven is going to handle Brock Jonas, and I seriously hope he finds something he can use to blackmail the bastard into returning the copies he made of that recording.

"That's a great idea." Keats pulls out his cell and taps away. "I should've thought of it. Even if we don't find anything, Kev can track his emails and messages, so if he reaches out to anyone, we'll have a heads-up."

The next few weeks are blissfully uneventful, and I hope it stays this way. Although there's no resolution to the Brock Jonas issue yet, he hasn't come near Keaton, and I seriously hope my threat worked and he's dropped it.

But I've got other, more pressing, issues.

Namely, Keaton's birthday celebration is this weekend, and I still haven't bought him anything. "What do you buy the man who has everything?" I ask Colton as we stroll through the busy shopping mall after practice.

"That's the million-dollar question," he says, winking at two college-aged girls as they pass by us, their interest obvious from the way they are undressing both of us with their eyes.

"That's super helpful. Thanks." Sarcasm drips from my tone as I stop in front of a large jewelry store, squinting in the window at the watch selection.

"Not a watch," Colton says over my shoulder. "Way too cliché and not personal enough." He leans his back against the glass, looking thoughtful. "Keaton's a real genuine guy, and I think no matter what you give him, he'll love it."

"You are zero help," I mumble. "Remind me why I asked you to come with me again?"

"Because you adore my pretty face, my sharp wit, and my scintillating personality."

I mock gag, shoulder checking him, as we walk away from the jewelry store. "I'm not going to find anything here," I admit, passing store after store that holds no interest.

"Now, we're getting somewhere."

I flip Colton the bird, and he chuckles.

"Man, this is too funny." He flashes me a blinding grin.

"I'm glad I amuse you," I drawl.

His face sobers. "I've never seen you this rattled. You're always so confident and self-assured. It's good to know you're human."

"I just want this weekend to be perfect for him. Kent is still not talking to him, which is bound to make it tense, and he has to break the news to his ex-girlfriend, plus his other brother hasn't updated us yet on Brock or Dax. Keats has a tendency to worry obsessively about things, and I want to remove all the strain from his life. I want to get him something that will help him escape."

"So, book a weekend away for you two. Your schedule will free up in the new year once the season is over. You could book a romantic getaway for January."

"Isn't that cliché?" I ask, pulling the car keys from my

pocket. "Let's get out of here. Perhaps the answer will come to me over a steak."

"New menu?" Colton asks the waitress when we're settled in our usual booth at the restaurant.

"The chef is trying some new healthy options," she supplies. "You can thank that Kennedy boy. His new cooking column gave Danny the idea."

"Yeah?" Pride rushes through me. Although Keaton writes for the student college paper, it's all online, and anyone can sign up for a digital subscription.

She nods. "I recommend the steak with the arrabbiata sauce. It's divine."

We both order it with salad and a baked potato on the side, and as the waitress is writing our order down, a light bulb goes off in my head. I whip out my cell and tap the words into Google, grinning like a loon as options pop up before me.

"What's that cheesy grin for?" Colton asks, noisily slurping his soda.

"I know what I'm getting him," I say, as I click on the link for the culinary weekend in Half Moon Bay. "A cooking vacay," I add, before he asks, scrolling through the description. "They have personalized classes as well as a private tour of a farmer's market and a meeting with a wine ambassador. The hotel is boutique and it's private, in a little seaside town."

It's going to make a considerable dent in my savings account, but I don't care. Keaton will love it, and I love the idea of helping him explore his passion. Maybe I'm wrong, but I think cooking is where his future lies. He just doesn't see it yet. And even if he doesn't end up pursuing it as a career, I know he'll always have it as a hobby, so the weekend will be worthwhile either way. Plus, we'll get to spend time together away from prying eyes on campus.

I lift my head, feeling relaxed for the first time all week. "It's perfect." Between that and the framed tattoo drawing I already have stashed in the back of my closet, I hope my boyfriend agrees, because I want to make his birthday extra special and one he'll remember for years to come.

Chapter Twenty-Seven
Keaton

Standing at Melissa's front door on Friday night, I steel my nerves before pressing the bell. She knows I'm coming, but not why, and I really hope she meant what she said the last time we talked in July and that she's not anticipating a reunion. Because it would kill me to do that to her. It's already going to be difficult enough without that.

The door swings open to reveal my ex. She's wearing skinny jeans and an off-the-shoulder sweater, and her long hair is down, her face devoid of makeup. "Hey, Mel. You look pretty." I inwardly cringe as the words leave my mouth. I don't want her reading into that. I was just speaking my mind and stating facts. Melissa is a gorgeous woman, but I don't think she sees that.

"Flattery won't work, Keats," she says though her cheeks tinge pink. "I'm not doing this dance with you again."

"That's not why I'm here. I swear." I rock back on my heels, stuffing my clammy hands in the back pockets of my jeans.

"Why *are* you here?" She props one hip against the doorjamb.

"I owe you an explanation and an apology. I hate how things ended, and there are some things I really need to tell you."

Her eyes drink me in, and she bites down on her lip. "Okay." She steps aside to let me in. "But you should know my brother will be home in an hour, and he's quite likely to punch you on sight if you're still here."

Quentin is a raging asshole, and he's never liked me, but my behavior the past couple years has given him due cause to punch me, and I can't fault him for looking out for his little sister. "I'll be gone by then." This won't take long. I'm pretty sure once I tell her the truth she'll kick my ass out.

Melissa leads me down a familiar hallway, out into the sunroom at the back of the two-story house. She closes the door behind me, sitting on the soft couch we spent many evenings on. I purposely sit on the chair across from her, staring out at the bleak gray sky, watching the thunderclouds rolling in, hoping it's not an omen.

"How are you?" I ask, leaning forward on my elbows, trying my best not to fidget.

She shrugs. "I'm fine." Tucking her legs into her chest, she rests her chin on her knees. "We don't have to do this." She gestures between us. "Pretend to be polite. I can tell you don't want to be here. Just say what you came to say."

"It's not that, Mel. I'm nervous because what I need to tell you is going to hurt and I swore I wouldn't hurt you anymore."

"I'll be the judge of that, and I'm stronger than you've ever given me credit for."

"I care about you. I always will. I need you to know that." I knot my hands on my knees, swiping my tongue along my dry bottom lip.

Tears pool in her eyes. "You've met someone else?" she whispers, and the first knife penetrates my heart.

I nod, because I won't lie to her anymore. This is going to be painful. For both of us. But there's nothing I can do to soften the blow. "His name is Austen. He's my roommate at Berkeley."

Shock splays across her face, and she stares at me with the whole deer in the headlights look.

I forge on. "I'm gay, Melissa."

"What?" she splutters.

"I'm into guys."

"I don't understand." Silent tears roll down her face, and I fucking hate myself. I'm an asshole. A shitty pathetic excuse for a human being.

"I'm sorry, Mel. I've been so confused, and I just didn't know how to tell you."

"How long?"

She asks the one question I've been dreading. Acid swirls in my gut like poison.

"How long have you known you are gay, Keaton," she hisses, and I watch the emotion transform on her face.

I could fudge the reply, because the honest truth is, I only fully accepted it these past few months, but I won't insult her intelligence. If I'm to be completely transparent, I need to face the fact I've always known. I might not have wanted it, or accepted it, but I've always known. I just tried to deny it.

"Answer me," she snaps, hugging her arms around her knees, openly sobbing now.

"From before we started dating," I admit.

"Oh my God." She raises a shaky hand to her mouth, and I sink to my knees in front of her, struggling to hold back tears of my own.

"Mel." I reach for her hands, but she slaps me away. I fall back on my butt, watching her unravel before my eyes.

"Don't fucking touch me! You unimaginable asshole." Tears pour out of her eyes.

"I'm so, so sorry."

"Do you have any idea what you've done to me?! I have wasted years on you!" she yells, picking up the plant pot on the coffee table and throwing it across the room. It crashes to the tile floor, shattering to pieces.

I stand, moving to pick up the broken ceramic.

"Leave it!" she shrieks. "I can't believe this. You let me think there was something wrong with me!" She thumps a hand over her heart as she sobs. "I thought I wasn't pretty enough. Wasn't sexy enough. Wasn't good enough in bed." She swipes an angry hand across her face, swatting at her damp cheeks, and her eyes blaze with righteous indignation. "And all along it's because I have a vagina and not a penis?!" she roars.

"Melissa. Is everything—" Mel's mom enters the sunroom, slamming to a halt as she lays eyes on her daughter.

"What have you done to upset my daughter now?" she asks, rushing to Mel's side and pulling her into a hug. She glares at me with barely contained hatred. "I'd like you to leave."

"I'm very sorry, Mel. If you ever want to talk about—"

She lunges at me, slapping me across the face. "Get the fuck out of my life and stay out! I hate you! You selfish fucking prick."

I have never heard Melissa curse so blatantly or ever seen her so enraged. She has never hit me or reacted violently. Ever. I hate what I've done to her. This is all on me.

Hanging my head in shame, I walk out the door, barely feeling the stinging pain in my cheek. Mel's mother follows me out, and I feel her embedding imaginary daggers in my back the whole way.

"You're not welcome here anymore, Keaton," she says, stopping in the doorway. "I can't let you keep doing this to Melissa.

If you ever cared for her, you'll let her go. She deserves to move on, and she can't when you keep coming back."

Her words cut deep, but I'm guessing that's the point. "I won't be back. Melissa will explain. I have always cared for her, and it was never my intention to hurt her.

"Intentional or not, you did." She narrows her eyes at me. "Goodbye, Mr. Kennedy." She slams the door in my face, and I drag my body to my rental, climb in, and peel out of there.

"Oh, honey." Mom opens the door before I've put my key in the lock, confirming she was watching out for me. She knew I was going straight to Melissa's from the airport. She envelops me in her arms, and I cling to her, shutting my eyes as if that will block out the screaming in my head. "It's okay." She rubs a soothing hand up and down my back, ushering me inside the house.

"She hates me, and I don't blame her. Right now, I hate me too."

Mom wraps her arm around my back, steering me through the entryway. "She doesn't hate you. She loves you. That's the problem."

I walk as if on autopilot, letting Mom push me down on the couch in the living room.

"Is everything okay?" Dad asks, stepping into the room from the other direction.

"We need the good stuff," Mom says, looking over her shoulder. The sound of Dad's retreating footfalls confirms he's gone to retrieve his prized Macallan whisky.

"Tell me what happened." Mom circles her arms around my frozen body.

"It was awful, Mom." I squeeze my eyes shut to ward off

tears. "I hurt her so bad. She screamed. Cursed. Threw things. She slapped me."

"She what?" Mom's voice sharpens.

I lift my red-rimmed bloodshot eyes to hers. "Don't hate her for that. She had every right."

"She had *no* right." Mom kisses my reddened cheek. "I don't care what you've done, or how much she's hurting, there is no excuse for violence." She wets her lips, looking pensive. "I've done things I'm not proud of, so I won't judge Melissa even though I'm furious she raised her hand to you."

"Get that down ya," Dad says, handing me a glass of whisky from behind the couch. Aside from ice, it's pure alcohol, and though I don't usually drink whisky, right now, it's exactly what I need.

Dad hands Mom a glass before sitting on the coffee table in front of us, nursing his own whisky.

I gulp back a full mouthful, welcoming the bitter burn as it glides down my throat.

"I take it things didn't go well." Dad eyes me carefully.

"That's the understatement of the century." I swallow another mouthful of the amber-colored liquid, and at this rate, I'm going to need a refill soon.

"It's bound to have been a shock, but she's a sweet girl, and she cares for you. She will forgive you one day."

"I wouldn't if I was her." I rub at my eyes, sniffling. "I'm a piece of shit. Deep down, I knew I wasn't into girls, yet I dated her, took her virginity, and continued to keep her on a string while I tried to make sense of the mess in my head. I would never speak to me again if I was Melissa."

The dam breaks, and I put my whisky down, burying my head in my hands as I cry.

Dad sits beside me, offering silent comfort, while Mom

hugs me, rocking us as she whispers soothing reassurances in my ear.

When my crying jaunt ends, a new layer of shame washes over me. I'm so weak. Such a pussy. And I have no right to these tears. Melissa does, because she was wronged, but I have no right to feel sorry for myself. Even if I was confused, I knew what I was doing was wrong.

"I know what you're thinking," Mom says. "And it's not all your fault."

"How can you say that?" I look at her, realizing she's been crying too. "It *is* my fault. It's certainly not Mel's."

Mom and Dad exchange one of their looks.

"You're both young," Mom softly says. "And I know it seems like it's all your fault. I know you want to shoulder the entire burden, because it's in your nature, but relationships are two-way streets. You were not in that relationship alone. Melissa was in it too. I don't need to know the specifics to understand she knew something wasn't right because we could all see it, Keaton. We may not have known the reason for it, but it was completely obvious you two were not meant for one another." She caresses my cheek. "Honestly, I gave you six months when you first started dating."

"I was her first relationship. She had nothing to compare it to."

"It was your first relationship too," Dad says. "And from what I saw, you were attentive and caring and you treated her with respect."

I retrieve my whisky, cradling the glass between my hands. "I treated her like a really good friend, Dad. And I lied to her. In all the ways that matter, I wasn't attentive or caring or respectful."

"I don't want to hear about my kids' sex lives," Mom bluntly exclaims over a shudder, and if I wasn't so heartsore, I'd laugh at the irony. "But if you're saying what I think you're saying, then I'm sorry, sweetheart, but Melissa knew. Deep down, she knew that something was wrong."

"Your mom is right," Austen says an hour later when I finally get a hold of him. He's back at our apartment after practice, fixing something to eat. "Did Melissa ever ask you why you weren't that interested in sex?"

I lie on my side on the bed, holding my cell in front of my face as I tell my boyfriend everything that went down since I left California earlier today. "No. We didn't talk about sex."

"Then, I'm sorry, but *she* is partly responsible. She told you she knew something was wrong, but she never asked you about it. Who does that?"

"You don't understand. She's innocent and sweet, and I honestly don't think she'd know how to have a conversation like that."

"She wasn't so innocent and sweet when she was hitting you." That's touched a nerve with my boyfriend.

"She was wrong to hit me. Like I was wrong to lie to her."

"You were lying to yourself too, Keats," he says, placing a plate of food on the counter and pulling himself up on the stool. "You were confused, and you didn't deliberately set out to mislead her or hurt her. You were only trying to figure it all out. She had no right to hit you or call you selfish. I know what it's like to be your partner, and the very last thing you are is selfish, and she damn well knows it."

I love how quickly he jumps to defend me. How readily he believes it with his entire being. "She was angry, and it was a shock."

"It still doesn't excuse it."

"There have been wrongs on both sides." I'm willing to admit that much. I've spent a lot of time mulling over Mom's words since we spoke earlier. What she said is true.

Why did Melissa stay quiet? Why didn't she confront me with her suspicions? Why did she let me treat her less than she deserved?

"That's not the way it works, but you know what? Going over it isn't going to help. She knows the truth now, and you've apologized. You don't owe her anything else."

"I feel so responsible."

Austen sets his silverware down, chewing his food, his features softening. "I know you do. You wouldn't be the guy I love if you didn't want to take it all on yourself. But you need to let it go, Keats. Whether she wants to admit it or not, she shares in the responsibility. Maybe she will never accept that, but that's on *her*. You've done all you can now to make it right. It's time to put it behind you."

His words soothe me, and I know he's right. I don't want to dwell on the past at the expense of my future, and I'm determined to accept it for what it is and move forward. "How do you always know the right thing to say?"

"Because your boyfriend's not just gorgeous eye candy, he's hella smart too," Austen jokes, shoveling more food in his mouth.

"And so freaking humble. You forgot that part."

"I forgot the pathetic part too," he adds, grinning into the phone, "because I miss your face already."

"I wish you were here right now."

"Me too. I hate that I'm not there to chase your sadness away."

"You can make it up to me tomorrow night. By the way, did you get the flight details I sent?"

"I did." He gives me the stink eye. "I told you not to do that. I was happy to fly commercial."

"Don't rain on my parade, man. It's my birthday, and I want you here as early as possible. If you'd flown commercial you wouldn't have gotten here till like midnight."

"A slight exaggeration," he says in between mouthfuls.

"This way you'll only miss the first hour and a half of the party."

"I've never flown on a private jet before," he adds, getting up to rinse his plate when he's finished eating.

"Get used to it. It's Dad's plane, and it's usually how we travel." Dad won't be piloting it tomorrow, because he'll be busy getting things set up here, but his trusted copilot Michael is flying my boyfriend out.

"How the other half lives," he teases, flashing me a dazzling smile, and my heart does a twisty loop in my chest.

I love this guy so much. I don't have words to describe it. "Can't you just get here already," I whisper, needing his arms around me.

"I'll be with you before you know it." He blows me a kiss. "And I know exactly how to relax you in the meantime." He winks, and heat surges through my body.

"Hell yeah," I say, getting up to lock my bedroom door because I know where his mind is at. "Tell me where you want me."

Chapter Twenty-Eight
Austen

My eyes stay glued to the window of the Mercedes as we drive past opulent houses, many hidden behind high walls and tall gates. Getting a glimpse into Keaton's life has been eye-opening so far. From the luxury of the private plane to the chauffeur-driven car waiting for me at the private hangar, Keats' world is a million miles away from mine. Knowing this is how he's grown up only makes me appreciate the man he is even more. While the penthouse apartment we live in is levels above most student accommodations, Keaton leads a very normal life. He isn't extravagant, and he doesn't flaunt his wealth. Because he's a decent guy. He might have grown up surrounded by money, but he hasn't let it go to his head.

It only makes me love him more.

The car slows as we approach wrought-iron gates, and I strain forward in my seat as the gates open, revealing a long driveway, bordered by shrubs and plants and perfectly manicured lawns with colorful flowerbeds.

I whistle under my breath when the house comes into view.

Resting on a huge plot of land, and stretching endlessly on both sides of the estate, the one-story property is large and modern, comprised of wood and lots of glass with different peaked roofs, and I'm guessing it's stunning in the summer, letting lots of sunlight in.

Lines of cars are parked on the far left of the house, and it's obvious the party is in full swing.

I'm well versed in meeting new people, and rarely nervous, but I'm a little on edge, because this is my boyfriend's family, and I want to make a good impression. This is as new to them as it is for Keaton, and I want to assuage any concerns they may have. To ensure they know I care about him and that I have his back.

The driver swings the car in front of the open entranceway, and my heart swells when my boyfriend emerges from the house, his massive grin so wide it threatens to split his face. Pushing a few loose strands of hair back off my brow, I steady my nerves and climb out of the car before the driver has opened my door. He frowns a little, but I'm too busy ogling my boyfriend to care.

Keats is wearing a tight, white, designer T-shirt under a fitted navy blazer and dark jeans, ripped at the knees. He obviously got a haircut today, and I smile at the irony. The stylish layer of stubble on his face has me itching to drag my fingers through it, and with the way he's staring at me, it takes colossal willpower not to pull him into my arms and kiss the living daylights out of him. But we must play pretend tonight, because his parents invited tons of friends, including many prominent figures within Boston's high society, so I'm here as Keaton's friend and roommate and nothing more.

Which sucks, if I'm being honest. But I swore not to make things harder for him, and he's not ready to reveal his true self to the world at large yet.

"You cut your hair," Keats says, coming to a standstill in front of me.

"As did you."

"It's my birthday. I've got to look the part."

I lean in closer, pressing my mouth to his ear. "News flash. It's my boyfriend's twenty-first birthday. I've got to look the part too."

Keaton grins, his eyes oozing love and adoration, and if I don't get to kiss him soon, I'll self-combust.

"You look good, man," he says, his voice dropping a couple notches while his heated gaze roams over my fitted black shirt and tight, ripped black jeans.

"Good enough to eat?" I tease in a whisper.

His eyes dilate, and I know he's dying to touch me too.

"You know you do," he murmurs, glancing over my shoulder. "I'll take that," he says, stretching his hand out for my overnight bag. The driver hands it to him, and Keaton slings it over his shoulder. "Come on inside. Everyone is dying to meet you."

My boots thud on the gray stone pavement as we walk toward the door, and I brace myself for whatever the night may bring.

Something bright captures my eye, and I turn my head, a burst of laughter escaping my mouth when I spot the illuminous pink Porsche with a big white bow wrapped around it. "Is that what I think it is?" I ask, stopping to inspect the car. Two identical cars are parked on either side of it; the only difference is they are an understated silvery-gray color. "Wow." I whistle under my breath, running my fingers over the hood. "It's a 911 Carrera S. I didn't think you could get those in pink."

"My brothers are assholes," Keaton says, but there's zero heat behind the words. "Mom and Dad bought the three of us a car for our birthday, and my brothers thought it was funny to get mine spray-painted pink. Dickheads," he adds, fighting a smile.

"You're taking me out in this tomorrow." I press my mouth close to his ear. "If you're lucky, I'll let you fuck me in it."

Keaton adjusts himself behind his jeans, staring at me through hooded eyes. "You mean if *you're* lucky."

I slap him on the back. "Whatever you need to tell yourself works for me." I wink, and he flips me the bird.

Raucous laughter carries on the wind, mixing with the pulse-pounding beats of music, reminding us we've a party to get to.

"Get inside already," Keats says, jerking his head to the door. "Before I throw you against the wall and drive my cock in your ass."

"You won't hear me complaining," I tease, chuckling as I watch him adjust the bulge in his jeans.

"Is death by boner a real thing because I swear that's what's going to happen if you keep flirting with me," he says, guiding me into an impressively large, bright lobby. Keaton heads right, down a long hallway, moving us away from the noise of the party.

"I missed you," I truthfully admit, keeping pace with my boyfriend as he strides past successive closed doors. We pass through a large open-plan game room, complete with pool and foosball tables and two large leather sectionals positioned around a giant wall-mounted TV. Game consoles and accessories sit on a shelf underneath the TV, and the walls are adorned with tons of family photos. A jukebox sits tucked into a corner alongside a fully-stocked bar.

"Nice room," I supply, as Keaton presses forward into a back hallway. The noise from the party is muted here, because his house is just that big.

"We mostly hang out here," Keaton explains, leading me

past more closed doors. "We also have an indoor pool, theater room, and gym back here, as well as the bedrooms. My parents' master suite is on the mezzanine level just off the lobby, alongside Dad's study. The other side of the house is where the kitchen and living areas are, and it's where my parents entertain guests and host family get-togethers."

"I take it your mom designed everything," I say as Keats slows down in front of a closed door.

"She did. She's obsessed and always changing things."

Keats opens the door to a large bedroom, ushering me inside.

I've barely had time to look around before he shuts the door, grabbing me and pushing me up against it.

His lips are on mine in a nanosecond, his tongue plunging greedily into my mouth. I grab hold of his ass, yanking his body flush against mine while angling my head and kissing him back with the same pent-up desire. His stubble grazes along my smooth jawline, ramping my lust to new heights. My cock strains painfully against the crotch of my jeans, and we grind our erections together, both of us like steel behind our clothes.

"Fuck, man," Keaton rasps, pulling his lips from mine. "I need to be inside you." He fumbles with my belt as I reach for his jeans, popping the top button.

"You'll never hear me complaining or denying you," I admit, raking my teeth gently against his neck, inhaling the woodsy, musky smell of his cologne.

In a hurry, we shove our jeans and boxers down our legs, and I turn around, planting my palms on the door as I bend over, jutting my ass up in the air. Keaton covers his shaft with a condom and lube, teasing my ass open with slick fingers, before he eases inside me.

"Fucking hell." I grit my teeth as his hard length fills me all the way, pushing back against him when he begins thrusting.

With one hand, he grabs my hip to control our movements, and the other hand wraps around my erection. Keaton pumps me in his hand in sync with the rough thrusts of his cock in my ass, and pleasure whips through me when his dick presses against my prostate, sending me into sheer bliss. I arch my head back, straining toward him, and he leans forward, meeting my lips and kissing me as he rocks into my ass and strokes my cock.

We come in record time, within seconds of each other, my cum coating my boyfriend's hand.

"God, Austen." Keaton pulls out of my ass, and I straighten up, turning around to face him. He presses the softest of kisses to my lips. "Every time is better than the last with you. I will never get enough."

I cup one side of his face. "You never have to. I'm going nowhere."

"Stay put," Keats commands, tugging his jeans up and holding them around his waist with his clean hand. He walks to the en suite bathroom, returning a minute later, all cleaned up and dressed. Using a warm washcloth, he proceeds to clean me before pulling my boxers and jeans back up my legs. He tucks me in, and I smile at him as he rebuttons my jeans and my belt and smooths the wrinkles from my shirt.

Reeling him into me, I slant my mouth over his. We hold on to one another as we kiss in a more leisurely fashion, and Keaton is right. Every kiss, every touch, every fuck, is better than the last. I will never get enough of this guy. When we break apart, we stare at one another, drowning in sentiments we've never experienced before. Keats rests his brow against mine. "I'm so glad you're here."

"Me too." I grab the back of his neck, tracing my fingers across his smooth skin.

"I wish you were here as my boyfriend, not my roomie," he admits after a few beats.

I force his eyes to mine. "One step at a time, right?"

He nods, his eyes drifting to my mouth again.

Heat pulses in my veins, and I wet my lips, needing more. "If you keep looking at me like that, we'll never make it out of this room," I warn, my cock already thickening.

He takes a purposeful step back. "I know, man. I just can't keep my hands off you."

I push off the door, playfully messing his hair as I head toward my bag. "The feeling is mutual." Grabbing my bag, I sit on the side of Keaton's humongous king-sized bed, looking around his bedroom.

It's decorated in shades of blue, white, and gray, and it's tastefully designed. Matching bedside tables rest on either side of the bed, and a large TV is mounted on a white dresser off to the side, alongside a desk and chair. He has a huge walk-in closet on the left just before his private bathroom. A couch, coffee table, and window seat form a cozy area at the rear right-hand side of the room.

The room is spacious and comfortable and larger than most hotel suites I've stayed in. Two wide windows sit on either side of French doors, which open to the rear grounds. The curtains are pulled so I can't see outside, but I'm guessing it's as impressive as everything else I've seen so far.

"Sit for a sec," I tell Keaton, patting the space beside me as I open the zipper on my bag. I remove the wrapped package, handing it to him. "Happy birthday, Keats."

Excitement radiates from his every pore, and I smile as he tears at the blue and silver wrapping, uncovering the framed tattoo and plain white envelope.

"You framed it," he whispers, his gaze raking over the drawing I've painstakingly designed and etched.

"I thought it was the best way of preserving it until I'm ready to ink it on your skin."

He trails his finger along the glass covering the design. "I love this so much." When he lifts his head, his eyes are damp with unshed tears. "I can't wait to have it on my body."

"Open your second present," I urge, plucking the envelope from the bed and handing it to him.

A giant smile stretches across his mouth when he removes the sheet of paper, reading the details of our January culinary break. "This is too much." Emotion blares from his eyes as he stares at me, reaching out to thread his fingers in mine.

"Do you like it?"

"I love it! It's perfect." Leaning forward, he grabs the back of my head with his free hand and pulls me into him for a deep kiss. "And I love you. Thank you."

"I love you too." I clasp his neck, keeping him close, unable to tear myself away from him. Our mouths meet again, and we devour one another, lost in our own little world.

Until the door slams open and someone releases a whimper of pain.

We break apart in tandem, our heads darting to the open door, where a pretty girl with long hair and big eyes stares at us in disbelief.

Shit.

"It's true," she whispers as silent tears roll down her face and her lower lip wobbles.

"Mel." Keaton stands, the pain evident on his face and in his voice.

"I'm such an idiot," she adds, openly crying now.

Keaton walks toward her. "You're not," he softly replies, reaching for her.

"I can't..." She chokes on a sob, ducking out of his grasp and running off.

Chapter Twenty-Nine
Keaton

"Go after her," Austen says, as I stand helpless in the doorway. "Make sure she's okay." I hesitate, not knowing what the protocol is here. I've no clue why she's even here—I didn't invite her, and I'm pretty sure Mom didn't either.

"Keats." Austen stands, walking to my side. He clasps my face in his hands. "It's okay. I'm not threatened. She's upset, and you'll only worry." He presses a hard kiss to my lips, and I hold on to his shoulders.

A loud hissing sound has us drawing back, and I'm instantly on guard when I spot Kent in the doorway of his bedroom, glaring at me with clear disgust. From the minute he arrived home today, he has avoided me, and I've given him a wide berth. I'm still hurt over his callous treatment, and I don't want to cause a fight when Mom and Dad have gone to so much trouble.

But my brother doesn't get to eyeball my man the way he's currently eyeballing him—as if he's seconds away from tearing Austen limb to limb. Naked aggression and raw loathing seep from his every pore, as he casts a derogatory lens over my boyfriend.

Kent can be pissed at me all he wants, but Austen has done nothing to warrant such a hostile reception. Straightening my shoulders, I stand slightly in front of Austen, linking my hand in his. "Stop looking at my boyfriend like that. Hate me, but Austen has done nothing to you."

"He fucking exists," Kent spits, his nostrils flaring as a cruel sneer twists his mouth into an unattractive line. My brother shoulder checks me as he brushes past. "You make me sick." His gaze flits to our conjoined hands. "Fucking faggots."

Austen stiffens, every muscle in his body locking up tight, and he moves instinctively, taking a step forward. I push him back with my hands, shaking my head. "Let it go." I hold him against the wall with my palms braced on his chest until Kent has disappeared.

"What the hell is his problem?" Austen asks, blowing air out of his mouth.

"Where do you want to start?" I deadpan, twisting my head from side to side to loosen the kink in my neck.

"He can't speak to you that way. I don't care if he's got a problem with us. He doesn't get to throw homophobic insults at us."

"I know, but I can't fight him on it tonight. I won't do that to my parents."

He nods. "Agreed." He runs a hand along the back of his neck. "You need to find Melissa," Austen reminds me.

Sighing, I close my bedroom door. "She's probably long gone by now."

"Probably," he says, matching my strides as we walk down the hallway.

"I should've locked the fucking door."

"She shouldn't have barged in there without knocking,"

Austen coolly replies. "But I am sorry she saw that. I know it hurt her."

We step foot in the game room, and my eyes narrow on Kent. He's sprawled lengthways across one of the leather sectionals, his body covering the girl underneath him. Her purple hair is splayed across the seat of the couch, and I don't need to see her face to know it's Faye's half-sister, Whitney. She cries out as Kent's hands move under her dress, and I look away, disgusted and angrier than I've ever been in my life.

"Keep walking," Austen says, tugging on my hand and pulling me through the room. "Maybe she'll fuck some sense into him," he adds when we're past the room, walking along the second hallway that leads to the entrance lobby.

I snort out a bitter laugh. "I very much doubt it. That's Whitney. Faye's troubled half-sister, and Kent is supposedly finished with her. Let's hope Faye's dad, Adam, doesn't find them, or there'll be hell to pay." If I was vindictive, I'd tell him, but I don't want to get Kent in trouble—even if I'm seriously pissed at him right now.

A commotion up ahead claims my attention, and I quicken my pace. "Is it Melissa?" Austen asks, and I start running, terrified he's right and that she's doing something she'll regret—like outing me to the party guests.

But it's not Melissa.

It's unexpected guests. Very welcome unexpected guests.

A giant grin spreads across my mouth as I push past Mom, yanking Faye into my arms. "Oh my God. What are you doing here?" I hug her tight, and the feel of her arms around me is like a comfort blanket.

"You didn't honestly think we'd miss your twenty-first, did you?" she replies, squeezing me harder.

"There's no way we wouldn't be here," Kyler adds, wrapping me in a hug as soon as his wife releases me. "Especially not after your revelation." He pulls back, grinning. "Did you like your birthday present?" His lips twitch.

I shove at his chest. "It was your idea?"

He shakes his head. "I'd love to claim the credit, but it was—"

"Kal's idea," I finish for him, because Kal is the known joker in the pack.

"Oh my." Faye's raspy breath pulls me away from her husband. I examine my sister-in-law's face as she stares behind me, her eyes popping wide and her cheeks flushing.

Turning around, I urge Austen to come forward with a jerk of my head. He's been holding back on purpose. Giving me time to greet my brother and his wife. As I look around, it's only family here now, so I take hold of Austen's hand when he reaches my side, gripping it firmly. Though my guy is super confident, this has got to be daunting for him.

More of my family spills into the lobby from the living room, emitting excited shrieks when they spot Faye and Ky. You'd swear it was four years, not four months, since we last saw them. "This is Austen," I say, introducing my boyfriend to them.

"Um, wow. Keats was right," Faye says. "Your picture didn't do you justice."

Ky rolls his eyes, sliding a protective arm around his wife's shoulders. "We didn't travel all this way for you to drool over Austen. Show some restraint, woman."

Austen grins. "It's good to meet you both. I know how happy Keats is to have you here."

Ky stretches out his arm, and my heart soars like it has wings as I watch my boyfriend shake hands with my brother.

I love all my brothers, but I'll always have a special bond with Ky. He was the one I was closest to—outside of Kent and

Keanu—growing up. He looked out for us in a way the others didn't, and I've never forgotten that.

"Good to meet you too. It's nice to see a smile on my brother's face again."

Faye and Ky get swallowed up by some of the others, and I spot my parents moving this way.

"Incoming," I warn just as Mom grabs Austen, hauling him into her arms for a hug. Mom is a big hugger, and I'd already forewarned Austen, so he's not fazed by her exuberance. She looks so petite bundled up against his tall frame, and it's almost comical.

"Austen. We are so happy to finally meet you." She pulls him down so she can kiss both his cheeks.

"Likewise, Mrs. Kennedy. Thank you for inviting me."

"Please call me Alex." She turns to my dad, yanking him forward. "This is my husband, James."

"You're very welcome, Austen," Dad says, clapping him on the back. "We look forward to getting to know you."

"Same, although Keaton talks about you all so much I feel like I know you already."

Mom beams, pulling me into her arms. "He's gorgeous," she says, way too loud. "And very polite. I approve."

Austen fights a smirk as he shares a knowing look with my dad.

I spy Lana peeking at me, and I haul her over. "This is my very talented famous writer sister-in-law," I say, introducing her to my man.

Her cheeks flush a little, from my compliment and my guy, I'm guessing. "Lovely to meet you, Austen," she says.

"It's good to meet you too." Taking her hand, he brings it to his lips. "Keats never misses an opportunity to boast about how amazing you are."

"Hmm," Kal says, slapping me on the back as he sidles up

next to us, eyeing my boyfriend holding his wife's hand. "You sure he's not into women too? Or is my wife so beautiful she can turn any gay man straight?"

"Kal!" Lana shrieks, her cheeks turning fire-engine red. "You promised to be on your best behavior!" She faces Austen. "Don't listen to him. He has zero filter, and he loves to shock." She pins her husband with a pointed look. "It's like having three children," she admits.

I chuckle, sliding closer to Austen out of a sense of protectiveness. "It's okay, Lana. I made sure Austen came here prepared. He knows exactly who to watch out for."

Kal tucks his wife into his side, pressing a kiss to her temple. "Don't pretend like you don't love it, honeybun. You love that I spout the shit most men don't have the balls to admit." He flashes Austen a wide smile. "All joking aside, it's good to meet you, man." He thrusts out his arm, and they shake hands. "I was just messing around."

"Like with the Porsche?" Austen asks, grinning. "Nice touch."

Kal puffs out his chest. "I thought so too. Keats *does* love his pink."

"You're so funny." I flip him the bird. "And I might just keep it that color, purely to spite you."

"Please do," he begs, wrapping his arms around his wife. "That I have got to see."

Keanu and Selena step forward, and Keanu shoots me an approving grin. Thank God for my other triplet.

Keanu has gone out of his way to touch base with me several times this week to ensure I'm okay, and we had a good talk this morning over breakfast. I know he's talked to Kent and he's trying to play peacemaker, which I love, but I told him not to do that, because I don't want him dragged into this any more than he is. I don't want him backed into a corner where he has to choose sides.

"I'm Keanu, and this is my wife Selena," he says, smiling at Austen. "We're glad to finally meet you." Selena gives me a subtle thumbs-up when Austen isn't looking, and I grin.

"Me too," Austen says. "Keats has been telling me all about Moonlight, and I think what you're doing is really great. I don't have a ton of spare time, but if I can do anything to help, you only need to ask."

"Thanks, man. Appreciate it," Keanu says.

"Perhaps, later, if you have time, you could look over the plans for the football field and assist us when it comes to recruiting a coach?" Selena suggests, smiling warmly at him.

"Consider it done. I'd love to."

I spend another few minutes introducing Austen to everyone else, and then we move into the main body of the house, where the party is raging.

Leaving Austen with Eva and Kade, I do a quick search of the house for Melissa, but she appears to be gone. Taking the steps to the mezzanine level, I duck into Dad's study to call her, leaving a message when she doesn't pick up. There isn't anything more I can do, so I head back to the party, trying not to worry about the mess I've caused.

We dance and drink until the early hours of the morning, eventually falling into bed sometime after four a.m.

"How's your head, birthday boy?" Austen asks the following morning, placing a kiss on the back of my shoulder.

"I've felt better," I admit, groaning when I lift my sore head from the pillow, wishing I hadn't drunk so many shots.

Austen chuckles. "Told you to drink more water." He tried plying me with water in between alcohol, but I was having too good of a time to listen to reason.

Hauling myself upright in the bed, I lean my pounding

skull back against the headrest as the covers pool in my lap. "I'm sure getting trashed on your twenty-first is a rite of passage," I say, gratefully accepting the bottle of water and pain pills he hands me. "The hangover from hell too," I add.

"I wouldn't know. Mine occurred at the start of our summer practice season, so I couldn't go wild."

"I'm thinking you had the right idea," I mumble, noticing he's dressed in sweats and a tee. "You got up?"

He chuckles. "Your observational skills still suck," he teases, planting a kiss on the top of my head. "I got up to find water and pain pills for you."

"Uh-oh," I say, grinning. "Did Mom corner you?" Mom is a super early riser. Comes from years of running her own global business and tons of early starts.

"She did." Austen crosses his feet at the ankles, looking relaxed. "Forced a ton of pancakes and bacon on me as she and your dad and Kaden and Keven grilled me."

I jerk up, banging my head off the wall, cussing. "Shit. You should've woken me."

Austen tilts his head, smiling. "It's cute you think I can't handle it on my own." He leans in, kissing me on the mouth, but I pull back, shaking my head.

"I'm sure I have the worst boozy morning breath."

"I don't care." He rubs my arm. "If I want to kiss you, I'll fucking kiss you."

My eyes search his. "Did it piss you off that we couldn't kiss at the party last night? Be honest."

"Truthfully? I hate hiding, but we found plenty of opportunities to steal a few kisses, and it was a great night. I've no regrets." He pecks my lips. "Stop worrying. It's cool."

"You sure you're okay to do the lunch thing today? Because I can make our excuses if you like."

We all chipped in to buy Keanu and Selena a boat as a

wedding present, but it's as much for our use as theirs. When Mom found out this is Austen's first trip to Boston, she spoke to Keanu, and he arranged to take it out today. The plan is to show Austen some of the sights from the water while we have a nice family lunch. It was a thoughtful gesture, and one I'd hate to turn down, but I don't want Austen to feel like he's being ambushed into it either. My family is a lot to take on.

He taps his fingers on his chin. "Do I want to have lunch onboard a luxury boat off Boston Harbor?" His smile is knowing as he holds my gaze. "I'm cool with lunch. You can't bail on your family. Especially when Faye and Ky came all the way from Australia to be here. I'm happy to hang with your family. I like them."

With one noticeable exception.

That sentiment doesn't need to be verbalized for me to know his comment doesn't extend to Kent. And I don't blame my boyfriend. Though Kent made himself scarce most of the night, whenever he was around, he made his disgust clear through pointed comments and poisonous looks.

I want to throttle him.

I am so mad and hurt on Austen's behalf. Mine too.

At least everyone else has made up for it, openly welcoming him, and it's helped to offset Kent's cold disdain.

A loud crash resonates from the hallway outside, and we jump up as one, dashing out into the corridor. A secondary crash echoes from Kent's bedroom, and I rush to his door without hesitation, yanking it open, scared something has happened to him.

All the blood drains from my face as I confront the scene in front of me. Kent is lying on his stomach in the bed, the covers only covering him from the lower legs down, his naked upper body on full display. His blue eyes, identical to mine, are wide-open, and the smug grin on his mouth is obvious in the extreme.

Melissa is sitting on the floor, in front of a bedside table that's fallen on its side, her hair all messed up, her red-rimmed eyes bloodshot and swollen. Her skin is flushed, and the red splotches on her cheeks confirm she was crying. Shards of broken glass surround her as she stares up at me with horror-stricken eyes. Used condoms litter the ground, leaving an even nastier taste in my mouth.

As if she's just noticed she's completely naked, Mel pins her legs to her chest, wrapping her arms around herself. "Keats, I—" She cuts herself off, sobbing.

"You fucking asshole," I seethe, pinning the full extent of my glare on my brother. "What the fuck have you done?"

Chapter Thirty
Austen

"**I** think that's pretty obvious," Kent says, the ugly sneer on his mouth enlarging. "Your ex deserved a proper dicking." Tugging the covers up to his waist, he wraps the sheet around himself, sitting upright and planting his feet on the ground. "It's not like you ever fucked her right."

Melissa continues to sob, her eyes flitting between Kent and Keaton, and I'm wondering what he ever saw in this girl. I get that she's hurting, but fucking his brother, his *triplet*, to get back at him is a real low blow. I work hard to maintain a neutral expression, but I want to rip both of them a new one. How fucking dare they hurt Keaton like this.

"What did you do to get her to agree to this?" Keaton asks, moving into the room in only his boxers. Swiping a T-shirt from the ground, he wordlessly hands it to Melissa.

Kent barks out a laugh. "I didn't have to do anything, brother." Kent stares at Keaton's ex as she pulls his shirt on over her head. "Mel has always had the hots for me."

"That's not true," Melissa blurts, swiping at the tears still flowing down her face.

She moves to stand, but Keaton shakes his head. "Don't move," he cautions. "You could cut yourself."

Kent snorts. "You're such a pussy. She just *fucked* me. Repeatedly, all night long," he says, really digging the knife in. "And all you care about is that she doesn't cut herself?"

"Melissa is single, and it's none of my business who she fucks, but I still care about her, and I don't want to see her hurt." He narrows his eyes at his brother. "I know that's a foreign concept to you, because you're a selfish prick who never thinks about anyone else." Keats looks to me over his shoulder. "Could you grab me some sweats and sneakers from my room?"

I leave, returning a minute later with his things. I hand them to Keaton, watching him get dressed so I don't have to look at his jerk of a brother, because right now, I want to wring his neck. This was a clear intentional move to hurt Keaton—on both their parts—and I've little patience or tolerance for either of them.

"Quit your sniveling," Kent snaps at Melissa, rubbing his brows. "Own your fucking shit like a grown-up." He lights a joint, taking a long drag on it, as he stares at the girl. "You weren't crying last night when my cock was in your cunt and I was fingering your ass."

Melissa's cheeks stain red, and she hangs her head as Keaton walks to her, lifting her up and over the broken glass. He sets her down before pushing the glass aside with the toe of his sneaker.

"Keats. I'm so sorry," she blurts, panic evident on her face. "I was drunk and hurting and—"

"What the actual fuck is going on here?" someone screeches in a high-pitched voice behind me, and I know things are about to head south.

Whitney barges into the room, pushing past me like a tornado hell-bent on causing maximum destruction. Her gaze bounces from Kent to Keaton to Melissa before landing on the used rubbers on the floor. Her hands ball up, and her nostrils flare as steam practically billows from her ears.

"Did you fuck her after fucking me?" she roars at Kent, shoving his shoulders.

He smirks, taking another drag from his joint. "Relax, babe. You're still queen slut. She was a lousy fuck."

I honestly don't have words for this guy.

Kent fixes Melissa with a look that has her whimpering and clutching on to Keats. I'm two seconds away from ripping her hands off him when my boyfriend does it for me, positioning her arms back at her sides and warning her with an obvious look.

Kent smirks before delivering his next blow. "She just lay there like a fucking retard while I drove my cock, my fingers, and my tongue into every hole. But I'm guessing that's all she knows."

"Kent. I'm warning you," Keats grits out, shaking his head as a sobbing Melissa reaches for him again. Keaton takes a step back, adding more distance between them. He glares at his brother, and I can tell he's close to his breaking point. At this stage, I *want* Keats to wipe that smug grin off Kent's face. "Shut your fucking mouth."

"A faggot doesn't know how to satisfy a woman," Kent continues, regardless. "It's no wonder the poor bitch just lies back and zones out."

Keats lunges at Kent at the same time Whitney charges at Melissa, pushing her to the floor. Keaton throws a punch in Kent's face, and it's hugely satisfying. Although, I wish I was the one swinging fists, because this is going to hurt my boyfriend in the long run.

Melissa screams, and I divert my attention to the girls, moving toward them while keeping an eye on the guys.

Whitney is sitting on Melissa's chest with one hand fisted in her hair as she yanks Melissa's head up and then slams it back down on the ground. Melissa claws her nails down Whitney's cheek as she fights to shove her off, and Whitney loses her shit, shouting obscenities as she punches Melissa in the face. Melissa screams again, bucking and thrashing as she tries to fight Whitney off.

Kent and Keaton roll off the bed onto the floor, swinging punches. My instinct is to protect my boyfriend, but I know he won't thank me for it, even if he'll regret this later. Instead, I pull an out-of-control Whitney off Melissa, knowing it's what Keats would want.

Kyler and Kalvin rush into the room, cursing under their breath as they race to their brothers, pulling them apart. I'm grateful Alex, James, Adam, and his girlfriend, Callie, are out walking and not here to witness this.

"Oh my God," Faye says from the doorway, a hand over her mouth as she surveys the mayhem.

Melissa is full-scale sobbing again, watching the mess she created from her position on the floor. Her nose is bleeding, her lip is busted, and her cheek is red and will most likely bruise. I have zero fucks to give, and little sympathy, because she started this when she chose to get revenge on her ex by sleeping with his brother.

"Stay out of this, Faye," Kyler shouts, attempting to wrestle Kent back. Vitriol is spewing from Kent's mouth, and if it wasn't for the raving lunatic female thrashing in my arms, I'd be all over his ass, beating him to a pulp.

Keanu sprints into the room, and I thrust Whitney at him, just as her elbow connects with my cheekbone. Stinging pain rips across my face as I reach for Melissa, offering her my hand, because she's going to get trampled if she doesn't stand up.

"Austen!" Keaton yells, wriggling in Kalvin's arms, still looking enraged. "Get Mel out of here."

"Lose my number, *Mel*," Kent roars. "I'm done with your boring ass."

Whitney goes apeshit, shouting insults and death threats at Melissa as Keven enters the room, his intelligent eyes quickly assessing the situation. "Whitney. Shut the hell up," he says. "Unless you want me to retrieve your father to come control you." His heated glare extends around the room. "Everyone, calm the fuck down." Cheryl pushes into the room, shaking her head. Keven looks at his fiancée, and some unspoken communication passes between them. He swings his gaze to me. "Get Melissa out of the house, Austen. Cheryl will meet you out front, and she'll drive her home."

I steer a trembling, sobbing Melissa out through the door, past the women gathered there. Cheryl has disappeared to get the car, I'm assuming.

"Austen," Faye says, appearing alongside me. "I'll come with you." I nod, appreciating the moral support. "Melissa." Faye gently touches her arm as we walk. "Are you okay?" She hands her a tissue.

Melissa shakes her head, sobbing as she dabs at her nose. "I didn't mean to do it. I don't even like Kent. He's always so horrible to me."

As if she just fell on Kent's cock. I resist an eye roll.

Faye perceptibly stiffens, and her worried eyes flit to mine. Her mouth opens and closes, and I take pity on her, voicing what I believe to be her concern.

"Were you aware of what you were doing?" I ask Melissa. "Was it consensual?"

She hangs her head, and Faye and I share another look.

"He didn't force me," she admits after a few tense beats. "In fact, he asked me several times if I wanted to do it. If I wanted to keep going." A strangled sob escapes her mouth. "We were both drunk, but he made sure." She lifts her head. "I willingly cheated on Keats."

A muscle clenches in my jaw, and I'm done holding back. "He's not your boyfriend, so you can't cheat on him," I say. "And using his brother in a deliberate attempt to hurt him for being true to himself is a really shitty thing to do. I hope you're proud of yourself."

"Don't fucking pretend like you know me." Her lips pull into a sneer, and I'm sensing I'm finally getting a glimpse of the real Melissa. "And I know Keaton better than you'll *ever* know him."

I glare at her, done trying to be nice. "I already know more about him after a few months than you know after years, because you never made any attempt to understand him. I don't know what your agenda was or is, but you're done. You should cut your losses and run."

"Keats has done nothing to deserve your petty revenge," Faye says, stomping to the front door and swinging it wide-open. "You may not want my advice, but I'm giving it to you anyway. Stay away from Keaton, and stay away from Kent. There is no scenario where this ends well." She drills her with a look I wouldn't want to be on the receiving end of. "I wasn't going to say anything, but screw that shit. I'm not holding back now."

I smother my proud smile, encouraging Faye to bring it all —claws, fangs, and everything.

"I've never been able to figure you out," she says. "And it always bugged me, but I see it clearly now. You're a fucking gold-digger. You just wanted to stick your claws into a Kennedy. You tried with Kent first, and when he brushed you off, you latched on to Keaton because he always sees the good in everyone and he would never have accepted your interest in him as anything but genuine. You've made little effort to get to know us, and you haven't integrated into the family like the other girls, because you honestly couldn't give a fuck about us. You just wanted the ring, the name, and the bank balance, and you were going to do your own thing. I'm betting you would've turned on the waterworks and refused to sign a pre-nup so you'd walk away wealthy after the inevitable divorce."

And there we have it, ladies and gentlemen.

The ugly truth, fully exposed.

I don't need to have been around these past few years to know that Faye has hit the nail on the head.

It all stacks up.

Why Melissa never pushed Keats when it was clear he wasn't into their relationship.

Why she didn't challenge him on his lack of interest in sex.

Why she tolerated the on-off nature of their relationship in recent times.

Keats even mentioned she was pressuring him to get engaged after they graduated high school.

Now it all makes sense.

That stupid, conniving bitch never truly cared for him. Keaton was just a means to an end for her. But now the ruse is up, and in a twisted form of poetic justice, Kent has just freed his brother from his residual guilt.

Karma is a beautiful thing.

Melissa glowers at Faye, with thinly concealed rage, before her face transforms to a more familiar mask. Her lower lip wobbles, and tears build in her eyes.

"You can drop the sob story because I'm not buying it," Faye says, crossing her arms. "You set out to reel Kent in, thinking you could switch your affections to him. Well, news flash. That will happen over my dead fucking body."

"Fuck you, whore," Melissa spits out, lunging at Faye.

I jump in between them, shielding Faye with my body as I push Melissa back. "It's time you left," I say, my tone cold and unforgiving. I don't care how the bitch is getting home. She can walk in her bare feet for all I care.

She spins around, as if to head back into the house, and I grab her elbow, stalling her. "The door is that way." I jerk my head at the open door.

"I'm not leaving without my purse and my clothes," she snaps, attempting to wrestle out of my grip. She didn't seem concerned about them before, and I'm guessing she planned to use that as an excuse to call Kent and try to manipulate him into meeting her.

"Here," Kyler says, storming toward us with a face like thunder. He shoves her clothes, shoes, and purse at her. "Leave and never come back here. You're not welcome." He looks over my shoulder, to where Faye is shielded behind my back, his face paling. "Are you okay?"

"I'm fine. Austen protected me."

Kyler nods at me, his eyes conveying respect and gratitude.

Faye slides out from behind me, moving to meet Kyler as he walks to her side. His eyes lower to her stomach before he checks every inch of her face. Seemingly satisfied, he pulls her into his arms before turning them around as the sound of a car engine rumbles from outside.

"That's your cue to leave," he tells Melissa.

"Fuck you all," she says as Cheryl pulls up in a black X5. Melissa flips us the bird before stalking outside and climbing into the car.

"At least we finally put the trash out," Faye says, resting her head on her husband's chest as she taps out a message on her cell. If I had to guess, she's warning Cheryl about what's transpired in the last few minutes.

"I never liked that girl," Kyler says.

"You haven't heard the half of it," Faye says, stifling a yawn.

"Welcome home," Kyler deadpans, shutting the door with his wife still in his arms. It's like he physically can't let her go. Like it would pain him to do so. They have this epic kind of love—the kind I want with his brother.

Faye looks over at me, and her lips kick up at the corner. "It wouldn't be a Kennedy family party without drama."

"So I've heard." I rub the back of my neck. "I know Kent is struggling to accept who Keaton is, but why would he treat his brother like this?"

"Kent is complicated," Kyler says.

"That's no excuse."

"It isn't, and he's really done it now," Faye says, sighing. She rubs her stomach absentmindedly, and it clicks in my head. "He's regressing, and Whitney is in a bad place again, and I just wish they would stay away from one another because it's making things worse."

"Wait? He was with Whitney again?" Kyler asks.

Faye nods. "I only found out last night. Whitney was upset because she had sex with him and then he brushed her off. Apparently, he's been meeting up with her on occasion in New York."

Wow. Kent really is a selfish asshole. *How does he get away with treating people he claims to love in such a shitty manner?* He doesn't get a free pass just because he's family. He has been vicious and vindictive, and unless he grovels at Keaton's feet, he is undeserving of forgiveness, in my opinion. I will respect whatever decision Keats makes, and I will hold my own feelings aside, but if Kent continues to treat my boyfriend like this, then all bets are off.

Chapter Thirty-One
Keaton

"Sorry everything turned to shit today," I tell Austen as we enter our apartment later that evening.

"It's cool. I'm happy to go with the flow." He deposits our bags on the floor in the hall and pulls me into his arms. His eyes scrutinize mine. "Are you doing okay?"

I place my hands on his shoulders while he grips my waist. "I'm fine." He arches a brow, and I smile. "Truthfully, I am."

"I thought learning the truth about Melissa would set you back, and I know you're pissed at Kent."

I shuck out of his arms, clawing my hands through my hair. "Let's order takeout and then talk."

Austen calls our order in with the Chinese place down the street while I grab a quick shower and change. When I emerge from my bedroom a short while later, I find my boyfriend lying lengthways on the couch, in sweats, yawning. "Tired?" I bend down to kiss his brow.

"It's been an eventful twenty-four hours," he says, lifting so I can sit down. He rests his head in my lap, and I wind my fingers in his hair, admiring his perfect face.

"It has." A smile plays across my lips. "I'm so happy for Faye and Kyler, and Rachel and Brad."

Lunch got canceled today after the showdown this morning. Kent stormed off back to Boston without telling anyone, so he missed my brother's big news—Faye is three months pregnant, and they're not returning to Australia. It was double the joy when Rachel started crying, which forced Brad to admit they are also expecting a baby, and the girls were an emotional mess when they discovered they are due to give birth only ten days apart. Of course, Mom was beside herself, and she's already planning baby showers and the addition of a new wing at the house for more rooms for her grandbabies, and it helped to defuse the tension from this rift between Kent and me.

"I figured it out when we were escorting Melissa out," Austen admits. "Kyler was very protective of Faye."

"He's like that on a normal day. I bet he barely leaves her side the entire pregnancy." Gently, I probe the bruise blossoming on Austen's cheek, thanks to Whitney's stray elbow. "Does that hurt?" I ask.

He shakes his head, looking amused. "It's a bruise, Keats. Relax."

His hands move to my face, his finger tracing over my cut lip and the swelling on my jawline. "Does that?"

"Not much," I reply, flexing my sore jaw. "And it was worth it, because I feel better after punching him a few times." It's a miracle Kent didn't inflict more damage because he's the stronger out of the two of us. Either he was subconsciously holding back or my anger leveled the playing field.

"He fucking deserved it," Austin seethes. His piercing green eyes lock on mine. "What are you going to do about him?"

"Nothing." I've thought this through on the plane ride home. "Kent is the one who owes me an apology, and I'm not reaching out to him to be rejected and verbally abused. If he wants to make this right, he needs to make the first move. I'm done making excuses for him, and I think we haven't done him any favors by always making allowances. He needs to be held accountable, and that's the standard I'm setting from now on."

"I agree." Austen peers at me curiously.

"What?"

"I'm surprised is all. I know you don't like conflict, and I know how much your family means to you. I thought for sure you'd be the one to extend the olive branch."

"I usually am, but that doesn't mean it's right. What transpired with Melissa today actually did me a favor. I can't continue being so fucking naïve. And I can't always be the one to make things right. I'm not carrying that responsibility anymore. I will accept responsibility for my own actions, and that's it."

He leans up, pecking my lips. "I'm proud of you."

"I'm not sure there's much to be proud of. I dated a girl who deliberately used me, and I didn't see it. And I punched my brother."

"Your brother deserved it, and Melissa is a bitch." Austen runs his hand up my chest. "I thought you'd still beat yourself up for it though. This is progress." He smiles, and I melt.

"It doesn't condone what I did, but it's helped me make my peace with it. She was deceiving me, and I was deceiving her."

"I don't think it's the same, but I get what you mean, and I'm just glad you've put it behind you."

"It's funny how I feel lighter today," I admit as the doorbell chimes.

Austen jumps off the couch to answer it while I wander to the kitchen to grab plates and silverware.

"Not really, when you think about it," Austen says, continuing the conversation when he enters the kitchen a minute later. He starts unpacking cartons from the paper bag. "Though Melissa didn't confirm Faye's theories, it was clearly the truth, and that knowledge has released you of the guilt you felt toward her. If she's miserable, it's her own fault because she knowingly targeted you. And as for your brother, he knew what he was doing when he slept with her."

"He'll regret it." I grab two waters from the fridge. "Someday, Kent is going to regret so much of the shit he's pulled. I'm really mad at him, but I can't help feeling sorry for him too. I know what it's like to be lost, and I don't wish that for my brother."

"You sure you don't want to come home with me on Wednesday?" Austen asks when we're in bed later that night.

"And watch you and Gia in action?" I shake my head. "No thanks. Besides, Mom will kill me if I don't come home for Thanksgiving." If it wasn't for Austen's football and a few tests I have to take, I probably would've just stayed at home all week.

He's quiet, too quiet, and I turn on my side so I'm facing him. "What's on your mind?"

He's flat on his back in bed, staring at the ceiling.

I rub circles on his chest with my finger, waiting him out.

Austen twists his head sideways, looking at me. "I think, when I come back from Thanksgiving break, I'm going to tell Coach and the team I'm gay."

"You're sure?"

He nods, taking my hand and placing it over his heart. He rests his hand atop mine. "Being with you has reminded me of how good it feels to be *me*. I can't hide who I am anymore." His eyes peer deep into mine.

"What about us?" I ask, understanding why Austen needs

to do this, but I'm not ready to be part of an openly gay relationship on campus.

"Nothing changes. I know you're not ready, and I'm okay with that."

"Will it be enough?"

"Yes." Confidence rings through his tone, and he pulls my hands to his lips, kissing my knuckles. "I'll be much happier when it's all out on the table, but I understand why that can't happen now, and I will never force you, Keaton. Never."

"What about the NFL?"

Austen shrugs. "I've thought of this for more than two years, Keats. I'll handle the fallout. If the NFL doesn't want me, purely because I'm gay, then fuck them. I don't want to play with a team who judges me on my sexuality and not my performance. I'm prepared to live with the consequences."

I lean down, kissing his mouth. "Every day, you give me more reasons to be proud I'm your boyfriend. I only hope I can be as brave as you one day."

He sits up, pushing me back on the bed. "You already are." He fuses his mouth to mine, and we kiss as our hands roam naked flesh.

Sex with Austen is out of this world, and we're very active, but I still haven't bridged that last distance, and I want to now. Maybe it's because I've let go of a lot of guilt today, or the prep we've taken to get to this point has paid off, or I just love this guy so fucking much I want to do this with him, but I'm ready now, and I don't want to waste another second.

Ripping my lips from Austen's, I grab his shoulders as I stare into his eyes. "Fuck me, man. I want you inside me."

Austen examines my face, and a slow smile graces his gorgeous mouth. "You're one hundred percent sure?"

"Yes. I want this with you. I want your dick in my ass."

Austen strips back the covers while I retrieve lube and condoms from the drawer.

He hovers over me, his eyes awash with desire and searing-hot emotion. "Thank you for trusting me with this. If I do anything you don't like or you want me to stop, just say the words."

"Kiss me, man." I grab the back of his head, yanking his mouth down to mine. We thrust and grind against one another, our cocks sliding together as we kiss, and I fondle the cheeks of his ass, pushing my finger into his hole like I know he likes.

"You keep doing that, and this'll be over before it's started," he rasps, grazing his teeth along my neck.

"Don't draw this out. I need you now," I admit as he moves slowly down my body, nipping, licking, and sucking. When he reaches my cock, he lowers his mouth over my crown while nudging my thighs apart. I spread for him, not feeling the slightest bit vulnerable, purposely relaxing myself, refusing to let my head interfere with this. Austen lubes his fingers before sliding them in my ass, gently teasing me open. I've had his fingers in my hole before, and I love how he strokes my inner walls and the care he brings to his every touch.

My cock jumps in his mouth, the muscles on my shaft straining as my balls tighten a little. I don't want to come like this, but I don't need to voice that, because my boyfriend knows me by now. I slide out of his mouth with a pop as he kneels, grabbing a condom. "How do you want this?" he inquires, his eyes never leaving my face as he rolls the latex over his hard cock.

"Same way we did it the first time. Like this. I want to look into your eyes when you thrust inside me for the first time."

Austen leans down, kissing me hard. "Do you have any idea how hot you are? How horny you make me?"

I shoot him a teasing smile, staring at his long, thick, straining length. "I think I have some clue."

Austen pulls one of my legs over his shoulder, pressing my other leg up and into my chest as he positions himself at my entrance. His cock inches in a little, and I instinctively tense up. "Relax, babe." He massages my lower belly while his lips brush against my lips in a tender kiss. He eases in a little more, and I focus on his face and the feel of his warm mouth against mine, letting my limbs sink into the bed. "Fuck, you are so tight," he grits out, pushing in a bit more.

"You feel good, but I need more," I say, tugging his mouth down and pressing a firm kiss to his lips. "I'm not fragile, man. Move."

Austen inspects my face, ensuring I'm telling the truth before he thrusts the rest of the way in, and my muscles hug him tight.

"Oh, holy fuck." I squeeze my eyes shut, letting my body adjust to the fullness and the feel of him pressed deep inside me.

"You good?" He sweeps his fingers across my face.

"Yeah." My scratched throat is hoarse, and my eyes are damp as I open them and look at him. "I love you, and I want you to hold nothing back." I grab his ass, pulling him in even closer, and fiery tingles shoot up my spine when he starts to move.

We kiss as we fuck, and I wrap one ankle around his back, holding him close, as he picks up his pace. The sensations are like nothing I've ever experienced, and I know I could get addicted to this feeling like I'm already addicted to him.

Austen circles his hand around my shaft, matching his strokes with the thrusts of his hips, and the outside world ceases to exist for me. There is just us, and the sound of skin slapping against skin, and the pleasure building and building inside me.

Austen pivots his hips, thrusting deeper, his eyes flashing with dark desire, as he presses against my prostate, once, twice, three times, and I'm a goner.

I roar out his name as I detonate, surrendering to the headiest orgasm of my life. Cum oozes from my cock, and my hole tightens around Austen's dick as he continues rocking into me. Sweat beads his brow and glistens on his chest as he pulls out abruptly and rips off the condom, hovering over me as he jacks off. Ropes of cum spray against my chest as my boyfriend orgasms on me, and I can't stop the tears from leaking from my eyes.

Austen slides onto his side alongside me, his eyes scrunching with concern as he watches me cry.

I shake my head before he reaches the wrong conclusion. "Happy tears," I croak, barely able to speak over such powerful emotions.

"I love you." Austen pulls me into him, ignoring our sticky chests and abs. He plants a line of kisses all over my face and my jaw. "And that was incredible." He holds my face in his palms. "Was it good for you?"

A burst of laughter erupts from my mouth, and I press my forehead to his, staring into his eyes, my heart so full of love for this man who has turned my world upside down. "It was everything, Austen. You're everything, and I never want this feeling to end."

Chapter Thirty-Two
Austen

"**I** didn't find anything we could use against him, but I've wiped all copies of the video from Brock's hard drives and the cloud," Keven Kennedy explains through the phone. Keats has me on speakerphone while he talks face to face with his FBI-agent brother, at their parent's house, about his blackmailer. "But I don't know if he took any physical copies. I can send a guy to his place to search it."

"Don't bother," Keats says. "Austen already checked his place and found nothing."

"That wasn't wise," Keven says. "You both need to stay out of this. You've too much to lose if this gets out."

I think Keven has a lot to lose too, except he's a genius hacker who knows how to completely hide his less-than-legal activities. "I covered my tracks, and it was weeks ago," I say. "If Brock was aware I'd been in his place, we'd know by now."

"From now on, leave it up to me. I'll keep monitoring his cell and email activity, but I see nothing which gives me cause for concern," Keven says.

"What about Dax Madden?" Keats asks. "Did you find anything on him?"

"Actually, I did." Keven pauses for a second, and I hear a door close. "It seems Dax was having an affair with one of his married professors back in Denver. He blackmailed him into calling in a favor with a friend who sits on the Berkeley board."

It's like I never knew the guy. "That son of a bitch didn't earn his MFA place. He used his lover's contacts to secure him a position."

"That makes me sick," Keats says. "There are only twelve places available for that program, and he stole one from someone more deserving."

I don't mention that Dax is actually a phenomenal artist because it's neither here nor there, and I won't defend that lying, cheating piece of shit. "You have proof?" I ask.

"Enough to be damning," Keven replies.

"Send me the files."

"What are you planning to do?" Keats asks.

I lean back in my chair, eyeing the door when I hear footsteps in the hallway outside. Dinner is nearly ready, so I'll need to wrap this up quick. "I don't know. It's a tough call."

It's a tricky situation. Now that I've decided to come clean with Coach and the team, Dax is no longer a threat to me. However, he's a threat to Keaton, and I'll do everything in my power to protect his secret. I could go to Dax with this knowledge and threaten him into keeping quiet, but it would show my hand. It indicates how desperate I am to keep Keaton's sexuality and our relationship on the down low and that worries me. I've no clue how much Dax actually values the MFA. I'm not arrogant enough to think he manipulated the situation to come here specifically for me, so I guess the MFA holds some value for him.

But enough to stop him from destroying my boyfriend and

trying to split us up? That, I don't know. And it's why it might make more sense to hold this in reserve. "Are you monitoring his email and cell activity too?" I ask Keven.

"Yes, and I can continue doing so, for both guys, as long as they present a threat. I've also set up keyword alerts on my system, so if either of them mention anything about either of you, I will receive a notification."

"What do you think we should do, Kev?" Keats asks.

"I think you should sit tight and let me handle this. For now, we've done all we can. I'll monitor both guys and let you know if I spot anything suspicious in their communications. If either of them plan to cause trouble, I'll see something in their call or email logs, and we can take preventive action then."

The door opens, and Mom pokes her head through. "Who are you talking with?" she asks, frowning a little.

"My roommate and his brother." I don't feel the need to lie.

"Dinner is almost ready, but I need you to check on Gia. I think she's had a little too much to drink. I sent her up to your room to lie down."

"Okay. I'll be right there." I implore her with my eyes until she backs out, closing the door. "I've got to go," I say into my phone.

"Happy Thanksgiving, man," Keven says.

"Same to you, and thanks again."

"No worries. Family comes first." Footsteps echo down the line as he walks off.

"I miss you," Keaton says, the instant I hear the door closing. "It's becoming problematic how I can't seem to be apart from you these days."

"He loves me," I tease, deliberately lowering my voice.

"I do." His wistful sigh filters down the line.

"You'll be at the game on Saturday?"

"Wild horses couldn't keep me away."

I grin. "Only two more days. You can manage." I stand, stretching my arms up over my head. "I best go check on Gia. FaceTime you later?"

Keaton snorts out a laugh. "As if you have to ask. Enjoy your dinner. Say hi to Orwell for me." He doesn't ask after Gia, but I don't blame him. If the situation was in reverse, I wouldn't be pleased at the thought of him sharing Thanksgiving with his fake girlfriend.

"This will be the last time," I promise, in an attempt to reassure him. "After I've told Coach and the team next week, I won't need to hide. I'm planning to fly home that weekend and tell my parents."

"You're really going through with it," he murmurs. I know I've given him a lot of food for thought this week.

"Yep, and I already feel happier having made that decision. I've set up a meeting with Coach for first thing on Monday."

"Good for you, man."

"Do you really mean that?"

"Yes." There is no hesitation in his voice. "Your strength inspires me, and each day I'm feeling stronger and…"

"And?" I coax, encouraging him to go on.

"And I'm wondering now if it's better to control the narrative."

"I'm not following," I say, walking to the window and looking out over the front lawn.

"Maybe I should fess up. Like you said a few weeks ago, not make a big deal of it. Release a two-line statement and just get on with my life."

"Why?" I ask, because I know he's terrified of coming out to the world. And with due cause. Silence pursues, and I drop back down in the chair. "What's going through your head, dude?"

"I know what Kev just said, but I don't trust Brock."

"I don't either. Or Dax," I add.

"I just know this hasn't gone away. Brock is a shrewd bastard, and it would be better if I outed myself to the world before he releases that tape, because I've got to face the facts. That tape is a gold mine, and he needs money. He's smart enough to have made a physical copy of it."

I agree, but I don't articulate that thought.

"I support you coming out, on your own terms, but I don't want you feeling pushed into a corner. Especially not on my account," I add, because I know he's holding some stuff back.

He sighs. "It's impossible to hide anything from you."

I grin, even though he can't see me. "We don't keep secrets from one another, Keats. Spill."

"Right now, he doesn't know about you. You're going public, and it won't take much to connect the dots. He could use that tape to try and discredit you as much as me, especially when I know he'll want revenge for the beatdown you gave him. I don't want my mistake to blow back on you."

"It won't."

"You don't know that." Exasperation is clear in his tone.

"It's a risk I'm willing to take."

"That there!" Keats says, his voice elevating a few levels. "That's what I'm talking about."

A loud rapping on the door reminds me Mom is still waiting on me to attend to my fake girlfriend.

"Look, we need to talk about this face to face not over the phone. I'll let you cook me dinner on Saturday night after the game, and we can talk it all through then."

"I just don't want to be a burden, man," he quietly says, and I fucking hate that I'm not there to pull him into my arms and reassure him.

"Keaton. You could never be a burden. Never. This is a complex situation, but we'll figure it out."

"I love you." He says it loud and proud.

"I love you too."

"Go. I'll talk to you later."

"Gia." I gently shake her shoulders, urging her to look at me. She's rolling around my bed, laughing and talking to herself, and it's clear she's in some other realm. "Gia!" I raise my voice, lightly gripping her chin and forcing her face to mine.

"Austen!" She singsongs, flinging her arms around my neck. She tries to pull me down on top of her, and I grab her wrists, pinning them lightly above her head as I stare into her eyes, silently cursing.

"What the fuck did you take?" I hiss, knowing she's not drunk.

She's high.

During Thanksgiving, when we're surrounded by family.

She writhes underneath me, bucking her hips up. "I'm horny. Fuck me."

"What the actual fuck, Gia?" I release her wrists, sitting on the side of the bed with my head in my hands. I have never seen her like this, and it scares me. This slaps of addiction and an out-of-control habit I'm ill-equipped to deal with. It's also a wakeup call because I'm realizing I don't know who she is anymore.

"Baby." She crawls toward me, dropping into my lap in only her underwear. She rotates her hips against my pelvis, and I lift her off me.

"Stop it. Stop touching me."

She kneels, unclasping her bra and baring her breasts.

Spying her phone on the bedside table, I snatch it up. "I'm

calling Hendrix." Let her actual boyfriend deal with this, because he's the reason she's in this mess.

"It doesn't matter," she says, reaching out for my dick. "He can't answer from the police station."

"What?" My finger hovers over the keypad of her phone. "Why is he at the police station?"

"He was arrested. Someone ratted him out for dealing. He got caught red-handed."

He managed to evade jail time the first time he was caught with drugs, but there's no way he'll avoid it a second time. "When did it happen?"

"Last night."

She makes a grab for my dick, and I swat her hand away. At least I know why she's trashed.

"I love him, and I can't lose him again." Gia flops back down on the bed, and a sob rips through the air.

"Maybe stop trying to fuck *me* then." I throw her bra and her dress at her. "And put your damn clothes back on."

She turns on her side, flicking her fingers against her nipples. "Don't you find me attractive, Woody?" Her fingers glide down her stomach, dipping into her panties. "Don't you want to see how I taste?"

"No, Gia." I stand, running my hands through my hair. I officially have no clue what to do. I'm not experienced at handling horny, high women.

"I need sex now, baby. And you're my boyfriend. You owe me."

Anger pounds through my veins. "I'm not your fucking boyfriend, and I owe you nothing, Gia." I glare at her, but it's pointless because she most likely won't remember this. "You're the one who owes me the truth. How long have you been doing drugs?"

She shrugs. "Who cares?"

"I. Care. And I'm betting your parents will too." I storm across the room, ready to get her parents, because I'm done. It's clear she needs help, and I can't do it alone.

"Austen! Wait." She stumbles off the bed, falling to the floor. "Oh my God."

I turn around in time to watch her vomit all over the carpet.

I run to her side, shoving the trash can under her face.

"I'm sorry, Woody," she cries, in between heaving. "I'm sorry for hitting on you. Don't tell them, and don't leave me. You can't leave me too."

I'm still thinking about Gia, wondering what the fuck to do about her, as I enter the locker room on Saturday morning. Keats suggested I tell our parents the truth so Gia can get the help she obviously needs, but I couldn't do it to her. She turned up sober and apologetic yesterday morning, begging me not to tell them yet. While she's promised she's going to stop, I don't believe her. I've never seen her like that. She spent the entire Thanksgiving dinner asleep in my bed. I made excuses for her. Told them she had a stomach bug, and they seemed to buy it, but for how long?

Anyway, I've told her I'm telling them the truth about our fake relationship next weekend because I'm done lying, so she has one week to decide what she wants to do.

All heads turn in my direction as I dump my bag on the bench. "What?" I ask, looking at my teammates as they stare at me. Bile swims up my throat as trepidation mounts. A group of guys are huddled around Nolan, watching something on his cell.

Fuck, no!

"Did you know Kennedy was a fucking pervert before you

moved in with him?" Nolan shouts, walking toward me with a hard-to-read expression on his face.

"I don't know what you're talking about," I lie, rolling my shoulders, getting battle-ready.

"Your roomie is a sick bastard," he hisses, shoving his cell in my face.

All the blood drains from my body as I watch the clip. Keaton is clearly visible in the video, but Brock's and Rod's faces have been hidden.

Red-hot rage races through my veins, and visions of squeezing the life out of Brock Jonas swarm my mind. This is going to devastate Keaton, just as he found the courage to take the situation by the balls. Now Jonas has robbed him of that control, and he'll spiral. Nolan's sneering, jeering face enrages me further, and I grab his cell, throwing it at the wall, watching it smash into smithereens with grim satisfaction.

"What the fuck, man?!" Nolan shoves me, and I stumble back into my locker.

"That's an invasion of his privacy," I say through gritted teeth, talking loudly for the whole room to hear. "And none of you should be looking at it."

"Protective, aren't we?" Nolan tilts his head to the side. "Why is that? Huh?" He moves to shove me, but I get there first, slamming my hands into his shoulders, pushing him away from me.

"He's my friend and a decent human being who's been shit on." I glare at the other guys in the room. "How the fuck can you all stand there and look at that when it's obvious it was filmed and posted without his consent?"

"The fucking faggot deserves it for screwing two guys at once and letting them film it," Nolan says, deliberately ignoring my comment. "That asshole deserves to be taken down a few notches. He thinks he's so fucking superior to all of us."

"Watch your filthy fucking mouth," I yell, clenching my fists and digging my nails into the palms of my hand. I'm seconds away from tearing into this dickhead.

"Austen." A heavy hand lands on my shoulder, and I look up at Colton. "He's baiting you on purpose. Ignore him."

"Anyone would think," Nolan continues, puffing out his chest and sneering, "that you're a fucking faggot too by the way you're jumping to his defense." Alan nods in agreement at Nolan's side.

"I think that's enough, Nolan," Preston says the same time I say, "So what if I am? What difference does it make?"

Colton subtly shakes his head, but I'm in way too deep now. Screw this. I jump up on the bench, casting a glance around the room. "This wasn't the way I wanted to tell you, but I'm not ashamed to admit I'm gay. If anyone has a problem with it, take it up with Coach."

Coach will be pissed I've blurted it out without talking to him first, but I'm not going to stand here and let Nolan verbally abuse Keats and drop homophobic slurs.

"I fucking knew it!" Nolan glares at me. "I fucking knew shit didn't add up with you." His gaze roams me from head to toe, and his lips curl into a snarl. "You sick motherfucker." He raises his voice, addressing the room. "That twisted pervert has been ogling us naked for more than two years! Bet he jerks off in the shower the second he leaves the field."

Jumping from the bench, I lunge at the asshole, but Colton and Preston hold me back. "Fuck you!"

"No thanks!" he snaps, shoving his face in mine. Alan squares up alongside him while most of the rest of the team hold back, sharing troubled looks, unsure what to do.

I glance around the room. "That's a ridiculous accusation and completely unfounded. I would never disrespect any of you like that. I'm gay, not some deviant sexual predator."

Nolan snorts. "You said it."

I work hard to put a leash on my anger. "Why do you feel so threatened, huh? Are you worried about your own sexuality, or you think you're so irresistible that no gay man could control himself around you?"

He gnashes his teeth, and his eyes narrow as he steps toward me, shoving his chest up against mine, and I'm guessing that's to try to prove a point. "How typical of you to deflect from the real situation. The point is, you lied to us."

"Quit the bullshit," Colton says. "You don't give a fuck about that. You've always felt threatened by Austen. Now you think you have an opportunity to redress the power balance, but you're wrong. That's not happening on my watch."

"You're an asshole, Nolan, and you're the last man I'd check out because everything about you is abhorrent to me." I struggle against Colton's and Preston's holds. "Let me go."

"Don't do anything stupid, man," Colton says low under his breath. "He's not worth losing your career over."

"I know that. I just want to explain," I murmur under my breath, and my friends release me.

Ignoring the homophobic jerk in front of me, I address the rest of my teammates. "I'm sorry I didn't tell you the truth from day one. My high school coach advised me against coming here as an openly gay football player, and I've regretted making that decision because not being true to myself has slowly been killing me. I was openly gay the whole way through high school, and it's not something I've ever felt ashamed about. My coach convinced me it would hurt my career, so that's why I hid that part of myself. But I've had enough. I didn't want to lie to anyone. Especially not any of you." I take my time looking at each of my teammates, hoping they see the truth on my face.

"I scheduled a meeting with Coach for Monday, and I was going to tell him and then talk to all of you. I assure you I'm the same person you've known for the past few years. This doesn't change anything for me, and I hope it doesn't change anything for you. I don't judge you based on who you sleep with, and that's all I ask in return."

"This doesn't change anything for me," Preston says.

"Or me," Colton adds, looking around the room. "Austen nails it on the field, and that's all that counts."

"You honestly expect us to be okay with this?" Nolan says, incredulity dripping from his tone. He looks at the confused faces surrounding us. "We're expected to be okay changing and showering with a faggot knowing he's imagining a hundred different ways to fuck us in the ass?"

I see red, and I explode, grabbing hold of his shirt and slamming him back against the lockers. His fist darts out, and I don't move fast enough. Pain splinters along my bruised cheekbone, and I stumble back. Alan swings his fist, and Colton moves to block him, and they get into it as Nolan comes at me again. I thrust my fist in his face, enjoying the pained sound he releases and the burst of blood sprouting from his nose. Recovering fast, he comes at me again, but Preston pushes him back, screaming at both of us to stand down.

A shrill whistle rings out, and my stomach drops to my toes as the room instantly mutes.

"Hayes, Nolan, Cummings, and Barnes!" Coach roars, his face like thunder. "In my office now!"

Chapter Thirty-Three
Keaton

"I'm sorry, Mom. I'm so, so sorry," I say for the umpteenth time. This is my every worst nightmare come to life, and I'm so ashamed. I can barely look my family in the eye.

"Honey, stop, please." Mom hugs me tighter while Dad makes coffees for everyone in the kitchen.

The instant Keven became aware of the video, he rallied the family, and Dad flew Mom, Keven, Kaden, and Eva here. Kyler and Faye called in the middle of a massive argument because she wanted to come to support me, but Kyler was worried about her safety, and I had to agree. She's pregnant, and we can't risk anything happening to her. Faye hates having to stay in Wellesley, but she won't put her unborn child's life at risk either, so she eventually conceded.

Reporters and TV crews have descended on Berkeley in droves, and there's a bunch of vultures camped outside my apartment building, salivating at another Kennedy scandal, just waiting to slice the second layer off my sanity.

I called the rest of my family, telling them not to come here. Having all the Kennedys show up en masse would only create a bigger media storm. I couldn't keep my parents away, and I need Keven. Kade and Eva are talking to the college administration right now, seeing what measures they can put in place. An ex-colleague of Eva's is a professor here, and she helped to set up some meetings for them. I'd be a fool to have turned down their help, so I didn't object to them coming either.

"This isn't your fault, son." Dad hands me a coffee. "Though you should have come to us the minute that asshole threatened you."

"I was embarrassed, Dad." I look up at him as pain hammers my skull. "I *am* embarrassed." I squeeze my eyes shut. "Now the whole world knows my secret. And everyone has seen me like that." I collapse against my mother, and I just want to die.

"It could be worse," Keven says. "At least it's only a two-minute clip."

I jump up, shouting at my brother. "Two minutes is enough to ruin my reputation for life!" I yell. "And how long do you think it'll take before someone uploads the full video?"

"The lawyers are working on it," Dad confirms. "Dan Evans just called. He says GayPornNet4U will have to remove it from their site within the hour."

"The PR people are working with the lawyers on a blanket statement to issue to the media and all social media sites. If they publish it or facilitate anyone else to publish it, we will sue. They will be left in no uncertain terms about that," Mom says.

"My colleagues are working with the FBI specialist technical team to remove it from the web," Kev says, adding, "And I've set up a ton of search terms to track any they might miss. It'll be blacklisted in next to no time."

I flop back down on the couch, elbows on my knees,

burying my head in my hands. "Sorry for shouting at you," I tell my brother. Kev nods in understanding. "I know you're doing everything you can to help. But it's too late. It's out there now. We'll never be able to remove every trace of it." People will still share it privately, and there isn't a thing I can do about that.

"We will damn well try." Steeliness reverberates through Mom's tone. "Our PR people are preparing a press release. Our lawyers will get an injunction to stop that horrid porn company from selling the video, and arrests will be issued for Brock Jonas, Rod Williams, and Dax Madden in a matter of hours."

"What has Dax got to do with it?" Austen asks from behind me, and I jump up, racing toward my boyfriend. I haven't spoken to him in hours. I don't even know how the game went or if Coach made him sit for the first quarter like he threatened after the altercation in the locker room.

"Are you okay?" I ask, examining the swelling on his cheek, right in the place where Whitney bruised him.

He presses his forehead to mine, clasping my shoulders. "I'm fine. Are you okay?"

Tears prick my eyes, and I can't speak over the lump in my throat.

Austen grabs the back of my head, wrapping his arms fully around me, holding me close. "It will be okay," he murmurs. "We'll get through this together."

"How?" I croak. "I can't show my face around campus after this."

Austen cradles my face between his palms. "You can and you will, because I'll be with you every step of the way."

"And we've got your back too," Kate says, sauntering into the apartment, followed by Seb and Mol. I hug my friends, grateful they're here.

"I've assigned a protective detail to you and to Austen,"

Keven adds. "You'll have twenty-four-seven security. No one is getting near either of you."

He doesn't get it. The physical threat isn't the one I'm worried about. It's the looks, whispers, and taunts that will now follow me everywhere I go. Plus the inevitable blowback on Austen, especially when his news becomes public knowledge, and then the obvious connection will be made. I won't let this hurt his career. I can't do that to him.

"I know this is really shitty, Keats, and that bastard deserves to rot in jail for what he's done to you," Mol says, squeezing my arm. "But at least you don't have to hide who you are anymore." She looks between me and Austen. "You don't have to hide anything anymore."

"I know this isn't the way you wanted it to come out," Colton says, and I didn't even see him lurking at the back of the living area. "But Molly is right. It's out now, and you can still control the situation. No one knows about your relationship, so maybe you use that to put a positive spin on this."

"No." Austen and I speak at the same time, and I'm glad we're on the same page.

"I don't want this tarnishing Austen. He has enough to contend with without this damn media circus."

Austen squeezes my hand. "And I don't want Nolan and other homophobic jerks like him having further ammunition to go after you. Right now, keeping our relationship out of this is the right thing to do."

"Maybe we should ask our PR company for their input," Mom says, leaning in to kiss Austen on the cheek. "I understand you both want to protect one another, but it could end up helping." She looks to me. "Being in a loving, committed relationship will help negate some of the seedier allegations, and it might appease the NFL," she adds, looking at Austen. "Having an openly gay player in a committed relationship will be an easier sell for your agent."

"No," we both repeat again, smiling softly at one another.

Mom sighs. "Just think about it, and I'll see what Christina says." She moves away, to call our family's chief publicist. Christina is an expert at putting the right spin on things. Even so, I'm not going to use Austen to try to win back some brownie points with the media.

I made this mess, and I want to keep him out of it.

"You didn't answer my question about Dax," Austen says, glancing between me and Keven. Mom is on the phone, and Dad is ushering our friends into the living room, plying them with coffee and cookies.

Kev props one hip against the island unit. "Brock and Dax partnered up, and they sold the video to the porn company for a seven-figure sum." A muscle flexes in Austen's jaw. "It appears that Dax's uncle is part owner of the porn company, so he likely set up the deal."

"What the fuck?" Austen blows air out of his mouth, his confused expression fixated on me. "How did this happen?"

I shrug. "Our best guess is they somehow figured out that both of them were watching us, and they got talking and realized their goals aligned."

"That fucking asshole. I'm going to fucking kill him," Austen seethes.

"Get in line." I rub a hand across the back of my neck.

"How did they do this without us knowing?" Austen asks.

"There is no communication chain between them," Kev says. "At least not on their usual phones and email accounts. They obviously used burner phones and fake email accounts."

"So how did you even know Dax was involved?" Austen asks, still looking confused.

"The porn company was quick to confirm the identity of the sellers. They're hoping to pass the blame," Kev says.

"What will happen to them?" Austen asks.

"Brock and Dax are MIA," Kev says, "but not for long. As soon as those warrants are processed, we'll put out an APB on them, and we'll catch them. They're looking at forgery, extortion, and fraud charges. Trust me, they're going to get what's coming to them."

"Forgery?" Austen asks.

"The porn company anticipated this would happen, and they supplied paperwork this morning which we've already reviewed," Kev says.

"The bastards forged my signature on the consent papers," I hiss. It's not that difficult to find a copy of my signature online.

"It's a bad forgery," Kev confirms. "Our handwriting experts will discredit it, and the company won't have a leg to stand on. We just need to line everything up, and it takes time to cut through some red tape, but we will get it handled."

Austen nods, before turning to me. "I'm sorry, Keats."

I shake my head. "It's not your fault your ex is an asshole."

"I still brought him down on you. If he hadn't come here, Brock would never have met him and had a way to monetize the video." He looks away, and his shoulders slump.

"Hey." I grip his chin, forcing his gaze to mine. "Don't do that. The only ones responsible are Dax, Brock and Rod."

"What's Rod's part in all this?" he asks as Mom hangs up the phone. She moves to the living room, patting my arm as she passes by me.

"His signature is on the consent paperwork, but he's in a private rehab facility. I'm going up there with a colleague to interview him. He was either complicit—"

"Or they forged his signature too," I surmise, finishing Kev's sentence.

Kev nods. "Either way, I'll have that answer tomorrow."

Mom orders takeout when Kade and Eva return, and our friends take off, leaving us with my family.

I toss my prawn stir fry around my plate as I listen to my brother and his wife update us on the meetings they held today with campus administration and security.

The college has agreed to allow our security guards to enter school buildings and lecture halls, on the provision they're not armed, and they'll instruct campus security to keep reporters and TV crews off the grounds, but it's a tall order because the campus is large and the media is sneaky. But I can't fault their willingness to help.

It seems Austen's coach attended one of the meetings, and he's given his support to the measures, because he wants to keep Austen's focus on the game and he's keen to keep all mention of Austen's revelation from the media until this furor over me dies down.

The administration will allow me to attend classes online, if I want. I'm sorely tempted to take them up on their offer, but hiding away will only make things worse. If I want to stay at Berkeley, I've got to face this head-on.

I just hope I'm strong enough to do it.

"What happened with the game?" I ask Austen a couple hours later when we're in bed. Mom and Keven are still here, sleeping in the other two bedrooms, while Dad took Kaden and Eva home. They wanted to return to their kids, and there's nothing more they can do here. I tried to encourage Mom to go home too, but I know she's worried about me, and she refuses to leave.

"We lost, and Coach threw an epic hissy fit." He leans on his side, brushing his thumb along my lower lip. "I played my worst game ever. I couldn't concentrate for shit. I was too worried about you."

I don't want that for him. A new layer of guilt settles on my shoulders. "How were your teammates when you were leaving?"

He shrugs. "Most of them are still processing. Preston's and Colton's support will go a long way toward bringing the others onboard. Coach has warned everyone to keep their lips sealed. He wants to contain it to the team for the moment. He didn't hold back. He said anyone who talks about it outside will be kicked off the team."

"I'm glad he's stepped up for you."

Austen traces circles on my chest with his finger. "I'm not sure it's for me. He's in damage control mode, and he'll do what he has to, to protect the team."

"He wasn't outwardly hostile to you though, right?"

Austen nods. "He was pissed I didn't come clean from the start, but he seemed to accept my explanation."

"I think it's going to be okay for you." I smile. At least one of us might come out of this relatively unscathed, and I'd rather it was Austen.

"Nolan and Alan are going to be a problem."

"I want to lay that motherfucking asshole out cold." Anger resurfaces, and I know Austen didn't tell me the worst of it. I know he's sheltering me from a lot of the shit that went down in the locker room, and I hate he has to do that.

"You seem to be handling this okay," he says, staring lovingly into my eyes.

"I think I'm still in shock. Thank fuck tomorrow's Sunday and I have a day to prepare for next week. It's not going to be fun."

"You'll survive this, Keats. You're tougher than you think."

"I couldn't do this without you, and yet I hate that this exposes you too."

"Don't worry about me." He leans in, kissing me. "Just focus on yourself, and I'll focus on me, and then we'll be able to better support one another."

If only it were that simple.

Monday is a shitshow of epic proportions. Austen left first, for his usual early morning gym session, and he texted me to warn the media is out in full force in front of our apartment building.

Because we don't live on campus, there is nothing the college administration can do to help with the situation here. Mom and I spoke with the building manager yesterday, and she is less than pleased with me. This is an exclusive, highly sought-after building, and she fears my presence here will devalue the property.

Bitch.

She also said she's received several complaints from other tenants, and if the situation with the media doesn't die down soon, I will need to find somewhere else to live.

Mom quickly put her in her place, stating in no unequivocal terms that me living here for the past fifteen months has likely already increased the value. She also mentioned the fact the rent has been paid in advance, up until next summer, and she finished with a threat to sue the management company if they even attempt to throw me out.

I'd had an option to buy the place when I first moved in, but I chose to rent instead because I don't see myself staying permanently in Cali and it seemed smarter to just rent.

Now, I wish I'd given it more thought.

I don't know how long Mom's threat will work, but for now,

it seems I don't need to worry about being kicked out of my place. It's pretty pathetic to admit, at twenty-one-years of age, that I'm so fucking grateful my mom is here. Although I drew the line at her coming with me to campus today. That's something I've got to do by myself.

Reporters swamp my SUV when I exit the parking garage, and I'm grateful my brothers forced me to buy a car with blacked-out windows. I press down on my horn repeatedly, inching the car forward at a snail's pace, until I make it out onto the road. I guess the days of walking to campus are over with. For now.

The day is long and arduous with expected and unexpected outcomes. While the obvious finger-pointing and whispering was expected, most students have left me alone. I've had a few sleazy looks and a few shouted slurs, but equally as many sympathetic looks and offers of support. A guy and a girl from QARC, one of the LGBTQ groups on campus, approached me with an offer to join the group and attend one of their meetings. They gave me some info on other support groups, and it was the highlight of my day. I'm not sure I'll ever have the courage to actively participate, but knowing they took time out of their day to seek me out, to let me know I'm not alone, means a lot to me.

One of the reasons why I chose to come to Berkeley was the diverse student body, and they are known for their liberal views. I think, in time, things will probably settle down on campus, but I'll have to come to terms with the knowledge plenty of my fellow students have seen me at my most vulnerable, and that's the challenge.

Along with the media. Because it's clear they're not planning on letting this go anytime soon. At least, not until the next big scandal draws their attention away.

Despite having my bodyguard in the room and additional

security resources around the business campus, reporters managed to sneak into two of my classes, pouncing on me in the middle of lectures, forcing me to leave. Austen tried to leave too, but I wouldn't hear of it.

Now, more than ever, we need to create distance in public, because I won't let the media scum drag him down too.

Chapter Thirty-Four
Keaton

"I made dinner," I say when Austen arrives home after practice.

"Where's your mom?" He comes up behind me, resting his chin on my shoulder and placing his hands on my hips.

"I made her go home. There's nothing more she can do."

The video is gone from the porn site, and it's been removed from all the main social media sites, and the various teams are working to get it removed from everywhere else. However, that hasn't stopped gossip sites and news channels from reporting on it, and I'm still trending online.

I shut down all my social media accounts because I couldn't stomach the never-ending notifications, and reading the comments was doing nothing positive for my mental health. Though I have plenty of supporters, there are an equal number of trolls who are determined to tear me down.

I grab my wineglass, gulping back a few mouthfuls as Austen stares silently into space. "How was your day?" I ask, shucking out of his embrace to grab the vegetable mix I parcooked earlier.

"Fine."

Tossing the vegetables into the sizzling chicken in the skillet, I turn to face him, lifting a brow.

He leans back against the island unit. "Nolan and Alan were being their usual prick selves, but the rest of the team seem to have accepted it."

"So why the long face?"

He levels an intense gaze on me. "I'd have thought that's obvious. I'm worried about you."

"I'm fine," I say, returning my attention to the stir fry.

"You're guzzling wine at eight on a Monday night. You're not okay."

He's right. I'm not. Because a bunch of reporters were waiting in the parking garage when I came home and they heckled me all the way to the elevator. My bodyguard might have physically kept them away from me, but he couldn't magically glue their mouths shut.

"Are you gay or bi or pan, Keaton?"

"How often do you have threesomes?"

"Are you into orgies?"

"Are the guys in the video your boyfriends or fuck buddies?"

"Do you only bottom?"'

"Have you topped?"

"What do you have to say to those parents who state you are a bad role model?"

"What do your brothers think about you being gay?"

"Did you cheat on Melissa with other men?"

"Have you fucked any famous men?"

"Are you into BDSM?"

The questions came at me relentlessly, in quick-fire succession, and I tried to blank my mind, to ignore their rude, invasive questions, but I wasn't fast enough to block them out, and now they churn in my mind, tormenting me on a continuous loop.

And I just want it to stop.

The thought of everyone thinking they know me now, when they know even less about me, is suffocating. Everyone thinks they have a right to comment on my sexuality and my sex life, and I can't bear it.

At least in class, I had something to distract me from my own thoughts. Since I came home, all I've thought about is the shitshow that's my life, and it's the last thing I want to discuss with my boyfriend.

I just want everything to go back to the way it was. When I was happy. Not this miserable shell I'm barely existing behind.

"Just drop it, please," I implore Austen, turning the heat off on the stove and dividing the food between two plates.

"You can't bottle this shit up, Keats," Austen quietly says. "It'll rot your insides."

"You think I don't know that?" I say, handing him his plate. I hop up on a stool, and Austen sits on the one beside me. "Today pushed me to my limits. It wasn't all bad, but I don't want to talk about it. I want to leave all that crap at the front door when I come home every day, because it's the only way I can do this, man." I hang my head as intense pain threatens to drown me.

"Okay." Austen squeezes my shoulder. "Just know I'm here anytime you want to talk. Whatever you need, it's yours."

"I just want to return to pretending," I whisper, not able to look him in the eye when I say it. "I just want to pretend."

One week turns into two, and the media attention shows no sign of abating. Daily interview requests continue to pour in, especially in the wake of Brock's and Dax's arrests. Kev and his team located them in Hawaii, holed up in a five-star hotel, where they were apparently fucking their brains out. Oh, the irony.

Rod Williams was pivotal in helping track them down, and he's critical to the civil and criminal proceedings against them. It turns out Rod was a victim in this as well. Brock was holding something over him which forced his participation that night. Then he used the video as further blackmail, causing the guy to overdose and almost die. His parents intervened, getting him into a private rehab in SoCal. He didn't give his permission to release the video either, and it's already been proven that his signature was forged too.

Our legal team has spoken with Rod's, and we've joined forces to issue civil proceedings for damages against both guys and the porn company. Our attorneys are cooperating with the criminal proceedings the state is taking, and there's no doubt the guys are going down for this. Brock is also facing drug charges, because the police raid on his home found his stash, and both have been kicked out of Berkeley.

I've had little to do with all this, but Mom calls me daily, and she runs everything by me. Instead, I've retreated into my shell, and I'm comfortable inside it. I go to classes, do my best to avoid the paps, and keep my head down, and I'm a virtual recluse the rest of the time.

I know Austen is worried about me, and there's a distance growing between us that wasn't there before. I hate it, and I don't want to push him away, but I can't help how I feel. And right now, I just want to be alone.

"Keaton," Austen shouts from the living area of the apartment, and I drag my weary body from my bed, shuffling out to meet him.

"What's wrong?" I ask the second I see his face.

"That bastard Nolan went to the press," he confirms, holding out his cell. "He outed me, and he also alluded to a sexual relationship between us."

"Great." I sigh, rubbing at my temples. "Even I didn't think he'd be that foolish."

"He wasn't named in the article," Austen says, pocketing his cell before I've had time to read it. "It referred to him as a reliable source. Coach went apeshit. Called us all in early. Asked the guilty party to own up, but no one came forward. So, I spoke to Coach about Keven, and I called him from the office. Keven ran a cell trace and within an hour was able to prove Nolan had been in touch with the reporter. The idiot used his own phone."

"Please tell me Coach didn't lose his nerve. That the bastard was kicked off the team."

"It has to go before a disciplinary board, but he's been suspended, and I know Coach to be a man of his word. I doubt Nolan will be back on the team. At least something good has come out of it."

"Glad you can see the bright side," I mumble, crossing to the counter and grabbing the half-empty bottle of shiraz.

"Keats. I really don't think—"

"I'm not in the mood for a lecture, man." I pour a large glass of wine. "You know what this means?"

"We don't have to hide anymore. It's out there now, and there's no point denying our relationship." He takes the glass from my hand, putting it down on the counter. He holds my hips, pressing his forehead to mine. "Let the chips fall where they may."

I slide out of his hold. "I don't know how you can be so flippant about this! This will ruin your NFL career."

"I'm prepared for all outcomes," he says, and his cool demeanor irritates me.

"Don't do that! The NFL is your dream, and I've probably just cost you that."

"We don't know what's going to happen, and the fact we're in a relationship might actually help. I've been thinking about what your mom said and—"

"No!" I shake my head. "Don't downplay this. Tying yourself to me is a bad career move right now, Austen. I won't be the reason you lose out on the NFL."

Austen's jaw pulls tight. "Just say what you mean, Keats."

"Maybe you should move out." The words feel like poison as they leave my lips, and my throat constricts, like someone is strangling me.

"If you want to break up with me, at least have the balls to say it."

I don't.

I don't want to lose you.

I love you.

I think all those things, but I can't voice them. "This doesn't have to be permanent. I think putting some space between us right now is the best thing for both of us." I make a spur of the moment decision. "I'm going to go home until after Christmas. The administration has already said I can take my tests online." Reporters are still sneaking into lecture halls, and more than a few of my professors have suggested I log in for lectures instead of attending in person because I'm disrupting their classes, which isn't fair for them or the other students.

"You don't have to do that," Austen says, his voice cold and devoid of his usual warmth. "I'm flying to Denver after the game on Saturday night. I need to speak to my parents because this is going to blow up in the coming days. Coach said I could take a few extra days off." Austen was originally supposed to go home to tell his parents two weeks ago, but he didn't want to leave me alone with all this crap going on.

"I'd rather not be here," I say, reaching for him when his face drops. "It's not that I want to be apart from you, but I can't handle the media as it is. It's only going to get worse now they know about you and think they know about us."

"I know you're depressed," Austen says. "And I understand it, but don't push me away, Keats. Please."

I lift my damp eyes to his agonized gaze, and we move as one, our arms winding around each other. "I don't want to push you away, Austen. But I won't be the reason you miss out on your dream."

"That's not your decision to make," he says in my ear. "And if it happens, it won't be because of you or the fact we love each other. It will be down to narrow-minded judgmental assholes." He eases back, holding my face. "I've prepared myself for this scenario. I have my Plan B. But I haven't prepared myself for losing you, and I wouldn't survive that."

"I'm not more important than your career," I say, batting down the warmth trying to spread through me. "I'm just a guy."

"You're *the* guy, Keats. You've never been just *a* guy to me."

I press my mouth to his, kissing him tenderly, trying to pretend the pain rupturing my heart isn't almost killing me. "And you're that person for me too, but you don't know that you won't resent me in the future if I'm the reason you lose out on a place in the NFL. *I'll* resent *me*."

"Please, just promise me you won't make any rash decisions without talking to me. I know you're hurting. I am too. But that only means we need each other even more," Austen pleads, threading his fingers in my hair. "Don't give up on us, Keats. I'm begging you."

"I won't," I say, and it's the first time I've ever deliberately, willingly, lied to Austen's face.

I'm staring at the ceiling, listening to music, when my bedroom door swings open and Faye storms into my space. She flops down on the bed alongside me, tugging one of my EarPods out. "I need to speak to you."

I stop the music on my cell and remove my other EarPod, setting them on my bedside table. "What's up?"

"This has to stop because you're breaking my heart, and that can't be good for the baby."

I narrow my eyes at her. "Using your unborn child is a low blow and so beneath you."

"Keats." She rests her head on my shoulder, and I wrap my arm around her back, pulling her in close. "I'm worried about you. We all are."

I snort, because everyone knows Kent doesn't give a rat's ass about anything I'm going through. But I won't mention it, because everyone's treading on eggshells around both of us these days. "It's better here," I admit, because it's not as stressful at home as it was back in Cali.

"Liar," she replies, snuggling into my neck. "You're miserable as sin."

"At least I don't have to contend with the media here."

"You can't be a hermit for the rest of your life."

"I know, but it's more peaceful here, and I need to wallow in that for a while."

"I can't believe Melissa gave that interview. I want to go over there and slap her into the next century. It's either that or make a voodoo doll in her likeness and stab the shit out of it."

"I don't care about that," I truthfully reply. I mean, I'm hurt she'd try to kick me when I'm down, but it confirms what we already figured out. She was in it for the money and I'm sure she got a nice payday for that primetime interview. She really threw me to the wolves. "Except for the part where she criticized Austen and implied I'd been cheating on her with him. That pisses me off."

The PR people put out a press release denying her claims, subtly insinuating she's brokenhearted and saying things to spite me, but who knows what people will believe.

"You could sue her." Faye lifts her head, staring me in the eyes. "You *should* sue her."

"That will only prolong things in the media, and I want it to die down. The last thing I want is to be forced to confirm the details of my relationship with Austen in a televised courtroom. I'm trying to protect him, not make things worse." If we say nothing, and we're not seen together, the rumors will eventually die out.

"How is pushing him away protecting him?" she inquires, her features softening. "Because I know that's what you're doing."

"He's dealing with enough shit as it is without me adding to it." The media is having a field day with both of us. Every day, the headlines are dominated with Austen Hayes, Keaton Kennedy, and speculation over our relationship. It's a clusterfuck of epic proportions, and it shows no signs of going away.

We speak every night by phone, but there's a gulf separating us, and I'm not just talking about the physical miles separating us. "Things are tense, and I don't know what to say, or how to make it right, or if I even should."

"I hate this for you. You were so happy a few weeks ago. I want to round up the world's media, put them on an isolated island, and then push it out into the middle of the sea. A bit like *Survivor*. Except the end game is no one survives."

I chuckle, and she's the first one to make me smile in weeks.

She sits up, forcing me to sit up too. "I'm going to level with you. Austen is the best fucking thing that's ever happened to you, and I think you're making a mistake."

"I'm trying to do the right thing by him, and it's killing me. You think I want this?" I wave my hands in the air. "I don't fucking want this. I love him, and I miss him so much, but I've got nothing to offer him right now."

"Bullshit." Faye takes my hands in hers. "You have everything he wants and needs."

"I'm in a bad place, Faye," I confess. "And I'm scared I'm only going to drag him down to the gutter with me. And he's so good. So loyal. So talented. So dedicated. He deserves to see his dream come true. I couldn't live with myself if I ruined it for him."

"Every relationship has its ups and downs, Keats, and every relationship has outside pressures that threaten its very foundation. That's when it's time to batten down the hatches and fight, but you're giving up."

I open my mouth to protest, but she shakes her head.

"I know why you're doing this. This is classic Keaton. Your default setting is to put everyone else first, but it's time you put yourself first. I know it's what Austen wants you to do. Don't push him away. *Fight* for him. If you truly love him, don't let the media or Melissa or any other judgmental asshole take that from you. He's going through a hard time too, and he needs you. You need one another." She climbs off the bed, leaning down to kiss my cheek. "I just want you to be happy, and that guy is your happy place. Don't give it up. At least, not without fighting."

Chapter Thirty-Five
Keaton

I clasp my hands in my lap, staring at the landscape flashing by through the window of the taxi, hoping I'm doing the right thing. Austen says his parents are conservative, and they're bound to be pissed when they discover Austen and Gia have been lying, so Austen's boyfriend showing up out of the blue probably won't go down well. But I'm mere minutes from their house, so there's no backing out now.

Faye's pep talk cracked through my inner walls, and it was exactly what I needed to hear. I'm ashamed I've been so wrapped up in myself I haven't given any thought to my boyfriend's needs. He's got a lot on his plate too, and I can't abandon him. Especially when he's made it clear it's not what he wants.

So, I'm here to offer my physical, moral, and emotional support and to ask for his forgiveness, because he's been carrying our relationship since the video leak. And it's time I started pulling my weight.

The driver pulls up alongside the curb, pointing at the neat two-story house across the road. "It's that one there."

"Thanks, man." I hand him two hundred-dollar bills. "Keep the change."

I grab my overnight bag and climb out of the back seat, pulling the collar of my black, double-breasted wool coat up around my neck to combat the icy chill in the air. Austen wasn't wrong when he said it was cold in December, but it's not that different from home, and I came prepared.

Christmas is only five days away, and every house is decorated for the holidays, bringing a smile to my face. Christmas is one of my favorite times of the year, and I love spending the holidays with my extended family. Since my nieces and nephews arrived on the scene, it's become truly magical again, and I love seeing their excited faces and hearing their squeals of delight when they open their gifts.

I look left and right before crossing the road, gripping the strap of my bag firmly as I head toward Austen's house.

The sound of laughter trickles out through the open door, and from the myriad of voices conversing and laughing, it's obvious they have guests. It's Sunday lunchtime, so it's not that unusual, and I know Austen's flight got in late last night, so he probably hasn't had a chance to tell them yet.

I wet my lips, wondering if I should turn around and retreat. Maybe get a hotel room and call Austen from there? I'm still debating my options when the *click-clack* of heels alerts me to someone's impending presence. I dart to the side of the door, flattening my back to the wall, hoping whomever it is doesn't stick their head out the door and notice me.

"Pamela, there you are," a woman says.

"Why is the front door open?" the second woman asks, and I'm guessing she's Pamela Hayes, Austen's mom.

"Gia has gone to our house to get more champagne."

"Can you believe it?" Pamela says. "Everything we hoped for is coming true."

"They've always been sweet on one another, so this isn't a surprise," the other woman says.

"At least it will put an end to all that nonsense about Austen in the papers. A baby and a wedding will reassure the NFL that he's a good Christian heterosexual man," Pamela says.

Pressure settles on my chest, and I swallow thickly over the lump in my throat. *What the hell are they talking about?*

"I'm going to close it. All the heat is escaping," Pamela says a second before the door slams shut, and she leaves me out in the cold, confused and in a panic.

My heart pounds in my ears, and I'm rooted to the spot, my brain whirling with different explanations, because it can't be what I just heard, right? There is no baby. At least, no baby he fathered.

Unless.

Fuck.

Is Gia pregnant by her boyfriend and she's asked Austen to continue the lie?

"Keaton."

I jump, dropping my bag on the ground, startled at the unexpected voice.

Gia walks toward me, holding a bottle of champagne in one hand. Her other hand is pressed against her wooly cardigan, keeping it closed around her body.

"Does Austen know you're here?" She stops in front of me.

I shake my head, my eyes lowering to the hand on her stomach and the sparkling diamond on her ring finger.

"What the hell is going on?" I splutter, lifting my gaze to hers.

She thrusts her hand at me, almost shoving the ring up my

nose. "It was Austen's grandmother's ring. It's beautiful. Isn't it?"

"Austen…proposed?" I choke out, and it feels like every organ in my body stops functioning.

Her face drops, and she brings the hand to her mouth. "Oh my God. He didn't tell you?"

"Tell me what exactly?" I ask, folding my arms around my midriff.

"Keaton. I'm so sorry. When Austen came home for Thanksgiving, we ended up sleeping together, and I just discovered I'm pregnant."

"But he's gay," I blurt, horrified by what I'm hearing. There is no way that could be true. Austen isn't into women, isn't into Gia, and there's no way he'd cheat on me. He wouldn't.

She slants me a pitiful look while my brain turns somersaults. "Austen popped the question as soon as he heard, because we both know he's not the type of guy to shirk his responsibilities."

"But Hendrix—"

"We broke up. I've always loved Austen, and I knew one day he'd come around."

"But he's with me." On autopilot, I bend down, retrieving my bag. "This doesn't make sense. I need to speak with him."

"Oh, Keaton." She tips her head to one side, placing her hand—the one with the ring—on my arm. "I really don't think that's a good idea. Pamela has already told Austen he needs to stop rooming with you because your reputation will only tarnish his family-man image. She won't be pleased if you show up at her door. And you'll only make it awkward for Austen."

She flashes the ring in my face, and if she does it again, I'm going to shove it down her throat, pregnant or not.

"Our mothers are already talking about a March wedding," she continues. "This is a done deal. You know Austen will never let another man raise his child. Just walk away with some pride. And if you ever cared for Austen, you'll do the right thing." She moves to pat my arm again, and I sidestep her.

If she touches me one more time, I won't be responsible for my actions.

"I knew I didn't like you for a reason," I say, holding onto my bag for dear life. "My gut instincts rarely let me down." Except when I don't listen to them, of course.

"I know you're upset. I get it. I know what it's like to love and lose Austen, but you'll get over it." She walks up to the door, turning to look at me over her shoulder. "I'm sure the degenerates are lining up for a turn in your ass now you're famous for more than just your name."

If she wasn't a woman, and she wasn't pregnant, I would kick her ass for that comment. Instead, I do what I'm good at—I turn and run.

Christmas comes and goes, and Ebenezer Scrooge has nothing on Keaton Kennedy. It takes effort to haul my ass out of bed every day, and I only do that because of Mom. She's freaking out, over me, over Kent, and I hate hurting her. But I'm in a world of pain, and I don't know how to cope without Austen. He's sent me tons of texts and left voice messages for me, but I can't bear to talk to him. I don't want to hear his excuses.

I spent the plane ride home from Denver convincing myself Gia was lying. Because I know Austen. I know he's not into women. I know he wouldn't cheat on me. And I know he wouldn't go to all that risk to come out as gay only to throw it away for a hookup.

I got off the plane determined to call him and find out the truth—until I saw the news report on the TV in the airport, confirming Austen Hayes' engagement, accompanied by a picture of Austen with his arm around Gia. That hideous fucking ring was front and center in the photo, and everything I thought I knew went flying out the window.

No one knows what to say to me, and I've refused to talk about it until Faye comes storming into my room again, the week before I'm due to fly back to Cali for spring semester. Austen and I were supposed to be on our cooking mini vacay this week, and my depression has reached new lows. I considered going by myself for all of one second. There is no way I could take that trip without him.

"This feels like déjà vu," I say as Faye walks toward me with a face like thunder.

She plops onto the bed beside me, holding her cell in one hand. "I want to know what the fuck is going on, and you're going to tell me right now."

"Babe."

I glance up, spotting Kyler in the doorway. His brows are drawn together, his features a mask of worry. Seeing these two pregnant has been the only highlight of Christmas for me. He's in uber protective mode, and it's driving Faye nuts.

"Please stop stressing out. It's not good for you or the baby."

She flips him the bird while hissing at him. Like, she legit hisses. I half-expect fangs to drop from her mouth.

Pregnancy hormones are terrifying, with a capital T.

"Butt out, buttface. Go harass some other pregnant woman." She rubs a hand over her baby bump, which seems to have sprouted almost overnight. "Tell Daddy to stop being such a worrywart and to chill the fuck out."

"You shouldn't curse," Kyler and I say at the same time.

"Ha." Ky straightens up. "Keats agrees with me."

I hold up my hands. "Don't bring me into this. I was just sitting here, minding my own business—"

"You were sitting here wallowing in a pity party for one, and that stops right fucking now." Faye pins the full extent of her erratic hormones on me, and I cower in fear.

Ky chuckles. "You're scaring him, babe."

"Good." Faye pats her stomach lovingly, and it's at odds with the fierce determination on her face. "He needs a good scare, because if he doesn't pull his head out of his ass, he's going to lose Austen for good."

"I've already lost him. He's having a baby with the She-Devil, and they're getting married."

"And he told you this?" Faye asks, her tone laced with suspicion.

"Well, no, but—"

"Have you even talked to him?" The truth is written all over my face, and she slaps me in the chest. "Oh my God. You're an idiot. Like certifiable." She shakes her head before looking up at Ky. "Babe. I need a hug, because otherwise, I'm going to keep slapping your brother until I've slapped the stupid out of him."

Ky chuckles, strolling to his wife and pulling her up into his arms.

"You're so strange," I mutter, still a little afraid of her.

"And you're stupid."

I sigh. "I think we've determined that."

"Keats, please tell me why you think Austen is having a baby with some nutjob and marrying her?"

"You're not going to drop this, are you?"

"I've been biting my tongue since you returned from Colorado like a different man. Everyone told me to give you space, but they're all stupid too." She sniffles, and I share a concerned look with my brother.

I've been around my other sisters-in-law when they've been pregnant, and I've witnessed some emotional, hormonal outbursts, but nothing like Faye. It's like her hormones are on super overdrive.

But I still love the bones of the girl.

"Okay, everyone's stupid," I say. "We've determined that now too."

"Not Ky," Faye says, resting her head on her husband's chest.

"Babe. Just tell him," Ky implores.

Faye thrusts her cell at me. "Austen just made a statement, and the TV station who originally reported the engagement has retracted it and made a public apology."

I watch a representative from Berkeley read out the statement from Austen with mounting horror and the largest lump in my throat.

"It wasn't real," I croak, staring up at her through glassy eyes.

"You need to talk to him, Keats. I can't believe you haven't talked to him already," Ky says.

"I fucked up." I drop the cell on the bed, burying my head in my hands. "I majorly fucked up." I don't know exactly what has happened, but Austen's statement confirms he's not going to be a father, he's not getting married, and he's most definitely gay.

I jump up. "I need to get back to Cali."

"Halle-fucking-lujah." Faye visibly relaxes.

I grab my tablet and pull up the travel app, booking myself on the next available flight back to Berkeley.

Chapter Thirty-Six
Keaton

My palms are sweaty as I approach the door to our apartment, and I wonder if I should have given Austen advance warning I was returning early. I've no idea what kind of reception I'll receive after weeks of ghosting him, but I'm prepared to grovel like no one has groveled in the history of time.

When I step into the hallway, the first thing I notice is moving boxes lined up against the wall. Panic jumps up and slaps me in the face, and I drop my bag, racing into the main living space.

I know he's here somewhere because it's late and all the lights are on. If he'd gone out, or he was asleep, the place would be in darkness. "Austen?" I call out, walking toward the bedrooms.

He appears in the doorway of his room, holding a box and wearing an emotionless expression.

We stare at one another, and the air is heavy with unspoken words. He's only wearing sweats, and the sight of his gorgeous body reminds me of everything I've been missing. He cut his hair since I last saw him, and it's shorter and tighter on top, but damn, he looks so good, and a pang of longing hits me square in the chest.

I have missed him so much. Even when I was trying to deny that I missed him to myself.

He clears his throat, staring at me as if he's staring right through me. "I wasn't expecting you for another week." His voice is cold, so cold, and acid crawls up my throat and swims in my belly.

"You're leaving?" I rasp, my eyes flitting to the piles of clothes on his bed and the boxes littering the floor.

"Yup." He pushes past me, without making eye contact, walking off like he's not aware my heart is lying in pieces on the floor at his feet.

"Austen," I call out after him, rushing to catch up with him. "I'm sorry. So fucking sorry."

He puts the box down on the island unit, turning to face me.

"Can we talk?" I ask. "Please."

"Now he wants to talk." He harrumphs. "Typical." He crosses his arms over his chest. "Let me guess. You saw the news. Heard my statement, and you've come to beg for forgiveness."

God, when he puts it like that, I see how utterly stupid and pathetic I am. And weak. Let's not forget that. "That's pretty much it. Yes."

"Tell me, would you have shown up here if you hadn't discovered the truth?"

My mouth is as dry as the Gobi Desert, and this is probably one of those times where I should lie, but I can't lie to him. "I don't know," I truthfully admit.

"That's what I thought." Hurt glimmers in his eyes, but he composes himself quickly.

"I made a mistake, Austen. I fucked up. Gia messed with my head, but I thought about it on the plane ride home, and I—"

"What are you talking about?" He interrupts me. "When did you see Gia?" His brows knit together.

"The day I showed up at your house. The day of the engagement dinner."

Shock splays across his face.

"Of course, she didn't tell you I was there." That bitch is a real piece of work, but I don't think admitting that will help my cause. I've no clue what's happened or how Austen feels about her now.

"Tell me everything," he demands, staring at me with those gorgeous green eyes, and I just want to fall at his feet and beg for forgiveness. But he needs the truth first. So, I tell him how I came to be at his house that day and what transpired.

"That stupid conniving cunt," he seethes, locking his hands behind his head. I'm shocked to hear Austen speaking like that, especially about his so-called best friend.

"What happened?" I ask. "Just tell me what she did."

He exhales heavily, walking silently into the living room, and I follow. He sits down on the couch, and I drop onto the recliner chair.

"I went home to tell my parents the truth about my sexuality and the fake relationship with Gia. I got in late, crashed like the dead, and I woke up to everyone in the house that Sunday morning. Mom was ecstatic at the news Gia and I were having a baby, and I almost keeled over in shock."

"She ambushed you," I say, and he nods. "And your mom had no issue with you having a baby young and out of wedlock."

"It was her every fantasy come to life and a far better outcome than believing the reports in the news about her son being gay." He scrubs a hand over the thin layer of stubble on his face, and I notice the strain etched into his features and the dark shadows under his eyes, for the first time.

I haven't been suffering alone. That much is clear. Except where my suffering was self-inflicted, Austen's was wholly undeserved.

"I'm so sorry, man. I—"

"Do you want to hear this or not?" he snaps in a manner that is uncharacteristic for him. He's angry with me, and I don't fault him at all. I'd feel the same if the roles were reversed.

I nod, encouraging him to go on, promising myself I'll stay quiet until he's got it all out.

"Gia was pregnant with Hendrix's baby, except Hendrix is going down for drug possession and dealing, and it's likely to be years before he gets out of jail." A muscle pops in his jaw as he looks off into space. "In her spaced-out brain, she concocted this new plan and decided to announce it to our parents without consulting me."

He sighs again, leaning back in the chair, and I can see the toll this has taken on him. "I was furious, but I said nothing at first, because I wanted to get Gia alone to find out what the fuck she was playing at. She avoided me most of the day while our mothers discussed wedding dates. Gia had lied about that too. She told my mom I had already proposed and that I was hoping to give her her mother's ring." He shakes his head, a look of disgust washing over his face. "She was wearing the fucking ring when I came down that morning."

Yeah. Tell me about it.

I say nothing.

"Later that night, I got Gia upstairs and forced the truth out of her. She admitted she was pregnant and begged me to go along with the plan."

"That's why you released that report to the news," I blurt.

He just stares at me. "You're unbelievable." He shakes his head repeatedly. "Did you ever know me at all?" His voice raises a few octaves.

"You didn't go along with it," I say, instantly understanding.

"Of course, I fucking didn't!" he yells, standing. "She doctored an old picture of us and sent the report to the media. She thought I'd go along with it if she made it public, but I guess she never really knew me either."

The blow slices through skin, bone, sinew, and blood, cutting me to shreds on the insides, like intended.

But I can give Austen this. He can take it all out on me because I deserve it.

"I told her bluntly that she had until the next morning to come clean with her parents or I would do it. I told her all the lies ended now." He paces the room. "I told her I was in love *with you*, and I wanted to spend my life *with you*."

I am such a fool. If only I had given my boyfriend the benefit of the doubt. If only I had given him an opportunity to explain. I'm like one of those sad fucks you read about in books who wrecks everything by believing a lie and refusing to communicate.

Guilty as charged.

It doesn't matter that my head was fucked from the media storm and that I was depressed. I failed my boyfriend. I failed myself. And if I can't fix this, I'll have lost the best thing that's ever happened to me.

Sobs build at the base of my throat and tears stab my eyes, but I hold everything back, giving Austen the floor.

"She knew I wasn't bluffing," he says. "That's why she deliberately took an overdose and almost died."

My eyes widen in horror.

"She lost the baby," he says, sitting back down, resting his elbows on his knees. "And our parents blame me."

"Wait? What?"

He barks out a bitter laugh. "She confessed to everything. Hendrix. The drugs. Our relationship being fake. I think that was her way of trying to make it up to me, but it was too late. Our parents had twisted it into a story of their own making."

Pain rips across his face, and he shields nothing from me. "They said I put her in harm's way by agreeing to the fake relationship in the first place, because I facilitated her continuing to see Hendrix. That I stood by and did nothing when it was clear she had a drug problem, and my biggest failure was not coming clean straightaway about the baby and the wedding. According to my mom, if I'd told them, then Gia wouldn't have tried to commit suicide and she wouldn't have lost her baby."

"They said that to you?" I'm appalled, and my heart breaks for him.

"Yeah, oh, and Mom's disgusted I came out. Apparently, I've made her look foolish, and she can't show her face around town."

"I'm sorry, Austen. I hope you know none of that is your fault. What happened to Gia is on her. Not you."

"I needed you, man." His voice breaks, and I hate myself.

"I didn't know. I thought—"

"That I was off playing happy family with my best friend?" he hisses, and I deserve every ounce of his hatred. "How could you, Keats? I know she manipulated both of us, but how could you believe the crap that came out of her mouth? How could you shut me out like that? I called and texted so many times, and you never picked up!"

He shouts out the last part, and I move toward him, to take his hands, but he shakes his head, moving sideways on the couch until he's out of reach. "Don't touch me. I don't want you to touch me."

"Austen, please let me make this right. Tell me what I can

do? I'll do anything to make it up to you. I'm an idiot. And it's not enough to say I was depressed and stressed and not thinking clearly. You're right. I should've let you explain. I got off that plane convinced she was lying, but the TV report seemed to confirm her lies." A harsh laugh escapes my lips. "And I know better than anyone how the media twists things. I never should've believed it."

"No, you shouldn't." Austen stands, and the sad look on his face has my heart breaking all over again. "I needed you, Keaton. I've been there for you, and when I needed you the most, you ghosted me."

I stand, begging him with my eyes. "I hate myself, Austen. I hate that you went through that alone."

"I wasn't alone. Colton came through for me after it became clear you wanted nothing more to do with me."

"I'm glad he was there for you. That you had some support, and as long as I live, I'll never forgive myself for abandoning you like I did. But I promise, if you give me another chance, I swear I won't let you down again." I step closer, my heart aching when he steps back, folding his arms around himself, as if to protect himself from me. "Please, Austen. I love you. Please give me another chance."

"If you really loved me, you wouldn't have been so quick to believe all the lies. If you were really accepting of who you are, and you believed in us, you wouldn't have shut me out like that."

Tears glide down my cheeks, and I do nothing to stop them. I want him to see them. To know how much I hate that I tore us apart. I knew I would ruin us in the end, and it seems I was right. "Tell me what to say," I plead, in between sobs. "Tell me how to make this right because I can't lose you, Austen. I can't live without you."

"Don't do this." His eyes fill up, and tears roll down his

face. "Don't make this worse. Let's just walk away and try to remember the good times before it all went to shit."

Drawing a brave breath, I close the gap between us, grab his face, and slam my lips down on his. If I can't get through to him using words, I'll resort to anything I can, because there is no reality for me where he doesn't exist in my world.

He kisses me back, but I don't rejoice, because this kiss is rough and brutal, laced with dark emotions that have no place in our love. We devour one another, in one last desperate battle cry, even though we know the war is already lost. When he softens the kiss, and his fingers wind into my hair, I know this is goodbye, and I break apart, sobbing uncontrollably, unable to accept this is the end.

"Please, Austen. Please don't do this." I don't care how pathetic I am. I came here to grovel, and I'm not going back on my word. "I love you so much. I was weak, but it doesn't mean I don't love you."

"I can't be with someone who runs away at the first sign of trouble instead of pulling me close. I can't be with someone who doesn't prioritize me when I need him." He palms my cheek, brushing my tears away with his thumb. "I can't be with someone who doesn't fight for me." His voice cracks, and he breaks down in my arms. I hold him close, in the only way I can comfort him now.

"I want to fight for you, Austen," I say when I'm composed enough to speak. "This *is* me fighting for you."

He pulls back, swiping at his eyes. "It's too late."

"It's not. We're so good together. This is just a bump in the road. Albeit a big one, but we can get through this. Just give me a chance to prove I can be all those things for you."

"You're not ready, man." His smile is sad. "Maybe I'm not either." He pulls himself together, and I force myself to stop crying, because I recognize defeat when I see it. "I'm focusing on football, and I want to give it my sole dedication. Tomorrow, I'm announcing that I'm entering the draft."

My jaw hangs open. "You are?"

He nods. "I've spoken with scouts from the Baltimore Ravens. They want me, man. They've had their eye on me, and after my performance at the bowl game, they believe the time is right. They're one of the more liberal teams in the NFL, and they think I'll feel at home there."

"Oh my God, Austen. That's amazing. I'm so proud of you."

"Thank you. They helped me get an agent and a trainer, and I'm moving to Baltimore in three days. I'll train at a place up there, and Berkeley has agreed to let me finish my degree online."

I've been absent for so much, and it's all moving forward without me. I don't know how I'll survive without Austen Hayes, but I'm happy he's getting to live his dream because no one deserves it more.

"I'm happy for you, man. I hope it all works out because you deserve it."

"Thanks." He shoves his hands in his pockets. "This isn't how I expected things to end up, and I'll always cherish the time we shared."

His eyes penetrate mine and tears pour down my face, as I'm unable to hold my devastation inside. "I take full responsibility for this, and you should know I don't ever see myself loving anyone the way I love you."

His Adam's apple bobs in his throat, and I can tell he's fighting to hold on to his composure. "A part of me will always love you, Keaton, and I hope you find happiness within yourself, because you deserve that too."

Chapter Thirty-Seven

Austen

Baltimore. Twenty Months Later.

"**G**ood game, dude." Colton slaps me on the back as we emerge from the showers after a blistering win over the Denver Broncos. It's the first time we've played my home team, and I get a sick thrill out of beating their asses.

"We still make a damn good team." I raise my fist for a knuckle touch. Colton was a third-round pick in last April's draft, and I was fucking ecstatic when I realized my college buddy was joining me here. We've stayed in regular contact since I joined the Baltimore Ravens the previous April, but I've missed having him around.

Don't misunderstand, the guys on my team are great, and despite my concerns, they have welcomed me with open arms. Sure, a couple of them are lukewarm, but no one has been openly hostile, and it's more than I hoped for. Having the support of the coaching team helps enormously, and having a stellar first-year performance has helped win the fans over too.

Still, there have been periods where I've been lonely. Where I've missed Orwell and Charlotte and Colton.

When Colton moved out here, I insisted he stay with me, because I fucking hate living alone.

Too much time with my thoughts isn't good for me. Because my brain instantly returns to thoughts of the guy I left behind. The one guy I'm still struggling to evict from my heart and my head.

I don't let myself miss Keaton, except at night when I'm alone in my bed, remembering how good it felt to fall asleep and wake up with him by my side, and I give in to my heartache, indulging my memories, if only to remind me what it feels like to love and be loved.

"Damn straight!" Colton slaps me on the back as we walk to our lockers. "Please tell me I'm not going solo tonight? I need my wingman."

I roll my eyes. "We both know I'm no wingman, and you need zero help with the ladies."

"We can go to a gay bar," he offers. "I don't mind playing third wheel though I still think you should consider another date with Jon."

Colton badgered me for months about meeting his bestie, Jon, and I finally relented, purely to get him off my back. And you know what? Under different circumstances, Jon would definitely be my type. He's hot. He's smart. He's funny.

But he's not Keats.

And therein lies my problem.

I have no interest in any other guy.

I've tried to move on. I've gone on a couple of dates, but none of them went anywhere, because I can't forget the guy I gave my heart to back in California.

"Don't start that shit again. Jon is a great guy. But he's not for me."

"Dude." Colton leans in close, lowering his voice as we get dressed. "You can't keep pining after him. Either move on or do something about it."

"You think it's that easy?"

"I know it's not. But you can't live the best years of your life like this. And all that jerking off is not good for your wrists."

I shoulder check him, rolling my eyes again. "You can't force these things. And I'm only twenty-three."

Colton's serious face makes an appearance. "You should call him."

"I've thought about it, but too much time has passed. And it was so painful at the end. I don't know that I could ever go back. Besides," I say, shoving my feet into my sneakers. "He seems to be in a good place, and I think the past is best left in the past."

"His vlog has fifty million followers now," Colton says, pride lacing his words. "And his cookbook releases next week. According to an article I read, the preorder numbers guarantee him a place on the New York Times bestseller's list."

I'm well aware of Keaton's success, and I've followed his vlog—now a cooking show called *The Queer Kitchen Revolution*—since his first video.

Ironically, he started it shortly after we broke up, purely as a way of sharing who he was with the world, fed up with the way he was being portrayed in the media. He cooked while he was talking, because it keeps him calm, and it was the combination of his winning personality, his willingness to be vulnerable in front of his audience, and his obvious skill in the kitchen that was an instant hit. Within a month, he had five million followers, and it's mushroomed since then.

I've watched each and every one even though I've promised myself, time and time again, I'll stop because it hurts so much. Every time I look at him, I remember how amazing it felt to kiss him, hold him, fuck him, and the pain feels as raw as it did in those horrible first few months after we broke up when it felt like I'd lost a limb.

Colton is staring at me, waiting for me to come back to the land of the living. I clear my throat and finish lacing my sneakers. "I know. I'm so fucking proud of him."

"You should text him that. Open up communication and see where it goes."

"He probably wouldn't answer me." Not after I ignored him last year when he texted to congratulate me on being a second-round pick. I wanted to reply, so fucking badly, because there was no one else on this planet I wanted to celebrate with more than him, but I didn't, because there was no point in either of us going down a road that only led to more heartache.

"You won't know unless you try."

We grab our bags, say goodbye to our teammates, and leave the locker room. "I walked away for valid reasons, Colton," I remind him, slinging my bag over my shoulder.

"He made a mistake, and it was a really stressful time for both of you. If you still love him, isn't he worth fighting for?" he asks.

"If he still loves me, am *I* not worth fighting for?" I state, because that's really the crux of the matter for me.

Chapter Thirty-Eight
Keaton

I'm going to vomit any second now, I think, as I wipe my clammy hands down the front of my jeans. Exhaling heavily, I remind myself of why I'm here and how far I've come since I last saw Austen Hayes.

It was exactly twenty months, three days, and six hours since I watched the love of my life walk away from me.

I'm not going to lie. Those first few months without him were a blur, and I only got through it because Mol, Kate, and Seb refused to let me drown in grief and self-pity.

Kate suggested I start my vlog when the pressure of the media intrusion in my life got too much and I'd reached my breaking point. It started as a form of therapy, and it was risky, because I knew the same assholes who continue to hound me online would misinterpret my heartfelt words, but I took a chance, and I've never looked back.

The world never discovered the truth about Austen and me, and I'm grateful for that. There was a massive spotlight on his head when he first entered the draft, and then again when he signed with the Baltimore Ravens, and that light hasn't diminished. I've watched his career proudly from the sidelines and celebrated every milestone he's achieved, despite the near constant ache in my heart.

I didn't contemplate going after him for a long time. Because he made his feelings clear. His star was rising, and I didn't want to complicate his life. But I also realized Austen was right. I wasn't ready to embrace everything about my life, his life, and our relationship, and though our separation has killed me, I know we needed that time apart.

Today, I have the kind of career I never imagined I'd have, and a lot of it is thanks to Austen. He was the one who first planted the idea in my head, then Kate nurtured the seeds, and I made it grow—into a passion I love almost as much as the man I'm here to see.

I glance at my watch, hoping I haven't missed him. Colton assured me they always come out this way, and I arrived at the Under Armour Performance Center early in case their practice ended sooner than expected.

The longer I stand here like a tool, the more I grow restless. I've waited a long time to fight for Austen, and now I've reached the point where it's within grasp, I am impatient.

Footsteps thud on the pavement as some of the players emerge from the tunnel into the staff parking lot.

I wouldn't be here without Colton's help, and I'm grateful he accepted my phone call and listened to what I had to say. He didn't divulge much, and he needed time to think about it, but when he called me back to say he'd left a pass for me at the front gate, I could have kissed the guy—if he wasn't Austen's best friend and I wasn't still hopelessly in love with the Baltimore Raven's star wide receiver.

I went through a period where I tried to put Austen out of my mind. Where I tried to move on. I went on a few dates, and they were nice guys, but they weren't him, and my heart just wasn't in it.

More players appear, and I scan their faces, looking for the guy with the gorgeous green eyes, full lips, and dark hair, growing frustrated when I don't find him. A few of them glance my way, and I spot the recognition in their eyes. Thankfully, none of them approach me, because I hadn't considered what I'd say if anyone noticed me.

I'm contemplating calling Colton when he materializes on the sidewalk, standing beside Austen, and my heart starts beating out of control.

Austen looks so good, even in team sweats and his training top. He's still all corded muscle with wide shoulders, a broad chest, chiseled abs, powerful thighs, and long legs. His strong arms showcase the ink I'm well acquainted with, along with a few new tattoos I haven't gotten up close and personal with. He wears his hair the same, but it's a little tighter on top. The eyebrow piercing is new, and there's a new air of confidence around him. Austen was always confident and self-assured, but I can tell he's really comfortable in his skin now, and he exudes confidence by the bucketload.

Colton eyeballs me, urging me to move with his facial expression, and I push off the wall I've been leaning against, walking toward them.

Austen turns his head, and it's as if it happens in slow motion. I hold my chin up, keeping my shoulders back, forcing the last-minute surge of nerves aside, because I'm not fucking up this moment. Not when I've dreamed of it from the minute we broke up.

Austen stares at me, barely blinking, and I can't get a read on him because his face is giving nothing away. Undeterred, I step right up to him, smiling. "Hey, man. It's good to see you."

Colton nods at me as he walks away, giving us privacy.

Austen watches his friend for a few beats, instantly realizing he helped to make this happen. I hope he won't be mad at him, because Colton had the best of intentions. I was encouraged when he didn't outrightly turn me away, and maybe I was wrong to read into it, but I saw it as a positive sign that he believes Austen would be amenable to me reaching out.

"Keaton." Austen clears his throat, and now I'm up close I can see the shock he's working hard to disguise. "What are you doing here?"

"I'm in town to do an interview, and I wanted to see you. I was hoping we could talk."

Austen stares at me, and I hold his gaze, ignoring the butterflies in my stomach and standing firm. A frisson of electricity charges the air, reminding both of us of the intense connection between us. A connection that was only broken by my immaturity and my tendency to press the self-destruct button.

The attraction we shared never died.

The love we shared never died.

At least, it didn't on my side.

I've scoured the news for information on his love life, but there's been next to nothing. Still, that didn't necessarily mean anything, so the only other thing I asked of Colton before I came here today was whether Austen was single. If he'd been in a relationship, I would've had to wait. Thankfully, Colton confirmed he wasn't, and I didn't waste another minute second-guessing myself.

Even as Austen stares at me, with obvious conflict written on his face, I don't regret my decision to come here.

"I don't think that would be a good idea," he finally says, grabbing the strap of his bag like it's a lifeline.

"Why?" I ask, holding firm.

"Going over old ground won't do either of us any favors. It's good to see you looking so well, and congratulations on your career, but I think it's best we leave the past in the past."

"I disagree, and I don't expect you to make this easy for me. I'm in town for the next few days," I explain. "I'm staying at the Four Seasons. Room four-twelve. Call me or drop by if you change your mind."

"What. That's it?" he says, arching a brow.

My lips kick up. "I'm not going to beg this time, man." I take a step closer, and my eyes drop to his lush mouth for a second. "But I *am* going to fight. I'm going to fight harder than I've ever fought for anything in my life." I peer deep into his eyes. "Because there is no one else I *want* to fight for. No other man worthy of fighting for." I shove my hands in my pocket, smiling as I step back. "Consider yourself warned."

"Let's give a big WBAL-TV welcome to Mr. Keaton Kennedy," Cherie, the daytime talk show host says, and the studio audience breaks out in a round of applause.

I smile and wave as I walk to the couch, sitting in the spot the producer told me to sit in. I'm not exactly an expert at giving TV interviews—certainly not in Mom's league—but my publisher has organized a ton of interviews in various cities across the US to celebrate the impending release of my first cookbook, and it's not as nerve-wracking as it was at the start. Mom gave me some tips, as did Christina, my family's chief publicist, and the publisher's PR division gave me pointers too.

"Welcome, Keaton," Cherie says, leaning across the desk to shake my hand. "We're delighted you could be with us today."

"Thanks for having me. I'm delighted to be in Baltimore and looking forward to exploring your wonderful city."

"First time here?" she asks, easing me into the interview.

"Yes," I confirm, settling back on the couch. "And I want to do the whole tourist thing. What would you recommend?"

We spend a few minutes talking about some of the best places to visit, best restaurants to eat at, and I have to smother a laugh when she suggests I stay to watch the Ravens game on Sunday. The TV station is affiliated with the NFL, so it's no surprise she's plugging the local team.

"So, Keaton. Tell me, what are your plans now you've graduated from Berkeley?"

"Right now, I'm focused on my cooking show, *The Queer Kitchen Revolution*, and, as you know, my first cookbook releases next week. I have a couple of other business ideas I'm exploring, but for now, my passion most definitely is food related."

"For those of you who have been living under a rock," Cherie says, addressing the audience and the cameraman. "Keaton's focus is on developing delicious healthy meals with a specific emphasis on athletes and those who want to follow a calorie-controlled diet without compromising on flavor. How did that come about?" she asks me. "Was it a conscious decision to go down this route or you just fell into it?"

"It was a bit of both," I say, taking a sip from the glass of water on the table beside me. "My roommate in college was a football player," I admit, because that aspect of my relationship with Austen is not a secret, but this is the first time I'm talking about it in public. Even on my vlog, I couldn't admit how the idea for the show started, because my breakup was still too raw and Austen was a part of my life I wasn't comfortable talking about then, not when there was still so much media interest in both of us.

"And he used to do all the cooking," I continue, "until I got sick of eating steak and broccoli medley, and I insisted we take turns cooking dinner."

The audience chuckles.

"Austen was very strict about his diet, because he was dedicated to football and maintaining peak fitness, and I wanted to ensure I stayed within the confines of his diet while offering more variety and tastier meals. Over time, I developed more and more recipes, started a column for the student paper back in Cali, and then I started my vlog, and people were really interested in the cooking segments, and it took off from there."

"That's a wonderful story," Cherie gushes before swinging her gaze to the audience. "And in case you didn't realize, the Austen Keaton refers to is none other than our own Austen Hayes." Whoops, hollers, and another round of applause breaks out, and I can't help smiling, because the adoration is obvious, and it warms my heart.

"What was Austen like back then?" Cherie asks, leaning forward on the desk with her elbows.

"Austen is a great guy. Hardworking and driven. So damn talented. Smart and funny and a loyal friend."

"It sounds like you two were good friends."

"We were." I smile, working hard to smother the pang of sadness that hits me from left field.

"It must have helped having a roommate who was also gay," she says, and I grow a little hot under the collar.

While I haven't vetoed questions about my sexuality, I've made it clear I won't discuss my love life. Most of the interviewers I've met have tried pushing me, but no one has asked me about Austen Hayes and my gay status in the same breath, and it makes me uncomfortable. At the same time, I won't shy away from answering, and I can speak the truth while still protecting our secret.

"It did. Austen helped me come to terms with who I am. He helped me to accept that my sexuality didn't define who I was as a person, and he was there for me during a very difficult period in my life." I sit up straighter. "More than that, he showed me the value of loyalty and honesty and true courage, and he made me realize some things about myself."

"Like what?" she asks, grabbing the bone like a dog who hasn't chewed one in weeks.

"That it takes time to fully accept who you are as a person when you've spent years hiding the truth and that sometimes you need to take a step back to fully appreciate everything good you have in your life."

"It sounds like you had a very close friendship with Mr. Hayes. Was it ever anything more?"

I plaster a smile on my face and use humor to deflect when I really want to throttle her. "Now, now, Cherie, you know I'm here to discuss my new book, not talk about my love life."

The audience chuckles, and I take another sip of my water, praying she drops the subject.

"Just indulge me one final question," she says, and I guess no one up there is listening to me today.

"Have you ever been in love?"

Such a simple question with a simple answer, and yet it's like she's cut a line straight through my middle and is asking me to rip my heart out and serve it to her on a silver platter.

"I can tell from your expression that you have," she adds, smiling encouragingly at me.

"One time," I admit.

"It ended badly?" she surmises.

"Something like that." My chest heaves, and I don't know why I say what I say next. Maybe I've a sixth sense that he's watching and it might be the only opportunity I get to tell him these things. Or I just need to admit these things out loud for myself.

"He was the love of my life, and losing him broke me yet rebuilt me at the same time. I know I'm the man I am today because he helped shape my life in so many different ways. Things ended because I messed up. I abandoned him when he needed me the most, and I was too wrapped up in my own stuff to see what was in front of my eyes."

The audience is waiting with bated breath for me to go on, and I can tell I've captured the attention of every person sitting in those seats. "He was always so self-assured, so confident, and he was my rock. I thought he was infallible. That nothing fazed him. But I forgot he was still human. And I didn't know it at the time, because I was still a novice when it came to relationships, but there were times when he was low and he needed me to lift him up, like he'd done for me."

"It sounds like you never got over him," Cherie says, looking as enchanted as the audience.

"I haven't." I stare right into the camera, speaking directly to Austen. "I still love him as much as I did back then, and I'm stronger today. My eyes are fully open, and I have the confidence to go after what I want now. And what I want is him. It will always be him. Even if he never gives me a second chance, I know he is the only man for me."

Chapter Thirty-Nine
Austen

"Your guest is in meeting room A12 on level one," Shelby, one of the stadium coordinators, tells me when I exit the press conference after the game. She was the only one I trusted to escort Keaton from the VIP area, where he watched the game, to a private room where we can talk.

"Thanks, Shelby. I'll be right there." She hovers, chewing on her lip, and I arch a brow. "Was there something else?"

"Do you think he's really gay?" she whispers, leaning in. "Because I heard he's into women too."

An amused grin spreads across my mouth. "Nope. Definitely gay."

"Well, darn it." She looks genuinely disappointed. "He's so hot, and he was really sweet and polite. I could see myself as a cougar with the right guy." She waggles her brows, grinning.

Shelby recently went through a bitter divorce, and she's on the dating scene for the first time in ten years. She keeps me entertained with her stories every time I see her.

"I swear all the good ones are either too young, taken, or gay."

"I'll be sure to pass on your regards to Keaton," I tease.

"Oh." Her eyes light up, and she places her hand on my arm. "Could you get me his autograph? You'll have my undying love for eternity."

I can't contain my grin. "I think I can manage that, but why didn't you just ask him yourself?"

"I was too starstruck, and I have a feeling I was staring at his mouth for too long, so I got all tongue-tied, and I basically fled from the room."

I burst out laughing, pulling the older woman in for a hug. "You brighten up my days, Shelby. Don't ever change."

"Right back at ya." She tweaks my cheeks. "You're still my favorite."

"Word to the wise. Don't let Colton hear you say that. I don't think his ego could handle it."

"Handle what?" the man himself says, coming up behind me.

"That's my cue to leave. Good night, boys." She waggles her fingers before disappearing out the door.

"He here?" Colton asks, lowering his voice.

"Yeah. He's upstairs." I run my hands through my hair, fighting a sudden bout of nerves.

Colton chuckles. "He's still the only man to ever ruffle your feathers."

I flip him the bird. "He's the only man who's ever mattered."

Colton feigns a heart attack.

"Besides you and my brother," I add, because I don't know if I've ever told Colton how much he means to me. "I hope you know how important your friendship is to me."

"I know, brother." He pulls me into a manly hug. "Now

stop deflecting and get upstairs and put that man out of his misery."

"Is it crazy to feel scared when you know everything you've ever wanted is in arm's reach?"

Colton slaps me on the back. "Nah, man. There'd be something wrong if you weren't scared, but Austen Hayes doesn't run from things that frighten him. He barrels headfirst toward them." A devilish glint appears in his eyes. "I should probably warn Kennedy there's a tornado heading his way, but that would be a lot less fun."

"Am I doing the right thing?" I ask.

"Don't have a crisis of confidence now, dude. You love him. He loves you. The stars have finally aligned, yada, yada." He shoves me toward the door. "Go get your man. Maybe if you finally get laid, you'll be more bearable to live with."

"I'm evicting you," I tease.

"You wouldn't dare," he retorts. "See you in the morning," he adds, walking backward out the door. "I'm gonna crash with Jennings. Give you guys some privacy."

I take the elevator to the first level and walk along the hallway toward the room where my future awaits me. Not stopping to second-guess myself anymore—because my gut knows this is right—I push into the room and come to an immediate standstill.

Keaton is staring out the window at the dark Baltimore night sky, standing regally, with his hands behind his back, his legs slightly parted, and his shoulders upright. I noticed it the other day, and again during the TV interview, that he holds himself with much more confidence these days, and it's clear he's grown into his skin and become the man I always knew he would be.

A burst of pride hits me in the chest, and though I know the time we were apart has undoubtedly changed both of us, I know it was the way things were meant to happen.

"Are you just going to stand there and stare at me all night or tell me why I'm here?" Keats says, slowly turning around to face me.

He's wearing a fitted blue-gray designer shirt that stretches tight across his chest and hugs his muscular biceps. That's another thing that's changed. He's bulked up a little more, and he's never looked sexier. From watching his show, I know he's added to his ink too, but his right arm is still tattoo-free, and I hope I know the reason why. His toned legs are encased behind dark jeans, and he's wearing navy-blue Vans. The musky, woodsy scent of his cologne takes me back, and emotion creeps up on me, threatening to overpower me.

"You know why you're here," I say, taking a step closer.

"Because you invited me. Put me up in the VIP box with the other WAGs." His lips twitch in amusement before his expression sobers again. "And now you've asked to meet me up here, away from everyone. So, am I still your secret or not, Austen?" he challenges.

"You've always been my secret," I say, stepping even closer. "My secret weapon," I add, staring into his beautiful blue eyes, instantly being swept up in their hidden depths. "Because it's you who's driven me to achieve all I've accomplished these past two years."

"Me?" Disbelief threads through his tone, and I don't blame him.

"Did you think I could ever forget you? That you weren't the biggest inspiration for everything I've done in my life from the moment I met you?"

"What's going on here, Austen?" His fingers twitch at his side, and I know he's dying to touch me as much as I'm dying to touch him.

"I watched your interview," I tell him. "And I felt like a pussy for turning you away in the parking lot that day."

"Why did you?"

"Because I'm scared, dude."

His jaw slackens, and I smile. "I'm not infallible, remember," I tease, giving in to my craving to touch him as I lift my hand to his face. I cup his cheek. "I'm human, and I've always been weak when it comes to you."

"What are you scared of exactly?" he asks, leaning into my hand, as his fingers wrap around my wrist.

"Losing you again," I say. "Because I barely survived it the first time. If we are doing this, I've got to know you're all in this time, Keaton."

He moves in, lacing his fingers in mine as his chest brushes against my chest. "I'm all in, Austen. I'm finally exactly where I need to be, and I know who I am and who I want to be with. No one else could ever compare to you. You have always been it for me."

I pull him into a hug, and we hold one another tight, neither of us talking, just holding one another and savoring the feeling of being back in each other's arms. There is so much I have missed about our relationship, and moments like this remind me how it's the simple things I've craved the most.

Like just being able to hold him at will.

Hugs are undervalued in my opinion. The power of a good hug should never be underestimated.

Right now, holding the love of my life in my arms feels like the best feeling in the world. My arms tighten around him, and I squeeze my eyes shut, just absorbing the feel of him against my body, how comforting his arms are around my back, and how fucking delicious he smells.

I allow myself another few minutes of self-indulgence before I reluctantly break our hug, easing back a little so I'm staring into his eyes. Eyes that return my hold confidently. Eyes that convey he's experiencing everything I'm experiencing.

"You have always been it for me too, Keats. I knew the day we broke up that it would kill me, even if it was the right thing to do. You needed to find who you were without me, and I needed to focus on football. Doing the long-distance thing, with all that stress and uncertainty, would've ruined us in the long run. And I was so hurt. Disappointed at how easily you had shut down on me. How easily you believed Gia's lies."

"I was a fool." His hands drop to my waist. "But you were right. I wasn't ready. I see that now, and though I've hated our separation, I'm glad you forced it." He presses his forehead against mine. "I'm glad you had the strength to do what was needed because we wouldn't be here now if you hadn't." He lifts his head, piercing me with eyes that are shielding nothing. "You saved us, and I have no regrets."

"You've always been the only one, Keats. And I have never stopped loving you."

"I've got to ask. Has there been anyone else in the time we were apart?"

I shake my head. "I went on a few dates, but my heart was never in it, and I didn't sleep with any of them."

Air whooshes out of his mouth, and then he smiles. "Thank fuck. That was my biggest fear. That you'd meet someone else and I'd cease to matter."

"Fuck, Keats." My eyes drop to his mouth before returning to his eyes. "There is no universe where that'd ever happen. No one exists for me but you."

"I haven't slept with anyone since you," he admits, and my shoulders relax.

I didn't realize how much that had been bothering me subconsciously. "Thank fuck I don't have to put the beat down on any guy for touching what's always been *mine*."

"So much for making me fight," he teases, kissing one corner of my mouth.

"I'm done fighting," I whisper over his lips. "We've spent enough time apart. Now it's time to truly start living our lives."

He closes the gap between us, fusing his mouth with mine as we taste one another again. His tongue licks against the seam of my lips, and I willingly open for him. Our tongues meet in languid strokes, and I quickly get lost in his kiss, because it's like coming home. I've never forgotten how good it feels to kiss this man because his kisses have always had the power to slay me.

It's as if we've never spent one second apart.

The past is gone, and all I see are endless moments like this in our future.

He grabs the back of my head, and I grip the nape of his neck as we kiss, over and over again, clinging to one another, hands roaming, mouths devouring, and I never want to stop.

But I have to, because I need to get this man into my bed, and it can't wait.

"Come home with me?" I whisper in his ear.

"Yes," he says, his voice thick with emotion. "I need you, man."

I peck his lips. "I love you."

"I love you too."

His words imprint on my soul for all eternity, and a serene sense of peace infiltrates every part of my body. It's deep contentment, and I know Keaton is my endgame. I've always known it, but now I live and breathe it, because there are no more obstacles in our path. There is nothing stopping us from living our best lives.

Together.

We hug again, and our mutual joy is like a blazing sun, burning bright, high in the sky, obvious for all to see.

Taking his hand, I lead him out of the room and out of the building. We hold hands, grinning at one another as we head toward the parking lot.

I slow down before we come out of the tunnel. "There will be press here."

"I know." He raises our conjoined hands, pressing a kiss to the back of my knuckles. "No more hiding, Austen. It's time to shout it from the rooftops."

A burst of laughter spurts from my throat, and tears prick the back of my eyes. I clasp his hand more firmly. "Let's do this."

We walk side by side, hand in hand, out of the tunnel, into the waiting media camped outside, grinning at one another as the flashbulbs go off and questions rain down on us.

Our eyes connect, silently communicating, and we move toward one another like magnets irresistibly drawn together, and the moment our lips meet, I know this is what forever feels like.

Epilogue
Keaton

Six Months Later

"**R**emind me again why I agreed to this?" I say, shivering under the sleeping bag as I snuggle in closer to Austen. The tent is top of the line, it's spacious, and we're on two camp beds pushed together, sharing a double sleeping bag, but it's fucking freezing, and I'm questioning how sane I was when I agreed to this camping trip.

He chuckles. "Because you love me, and you can't ever tell me no."

I scowl at him, scooting back, instantly missing his body heat. "Pretty sure I said no when you wanted to tie me up," I remind him.

He closes the gap between us when my teeth start chattering, pulling me in flush to his chest. "But you really wanted to say yes," he murmurs, brushing his lips along the column of my neck. "Admit it."

"Okay," I relent. "The thought of it might excite me, but why am *I* the one getting tied up?"

Austen's hands move toward the waistband of my boxers, and I'm down with where this is heading. "You know this is an equal relationship. Anything I do to you, you can do to me," he purrs, pressing a line of kisses along my collarbone. "If that's all you were worried about, you should have said so."

"Wait." I grab his chin, forcing his face to mine. "You're okay with me tying you up?"

He props up on one elbow, peering down at me. Strands of dark hair sweep over his brow, and his green eyes are dancing with amusement. "Hell yeah. We can take turns." He nudges his hard-on against my leg and all the blood in my body rushes straight to my cock.

"You're on," I say, grabbing his hips and pulling him on top of me. "But that'll have to wait. Until we have a bed. Right now, I need you to warm me up."

He pivots his hips, grinding his erection against mine through our boxers. "Oh, do you now?" he teases, leaning down to kiss me. "What if I need *you* to warm *me* up?"

I grab hold of his ass cheeks, squeezing. "It was your idea to come camping in Denver in March at the top of a fucking mountain where it's practically Arctic temperatures. That makes it *your* job to stop me from getting hypothermia."

He chuckles, brushing his nose against mine. "Always so dramatic."

I slide my hand underneath his boxers, palming his ass, skin on skin. "You love my drama."

God knows Austen has had to get used to it in the months since we became official and moved in together. We decided from the second we reunited that we weren't hiding anything, and we live our relationship under a spotlight, uncaring what the media or trolls say.

The majority of the public has embraced us as the "IT" gay

couple, and interest in our relationship shows no sign of waning.

Things blew up online last month when word of Brock Jonas's death hit the news. It seems he OD'd in jail, and it was another opportunity for the media to rehash everything from the past. Dax is still in jail, and he won't be seeing the light of day for at least another couple of years.

Having the cooking show helps because I'm happy to discuss Austen and my relationship in a way I can control, and it helps to keep us real and grounded. If the press prints some bullshit about us, I can address it while I am cooking, and that puts an end to the rumor. It means we don't stress about some of the crap that's written about us, and we don't have to do formal interviews. We completely control the narrative, and while there will always be jerks who try to twist things, we genuinely don't care.

The people that matter to us are the only ones we care about, and everyone is happy for us.

Even Austen's parents are coming around, but I doubt I will ever be good enough for Pamela Hayes. Gary, Austen's dad, has been warm and welcoming, but Austen's mom only *tolerates* me. Her relationship with Gia's mom has been strained since everything happened, and I know, deep down, she blames Austen. Which is so unfair, because it was never his fault.

Austen doesn't speak to Gia anymore. What she did sank the nail in the coffin of their friendship. We both understand she was strung out on drugs and desperate, but there are some things you just can't move past, no matter how much you might want to. In time, perhaps they can resume some kind of friendship, but it will never be what it was. Gia managed to get clean, graduating with her fine arts degree, and now she works in a gallery in Denver. Austen is happy she's in a good place, but he doesn't want to be around her anymore, and I respect and support his decision.

I suspect Austen accepted his parents' olive branch purely for Orwell and Charlotte, because the strain within their family has caused a divide, and it's been upsetting for his siblings, especially Charlotte. She's fifteen and at an age where everything is uncertain, and she needs her big brother now more than ever. So, when Gary and Pamela invited us to dinner a few months ago, we went, putting aside our differences for Austen's brother and sister.

I wish it was as easy with Kent, but my brother still refuses to speak to me. It's been over two years since we talked, and I miss him.

I will never understand it, because he has completely shut me out, and he won't speak to anyone else about it either. Not even Eva. He has distanced himself from the family, and I know it's killing my parents. I've reached out several times, in an attempt to reconcile, because it hurts me too, and he's ignored me every time.

I started sending him monthly texts recently, just to let him know I'm thinking of him, and I'm going to continue sending them even though I know he won't reply. There isn't anything more I can do.

"I do. I love your drama," Austen agrees, sitting up and sliding my boxers down my legs. "Because I love every part of who you are and everything that comes with it." His fingers trace over the design I finally got inked on my arm.

Austen has been training with a Baltimore tattoo parlor in his downtime, and one of the first things he did when we got back together was start inking his design on my skin. It's been a painstakingly slow process, as Austen wanted to take his time ensuring he did it right, a bit at a time. Now that it's finished, I can appreciate the care and attention to detail, and every time I look at the boat wheel and anchor on my arm, it reminds me of how lucky I am to have this second chance with the man of my dreams.

Of course, our fans went crazy when I revealed that the new ink on my arm was not only drawn by my boyfriend but lovingly inked by him too.

"I still get a boner every time I see this," he admits, grinning as he unzips the sleeping bag to remove his boxers and grab the lube.

We haven't used condoms since I moved into his penthouse apartment. We're clean, in a committed relationship, and there is nothing like the feel of him sliding in me bare or how incredible it feels when I drive my uncovered dick in his ass.

There are zero barriers between us anymore. In every aspect of our lives. And I love it.

I'm fortunate that I can film my cooking show and conduct my business from anywhere, so when Austen asked me to move in—the morning after we got back together—I didn't hesitate to agree. We've spent enough time apart, and I've enjoyed living with him again.

Our fans love that I film the show from our kitchen, and Austen makes the occasional impromptu appearance, which they go crazy for.

Colton moved out a couple months after I moved in, but neither of us put him under pressure to leave. Although we did our best to include him, I think he still felt like a third wheel, so when an apartment became available on the floor below, he put in an offer and moved out a couple weeks after it was accepted. Now, it's the best of both worlds, because we still spend a lot of time with our friend, but we have complete privacy, so it's a win-win.

And I love Baltimore. The people have made me feel very welcome, and most of Austen's teammates have become good friends. Not everyone on the team is one hundred percent comfortable with having a gay player onboard, even if he is in a loving relationship, but they keep their thoughts to themselves, and as long as they don't mistreat Austen, they are welcome to their silent narrow-mindedness.

"Of course, you do," I tease, watching his big dick spring free when he kicks his boxers away. "Because you're territorial as fuck."

"Guilty as charged. I was thinking maybe you could draw something that I can get tattooed on me." Austen crawls back under the sleeping bag, zipping it up.

"He wants me to brand him," I quip as he covers my body with his.

"I do. I want the world to know I'm yours."

I grab the back of his head. "They already do, man. But, if that's what you want, we'll do it. Though, I should warn you I can't draw for shit."

His lips kick up. "It can be something simple, and I honestly don't care." His mouth lands on mine, and we're done talking. We make out like horny teenagers before we lube up, and then he's sliding into my body as if it's the first time.

Every time with Austen is as incredible as the first time we made love, and I know I'll never get tired of him. It helps we both have a high sex drive, we're both vers, and we like experimenting with toys and positions. I have the kind of sex life I've only ever dreamed about, and it's all thanks to this man.

My eyes well up as Austen stares at me while plunging his cock in and out of my ass. His hand works my erection in sync with his thrusts, and it's the combination of his focused gaze and his searing touch that unravels me, in the best possible way.

Sex with Austen Hayes is never just physical. It's a connection I feel deep in my soul, and it only intensifies the more time we spend together and the closer we get. And still I crave more. Because he's everything, and I never want to be without him.

As we come together, I wish the clock would fast forward, because I'm in a huge hurry to propose to my boyfriend.

"Okay, wow," I say the following morning, standing beside my boyfriend at the edge of the mountain looking out at the most exquisite view. "Now I get why you like to camp here." The scenery is to die for, and it's so peaceful and calm up here. There isn't a soul around, and it's like we are the only two people in the world.

"Do you hear that?" Austen asks, looking at me. Wind blows strands of hair into his face, but it doesn't disguise the look of sheer contentment and joy on his face.

"I do. The silence is beautiful."

"I like to come here when I need to retreat from the world. In the past, I came here when I wanted all the noise in my head to stop. Up here, it's hard to imagine any worries or fears. Being here always reminds me what's important in life." Austen takes my hand in his, squeezing it. "All I need is this. You." He leans in, kissing me sweetly, and there will never be a more perfect moment.

When our kiss ends, I sink to one knee, pulling the box from my pants pocket.

Austen's mouth drops open, and shock splays across his face.

"I know we're young, and we still have so much living to do, but I already know you will be there, right by my side, for as long as there is breath in my body."

Tears pool in my eyes when Austen gets down on one knee with me.

"I love you, Austen. I would not be the man I am today without you, and I don't want to exist a single day on this planet without you by my side. Marry me, man. Be my husband."

"Yes," he says without hesitation, emotion spilling out of his eyes. "Yes, I want to be your husband. Nothing would make me happier than spending my life with you."

We fall into one another, kissing and kissing, and we're both smiling and crying when we break apart. I slide the plain platinum band on his ring finger. "That's a placeholder until the day we marry."

"I love it. We need to get you a ring," he says, lifting our conjoined hands to his mouth. He kisses the ring, and my heart melts.

"I'd like that."

He pulls me to my feet, clasping my face in his hands. "Just so you know, I would have proposed. It's been on my mind a lot since we got back together. You just beat me to it."

I beam at him. "I'm glad I did."

"I'm glad you did too." He kisses me hard, and my heart is doing cartwheels behind my chest.

He said yes! I'm going to be married to this amazing man for the rest of my life. It feels surreal, and I've never been happier.

"Your mom is going to go crazy. Especially when she finds out we want to marry in June," Austen says as we make our descent a couple of hours later. Neither of us wants a long engagement. Why bother waiting when we know our own minds and we have the resources to make it happen on short notice? We want to marry before the next football season starts, and we both love summer, so it's a no-brainer.

"For real." I lean over and kiss him. I haven't been able to stop kissing and touching him since we got engaged. I'm giddy even thinking the word. "She's been suffering wedding withdrawal symptoms since Kev and Cheryl tied the knot last year. You do know she's going to completely take over?"

He chuckles. "I wouldn't have it any other way. I love your mom."

"She loves you too." Watching the burgeoning relationship between Mom and Austen has been heartwarming. They've grown close quick, and I'm hella grateful because Austen needs a mother figure who supports him wholeheartedly, without any strings or agenda, and he's found that in Alex Kennedy. As if I needed other reasons to worship the ground Mom walks on.

He gets on well with the rest of the family too, and he's fit in like he's always been a part of the gang.

"Ciara and Cathal can be our flower girl and ring bearer," I say, already visualizing our special day. "They'll have just turned two, so we should be able to get them to focus long enough to walk up the aisle."

Kyler and Faye had twins, and to say they have their hands full is an understatement. Those two toddlers have an abundance of energy and they never seem to sleep. My brother and his wife sport matching shadows under their eyes these days, but they also wear the biggest smiles. Faye has been wanting kids for a long time, so it seems fitting she ended up with twins, even if it's double the work.

Rachel gave birth to her daughter, Elodie, one month after Faye prematurely delivered the twins. Brad whisked Rach away to Vegas six months later, and they were married with only their daughter and Faye and Ky and the twins in attendance. Mom insisted on throwing them a reception when they point-blank refused her offer to plan a full wedding. They didn't want all the fuss, but we partied in style at the reception and made sure the occasion was celebrated in proper Kennedy fashion.

"We'll involve all the kids," Austen says. "We'll find something special for each of them to do."

All my nieces and nephews adore Austen. Hewson, in particular, has taken a real shine to my fiancé, and Austen has been teaching him some cool football skills.

"Pinch me, man," I say when we reach the car, my grin threatening to explode across my face. "I'm getting married! I still can't believe it, and I need to know this is real."

Austen smiles, reeling me into his arms. "You and me are as real as it gets," he says, brushing his nose against mine. "All you ever need to do is reach out and touch me, because I will always be by your side."

"And I will always be by yours," I confirm, because there is nowhere else I would ever be.

Kent

"Hey, you!" I barely lift my head, clicking my fingers in the direction of the bartender. I slam my empty glass down on the counter. "Another whiskey."

Footsteps approach, and I raise my head fully, blinking repeatedly in an effort to focus on the blur in front of me.

"I think you've had enough," a sultry, female voice says, sending shivers of awareness cascading down my spine.

"Where's Ford?" I ask, still struggling to see clearly. "He always looks after me."

"Unlucky for you, Ford went home. I'm behind the bar now, and I'm saying you're done."

Fumbling in my pockets, I extract my wallet and slap a hundred-dollar bill down on the counter. I slide it toward her.

"I'm saying I'm not. Get me a whiskey, and you can keep the change."

She pushes the money back at me, folding her arms across her chest.

My vision solidifies, and I stare at her awesome rack. She's wearing a plain black T-shirt, but it's tight, highlighting the generous swells of her tits.

"Your money's no good here, Kennedy, and stop staring at my tits."

My lips curl into a seductive smile of their own volition. "Your tits are awesome," I say, examining her gorgeous face for the first time.

She has beautiful big, brown eyes, full lips, high cheekbones, and thick, long lashes that are the real deal. None of that fake, spidery shit for this girl. My eyes roam appreciatively over the rest of her. Ink adorns the inside of both her lower arms, and there's a hint of a tattoo peeking out from the top of her shirt. Leaning forward, I peruse the rest of her body, really liking what I see. She's wearing a short leather miniskirt with scuffed biker boots, and she's rocking an incredible body, one I want to get acquainted with.

My dick turns to steel behind my jeans, and I lick my lips as I meet her disgusted gaze full on.

It doesn't deter me.

It only spurs me on.

"You're hot, and I'm horny. A perfect combination." I stand, gripping the edge of the counter when I sway a little. Straightening up, I tower over her, flashing her the grin that makes countless women drop to their knees. "How about you bend over the counter, and I rock your world, baby."

She laughs. "Holy shit. Does that crap really work on women?"

"All the fucking time," I truthfully admit.

Her arm darts out, and she grabs a fistful of my shirt, yanking me toward her.

Hell yeah.

That's more like it.

"Word to the wise, Kennedy. That shit won't work on me. *You* won't work on me. Quit while you're ahead." She lets me go, stepping back. "And you're cut off. Go home."

This woman doesn't realize it, but she's just thrown down the gauntlet. I cannot remember the last time a woman rejected me, and my blood is ON. FIRE. "What's your name, beautiful?" I ask, undeterred.

She rolls her eyes. "You're drunk, Kennedy. Go home. Trust me, it's in your best interest. This isn't the type of place you should be hanging around anyway."

"I like it here," I reply. "Even more now I've met you."

She shakes her head while drying a few glasses. "Not happening, Kennedy. And if you won't go home, I'll have Bugger throw you out."

"Bugger?" I ask, frowning.

She points over my head. "That big motherfucker at the door. One whistle, and he'll haul your ass outside."

"I'll leave," I say, leaning my elbows on the counter. "On one condition."

Her lips twitch as she rolls her eyes again. "It's cute you think you hold any bargaining power here. I'm the bar manager on duty, and what I say goes."

"Your name," I say. "Just tell me your name, and I'll leave with no trouble."

"Why the hell does it matter?" she asks, placing the dry glasses on the shelf behind her head.

"Because I want to know."

She smirks, leaning her elbows on the counter so we're face

to face with barely any distance between us. "And I bet you always get what you want. Am I right?"

I shrug, flashing her another one of my trademark smiles.

I get no reaction.

Not even a flinch or a blink of her eye.

"Just tell me your name."

She straightens up. "No." She grabs a cloth, wiping down the counter. "Go home, Kennedy. I won't tell you again."

"Pres, is this guy bothering you?" a gruff voice says from behind me. I glance over my shoulder, and wouldn't you know it, it's Bugger, and he's even bigger in the flesh. But I'm not worried. I've got enough shit flowing through my veins to be completely unconcerned.

I grin, straightening up. "Pres?" I arch a brow at her in question.

"Presley. You need me to kick this asshole out?" Bugger asks, telling me exactly what I want to know.

Presley groans, pursing her lips. "I have it handled. Get back to the door."

He shuffles off, and I stand there grinning like a loon. "Presley. I like it. Were your parents big Elvis fans or something?"

She rolls her eyes again, and if she keeps doing it, she'll give herself eye strain. "Like I haven't heard that a million times." She leans into me again, and I silently fist pump the air when her gaze rakes me from head to toe. She might feign disinterest, but I know when a broad wants me, and Presley wants every inch of this body.

"Liking what you see, babe?"

She snorts. "How original. You got my name. Now, be a man of your word. And *leave.*"

I grab my jacket from the back of the bar stool. "I'll go, but this isn't the last you've seen of me, Presley baby." I blow her a kiss and walk off.

And for the first time in a long time, something, or some*one*, has pulled my head out from under the black hole I've been living in.

Presley thinks she's immune to my charms.

I can't wait to prove her wrong.

Reforming Kent is the next book in the series. Available now and free to read in Kindle Unlimited.

REFORMING KENT - The Kennedy Boys Book #10

Kent

Rogue. Troublemaker. Bad Boy. Delinquent.

Everyone thinks they know who I am, but they know *nothing*.

And that's how I prefer it.

Keeping my demons under lock and key is my only survival tactic.

Until a gorgeous feisty bartender enters my life, turning it upside down. Presley captivates me in a way no woman ever has, and I can't get her out of my mind.

She's determined to resist me, but I'm equally stubborn and more than up for the challenge.

Winning her trust, and her heart, becomes everything because she shows me a future worth fighting for.

But the consequences of my tortured past are far-reaching, and if I don't let her go, I'll only drag Presley down this dark hole with me.

Presley

Since I aged out of the foster system, I've worked hard for my dream future, and it's so close. Too close to let some arrogant rich playboy distract me.

I've heard all about Kent Kennedy, and with my history of troubled bad boys, I need his attention like a hole in the head.

Except he's nothing I expected and everything I never dared to dream of. As I slowly uncover the truth, I discover a broken man with a big heart who desperately needs someone to see him.

I want to be that person, but his demons loom large, and I don't know if I'm strong enough to do this again.

When the past rears its ugly head, shattering everything, will there be anything left of my heart to protect?

Available now in ebook, paperback, and audiobook.

CLAIM YOUR FREE EBOOK – ONLY AVAILABLE TO NEWSLETTER SUBSCRIBERS!

The boy who broke my heart is now the man who wants to mend it.

Jared was my everything until an ocean separated us and he abandoned me when I needed him most.

He forgot the promises he made.

Forgot the love he swore was eternal.

It was over before it began.

Now, he's a hot commodity, universally adored, and I'm the woman no one wants.

Pining for a boy who no longer exists is pathetic. Years pass, men come and go, but I cannot move on.

I didn't believe my fractured heart and broken soul could endure any more pain. Until Jared rocks up to the art gallery where I work, with his fiancée in tow, and I'm drowning again.

Seeing him brings everything to the surface, so I flee. Placing distance between us again, I'm determined to put him behind me once and for all.

Then he reappears at my door, begging me for another chance.

I know I should turn him away.

Try telling that to my heart.

This angsty, new adult romance is a FREE full-length ebook, exclusively available to newsletter subscribers.

Type this link into your browser to claim your free copy: https://bit.ly/TITMHFBB

OR

Scan this code to claim your free copy:

About the Author

Siobhan Davis is a *USA Today, Wall Street Journal*, and Amazon Top 5 bestselling romance author. **Siobhan** writes emotionally intense stories with swoon-worthy romance, complex characters, and tons of unexpected plot twists and turns that will have you flipping the pages beyond bedtime! She has sold over 2 million books, and her titles are translated into several languages.

Prior to becoming a full-time writer, Siobhan forged a successful corporate career in human resource management.

She lives in the Garden County of Ireland with her husband and two sons.

You can connect with Siobhan in the following ways:

Website: www.siobhandavis.com
Facebook: AuthorSiobhanDavis
Instagram: @siobhandavisauthor
Tiktok: @siobhandavisauthor
Email: siobhan@siobhandavis.com

Books by Siobhan Davis

KENNEDY BOYS SERIES

Upper Young Adult/New Adult Contemporary Romance

Finding Kyler

Losing Kyler

Keeping Kyler

The Irish Getaway

Loving Kalvin

Saving Brad

Seducing Kaden

Forgiving Keven

Summer in Nantucket

Releasing Keanu

Adoring Keaton

Reforming Kent

Moonlight in Massachusetts

STAND-ALONES

New Adult Contemporary Romance

Inseparable

Incognito

When Forever Changes

No Feelings Involved

Still Falling for You

Second Chances Box Set

Holding on to Forever

Always Meant to Be

Tell It to My Heart

The One I Want

Reverse Harem Romance

Surviving Amber Springs

Dark Mafia Romance

Vengeance of a Mafia Queen

RYDEVILLE ELITE SERIES

Dark High School Romance

Cruel Intentions

Twisted Betrayal

Sweet Retribution

Charlie

Jackson

Sawyer

*The Hate I Feel^*

*Drew^*

MAZZONE MAFIA SERIES

Dark Mafia Romance

Condemned to Love

Forbidden to Love

Scared to Love

Mazzone Mafia: The Complete Series

THE ACCARDI TWINS

Dark Mafia Romance

*CKONY #1^*

*CKONY #2^*

THE SAINTHOOD (BOYS OF LOWELL HIGH)

Dark HS Reverse Harem Romance

Resurrection

Rebellion

Reign

Revere

The Sainthood: The Complete Series

DIRTY CRAZY BAD DUET

Dark College Reverse Harem Romance

Dirty Crazy Bad - A Prequel Short Story

Dirty Crazy Bad # 1

Dirty Crazy Bad #2

ALL OF ME DUET

Angsty New Adult Romance

Say I'm The One

Let Me Love You

Hold Me Close

*Reeve**

All of Me: The Complete Series

ALINTHIA SERIES

Upper YA/NA Paranormal Romance/Reverse Harem

The Lost Savior

The Secret Heir

The Warrior Princess

The Chosen One

*The Rightful Queen^*

SAVEN SERIES

Young Adult Science Fiction/Paranormal Romance

Saven Deception

Logan

Saven Disclosure

Saven Denial

Saven Defiance

Axton

Saven Deliverance

Saven: The Complete Series

^Release date to be confirmed

* Coming 2023